KEEP ME CLOSE

A Gods of Hunger Novel

R.M. VIRTUES

Strange Hungers Publishing

Cover created by Covers in Color (coversincolor.com)

Print ISBN: 978-1-7367454-3-4

❀ Created with Vellum

AUTHOR'S NOTE

This book contains the following:

on page violence, explicit sex, rough sex, daddy kink, consensual sex work, physical violence, attempted murder, on page death, conversations around and about human trafficking (no sexual assault or violence within this topic on page, but the MCs are up against traffickers and so conversations surrounding trafficking are present albeit as vague as I could make them), guns, knives, bombs, ableist language (addressed on page).

Chapter One

HEPHAESTUS

"You can't keep doing shit like this, Aphrodite."

Hephaestus set his cane over his lap, leaning back in his chair with a heavy sigh as frustration gave way to exhaustion. It had been a long night, made longer still by Aphrodite's inability to see sense, and at this point, he was convinced that he was wasting his breath. If he would have known how much of his new position would involve her, he may have thought twice about it. He had committed to this arrangement already however, and if there was one thing Hades and Charon both had taught him thoroughly until they were hoarse, it was that they always fulfilled their commitments.

Combing a hand through his thick black hair, he studied her features with narrowed eyes. His voice was somber, his expression clear, but her face was contorted in conflated anger. Even with her lips pursed, he knew she was grinding her teeth. He could hear them in the silence. He caught the clench of her jaw as she stood, towering over him even with a desk between them. Hephaestus didn't flinch. He knew she was angry. That didn't change the reality.

"Doing shit like what, Hephaestus?" she at last managed, her tone strained. "Rescuing these women? Taking them out of harm's way?"

"You know that isn't what I mean."

"Then what do you mean?"

"We had a plan."

"A plan that would take months!"

"We needed time—"

"They didn't have time! When you took this job, you promised you would help—"

"And you promised we would do it together."

"I had to do something."

"No, you *think* you had to do something."

"Don't fucking patronize me, Hephaestus, I told you we could work together as long as it didn't put them at risk! And you taking your sweet ass time did exactly that!"

"What do you think you did to the next round of kids by taking them?"

"I did what I have always done, and I will do it again!"

"We needed to find the head before—"

"No, *you* needed to!"

The tension in the room was so dense that it was hard to breathe. Hephaestus felt as though he'd been submerged inside of a shark tank, and there was nothing but blood in the water. Still, he remained calm, reminding himself that he would get nowhere if he fought fire with fire. Besides, even if he tried, Aphrodite would burn the whole place down if only to prove a point.

Pushing himself to his feet, he leaned heavily upon his cane and smoothed out his composure with a click of his tongue.

"You saved them," he started slowly, "but how many others have you damned by doing so? Now they know we were onto them. They probably know it was you, and they know where we'll go looking for them next. They could flee the city or go underground, and we won't have any way to find them. And so you know what they'll do next? They'll find more victims."

"Then we'll find them again," she snarled, defiant.

"You don't know that, and to think you do is a disservice to them."

"You think I didn't think of that, Hephaestus, but I—"

"To tell you the truth, I don't think you thought at all."

He said it with a distinct air of nonchalance, but his voice was louder now, loud enough to quiet her, but he didn't yell. He rarely yelled. Yelling reminded him too much of Zeus, and Hades and Charon didn't yell. As Hades always said, they didn't need to. *If you have to yell to prove a point, it probably isn't a very good one.*

So he kept his composure even amidst his own anger and upset, and it had served him well in the past. It was also a skill crucial to his position, and Aphrodite confirmed that each and every time they shared a space. He simply could not afford the headache of a screaming match with her however. He had other things to do that required his focus. Like ensuring her safety and trying to salvage this investigation.

"Well, it's done, ain't it?" she retorted, her palms pressed into the desk. "Whatever foolish mistake I made, those survivors are safe now, and I can live with that."

"Yeah, let's just hope they stay that way."

"Fuck you, Hephaestus, I've been doing this without you for years!"

He turned his head slightly, staring at her through his better eye for a long moment before he exhaled. This was what it tended to be like, working with Aphrodite. She made it quite clear that she didn't like him to begin with, but on top of that, she had a tendency to be bullheaded and reckless where applicable, more so if he was involved. It wasn't at all for no reason. Hephaestus did understand her frustrations, but her methods of relieving those frustrations were shortsighted and rife with consequence. He simply didn't know how to get her to understand that.

Annoying as she could be though, her impact could not be disregarded. Aphrodite was divinity incarnate. Modest curves, dark eyes, and voluminous brown hair that she did art with on a regular basis, it was no wonder she was more celebrated in this city than anyone else. The Lush District was a place where the people of Khaos Falls could watch their wildest dreams come true, including the people she rescued from local trafficking rings. Every single one of her pleasure dens were endlessly busy, and all of her people were well taken care of. Those who declined sex work often took positions in the fashion mall or her security detail, and others still were sent to the Market District. His brothers, Hermes and Dionysos, always had work to hand down, and Hephaestus had also agreed to offer additional security positions now that he had the means. After all, you could never have too much security, especially in a popular city like Khaos Falls.

Prior to Hades' leadership, security in the city had been a fragmented affair, each of the districts handling their own security in a way that left far too many grey areas for Hades' taste. His concern was only magnified by Tartarus' full lockdown a few months ago, where they had robbed the city of naval support and left its entire coast vulnerable. To alleviate that, he created one entity, putting Hephaestus at its head and Artemis and Achilles on the wings. Since then, Khaos Falls was the most secure city in the Aegean, but it did not mean it was perfect. Hephaestus sought to do so much more, but it was easier said than done with so many voices to take into consideration. At the moment, Aphrodite's was loudest of all, and not just metaphorically.

The day after Hephaestus was instated, he and Aphrodite had agreed they would start tackling the trafficking rings together so that they could not only save the victims but end the cycle. She had in fact been tracking down missing people who were suspected of having been forced into these rings for years, but Hephaestus had wanted to permanently abolish the practice for good. That was what he had agreed to at least. It seemed they were still learning to trust one another.

Or just simply think shit through.

" I don't want to do this for years, Aphrodite," he concluded. "I want to help them, but I want to help all of them, not just some of them, and I know you do too, but that's going to require some patience. If we keep going like this, we'll be doing it forever, and eventually, those we lose will outnumber those we save. If we start cracking down on the traffickers though, we can shut down their business. Then, if we can clean out Khaos Falls, maybe we can help other places, but we need to be smarter than them. We need to get ahead of them, and we can't do that if you keep rushing in head first."

She scoffed. "That's not what I'm doing. I'm—"

He waved a hand. "It ends now. Going forward, you don't make any moves without my knowledge. Because you may have gotten those girls out, but you didn't get them out of danger. It doesn't take a genius to figure out who took 'em, does it? Now all of you got targets on your back."

"You do not own me, Hephaestus, and I do not answer to you."

"I'm not getting into this childish argument with you, Aphrodite. I said what I said. We do this together, or I do it alone. Those are the options."

"And if I don't agree to that?"

He leveled her with a stare that she met head on like a cobra. He couldn't threaten her, not with his capabilities and not with his uncle's. She was Persephone's best friend and the most beloved leader in Khaos Falls. Both of those facts were half the reason people had taken to Hades' leadership so well, having put their faith in Aphrodite's endorsement before anything else. Hephaestus may be the closest thing Khaos Falls had to the law, but she was everything else around it. And above it. So really, all he could do was tell her the truth.

Tapping his fingers against the desk, he wet his lips. "Then the blood of every person that gets roped into one of these rings after today and doesn't make it out is on your hands, and I hope you can live with that."

Aphrodite pursed her lips, her hands gripping the edges of her desk, but she said nothing more. He didn't wait long for a response either, accepting that no response at all was the best possible outcome. Turning towards the door of her office, he saw himself out, hoping he had finally gotten through to her but not too keen on holding his breath.

It was late, and he'd been up for nearly 24 hours by now. He hadn't had any plans of working late into the night, but when he got the call from his lookouts that someone was moving on the warehouse they had been watching for the past few weeks, he knew exactly who it was. She was the reason he had lookouts in the first place.

He had been too late to intervene though. She had already been making a move, and all he could do was brace everyone for the fallout lest he run in there and make things worse. This wasn't the first time they had had this conversation, but it was the first time she'd betrayed his trust since they started working together. She still might not listen after tonight, but maybe he could buy himself some time before she went out looking for more trouble.

He made it to the service elevator and down to the parking garage before his agitation began to wane, leaving room for fatigue to barrel its way through him. Accompanying it was a familiar ache as well, one that seeped into his muscles and made a home there just out of reach. Winter had arrived without warning just days ago, and this was the first night with a temperature below what they had become accustomed to all fall. He could feel it in his bones, a deeper discomfort that underlined that of his sinew. He was used to his body's sensitivities by now, having been familiarizing himself with them since he was a child. Now, it was little more than an inconvenience, and he never allowed it to keep him from doing his job. Though not for lack of trying on its part.

Reaching into his coat pocket, he extracted a slim, black vapor pen and slipped it between his lips. The cartridge attached to it currently was one of Dionysos's making, the younger man always eager to experiment with herbs and vines alike. He had concocted this strain specifically for his brother's ailments with the help of Asklepios, the town physician. Dio had tried many times to find the perfect blend that would aid his brother best, and Hephaestus was certain he had finally succeeded with this one. Inhaling, he stood there a moment and allowed the medicinal blend to soothe the pain in his weaker leg and the rest of his body as well. At the very least, it kept the tremors at bay.

Looking around, he noticed just how quiet the parking garage was. There were very few cars still parked on this first level, but he supposed that was normal being that the early birds usually utilized these spots. However, he had never seen it so empty, even this close to closing time. There were few guards... Actually, there were no guards, which was odd for a place like Lush, the main club in the district. It was more odd considering the events that had taken place that night. Even on a normal night though, security was always plentiful, and now it seemed nonexistent. Immediately, he felt uncomfortable.

Hephaestus gripped the anvil that graced the top of his cane tighter and made his way around the perimeter, searching for any sign of a disturbance. His heart rate was slowly rising, but panic was still far off, and he would be able to run it out for as long as necessary. Unfortunately, that did not mean it wasn't warranted.

He moved carefully through the shadows, checking around corners, his fingers curling inward to brush against the blade he now slid further down his wrist. He at last saw a few bodies —alive and well— near the rear exterior doors, dressed in black vests with a red patch on the chest. Although he could not make out the details of the design from here, he recognized it with ease — Aphrodite's insignia. But if the entire point was to make it discernible from a distance...

The look of them made Hephaestus nervous. He watched them continually peer through the windows before checking their surroundings, whispering to one another with pistols in hand. It could of course be nothing. It could also be anything, but Hephaestus had learned long ago to trust his gut, and his gut was telling him something wasn't right.

Moving back towards the service elevator without being seen, he pulled his phone from his pocket and called Achilles.

"You got guys near Lush?" he asked the moment the man answered.

"Two squads, yeah," Achilles responded after a moment, no doubt looking at his logs. "Artemis has two at Twilight House too. She figured more females would make the rescues more comfortable. Why? What's up?"

"Leave her squads at Twilight, and send your two over." Hephaestus rushed back into the elevator, hitting the club floor button. "Have them surround the building and watch for any of the guards leaving."

"What's going on?"

"I don't know yet, but something feels off. I'm going up to check. If they get the code red from me, tell them that none of the guards leave. But be quick."

"Got it."

Hephaestus hung up, hitting the button over and over, but the car didn't move. There was a red light on the panel that was blinking incessantly at him. He checked his watch. Seventeen minutes after closing time. Which meant elevator access *into* the club required a code as of two minutes ago, a code he did not have.

"Fuck."

Phone still in hand, he dialed Aphrodite, opening the doors up once more and heading around the building to find another entrance. That panic was rising now, boiling beneath his acceptance of the situation. Something was definitely wrong. Security was too sparse, and the district was too quiet. Whatever was occurring was bigger than he could see at the moment, and he could not even begin to untangle what that could mean. Not right now. Right now, he had to get to Aphrodite, who of course didn't answer her fucking phone.

With a growl of frustration, he shoved his phone in his pocket, searching for the service exit. If he could reach it before the bartenders and servers made their way out, he could slip inside and go straight up the stairs to Aphrodite's office. There was no way she wasn't the target, but he was surprised that anyone would attack her right now with all this heat in the streets. Then again, considering his current knowledge, they had done exactly what no one would expect them to do *because* of that fact. And from the looks of it, they had inside help, so this seemed to all be playing out exactly as they'd planned.

But they hadn't planned for him.

Before he reached the service exit, he noticed another door slightly cracked open, the glowing red lights from within outlining its frame. He searched for a clue to where he was on the perimeter, but he could not make out anything of note with either eye in the dense dark. Inhaling a deep breath, Hephaestus lofted up his cane, wincing as his knee threatened to give way. A light tremor racked it, but he forced himself to straighten, allowing the joint and muscles there to settle. Once he could handle his weight, he proceeded into the club..

Pulling the door open slowly, he listened for any sounds before stepping over the threshold. The corridor before him was wide and cast in shadow beneath the vivid red glow, and he still wasn't sure where in the club he was entering from. The hall was bland and unfamiliar, no doubt one of the service corridors that ran within the walls of the club. He imagined Apollo had designed them much like those in Casino Asphodel, his uncle's establishment. Or at least he hoped.

He proceeded forward, keeping his eyes and ears peeled as he swept his cane back and forth before him. But it was hard to hear with his heart hammering so hard against his ribcage that they rattled in his ears. The thrumming was so loud that it muted the footsteps that suddenly fell behind him if only for a moment. That moment was all it took though. All Hephaestus felt was a sharp pain in the side of his head before he crumpled to the ground.

Chapter Two

APHRODITE

Aphrodite was seething by the time she left her office, her muscles tense and her face flushed. She had expected for Hephaestus to find out about her midnight rescue mission, and she had expected him to be angry about it. She had not expected him to somehow know the moment it happened and to be waiting at Lush for her when she returned at three in the morning, exhausted and not at all in the mood to hear his mouth.

He hadn't yelled. She wished more than anything that he had yelled. She would have rather faced his wrath than his disappointment. She could deal with his wrath. She could poke at it all day and never get bored. Or at least, she could poke at everyone else's. She had never seen Hephaestus's. He never got angry, and he rarely got loud. At this point, she was convinced he was more machine than man, and currently, his laser vision was fixed on her in a way that made her fucking skin crawl even when he wasn't present. Especially when he wasn't present.

It was almost as though he had expected her to do it, which meant she was predictable, and if she was predictable to him, she was probably becoming predictable to those she continued to go up against. So the worst part of all this was that she wasn't angry because he was wrong. She was angry because he was right, and she'd never felt more foolish in her life.

She fucking hated that he could make her feel that way, and he'd been doing it for years. Now that he was in a place of importance beyond resident blacksmith however, it was so much worse. And so much harder to avoid.

Hector, one of her heads of security, had just locked up the main inner doors of Lush when Aphrodite stepped out onto the landing outside of her second floor office, resting her hands on the elegant gold railing and looking out over the main room. It was now empty of the wanton sounds and writhing bodies that usually occupied it, which was far more peaceful to Aphrodite than the quiet of closing time.

"Hey, Aphrodite," Hector greeted with a wave.

"Hey, Hector. Where's Kleon?"

Kleon was her security team's night shift leader, and he'd been with her since the fall of her father's district and the rise of her own. He was older than her and wiser for it, but he'd helped her build this place from scratch. She always felt safest when he was present.

"He left a few hours ago," Hector answered.

"Oh, really? He didn't tell me."

"I think he said he texted you? He had an emergency."

"Oh, that makes sense. I haven't checked my phone in hours."

And she wasn't about to now. What she needed was rest. She would call him in the morning to make sure he was alright.

Hector offered her a warm smile before proceeding on his nightly rounds of the property. Some of the newer pleasure dens in the district ran 24 hours a day, but Lush still closed up at 4 am and opened again at noon. It had been her first establishment built over the ruin of her father's floundering district, and it remained her favorite with its dark leather furniture bathed in vivid red lights. The neon signs that adorned the walls were all items she had handpicked herself, each of them with some kind of sentimental meaning she had tucked away since then. The decor, the layout, the design of the building itself; she had been at the head of it all, and no matter how her other businesses flourished, this one felt most like home. It was an ode to both how far she'd come and how far she could still go.

When her father had passed, everyone had laughed, believing that the Silver District would fall, even with the belief at the time that he'd had a son to take up the helm. The Silver District did in fact fall, Aphrodite all but kicking down the last of its pillars herself, and from its ashes rose the Lush District. With grace and ambition, she brought the rest of the city to its knees in no metaphorical way, and no one even blinked an eye when it turned out Oceanus had a daughter. How could they, when she embodied every desire they had ever had?

Aphrodite was certainly proud of her progress, but she took more pride in her work outside of the pleasure dens than she did in her work within them. For years, she had been at the helm of an active resistance against trafficking rings coming into the city and ravaging its youth. She wanted to do right by the men and women, the boys and girls, forced and coerced into these horrible situations where they no longer had control over their own bodies, and she wanted to help them start over, even if it meant working with fucking Hephaestus.

As she surveyed the main floor, Eros appeared below, giving her a wave as he galloped up the stairs towards her. His freshly dyed, fiery red curls were windswept, his brown skin tinted with a faint red flush that disappeared beneath the salmon-colored button-up he was wearing. When she embraced him, his skin was so cold that she shuddered. It was certainly winter.

"You alright?" he asked.

"I'm good. How are they?"

"Good," he replied with a nod, scratching at the light scruff across his jaw. "Psyche has them settled in at Twilight, and Asklepsios sent nurses over to have them checked out. He'll be sending counselors in the morning, and then we can start reaching out to any families or loved ones."

"Are they well secured?"

"Oh, Artemis had guards waiting on the premises. She said they would be there for as long as we needed them, and the - *younger* ones are very comfortable with her."

Aphrodite flinched, and not just at the memory that there were teenagers on this particular run. Of course Artemis had guards waiting because of course Hephaestus had demanded it. Grateful as she may be, it only proved that he had anticipated her move. Before she could recover and offer Eros some kind of graceful response, her phone started ringing in her clutch. Pulling it out, she stared at the screen as Hephaestus's name scrolled across it like a taunt. She ground her teeth together. Then she dismissed the call. Anything else he had to say could wait until tomorrow. Or never. Either way, she'd heard enough of his holier-than-thou bullshit for the night.

"He means well, you know," Eros whispered slowly.

She sucked her teeth. "Oh, not you too."

"Hey, I'm just sayin', Mama." He held up his hands in faux surrender. "I know you two clash a lot, but you both got your hearts in the right place."

"That's assuming he has a heart," she mumbled petulantly.

Eros snickered and kissed her cheek. "I'll let you tell it. I'm gonna call Psyche and check in again before I call it a night."

"Mhm, you do that."

They bade each other good night before Aphrodite headed upstairs to the penthouse she kept on the top floor. She only stayed there when she was too tired to drive home —which was more than often enough — and tonight was certainly one of those nights considering it was now morning. Additionally, she wanted to be downstairs as soon as she awoke to ensure that she could begin promptly contacting the families of those they had rescued. It was the most difficult part of it all for her. Sometimes those they contacted simply hung up, unwilling to even admit they had a child that was missing. Sometimes, there was no one at all to contact. Either way, she did her best to ensure that everyone she took in was taken care of in a way that catered to them and not to her or anyone who would exploit them. If they requested they call no one, they obliged, and she would take up the role of provider for as long as necessary.

She climbed into the elevator with a quiet yawn, looking forward to slipping into a warm bath before she crawled into bed for a few hours. Before she could input the code that would allow the car to travel to the top floor, a man slipped in after her, startling her. He was tall with cropped brown hair and striking blue eyes, and she had never seen him before. Not here and not anywhere in the Lush District. She could say for certain that there weren't many people in Khaos Falls who hadn't been to the Lush District, and she always remembered a face. Yet he wore her insignia on the chest of his vest. Or at least, he wore something similar to her insignia on his chest, but the design of the dove was off, and the patchwork looked rushed at best. She inhaled through her nose, seeking calm.

"Can I help you?" she questioned as the elevator doors closed them inside, attempting to hide her annoyance. She didn't hit a button or punch in her code just yet. "This is a private elevator. It doesn't go up to—"

She was cut off by the unmistakable glint of a blade as he brandished it from his pocket. He thrusted it toward her, hitting her square in the middle of the chest. She managed to grip his wrist, keeping it from entering more than a few inches, but he immediately whipped his hand back and jabbed at her again. The point of the blade, now slick with her blood, struck her abdomen, but she didn't release him even as the pain overtook her. She reached beneath her dress with her free hand, extracting her own blade and flicking it open. He aimed at her gut again, but she sidestepped it and buried the blade in his side.

"Who sent you!" she demanded, twisting the blade, but he wasn't at all perturbed by the wound.

He came at her again, this time throwing his weight into her and slamming her against the elevator wall. Hephaestus's voice echoed like a broken record in the back of her head, even as it crashed against the wood paneling. *Gotta be smarter than them...* She gritted her teeth. She knew she needed to interrogate this man, to find out who had sent him so that they could go straight to the source and handle whatever this was. And that was all so easy to say when not in the thick of it, but right now, fuck Hephaestus and all of his wisdom. There was no alternative outcome here. This man wasn't going to stop. He had come here to do one thing, and it wasn't to talk.

Rearing her hand back again, she waited for him to try another strike. Once he did, catching her in her stomach with a shallow cut, she sidestepped and drove her own blade into his neck, ripping it sideways before pulling it out again. He swung wildly once more, but she was easily able to dodge it. Then he stumbled back into the opposite wall as blood poured from the wound, clutching his throat with a trembling hand. The wound at his side was weeping as well, staining the red carpet beneath their feet with a darker shade of crimson. His blade fell from his hand with a resounding thump.

"Who sent you!"

But he didn't answer. He couldn't. Within seconds, he went still, eyes falling shut as he slumped against the wall and slid down onto the ground. Aphrodite clutched her chest, staunching the blood as she reached out for the keypad. She hit the emergency alarm as she leaned on the wall for support, a siren blaring immediately as the doors flew apart. Her adrenaline kept most of the pain at bay, but fatigue had already been hot on her heels, and she was most vulnerable to it now.

Her eyes snapped wide open when Hephaestus appeared framed in the doors, sweat and blood pouring down his scarred face and his cane raised like a gun. Or *as* a gun. Seconds later, guards —hers *and* his— swarmed the area, helping her out of the elevator. It all happened in a blur, but all she could hear was the memory of her own voice. *Who sent you!* She may never get the answer now.

Eros appeared on the landing, and Hephaestus moved to Aphrodite's side, all but dragging his leg with a grimace distorting his mouth. She had noticed long ago that he did that when it was hurting him. Aphrodite had no clue how he'd managed to get up here so fast.

"Call for an ambulance," he instructed Eros, his voice like ice. "Then call Persephone and my uncle."

Eros nodded and moved back to do so as Hephaestus turned to one of his men. "I want every single one of her guards that are on site detained. No one leaves. Find out who was supposed to be manning this floor then get me a list of everyone on duty tonight. And get this bastard downstairs."

He pointed at the body in the elevator, and the man gave him a firm nod before instructing two other guards to carry the assassin out. Hephaestus then turned to Aphrodite, his dark eyes filled with turmoil. And question.

"I'm fine," she growled through gritted teeth before he could ask.

She was absolutely certain she wouldn't die. The wounds had been shallow, and while there was a fair amount of blood and a growing ache, it wouldn't be enough to take her down. Still, Hephaestus unbuttoned his shirt despite the slight shake of his hands, pulling it off and pressing it against her chest. He let it go once she put her hand over it, her eyes, still narrowed, traveling over his torso. She'd never seen him in anything but a black dress shirt buttoned all the way to the top and matching slacks. Beneath the white tank top he unveiled, his neck and shoulder were scarred, much like his face although the scar tissue was more pronounced in some places. The perpetual tilt of his shoulders was more evident, but his biceps and forearms bulged in a way so that the veins were explicitly defined against his tanned skin, and—

"Do you know him?" he inquired, gesturing towards the body as it passed them and yanking her from her thoughts.

She shook her head. "Not even vaguely. I've never seen him." She paused, eyeing Hephaestus. "How did you get up here?"

He raised a brow. "I would've been quicker if you would've answered your damn phone." She glared at him, but he just shook his head. " I found one of the doors near the private rooms propped open. The guy standing inside clubbed me one time in the head and took off when I came in. I couldn't catch him, so I just - I found Eros, and he told me you were headed upstairs. I got here when you hit the emergency button."

"How did you know?"

"There were no guards in the parking garage, and the two at the back door looked - suspicious. I'd never seen 'em around before, so I came up to check."

"So - my guards..."

"We don't know yet. I didn't find any of them layin' around, but we'll have to sweep the club, see if we find any other bodies."

When their eyes met however, they both knew the truth. It wasn't just about tonight, and it wasn't just an outside job. This had been planned. Her security team had been compromised.

Chapter Three

HEPHAESTUS

Hephaestus stared at the massive black helmet printed on the purple velvet carpet of his uncle's office, the plume atop it woven into the intricate border design that surrounded it. It was new, no doubt something to make his office more welcoming than it had been prior. Now that he was the leader of Khaos Falls, half of his job was to entertain it seemed. He'd even opted for a smaller desk, meaning the distance between him and Hephaestus at the moment was minimal in comparison to what it used to be. Yet it also made Hades look much larger which was difficult to believe considering how imposing he was already. No matter how much decorating was done, Heph could not imagine any citizen walking in here and not being intimidated.

Charon sat next to Hephaestus, both their heads cocked to the side in the same fashion as they awaited Hades' conclusion about next steps. Hecate and Thanatos had just come in, situating themselves on the couch perpendicular to Hades' desk beside a sleeping Cerberus. News of Aphrodite's attack had spread like a plague, and they had to move quickly in order to maintain public trust. In cities with new leadership, any instance of weakness could become fatal quite quickly, and neither Hades nor Hephaestus were willing to let this settle. Something had to be done and fast.

"Persephone at the hospital?" Hephaestus asked with a yawn.

Hades nodded, his dark eyes drawn to the stitches on the side of his nephew's head. Hephaestus just waved him off. It looked worse than it was. He guessed that he'd been hit over the head with something like a bat or maybe even a hammer, but he couldn't be sure. Either way, the headache it incited had long since quieted, and all that was left was the faint ache of the stitching now in place. It was nothing compared to Aphrodite's wounds, who had only agreed to go to the hospital after Persephone and Hestia arrived at Lush and demanded it of her. That was also when she finally stopped yelling at him about it.

"What happened last night?" Hades asked instead. "With these people Aphrodite rescued?"

Hephaestus shrugged. "We had been watching a warehouse in the Harvest District for a while, but we hadn't seen any concrete evidence. Apparently, she received confirmation that people were being held there. Didn't know by who, but we agreed we would work on getting them out together. I wanted the guys responsible, but she got antsy and made a move, took 'em out in the dead of night. I don't think this has anything to do with that though."

Hades raised a brow. "No?"

"I mean, if it does, the timing is either coincidental or the rescue was a diversion. This had to have been planned well in advance."

"Like a few weeks?" Hecate questioned.

Hephaestus shook his head. "Try months. They infiltrated her security, and if I had to guess, I'd say most of it too. I don't know how many were in on it for sure, but we found no bodies in the building, and like I said this morning, there was no one on the floor. Aphrodite said she only saw one guard before she got into that elevator, and he was leaving the area."

"Did she say who?" Hades asked.

"Hector, but we found him out cold in a hallway. Not that it means he's entirely innocent, but he doesn't seem like the strongest lead either."

"But he is a top member of her security."

"He is."

"And you don't know who the hitman was?"

Hephaestus shook his head. "Never seen him."

"I had a look too," Charon assured Hades. "No luck. He definitely isn't from here."

Hephaestus had been going back and forth in his mind, doing his very best to dredge up anything or anyone remotely similar to the man in the elevator. It was troubling for many reasons, each more frustrating than the last. Hephaestus never forgot a face, and paired with his hypervigilance, his photographic memory took stock of as many other details as possible. Charon was much the same. He had been Hades' eyes and ears for decades now, and most of his information came from observation and inference. He knew how to read people, and he was rarely ever wrong. As for the assassin, the man could've grown a beard and put glasses on, and Hephaestus still would've been able to identify him if he'd seen him before no matter when or where. This wasn't the case.

"She's taken down a lot of these rings though," Hephaestus went on. "In a lot of places. It could've been anyone."

"We need to narrow it down, with both haste and discretion," Hades stated. "I'll give you whatever resources you need."

"I've got eyes on the ports, and they're doing random checks, but odds are they came on a private ship without reporting it. They might be able to slip out of the city without us knowing."

"We'll see about that. I want all itineraries checked. I'll have Athena check with other ports to see if they had any suspicious activity."

"Honestly I wouldn't be surprised if they were still in the city. If they've been hiding out this long, they must have a lot of holes to disappear into."

Hades huffed. "That's a very real possibility."

The door opened behind Hephaestus then, and Hades stood as if on instinct. Hephaestus knew by the glint in his uncle's eyes that it was Persephone, and he stood as well.

"How is she?" Hades inquired.

"She's fine," Persephone huffed, the bags underlining her eyes pronounced beneath the fluorescent lights. "Agitated of course, but Eros is taking her back home now. I told her I'd meet her there, but I wanted to check in with you first. Any news?"

Hades shook his head. They were quiet for a moment, and Hephaestus went through the many mental images of everyone he'd seen the night before when he'd first arrived at Lush. He knew for a fact that there had been men in the garage because they'd checked his license plate as he parked. He'd greeted several guards on the way in, and he remembered a few names on the badges he'd looked at. None of them had looked suspicious. Yet now every one of them was a suspect. What had he missed? And how had they managed to swap out an entire security team in an hour?

"We have to start by installing new security around her," Hades concluded. "If the entire building was clear, there must be multiple breaches."

"Achilles and I have already designated units for Lush, and we'll try and see if we can spare more," Hephaestus reported. "He's on site right now seeing who still shows up for work, but we're questioning all of them first thing."

Persephone stopped pacing to speak. "We need someone close to her, someone who can be with her at all times, someone that we trust."

"Then we'll install someone from my own security," Hades said, "someone dedicated to her protection, a personal guard."

"Okay, but we can't leave you or the casino vulnerable either. The fire wasn't that long ago. If they think you have a weakness, they might come for you too."

"She's right," Hephaestus agreed. "Until we know how big this thing is, it's best not to assume the scale of their plans. They aren't the only ones with eyes on the city right now. With all these changes, who knows how many people are down bad enough to try something foolish."

Hades rested his hands on his desk and bowed his head. Hephaestus saw the concern on his uncle's face, ebbing and flowing under his dark skin. Lines creased Hades' forehead, his jaw tensing intermittently. His new position was certainly aging him much quicker than the casino alone had. Hephaestus wondered if he ever had any regrets.

He looked up, and the two of them locked eyes. Immediately, Hephaestus knew he wasn't going to like what came next.

"We'll put Hephaestus," Hades stated, looking back at Persephone.

Hephaestus felt Persephone freeze behind him, and he knew what she was thinking. She knew Aphrodite didn't like him, and it was anyone's guess how she would react to this. He wasn't sure how to react to it himself if he was being honest.

"Do you think that's necessary?" she questioned. "He's head of security. He's probably busy, and having him follow her around seems a bit unfair to him."

"He's the best I have," Hades went on. "And he's most capable of figuring out who did this. He's going to have to be close to her anyway working on this, and correct me if I'm wrong, but odds are Aphrodite isn't going to take this lying down. She's going to want to be in on the investigation. It's best to have Hephaestus close so that she doesn't fall into any further trouble. He's the only one who has the means to both find the culprit *and* protect her. We might miss something if we send someone else."

Hephaestus, for all of his effort, couldn't find fault with that argument. Aphrodite may annoy him to no end, but she was at risk and he had a job to do. What happened last night happened with him not more than 100 feet away, and then they'd attacked him too. This was personal as well as professional, and he wanted to get to the bottom of it, preferably before she took another knife to the chest. The best way to do that was to work from the inside out, and there was no better place to start than at her side. It gave him complete access to Lush and oversight of the security team. If he was sure of anything, he was sure of this: last night's events would not be happening again.

He turned to face Persephone.

"Look, I'm not opposed," she assured both him and Hades with a meaningful look. "I would rather have him looking out for her, but she's — I don't want either of them to be uncomfortable."

Hades now addressed his nephew. "Hephaestus?"

Standing up as straight as he could, he raised one shoulder and shook his head.

"I have no issue," he conceded, his voice gruff. "She and I have never - gotten along well, but - I don't have a problem protecting her. I know how much she means to you, Persephone."

Persephone smiled, and although she looked uneasy, she offered no further rebuttal.

"And I'm gonna figure this out," he continued. "Soon."

"Okay," Persephone said after a moment. "I'll - talk to her."

"It's okay, Persephone. I can talk to her."

She eyed him warily but didn't argue this either. "She should be home by now, so we should probably head over."

"Agreed," Hades nodded. "And Heph." Hephaestus sought out his gaze. "Thank you."

"Of course, Uncle," he replied with a bow of his head. "I'll get it done. I can promise you that."

"I know you will."

The others pushed themselves to their feet then, Hecate and Thanatos heading for the casino floor after a round of hurried goodbyes. Charon clapped a hand on Hephaestus's shoulder with a heavy breath. Hephaestus turned his head to meet the elder's dark gaze, watching the worry fade in and out across his expression. He was only a few inches taller than Heph, ink adorning his neck and the sides of his shaved head. His golden brown skin was also well acquainted with scars of many kinds, and while he looked quiet and stoic, he wasn't the kind of guy you wanted to see angry. He had known Hephaestus all his life, and Charon had helped Hades raise him for most of it as well. Thanatos and Hecate were just as familiar, but Charon and Heph were a lot alike in ways that had bound them together over the years. It was Charon who had introduced him to metalwork, and although Hephaestus quickly excelled beyond his teachings, it was the passion Charon instilled that remained vital.

"Trust yourself always," Charon urged him, not for the first time. "And keep your eyes open."

"I will," Heph nodded.

"I'll see if I can find out anything on my end, check in with all my informants. Make sure you switch those radio channels too, and keep your most trusted guys close."

Heph smirked. "I know what I'm doing. I got it."

"I know you do, but we all need a little bit of guidance every now and then." He leaned closer now, his own smirk sharp. "And don't get too distracted over at the club, yeah?"

Hephaestus snorted, shaking his head. "I don't get distracted, so don't even worry about that."

Charon's smile grew, and he ruffled Heph's hair before the younger shoved his hand away playfully and turned to follow Hades and Persephone from the office. While he could feel the pressure now weighing on his shoulders to figure this out, he could not take for granted the secondary thought. He reasoned with himself then if only to subdue his nerves. If he could survive Aphrodite's reaction to this new arrangement, everything after would be easy.

Chapter Four

APHRODITE

Now that the painkillers were finally kicking in, all Aphrodite had left was rage. Rage at her attacker, rage at herself, rage at the situation, and rage at the amount of trust she had put in the people assigned to her security detail. She had vetted almost everyone herself on multiple occasions, and those she didn't see were double and triple checked by Eros or Artemis, who had run a smaller security detail in Aphrodite's district before she was promoted to the new city security forces. Even Ares had insisted he do background checks on some of the newer guys, which only made this entire thing exceedingly frustrating. How long had she been lied to? How many had played her for a fool?

Confusion and embarrassment lingered above her head like heavy storm clouds, pouring white hot shame over her shoulders where it seeped into her skin. She wanted to return to work as soon as possible, and not only because she hated sitting around. The last thing she was willing to give any one of these traitors was the privilege of seeing her down. They had failed in their assassination attempt, and they would live to regret it or so help her. She just needed to gather her bearings first.

"Achilles is downstairs," Eros informed her as he entered the room, red rimming his hazel eyes. Neither of them had slept, and he had been up here at least half a dozen times to check on her since he'd brought her back from the hospital. "There are a few guys missing but nowhere near as many as they think must have been involved." Putting his hands on his hips, he bit his lip. "I should've been there."

"You were there," Aphrodite pointed out, beckoning him over until he came to sit beside her. "As were Hector and Hephaestus. It didn't matter. They were three steps ahead of us."

It was easier to accept that when she was trying to convince someone else of course, but that didn't negate her disappointment. She took his hand in hers, brushing her thumb over his knuckles in a soothing motion. Eros had been by her side for years now, always looking out for her and holding her down. He'd been just a kid when she'd rescued him, and he'd been one of the lucky ones. He had only just been picked up by traffickers in Deucalion Heights days before he arrived in Khaos Falls, and the ship he was on was raided by Aphrodite's guard mere hours after it docked. He'd been more or less unharmed save for a few cuts and bruises from being snatched up against his will, but she imagined very little force was needed.

He had been a small and lanky ten-year-old back then with very little meat on his bones, and although he had tried to fight his way out, it had been a futile effort. She had been young herself at the time as was the Lush District, nearly a ten-year difference between her and him, but he'd been working alongside her ever since. He hadn't had a family to call, his mother abandoning him in a group home when he was a baby, but Aphrodite had taken him in without hesitation. Something in his soul spoke to her, and she swore they were meant to find one another. There was no one she trusted more than him apart from Persephone and her Aunt Hestia, and she knew that he was the closest thing she would probably ever have to a son. Not that she was complaining. She couldn't imagine having a better one.

She could tell that he was struggling with this, the reality that he had been mere yards away as she was attacked in that elevator. She struggled just as well, not with the wounds themselves but with the fact that a threat had made it into her club, her private elevator, her inner circle. She vowed every single one of them would pay. Eros was not at all a soldier in any sense. He could defend himself if he had to, but he was soft in all the ways she thought good people should be. Truly, she would rather take a thousand attacks than ever see him hurt. She wouldn't tell him that though, at least not right now.

"Did you talk to Psyche?" she asked then, attempting to eat up the tension.

He perked up immediately. "Yeah, everything is good over there. They had no problems whatsoever. Artemis thought maybe they would have tried something if she hadn't had her forces in place, but she's planning to settle them in for the foreseeable future."

"Did Asklepios send those counselors over?"

He nodded. "There were some pretty bad stories. I'm sure you can guess, but some of them - this wasn't their first trip around the Aegean. They're still not convinced they're out of danger yet."

"I really fucked up, didn't I?" She muttered it more to herself than to him after a brief bout of silence, but he squeezed her hand nonetheless.

"I think you did what you thought you had to do. And I mean, you *did* save 'em. They're gonna be alright, and we'll protect them for as long as we need to. We always do."

She shook her head. "I should've gone for the ringleaders and shut the shit down for good. Hephaesus's annoying ass will probably never let me live it down once I'm outta this bed. The bastard."

Eros chuckled, moving to sit beside her against the headboard of her bed. She rested her head against his shoulder, smiling as he kissed the crown of it.

"Do you even know why you hate him so much?" he questioned. "Because y'all are wild. I feel like I'm gonna burst into flame every time I step between y'all."

Aphrodite rolled her eyes. "He's an asshole for one, and it seems like the only things he knows how to do are give orders and pass judgment. And he's *always* fuckin' judgin'. You can see it in his eyes. He never laughs or smiles or nothing either. He's like - an A.I. or something. That is not the type of company I'm tryna keep."

Eros burst into laughter. "I used to think the same thing about Hades until I went to his birthday party and watched him lose his mind over chocolates. Maybe you just haven't seen him in the right environment, you know. Like - *outside* of work."

"That is the last thing I ever plan to do. In fact, no matter when I see him next, it'll still be way too soon. I'm gonna need you and Achilles to be my liaisons or something."

"At least he's good at his job. He'll figure this out quick fast, and then you can go back to pretending he doesn't exist for the majority of the month."

"If only."

Eros hummed, stroking his chin. "Well, he does seem to have that whole grizzled look going for him, so at least you have something pretty to look at when you do gotta deal with him."

"Yeah, when his mouth is shut."

Eros chortled again, shaking his head as she managed another smile. Truth be told, she didn't want to get into it, the way Hephaestus had this air about him that always made her feel like some silly little girl who had no clue what she was doing. Despite being slightly younger than her, he had always been so quick to disregard her beyond the commonplace acknowledgement and respect of her position. Or maybe it wasn't disregard but - disenchantment? Yeah, maybe that was what irked her, how he always looked so damn bored when he had to be in the same room as her, as if he was too good to keep her company and too smart to carry a conversation with her. It had been so since they first met years ago as teenagers, and yet, she would never get used to it. And dammit, she shouldn't have to.

It shouldn't bother her of course. She had all the love and admiration in the Aegean at her disposal, so one man —especially a man, and especially Hephaestus of all people— should be inconsequential to her, more so when it appeared that he didn't feel anything for anyone at all. Instead, he somehow knew exactly how to make her feel small without meaning to, to make her question herself without looking at her, to make her squirm without saying a word. Stoic, sharp, and cold as stone, he offered nothing without a price while acting like he knew everything, and it got to her. And he didn't even fucking realize just how deeply it touched, which made it all that much fucking worse.

Not that she didn't have her own insecurities that easily inflamed these thoughts. Aphrodite still had those days where she struggled to find comfort in her own skin, what with transitioning in a spotlight with very little secrets to keep for herself. She was constantly under that spotlight to this day, and with every spotlight came an overwhelming amount of scrutiny. She would sometimes catch herself wondering if maybe that was the problem, that he didn't like women like her, but how could that be true when she'd watched him take to Persephone in just a few months? What the hell was it about Aphrodite that was so unforgivable to him?

Ugh, it didn't matter. He wasn't the type of person she needed validation from in any form. He had always been exactly who he was, and there was no way it had anything, much less everything, to do with her. Even if they did continue to work together on stopping the trafficking rings, she was not going to afford him any more time than was absolutely necessary.

"I'm just gonna—"

She paused as the sound of the elevator filled the suite, Aphrodite more hyper aware of that bell than she had ever been before. Eros froze too, which meant he wasn't expecting anybody, and both of them stared at the door as Aphrodite reached for the blade under the pillow beside her. Before she could pull it out however, the man in question him-fucking-self appeared like a shadow in the doorway, and her exhaustion bit down on her throat with unyielding strength.

Hephaestus was in all black as usual, his crisp shirt buttoned to the top and accentuating the thick muscles of his arms and chest. She remembered tracking them with her gaze earlier that morning, and now she couldn't seem to unsee them to her annoyance. His thick black hair was pushed back from his sharp face, the sides freshly shaved almost down to the skin. She imagined it was so that they could properly stitch up his head, no doubt another scar to add to his expansive collection. She could see how angry the skin around it still was, and she suppressed the desire to flinch. He'd shaven his face too, leaving only the faintest fuzz along his jawline and across the top of his lips. This left both of his eyes, the darker grey and slightly cloudy one, fully exposed, and they pierced her mercilessly, pinning her to the cushions. The wounds she had sustained last night were nothing compared to that stare. She would rather take the knife.

The scar running from forehead to cheek over his left eye caught the light as he stepped over the threshold. While it was harder to see without direct light, it branched out across his face like cracks in the surface of a frozen lake. He led with his sleek black cane, different from the one he had been carrying last night, the head of it shaped like that of a hammer. She imagined it could shatter a kneecap with the same efficiency as one too as well as many other tricks if last night was any indication. That was one problem that all too many people had. They underestimated the man. She never had, no matter how easily he grated on her nerves. She was reckless, not stupid.

"I'll go down and see if Achilles needs anything," Eros announced even as she glared at the side of his head. "Call me if you need to."

He gave her a pointed look as if warning her to behave before kissing her forehead and disengaging from her. He gave Hephaestus a curt nod, and once the other man returned it, Eros left the room. Aphrodite listened as the elevator bell dinged once more before she looked up at her unwanted visitor. She assumed he was here to question her again more fully, but she truly was not in the mood.

"Do you think that maybe we can do the questioning a bit later?" she huffed, laying back against her silk pillows. "I haven't slept yet, and I have a lot to do downstairs."

"We can," he agreed with a nod, "but that isn't what I'm here for."

She raised a perfectly shaped brow. "Then what are you here for? An apology, I hope."

He scoffed. "For what? I didn't stab you."

"If you would've helped me like you said—"

"If you hadn't rushed into it like... You know what? Let's not, alright? We need to get comfortable because we're stuck together for the foreseeable future."

She sat up. "What does that mean?"

"It means we can't trust your security, and I need to be as close to this as possible to figure out who tried to kill you before they decide to try again."

"—And?"

"And so I'm your new guard, alright?"

There was a brief beat of silence before she barked a laugh. "No, you are not."

"Yes, I am, and this will be much easier if you abstain from being a child about it."

"Oh? And would it be any easier if you abstained from being a jackass about it?"

He shrugged. "Possibly."

They stared at one another for what felt like forever, and Aphrodite hated how unnerved she was by his lack of emotion, of expression, of anything human at all. It was as though he was encased in an impenetrable armor, deflecting any and all kinds of feelings the moment they got too close. She could be expressive and eccentric at times, but Hephaestus never seemed to even smile beyond that cruel half smirk he donned when he knew something you didn't know — which was a lot more common than she cared to admit. She kept their interactions few and far between for a reason.

She also had no clue how he could be so different from every single one of his brothers. For one, she and Ares had far more in common, which was saying something because it always seemed like they had nothing in common outside of their sporadic fooling around. They shared passion though, and passion was one of the most important characteristics to Aphrodite. She valued few others above it. However, she also valued intellect and insight and intuition, and Ares seemed to lack each and every one of these more often than not. He was intelligent surely, but he didn't often use it, and when he did, it had the potential to do just as much harm as good. If Hephaestus thought *her* reckless, she couldn't imagine what he thought of his younger brother.

It wasn't that Ares was a bad guy. It was simply that he seemed misguided in common courtesy. Hephaestus seemed to exist on the opposite end of that spectrum, knowing only logic and nothing else. Her comment to Eros was absolutely on point now that she thought about it. He reminded her of a robot. She supposed being *mildly* raised by Hera and Zeus *and* being tempered by Hades may account for much of it, but there was something else too...

But what did she know? Maybe he was just different, and that was the beginning and the end of it. Either way, she wasn't looking to find out nor was she looking forward to having him stuck to her side at all times. She supposed she'd spoken too soon about making Eros and Achilles her liaisons.

"I'll be in here to sweep the room right before you go to bed every night and right as you wake up each morning." His gruff voice, paired with that bored look on his face, made her fists clench. She said nothing. "We'll be interviewing all of your guards, whether they were on duty that night or not."

"I don't think that's necessary," she sighed, laying back once more and shutting her eyes.

"And I don't think that matters." She bit her tongue as he continued. "We can't find the leak without knowing every brick in the wall. You can come if you'd like though. It might help. Seeing you could make people nervous, and nervous people make mistakes."

"Mm, and how long did it take you to learn that clever tidbit, Hephaestus?"

"About as long as it took me to accept that you were going to be a pain in the ass the entire time that we're stuck together, and I have to actually protect you while you are."

Her eyes slid open, meeting his gaze head on. Those vibrant orbs still bore into her in a way she almost could not stand, but she stood her ground. She would not be frightened away by any man, least of all a son of Zeus. And least of all of those, Hephaestus.

As her eyes scanned his face, she caught the gash on the side of his head from last night again.

"Why did you do it?" she questioned, her voice distant, filing away his insult for a later time.

"Why did I do what, Aphrodite?" he returned, nearly yawning as he leaned against the doorframe.

"Why did you agree to this?"

He sighed. "Certainly not to spite you, believe me. It's my job, remember? And it meant a lot to Persephone and my uncle. They know I'm the best option."

"Even if we end up killing each other before this is over?"

"As hard as it's gonna be, *I* know how to be a professional. As for you, I'll lock you up if I have to. That's not a problem."

She looked away, taking his reasoning with a grain of salt. She may respect —and even appreciate at the moment— the characteristics he shared with his uncle, but it was those that he garnered from his parents, or in spite of them, that made her wary. They were the ones she had to look out for.

"Okay, well, do you have to stand in the room with me the entire time?" she sighed, pinching the bridge of her nose. "I need to sleep."

"I haven't slept either, so I figured it's best I share your bed."

Her head whipped towards him so fast that she swore her neck cracked. And that was the first time she'd ever seen him grin, his scars shining and both of his eyes darkening with glee. *Bastard.*

"I'm kidding, Princess." His voice dripped with poison. "I'll be right outside."

Then he was gone, and Aphrodite found herself glaring at the empty space beside her.

Chapter Five

HEPHAESTUS

The clock on the wall counted off the seconds with a palpable tick, the sound echoing through the room and gliding through the compressed tension. Hephaestus tapped his fingers against the surface of the table before him, his eyes surveying the man sitting across from him. He looked as skittish as a mouse, fidgeting in his seat every few seconds as the silence wore down on him.

Hephaestus was all out of questions, the barest thread of patience holding his frustration at bay. Again, nothing. No information, no observations, no leads. He knew it was only a matter of time, but that didn't make the wait easier. It was just hard for him to believe that none of the 40 people he'd talked to today knew anything, and he'd taken various approaches to the questioning based on each individual he came across. Some were shy, some were egotistical, and some were desperate to do a good job. However, none of them offered any insight whatsoever.

"Alright," he sighed at last, causing the other man to jump. He was one of Aphrodite's newer guards, but if he was in on the assassination attempt, it wasn't of his own accord. Heph would get very little from any foot soldiers. "You can go, Titus. Back to work."

Titus immediately nodded, standing up so quickly that his leg banged against the table. He apologized vehemently before rushing out of the room, his face red and washed with sweat. Hephaestus turned to Hades now, who was seated beside him, Charon at their shoulders. Aphrodite had been with them most of the day, interrogating each of her guards in turn, but she'd stepped out for a break roughly three interviews back, and he hadn't seen her since. Persephone was with her though, so he didn't worry too much, and his forces were manning the club. She couldn't be much safer in his opinion.

"What are you thinking?" Hades inquired with a sharp gaze.

"None of them," Hephaestus concluded, shaking his head, and Charon squeezed his shoulder in agreement. "They'll come though. We still got a lot to go through, and I was careful with how I scheduled the interviews."

"I figured you were." Hades smirked as they each stood. "How are things going with Aphrodite thus far? Well?"

Hephaestus raised a brow. "She's not dead, right?"

His uncle chuckled as did Charon.

"None of us missed Persephone's - *hesitation* yesterday," Charon relayed to him with a knowing look. "What, did she break your heart or something?"

Heph snorted a laugh. "She's the one that doesn't like me. I don't know what it is, but there is just - something about me that makes her seethe with rage every time she sees my face."

"And you have no idea what?"

"Not at all." He shrugged, smoothing a hand down the front of his shirt. "But each time we have to share a space, the first thing I get from her is an ugly look or some snide remark."

"I appreciate you both being adults about it," Hades sighed.

He clapped a hand on Hephaestus's shoulder although he didn't look entirely convinced of the explanation. What could Heph say though? He wasn't sure what Aphrodite's problem with him was, not entirely. All he knew was that she hated to be called out on her bullshit. He didn't kiss her ass and bow to her every whim like so many others, and maybe the rest of the world had spoiled her to the point that any divergence from that was a personal attack. Either way, he wasn't about to go down on his knees and beg for her to be nice to him. She could deal with whatever problems she may have with him on her own. They're hers and hers alone after all, and he wasn't shouldering any of that blame.

"Have you heard from anyone else?" Hades went on.

Heph shook his head, clearing his thoughts. "I got word back from my contacts in Naxos and Thassos saying they were willing to help try and ID the assassin, but information has been hard to come by out in Thassos. They've just been taken under new leadership again, and there's a lot of movement."

"I have Hermes checking shipping logs for anyone new that had come into the city recently and hadn't left yet. Even if they're using private ships to move their victims, it's possible they sent others ahead to prep locations."

Heph nodded. "That's a good call. I'll check with Achilles in a bit. He's supposed to be looking over the discrepancies in scheduling last night. We wanna see who got swapped out, and who didn't come in at all. He's looking over the camera film too."

"Someone had to have slipped up."

"I'll go down there and take a look too," Charon assured them. "Give him some fresh eyes."

"And you should go check on your charge," Hades told Hephaestus with a pointed look.

"She's with Persephone," Heph grunted, rubbing the back of his neck. "I'm sure she's fine."

Hades smirked, moving his hand to Heph's back and patting him there. "I'm sure she is too, but you're the one tasked with confirming that, so go on."

With a sigh, Heph nodded. "You got it."

The three men left the office together, going their separate ways as they reached the main hall. Hephaestus made his way to one of the standard elevators in the front room, which was currently packed with people in various states of undress and intimacy. Despite his steady pace, he kept his eyes straight ahead, finding no pleasure in letting them wander. It wasn't that he minded the atmosphere. He liked the freedom that it offered people, and he respected all the good

Aphrodite did within these clubs. However, intimacy was hard to come by for him even when he actively sought it out, and he wasn't the type that could just have sex with no strings attached. Meaning he also wasn't the type that could get off on someone else's pleasure, permitted or not. He'd never worked like that, and he doubted he would start anytime soon.

Besides that, he preferred metalwork to mingling. He would rather be in his workshop than out in the city, and it had been so since he learned how to use his tools. Metalwork was his safety net and his first —perhaps only— love. Sometimes it still shocked him that Hades had talked him into taking this position when the whole reason he'd declined running the Olympus District was because he didn't see himself in place of leadership. Yet here he was, protecting an entire city despite feeling as though that same city would have let him drown if they had no further use of him.

It was nearing midnight now, and Hephaestus found Aphrodite in her office with Persephone as he expected, but the latter seemed to be on her way out. He waited at the door, leaning against the railing that overlooked the main floor and letting his eyes scan the boundaries of it to ensure his guards were properly stationed.

Minutes later, Persephone stepped out onto the landing, giving him a smile and embracing him without warning. He stiffened in her embrace for a moment, still not at all used to her unconditional affection with him and his brothers. It wasn't that Charon and Hades hadn't been affectionate, but both men and Hephaestus had always been less prone to it than say Dionysos. In fact, Heph imagined he and his uncle wouldn't care for affection at all if it weren't for his baby brother, but he didn't hate Dio for it. Sometimes, it was kind of nice, and he really did like Persephone. She was the best possible match for his uncle, and she seemed to take up the mantle of proud auntie rather quickly.

At last, he relaxed and wrapped an arm around her.

"Thank you again for watching over her," she muttered against his neck, and he swore she may have been crying. "You have no idea how much it means to me."

He nodded. "It's the least I could do. I'll make sure she's safe, I promise."

"I know you will. I trust you. And-" She pulled back then, and he released her. "I know she can be a bit difficult at times, but she means well."

He managed a smile. "I know she does. Her heart's in the right place. It just - takes some time for her head to catch up. That's what I'm here for."

He wasn't just saying that either. She was difficult as hell, but Aphrodite wanted to help people just as much as he did, probably even more so. The difference was that she wore her heart on her sleeve and let it guide her every action, and he just didn't do that. He couldn't. As Persephone looked at him with all that gratitude in her eyes though, he found that he truly wanted to try and make this work. He wanted to help Aphrodite.

Even if it felt like pulling teeth half the damn time.

"I'm gonna go find your uncle now," she said, patting his cheek softly in a way that almost made him recoil. Not because it was uncomfortable but because it was so unfamiliar. "You two behave."

His smile widened. "Of course. Good night."

As Persephone continued down the stairs, Hephaestus turned his attention back to Aphrodite, who had moved to the window at the back of her office. He couldn't make out much of her features due to the shadows cast around her, but from here, she looked angry and lost and out of her element. It was something Hephaestus had never seen on her in any capacity. He hated that he noticed it. He hated that it made him feel uneasy.

Against his better judgment, he stepped inside, but her eyes did not leave the moon framed in the glass. He took up the decanter on the bar across from her desk, pouring two glasses and balancing them in one hand before moving over to her with slow steps. He still hadn't had much sleep, and he feared it was beginning to show. He set the second glass on the sill, and only then did she acknowledge his presence. Or at least, she looked away from the window, picking up the glass and sloshing the contents around before she moved towards her desk.

"Did you see anything of note today?" she asked, her voice ragged.

"No," he responded, "but we started with the least likely. I remember every guard I saw that night. None of them were here today."

She paused, glancing up at him. "You remember all of them?"

"Yes." He took a sip from his glass. "And I have an idea of the most likely suspects, but I want to make sure there weren't any smaller pieces, people that had other roles outside of the club that night or even guys that were booted off the schedule last minute."

"And you think you'll catch them? Just by questioning them?"

"Not at all, but it creates pressure, urgency. I don't even expect everyone to show up tomorrow. The people we talked to today will no doubt tell the rest of your people how we're doing things. I have eyes on them though, so if they try to run, I'll know."

For a moment, he thought she might look impressed, but he didn't put much stock into it. Collapsing into a seat, he stared at his glass before bringing it to his lips. He could feel her watching him, but he refused to react, only awaiting whatever absurd thing came out of her mouth next.

Instead, she asked, "What if you're wrong?"

He didn't ask her to specify. "Then we start over."

"There will just be another one, someone else to come for me."

"Not if we shut them all down."

"We can never shut them *all* down."

"Not with that attitude."

He glanced over the lip of his cup to find her staring at him although her expression was entirely unreadable. That was new.

He took his time, drinking deeply before lowering it to his lap.

"It'll take time," he conceded. "And we'll obviously need a more permanent solution than my personal presence on you at all times, but I'll find the leaks. I'll find the cracks in the armor, and then I'll replace the armor and prevent those same cracks. And if I have to do it again, I will. That's what I do. It isn't perfect, and it isn't foolproof. There will always be someone else or something else because that is the world we live in, but my job is to deal with each and every one. Preferably in a timely manner."

After a moment, she chuckled. "Sounds very heroic."

"I'm not a hero."

She rolled her eyes. "Of course you aren't. You would rather play the bad guy."

"Only so that I can catch the real bad guys off guard."

"So then what are you?"

He sighed, running a hand through his hair. "I'm a realist, Aphrodite. I don't put together fairy tales and pick out protagonists. I am who I have to be for the job that I'm tasked with and the people that I care about."

"I'm surprised you care about anything at all."

He flinched without meaning to but caught himself quickly. It wasn't the first time someone had said it to him. It wasn't even the first time Aphrodite had said it to him, and he doubted it would be the last time either. He'd followed in his uncle's direct footsteps for so long, intent on being a mirror image in all but reflection, he had no clue what to do now that the path had changed. He had never planned for that. His uncle no longer sought out solitude. Instead, he was blooming into quite the celebrated leader, seeking out company and showing his face at every charity event and holiday festival. Hephaestus was happy for Hades of course, but it made him question how right the elder had been when he'd said that solitude was safest. If Hades no longer believed it, where did that leave Hephaestus?

He supposed in the same place. He had far too many secrets to protect to follow his uncle down that slope. Besides, Hades may have passed on many of his traits, but he and Hephaestus differed in all of the ways that mattered to a world like theirs. In every other aspect, he was far more like Charon, smoke in a room that you don't notice until you've left it when it lingers on your clothes. For that, he would never be alone in the dark corners of the world. But Hephaestus had not only chosen solitude. Solitude had chosen him too. He could never be the face of anything. He was born to the shadows and betrothed to obscurity. It was where he belonged.

He tipped his glass towards her. "You should be glad that I do."

"The guns don't count."

"But the job does. I'm sure you can agree to that."

"Does the job keep you warm at night?"

"The money damn sure does."

Out of the corner of his eye, he caught her roll hers again, and the grip on his glass tightened.

"You know what I mean," she pushed, and his jaw flexed.

"No, I don't think I do."

"Money isn't made to be loved like that, above all else. Above people."

"Not everyone needs a happily ever after that looks like yours, Princess. Just because you need someone to make you feel whole doesn't mean everyone does."

"Excuse me? Uh uh, you don't know a damn thing about me."

"Oh, you're making it pretty clear. Maybe I don't care about all the shit you care about like the worship and the warm sheets, but I know what matters to me. I know who I am. Do you?"

She jumped up so fast that he had to fight not to reach for a weapon, looking up at her just as she snatched the glass from his hand. There was a potent wrath in her eyes that made her skin flush and her hands tremble enough to where some of the rum splashed onto his pants. He could see it. Of all the nerves he'd touched, he'd never touched one like this. He almost felt ashamed. *Almost.*

After a moment of sheer surprise, he let out a bitter laugh.

"Aren't you supposed to be out in the hall guarding it?" she barked. "Or investigating something? What are you sitting here drinking on the job for?"

"My job is to watch you, and I doubt anyone's gonna try something with me sitting right here," he grunted, but he stood up anyway and straightened his shirt. "Besides, your rum is weak."

"Get out, Hephaestus."

Her eyes cut through him like the finest blades, and he didn't need telling twice. Turning around without another look, he left her alone in the office, ignoring the way that his heart pounded as he did so. Usually, seeing her riled up for some petty reason was the best kind of entertainment he could think of, but tonight, it felt irresponsible and out of place. Even if Persephone hadn't just thanked him for being grown about this whole thing, he would still feel like the arguments of old had no place here in this current climate. Instead, clashing heads with her had him on edge.

...Or maybe it was the argument itself, broken open in a time when things were so different and continued to change right before his eyes. What was a happy ending in a world like this for a man like him? Zeus was gone. His mother was off the radar. His uncle was in the spotlight, and his brothers and Athena were thriving. And he was still the blacksmith with the cane and the cloudy eye, an omen no one wished to cross. That was once a crown he wore with pride, the nephew of the Wraith, but now? He was no one's son. He was no one's celebrated leader. He was simply the shield that protected them all, and when he outlived his usefulness, they would simply find another one.

As he positioned himself outside of the door, Achilles appeared on the stairs, determination written across his face.

"We got a runner," he declared.

"Who?"

"Apparently one of the night managers. Kleon."

"How did you find him?"

Just as he said it, another man with bronzed skin and dark hair appeared behind Achilles, a few inches shorter with a barreled chest and one of Aphrodite's insignia patches on his chest — Hector. He raised his hand, indicating that he was the source of the information.

"He told me he'd cleared it with Aphrodite, but I know that's a lie," Hector explained. "She and I go through vacation requests together, especially when he's gonna be gone because I take over scheduling for him. There was no way she said yes without telling me. Plus, she asked about him that night, the night of the attack, and I told her he had called out. He told me he had an emergency."

"But that's not true," Achilles chimed in now. Hephaestus gave him a questioning look. "Artemis said he was there, at Twilight, welcoming the girls."

"After he called in?" Hephaestus raised a brow, and Hector nodded in reply. "Why did he tell you then? That he was leaving?"

"Well, he was here earlier. I overheard him talking to one of his new hires, saying he was heading to the Sarpedon Port, so I asked him."

"What new hire? Where is he?"

"Nikolaos. I put him down in the security office manning the cameras. I confronted Kleon in the parking lot, so I didn't spook him into running too."

"I doubt he would tell just anyone he was leaving if he didn't have to," Achilles pointed out.

"Well, he definitely didn't *want* to tell me," Hector huffed.

"If he's lying like that, it means he isn't planning on coming back, is he?"

"My thoughts exactly," Hephaestus agreed.

"I got guys headed for the ports," Achilles went on, folding his arms over his chest. "Even if he changes plans and tries to jump on a ship from the port in the Harvest District, they'll be waiting for him. He won't get far."

"No." Hephaestus shook his head, a thought striking him. "Put a tail on him. They go wherever he goes. I wanna see where he ends up."

Achilles nodded, pulling out his phone. "You got it. I'll send Patroclus. He was heading down there with the first squad."

"Perfect, I know he can handle it."

"And the kid?" Hector questioned.

Hephaestus still wasn't entirely sure he trusted the guy, but he'd been more helpful in the past ten minutes than anyone else had been all day, so he would take it. For now, he would consider Hector an asset. If he turned out to be otherwise, Hephaestus would weed him out soon enough.

"I've scheduled everyone's interview already. I'll talk to him when his time comes."

"And if he tries to run?"

Hephaestus smirked. "Even better."

Chapter Six

APHRODITE

Aphrodite was already awake when Hephaestus's characteristic knock graced her bedroom door that morning. She didn't bother answering, but as expected, he entered a few moments later for his morning sweep of the area. She was sitting in front of her custom crafted vanity, combing out her thick locks, and she caught a glimpse of him in the mirror.

Briefly, she wondered if his entire closet consisted of crisp, black button-ups that accentuated his chest and the harsh cut of his biceps, but she refrained from asking. He didn't seek her out, instead proceeding with checking the bathroom, the closet, and even underneath the bed. She'd already expressed her annoyance the first two times he'd done this. It would be a waste of breath now.

Since their little argument in her office a couple days ago, he'd made a habit of coming in, combing the space, and walking out. However today, once he finished, he instead moved towards her, a solemn look on his face. She continued to brush out her hair, focusing on that rather than his approaching form until he spoke.

"Kleon," he said simply.

Her hands froze, and her eyes met his in their reflection.

"What about him?" she questioned, her words slow.

"Tell me about him."

"He's one of my best guys, and - my friend. He's worked for me for years. I hired him myself pretty soon after I took over the district. Why?"

"He ever give you any trouble at all? Any reason to look at him funny?"

"No." She scoffed, not at Hephaestus per se but at the mere thought that Kleon would be trouble. "He's been in his position for nearly a decade now, making the schedules, training and recruiting guards. He trained Hector when I promoted him. He's always been dependable for me."

"So you talk to him a lot."

"Can you just get to the point, Hephaestus?" The conversation was making her anxious.

"Was he supposed to be on vacation this week? Did he clear that with you?"

Her stomach churned. "No, and I would know. I would have to know even if he didn't tell me himself, and I would like to think that he would. The night shift is the busiest, and Hector doesn't approve any long-term vacations without my okay."

"And he supposed to be here the night of the attack."

"Yeah, but Hector said he'd called out, that he had an emergency."

"He lied. He was at Twilight when the rescues arrived. He helped get them settled until Artemis told him it was best he leave. Then he jumped a ship in the Sarpedon Port the day we started interviews."

The brush fell from her hands as she turned to look at him fully.

"What?"

He nodded in confirmation. "Hector overheard him talking to another guard about leaving, and when Hector confronted him, he said he'd cleared it with you."

"No, he did not... So you're saying he had something to do with the attack?"

"Currently? It sure sounds like it."

"What do you mean 'currently'?"

"We didn't stop him from leaving. I put a tail on him to see where he went. He's in Thassos right now, but he's just been holed up in a hotel for the past two days, so we don't have anything solid yet."

She paused, her brows furrowing. "What other guard was he talking to?"

"Nikolaos. Hector said it was someone Kleon hired."

She nodded. "Kleon recommended him, and I gave him the okay."

"So now—"

"Wait." She put her hand up, a headache threatening to overtake her. "Nikolaos was on the raid that night."

"Really?" Hephaestus looked genuinely surprised. "He wasn't on the schedule, and the security log doesn't show that."

"I know he was there. I know that I saw him."

"Okay, and I believe you. I'm just laying out the rest of the facts."

"Did you talk to him?"

"He's on my schedule for this evening. You wanna come with me?"

"I think you can handle this one without me." She feared that if she saw him right now, she might break, and she had no clue what that would look like under the circumstances.

"How long has he been working here?"

"He's only been with us at Lush a year, but he was part of a third-party company we used for one of my other dens while we were still hiring. Kleon recruited him back then too." She paused, scraping mud off of the memory. "Actually, he's the one who did the hiring for that den. He found the third party."

"What was the name of the other company?"

"I don't remember, but—"

"But what?"

"It wasn't local. They sent people from Thassos."

They stared at one another for a long moment, his lips pursed and her mouth agape. She was glad to finally be able to connect some dots, but the cost was taking a toll already. Kleon... Kleon, who she considered a good friend and a great mentor, whom she trusted with her life, literally. After all this time together, what would possess him to turn on her? Worse than that, how long had he been plotting to?

Hephaestus seemed to notice how anxious she was growing, so he broke the silence.

"Alright, I'll check on that, see if I can find a name to give Patroclus. He's the one tailing Kleon. Achilles is gonna come up and stay with you for an hour or so. I've gotta go check something out."

She was still reeling from everything he'd just told her, and it took her a moment to register what he was saying now. Pushing the more treacherous thoughts away, she looked up at him again. He was close, close enough for her to catch the scent of his cologne, close enough for her to make out what lied beneath his scars. He was tired, the bags dark beneath his eyes, and the eyelid over his murkier one drooped heavily. She cleared her throat and gathered her bearings quickly.

"You can go," she urged. "I'll be just fine on my own for an hour, Hephaestus."

Although even as she said it, unease settled in her chest.

"After this? I'm not taking that risk." He straightened up with slow movements. "And if you see any of your men without one of mine..."

He reached behind his back and pulled out a pistol. The barrel was silver, but the handle was plated in white with black markings, and if she didn't know any better —which... she really didn't— she would say it was one of his own personal weapons. She eyed it warily. She'd only shot a gun on a few select occasions, none of them life or death, and she was certain that she would look foolish if she picked this one up for any reason. She would probably end up hurting herself before anyone else, but she wasn't about to tell him that. She didn't feel like drawing out his more villainous side at the moment. She was just getting comfortable with his work mode.

"I definitely don't need that," she chuckled, allowing her blade to slip from her sleeve into her hand before she flicked it open.

He placed it on the vanity beside her fallen brush and patted the handle.

"Let's hope not."

She watched him leave, allowing the onslaught of information to settle before she continued getting ready. She wasn't sure what to think at the moment or who to be angry with. Instead, she felt numb and unsure of what would happen next. It had been a long time since she'd felt so out of control, so helpless to the events unfolding around her. Nonetheless, she was fully intent on returning all of her attention to work today. She didn't want to sit around locked away in a tower any longer than she already had, and she wouldn't allow the morale of her district to be lowered in her absence. She'd survived so much worse than a few cuts and bruises, and she damn sure wasn't scared of anyone.

She placed Hephaestus's pistol in her purse to keep it safe nonetheless.

The walk down to her office had a pleasant effect on her nerves. The increasing volume of the music below seeped through the red felt walls and into her skin, soothing all of the places her stitches didn't touch and any crevices that the pain medications couldn't reach. She descended the last flight of stairs onto the second floor landing with her chin held high and her shoulders rolled back, eyes scanning the immediate area. She recognized none of the guards spread out across the floor. It was ironic how that was supposed to be a comfort. She did recognize the face coming up the stairs however.

Achilles was once a renowned mercenary before being employed by Hephaestus in Khaos Falls. He was a bear of a man, his dark brown skin taut over corded muscles in every visible place beneath his clothes, his head and face closely shaven and his molten brown eyes large and luminous. He was tall, much taller than Hephaestus, and his shoulders could fill the entire frame of her door when he breathed in. He also smiled, and despite the imposing size of him, that smile was boyish and comforting. He gifted her with it as he reached her.

"Aphrodite," he greeted her, bowing his head.

"Achilles," she returned. "Nice to see you."

"Oh, I'm sure you don't mean that, not under the circumstances, but thank you all the same."

She laughed. "I prefer you to your boss."

"Hey, he might be a bit - rough, but he's good at what he does. You've got the best protection in the Aegean by all accounts."

"I do appreciate that."

"I'll be right out here if you need anything. Just press that little button on your radio, and the call comes straight to me."

Aphrodite glanced down at her hip where the radio Hephaestus had given her the first day now hung. If she was honest, it felt a bit silly when she could see Achilles through the glass. Nonetheless, she nodded her understanding, deciding to save any objections for Hephaestus upon his return. Leaving Achilles with one more smile, she turned and entered her office.

All things considered, there hadn't been much fanfare around the events that had taken place in Lush several nights ago, and she was thankful for it. She knew the news had spread quickly through the city, but Hades seemed to gain control of the narrative twice as fast. That was one thing she loved most about their new leader. Where Zeus probably would've been nowhere to be found, Hades had been at her side and on the frontlines the moment things transpired, and not just because she was Persephone's best friend. The man handled his business, and he looked out for all the district leaders to the best of his ability. She was thankful to have that support, more so because she didn't even think it possible. Then again, Zeus had set the bar very low in his time as leader, and so naturally, everything Hades did felt over the top to some extent. Not that she would complain.

She had only just sat down at her desk when the door opened again, a massive figure eclipsing the doorway. It was not Achilles however. With dark locks falling around his face and a tumultuous gaze that made her freeze in place, Ares entered the office without preamble. He had always been an open book, much like her, his emotions in fine print upon his face and the more minute details expressed through the flex of his forearms and the clench of his fists. More often than not, she appreciated the simplicity it offered their engagement, but she was becoming acutely aware that Ares didn't want simple. It was certainly not what he'd come here for today. He was angry, and whether it was warranted or not, it wasn't something Aphrodite had the capacity to deal with at the moment. Setting her hands on her desk, she braced herself.

"You haven't been answering my calls or texts," he grunted.

"I've been a little busy, Ares," she drawled, recovering from the initial apprehension. Because of course *that* was why he was mad. "In case you hadn't heard, someone is trying to kill me."

"That's why I've been calling." His voice rose slightly as he closed the door behind him. "It's not safe for you here."

"If I worried that much about my safety, I wouldn't be running a district. Speaking of which, isn't that something you should be doing?"

"Don't be so callous about it, Aphrodite."

"I don't have time to be anything else right now, but if you would like to discuss this at a later time, I can definitely—"

"I want you to come to Olympus with me."

"For?"

"So that I can protect you."

Her eyes darted up to his, searching his face for the signs of a joke. She found only the tight knit of his brows and the deep lines of his forehead. She scoffed, laughter lingering in the wake of the sound as she shook her head.

"I don't have time for this, Ares."

"I'm serious, Aphrodite. You'd be safer with me."

"I'm just fine right here, and if I wasn't, I wouldn't be safe anywhere."

"I want you to come—"

"You want me to run, to hide behind you like some helpless damsel, and I'm not doing that."

Long ago, Aphrodite would have given anything and everything to be the helpless damsel that the brazen hero came to rescue, defeating some rancid villain before whisking her away towards her happily ever after. And sure, every now and again, she still fantasized about such things, but she was grown now. She still envisioned a happy ending. Of course she did. She believed she deserved it, but it had evolved into something more manageable, something that didn't cost her autonomy. Hephaestus liked to joke about it, but the truth was that Aphrodite was simply a lover of love, and she wouldn't apologize for that. It did not mean she had forgone standards.

"I want you to be safe, Aphrodite! And I want you with me!"

"Those things are not mutually exclusive." She breathed out slowly through her nose. "And I have a district to run."

"We can do that together, from Olympus."

"I don't care what we can and can't do. I'm telling you that I'm not going. I'm not running."

He growled. "Now really isn't the time for your pride."

"Oh, and it's a good time for yours? What do you really want me there for, Ares?"

"I just told you!"

"And then what? I move into your house and settle down? Be the woman at your shoulder?"

"That would be the logical thing eventually, yeah! We can get married like normal people, have kids. Or adopt them, something!"

"Ares, please."

"What?"

"I can't do this right now. I know you mean well, and I am flattered that you want those things with me, but it isn't what I need right now. Everything is hectic and - and demanding, and I have to focus on staying alive before I can think of anything like that."

"You always have an excuse."

"It isn't an excuse. You're the one using this attack as an excuse to push your agenda."

"Agenda?" He scoffed. "It isn't a fucking business deal, Aphrodite! This is our life together!"

"And I have told you before, but you never listen."

"Told me what!"

"Those things you keep trying to force me, they're..." She gestured vaguely with her hand. "They're not what I want."

"Why not?"

Her anxiety skyrocketed from one moment to the next, sweat trickling down the back of her neck. She felt like she was suffocating, heat clawing at her skin with relentless insistence. She did not want to hash this out with him right now. She didn't want to fight about something that had never been guaranteed, certainly not for her. The world was crumbling around her, and all she wanted to do was go back to work, to help someone and remind herself that she wasn't weak, that she wasn't helpless, that her father wasn't right. Looking down at her hands, she tried to focus on her breathing.

"Because I just don't," she said slowly. "—and I don't have to."

"That's not a reason, Aphrodite!"

"I don't need a reason that you approve of, Ares. It is my choice too."

Slowly, her nerves became malleable, giving way to a monolithic frustration. It picked at her exhaustion and nipped at the stress of the last few days, setting it ablaze like kindling.

"We have had this discussion already," she continued, clinging to the dregs of her composure. "I'm currently not interested in having it again."

"Why not!" His voice was growing louder, ricocheting off the walls of her office.

"Because I have more pressing matters on my plate right now, and I need you to respect that—"

"I'm trying to help with that. You would be safe in Olympus—"

"I'm not leaving, Ares. I'm not leaving my people or my district, and the fact that you would even ask that of me only proves my point. You don't value me beyond the role that you've written for me in your life, and I've already been with that kind of man. I won't do it again."

"Are you fucking kidding me!" He shoved a chair aside, stepping closer to the desk and jabbing a finger at her. It pressed the last possible button it could, her blood boiling. "What is your issue! Every time I bring up the future—"

"Because I don't see a future with you!"

The words shattered between them, cutting through the air like shrapnel before scattering across the floor like marbles. The silence that followed was a living, breathing thing, descending upon them with the weight and volume of a tidal wave. Aphrodite had yet to realize she was on her feet, bent over her desk and breathing hard. The words rang through the room, an echo at her back that came on the cusp of a cold wind. They were clear despite the blood singing in her ears. Ares' eyes glinted with an unbridled rage, his teeth bared and his face a bright red, but before either of them could react to what she'd said, the door opened again.

Hephaestus walked into the room as if Ares wasn't there, coming to a halt several feet in front of him beside her desk. Only once he met her eyes did he look over his shoulder at his younger brother with about as much interest as one would have for a plastic bag on the street.

"Brother," he said, voice dripping with faux surprise. "Sorry, did I interrupt something?"

"Actually, Heph, ye—" Ares began, but Hephaestus looked back at Aphrodite.

"I need to discuss something with you. It has to do with what I told you earlier, and it's kind of urgent, so..."

Aphrodite gawked at him, her own wrath still brimming just beneath the surface, scraping away at the inside of her skin as it searched for an exit. Truly she didn't know which brother was worse company at the moment, but she couldn't bear to even look at Ares, so she let that be enough. Inhaling a deep breath, she nodded.

"Ares was just leaving," she asserted, shifting her gaze back to the larger man. "I'll call you if I find the time."

Ares opened his mouth to retort but seemed to think better of it, clamping his lips shut with a hard swallow. He looked between her and Hephaestus, the latter of whom regarded him with a stiff nod, before turning around and leaving the office, shaking his head as he disappeared down the stairs. Aphrodite allowed herself a moment to calm herself, expelling the negative energy coursing through her veins with a heavy breath. Or at least some of it. When she'd done the best she could, she threw Hephaestus an expectant look. He shrugged his shoulders.

"It really wasn't that urgent," he confessed nonchalantly. "Just looked like you two needed a referee or something."

Her vision was suddenly tinted red. For some reason, that sentiment angered her more than anything Ares had said.

"I don't need you to save me," she growled coldly.

"Although I'd beg to differ under the circumstances, that's definitely not what I was doing, but I could hear you two from the first floor. So I imagine everyone else could too. It isn't good for morale when it sounds like the district leader is cracking under pressure."

Her eyes fell to the surface of her desk once more, her fingers pressing into the wood hard enough to leave a print. Her knuckles were sheet white, throbbing faintly from the pressure. She ground her teeth so hard that she feared one might shatter. In the corner of her eye, she saw his face fall.

"Seriously," he muttered, his voice absent of sarcasm. It sounded almost alien. "You okay?'

"I'm fine! Can I just have a fucking minute!"

She pushed away from the desk, moving around him and out of the office. She needed to breathe, to find some solace away from the matter —or rather, *matters*— at hand if only for a moment, otherwise she might implode. She longed for the days when the sons of Zeus weren't making her life more difficult, and she vowed to return to them the moment she had the chance.

Rather than retreat upstairs, she descended down onto the main floor, a place she felt most at ease. Signaling for a drink, she waded into the crowd of bodies who were playing spectator rather than participant in the ongoing scenes around them, some of them swaying to the music while others swayed against their partners or both. While there was a decently sized dance floor in one corner of the main room, Lush also had a dedicated nightclub downstairs for those who liked the atmosphere but did not fancy exhibitionism. She had tried to make it a place for everyone, and judging by the feedback over the years and the nights consistently at capacity, she would say she had succeeded. As she looked around, she reminded herself that she still had a purpose, one that had nothing to do with Ares or her father or any other man who had tried to derail her before.

As she found an open sofa near the back wall where the partitioned playrooms were located, someone called her name through the crowd. Looking up, she searched for the source, unable to find it until bodies parted before her to reveal Psyche, Eros striding up behind her like a proud puppy. As usual. He was dressed in a crisp white button-up with short sleeves, his curly hair dyed a glamorous blue on top and a single earring shaped like an arrow dangling from his left ear. Psyche wore a simple dress with a black skirt and a white top, the two of them color-coded in a way Aphrodite was used to by now although she wasn't sure it was ever on purpose. Psyche's natural hair was picked out in a perfectly shaped afro, her glasses perched on the edge of her nose and her brown skin catching the neon so that it looked like she herself was glowing. She had started out as Aphrodite's assistant several years ago after she graduated college, but she had just taken over Twilight

House, the main survivor's shelter in the Lush District. She had always been a calming presence, and after seeing her with the victims all these years, Aphrodite knew there was no one better for the job.

The two slid into the booth beside her, Eros sliding her the drink that the bartender must have handed him after taking a small sip of it himself.

"Just wanted to make sure it wasn't poisoned," he said with a wink, his tone cheeky.

"Mhm," Aphrodite hummed with narrowed eyes.

"And I came to check on you," Psyche interceded with a smile. "I'm sorry I haven't made it down here, but I've been texting Eros nonstop, and he told me to just come see for myself how you were."

"Girl, please, don't apologize," Aphrodite assured her. "You're doing the real work, and I could never thank you enough. How are things goin' over there?"

"As well as we can expect. A few of the counselors have stayed on site to help the younger ones cope. They've been having some trouble sleeping of course, but Artemis hasn't left the site. She's really made everyone feel safe, comfortable. Me included."

That didn't surprise Aphrodite. Artemis was one of the fiercest people she knew, a natural born protector, and she had been running various security ops in Khaos Falls for years as a third party including several for Aphrodite in the past. When Hades initially announced his plan for citywide security, she had been certain Artemis would be first on the list for a leadership position. Granted, that was when she was certain Hephaestus had no desire to help anyone directly, only supply the weapons.

"Have they found anything?" Psyche asked now, her voice quieter.

Aphrodite glanced around, making note of the nearest guards and making sure they weren't her own men. It was painful to do so, but her paranoia was sharp, and Hephaestus's constant warnings were now a mantra she couldn't get out of her head.

"They have a lead or two but nothing solid yet," she relayed then, Eros also leaning in over Psyche's shoulder. "Hopefully by tomorrow, I can give y'all some real updates. Just - don't let anyone in that house, okay? At least, none of my men."

Psyche's eyebrows lifted, but she didn't ask any further questions, seeing the look in Aphrodite's eyes. She picked up her drink instead, sipping it slowly as she glanced around the club. Aphrodite hated to put them on edge any more than they already were, but it was vital to their safety. It still left a bitter taste in her mouth though.

Vaguely, she could feel Hephaestus's piercing gaze on her from somewhere above, no doubt her office window. She forced herself not to seek it out. For now, she simply wished to exist for a few hours before she returned to an empty bed and a full plate of trouble.

Slipping out of the booth abruptly, she beckoned Eros and Psyche to follow.

"Where are you goin'?" Eros questioned.

"Come on," Aphrodite coaxed. "Let's go dance."

"Don't you have stitches?"

"I'm fine. Now come on."

Eros and Psyche glanced at each other, but Aphrodite quickly snapped her fingers between them.

"I'm happy to go by myself," she teased.

At last, with a collective sigh, the two got up and followed her out to the dance floor, the throng of people absorbing them with ease. Aphrodite didn't mind that they were soon separated by several feet, instead focusing on finding a body to move with herself. The hands of one of her regulars soon found her hips, and she melted into the simple pleasure of touch and affection as she melded into him.

Even then, she could still feel Hephaestus's hawk-like gaze, and no matter how she closed her eyes and let herself live in the moment, she couldn't shake the vision of him watching her. She moved more fervently against her partner, turning to face him instead. He had striking green eyes and light brown skin, and any other night, she could get lost in him. But not tonight. Tonight, there was something far too heavy on her back, and the harder she tried to ignore it, the deeper it cut.

Chapter Seven

HEPHAESTUS

Hephaestus's eyes tailed Aphrodite through the club, wandering every now and again to inspect her surroundings before they returned to her. She didn't seem all that concerned with doing so herself, but he can admit it. She looked like she needed whatever therapy that came from dancing with some random guy and so much seduction that members of the crowd had started turning from the actual sex scenes to watch them. Or maybe just to watch Aphrodite.

He supposed he could understand it though. It was easy to get mesmerized by the sway of her hips and the toss of her hair, the shape of her mouth as she laughed and the way her hands sought out her partner in any way they could. And then when she met his eyes every now and again, whether blatantly or by accident, there were these chills that...

He took a long drag of his pen, berating himself for his distraction. He couldn't afford it, even if she seemed to have that effect on everyone who gave her the attention she sought. He wasn't everyone. But what else was he supposed to do? He had to watch her anyway, didn't he? Besides, it wasn't all that hard to pretend she was someone else from up here. It didn't *have* to be her.

It had been hours since she'd stalked out of her office, and the discomfort had yet to leave him. It laid over his shoulders, bogging him down like waterlogged clothes. He thought it would be easier to work like this. She had her freedom, and he had his vantage point. Everyone was happy. And yet, he couldn't shake the feeling that he should have followed her or at least said something else to keep her from leaving.

But why should he care? Whatever she had going on with his brother was irrelevant to the job and irrelevant to him. He was meant to protect her from death threats, not the treachery of her own heart. She had made it pretty clear she didn't want his help in that department anyway. He had nothing to feel bad about. Nothing at all.

If only it were that easy to turn off.

He watched her move to the bar now, which spanned the center of the room amidst the poles and furniture that surrounded it. The end of it ran into the far wall, splitting two of the large windows that separated the main room from the playrooms that could be either public or private with the push of a button. They usually went live after eleven, putting far more focused scenes on display or just a few people going at it for the world to see. There were more props involved in them too from what Hephaestus had gathered, and they included actual beds that could be kept for the night by those who were too worn out to get home.

The exotic dancers were at work from open to close as were the public spaces and private rooms on the second, third, and fourth floors. Servers and workers littered the place in various states of dress, their dress code left in their hands at Aphrodite's behest. The sex workers in the business of private appointments were also able to choose when, where, and how to take clients so long as a guard accompanied them to and from the appointment and the client was thoroughly vetted. Those appointments very rarely took place outside of the dens though. As of now, none were, Aphrodite and Hephaestus in agreement that it was safer not to allow house calls. As for these appointments, workers could stop any and all acts with one utterance of a safeword, and most clients knew better than to test that boundary. Those who did, well... it never ended well for them.

Aphrodite had gone all out on her first establishment which was as much a nightclub as it was a pleasure den. Other dens in her district were strictly one or the other, but Lush was an oasis for all, him included. It was one of the easiest places for him to move around in, with elevators throughout and ramps rather than stairs wherever the two could be swapped out. He could appreciate that at least. Aphrodite had a good heart. It was just - surrounded by teeth.

Her gaze snagged on his own once again as she had a drink with a woman he didn't recognize. A deep smirk was etched across the stranger's face, the neon lights dancing across her skin, delighted just to be near Aphrodite. The crowd seemed to close in on her, her very presence magnetic, inviting. They were drawn to her like moths to flame, and if he peered over his own dislike, he could see why. Aphrodite was, at her core, the embodiment of love. It poured from her lips and burned behind her eyes. She exuded it in its purest form, a salve for the most critical malady.

He looked away first.

"Heph," came a voice from behind him at the door.

He turned around to find Achilles standing there with a man at his shoulder. He was much shorter than Achilles, his light brown hair pushed back from his face and his brown eyes darting this way and that. His nervous energy permeated the air with a tangible weight, and Hephaestus knew right away that this was Nikolaos. He beckoned them forward.

"Nikolaos is here for his interview," Achilles explained. "You want me to take him down to the security office?"

"Naw, we can do it in here, it's fine," Hephaestus assured them. "It shouldn't take too long."

He led them over to Aphrodite's desk where Nikolaos sat down before it and Hephaestus took up her chair. Achilles remained standing at Nikolaos's shoulder as if prepared for him to run. That was good. What could be more uncomfortable than being in the office of the woman you tried to help kill flanked by Hephaestus and Achilles?

Nikolaos squirmed in his seat.

"How long have you worked here at Lush, Nikolaos?" Hephaestus began, his tone friendly.

Nikolaos scratched his head. "Uh, about a year or so."

"How did you wind up working here?"

"Well, I-" He looked down at his hands, and it seemed like he was weighing his options on how much to reveal. Hephaestus was all too familiar with that look. "Kleon, one of the security managers, he hired me. I was working at the Wild Rose for a while before I was relocated here."

"And you were working independently or?"

"I - well, no. I was with a, uh, another security firm."

"Oh, okay. And what firm would that be?"

Nikolaos let out a nervous laugh. "Is that - I mean, is that relevant? They weren't really that, uh, happy that I left them for this job."

"I'm not calling them for a reference, Nikolaos, I just need to know the name."

"—Okay, I - it's Labyrinth Security."

"That's not here in Khaos Falls, is it?"

"No, it was in Thassos."

"Ah, okay. You're from there originally?"

"Oh, uh, no. I went there for work. I'm - I'm from Naxos originally."

"So you move around a lot."

He shrugged. "I guess so."

"How long were you with this Thassos firm?"

"Um, I'd say about a year or so?"

"You plannin' on staying here long then?"

"I - I mean, this is my favorite job I've had so far, so I'd like to."

Hephaestus nodded, his eyes briefly catching on Achilles as he pulled out his phone. "Alright, thank you for that information, Nikolaos. Now, Kleon. He hired you. Did you know him beforehand?"

"No." He was quick to answer. "I - no, I only met him when we were sent over from Thassos to work at the Wild Rose."

"But you're pretty close now, I imagine. Working together for over a year."

"I - well, not really. I mean he's cool, and we're familiar with each other, but I wouldn't say we're super close at all."

It was fascinating to Hephaestus how the truth behind every one of his lies was written across Nikolaos' face. It was as though someone on the other side of a mirror was rearranging his words and giving Hephaestus hints to what was real and what wasn't. The fact of the matter was that Nikolaos was a liar and a horrible one at that. Still, there was one more lie Hephaestus needed him to tell.

"And you worked the night of the attack?" Hephaestus asked slowly now.

"Oh, I - well, I helped on Aphrodite's raid. Kleon said he couldn't make it and asked me if I could fill in for him, give Aphrodite the numbers. I wasn't doing anything, so I agreed."

"But you left immediately after?"

"Yeah. Yeah, right after. I didn't even come back to the club."

He must have known Aphrodite had seen him. Shame. "And you haven't seen Kleon since?"

"Uh, no." *Ah.* "I haven't seen him or heard from him since."

"But you saw him that night?"

"No, I - I only talked to him on the phone."

Hephaestus regarded him, narrowing his focus on a single drop of sweat descending the side of his reddening face. It wasn't enough, but it was certainly a start. There was no doubt in Heph's mind that this man before him knew more than he was letting on.

"—Alright, well that's all the questions I have currently, Nikolaos, thank you. I'll be in touch if I think of anything else, and I would ask that you do the same."

"Of course, thank you," Nikolaos managed, looking almost surprised at the brevity of it all.

He didn't waste time leaving the room, giving Achilles a short nod before scurrying around him.

Both men watched him go until Achilles turned back around and took up the seat their interviewee had just vacated. Hephaestus let out a heavy breath and dug out his vapor pen again. He had no clue how long he'd been on his feet, but he was feeling the ache, creeping down along his lower back and into his legs. He had learned to live with the pain well enough to function for hours without feeling it, but as of late, it had begun to catch up with him much quicker. He knew it was due to the change in temperature, and he usually planned well for the transition, but he simply hadn't had the chance with everything else going on. He inhaled the hit before giving Achilles his full attention. The larger man held up his phone, waving it slightly.

"Got into his phone," he informed Hephaestus with a grin. "He's still making a whole lot of calls back to Thassos, specifically to a number registered under Labyrinth Security."

"Odd to be calling a firm that isn't happy with you, right?"

"Very."

"He was only working under Kleon for a short while before being brought into Lush. Seems like a short time to get such a big role."

"Working at the Wild Rose is a pretty important role on its own."

Hephaestus nodded. It was true. The Wild Rose was a niche place, reserved for more extreme kinks and specializations. Aside from Lush, it was arguably Aphrodite's most popular pleasure den, and it was frequented by the biggest names in the city, including the heirs of Tartarus and Heph's own brother Dionysos. Top dogs meant top security, so there was no way he had been placed there on a whim.

"I'm thinking Kleon put Nikolaos on the raid so that he could give updates on Aphrodite's whereabouts," Hephaestus said. "When he knew Aphrodite wasn't going to Twilight, he showed up there."

"But why?"

"To see the security setup? If they planned to get the girls back as soon as Aphrodite was down, he had to know what they were up against before they made a move. Does he have any other ties to that firm apart from hiring them?"

"I can check. Patroclus has been trying to get into his phone, but he's struggling to get close enough. He still hasn't left that hotel room though."

Hephaestus nodded, scratching his chin. There was something else bugging him that he couldn't quite put a finger on. Kleon was in a pretty high position with Aphrodite. He had even accompanied Eros on a few arms deals with Hephaestus back when that was Heph's primary gig. Kleon was older, his dark beard streaked with silver, and the hair on his head thinning considerably, but he was in good shape, and he'd seemed like a genuine guy. But in the Aegean —and especially in Khaos Falls—greed was God, and everyone had a price. If Kleon had decided he could make more money in trafficking, why wouldn't he dabble in it? Especially when he was trusted by the one threat they'd faced in the city before Hephaestus came along.

"How far do those phone records go back?" he questioned, his gaze still somewhere else.

"I've only gone back the past few months," Achilles returned.

"What about Aphrodite's employment records?"

"Uh, we went back on those like two months? Why?"

"Go back a little further on both.They must have planned this before my uncle established our security forces." Achilles watched him, expectant, so he went on. "Kleon found a side gig in the trafficking trade and realized he was making nothing compared to what he could be bringing in. He had all the tools to start planning this, including complete control over the night shift, and Aphrodite trusted him to make recruiting calls. He could have brought in all of his co-conspirators slowly over time, and they may have used fake names, but at least we'll have an idea of how many were involved if we can find a hiring pattern over the past year or so. With Aphrodite down, Kleon could've moved a lot of these girls back into the trade. They trust him. He takes care of them."

"So why did he run? He had to know what that would look like."

Heph's gaze snapped back to the room. "Her death was the only option. Once we had city forces, he knew how difficult it would be to keep things up. He was gonna get whatever he could from her death and probably skip town anyway. The point is, he isn't the mastermind here, and honestly, I'm not even sure he's a top dog. If this Labyrinth Security is at all important, that means Nikolaos might be calling the shots since he's the one taking the calls. He could be playing dumb with us just in case a connection comes to light, so he won't be seen as important."

"Which means Kleon was just the perfect link between whoever he's working for and Aphrodite."

"Exactly."

"I'll weed out the new hires over the last year, try and get a glimpse of their phone records."

Heph leaned back in the chair, Aphrodite's chair, as he chewed his lip. "Have Patroclus send someone over to check out this firm. Don't question anyone until I give the go ahead, but scope out the location and see what we can find out."

"You got it."

Achilles stood, obviously giddy with this new phase of the investigation, just as Aphrodite entered the office, glowing beneath a thin sheen of sweat and glitter. Hephaestus offered her an instinctive smile before he caught it, allowing it to fall unceremoniously from his face. Achilles offered her a more genuine one as he approached the door, bidding her goodnight before leaving them alone in the room. Hephaestus pushed himself to his feet, checking his watch. It was still an hour before closing.

"Tired?" he asked.

"A bit," she replied, still catching her breath.

"Did you have fun though?"

She stared at him hard as if trying to determine if he was baiting her. "Yes, thank you."

"I'll walk you up."

She looked absolutely prepared to protest, but once he moved past her, whatever she planned to say seemed to die in her throat. She retrieved her purse from inside one of the locked drawers of her desk and followed him to the elevators. Once they were safely inside and she'd entered her code, she turned to fully face him. He kept his eyes on the doors as though they might burst open and reveal another assassin, but the silence got to him in time, her eyes burning a hole in his neck. He spoke first.

"You keep my gun safe?"

She sucked her teeth before patting her purse at her side. "It's fine." A brief pause, and then, "What was that about? Did something happen?"

"We talked to Nikolaos. We have a few leads we're checking out. Patroclus is gonna have someone check out that security company Nikolaos worked for. He's apparently still in touch."

"And Kleon?"

"Still holed up in that hotel in Thassos. They're trying to get into his phones but no luck yet."

"Oh."

That was all she said, and it was only then that he realized she hadn't complained this entire time about how long the investigation was taking or how slow they were going. Sure, she complained about him personally, but since the first day, she hadn't been all too combative about having him as a bodyguard. For some reason, he found that amusing. Not that he was going to tell *her* that.

He granted her a side glance as the doors opened into the penthouse. They each took off their shoes —something she'd enforced by day two for him— and proceeded to her bedroom, where he began his usual scan of the space.

"Do you honestly think someone is going to get up here and hide in my closet?" she asked.

"Better safe than sorry," he said as though it were a mantra.

"What a refined code you live by."

"There's really no need to refine it if it works. It's not a code. It's simple logic."

"And you are definitely a man of logic."

He got up off of the floor with the help of his cane after checking under the bed, pushing his hair back out of his face to look at her.

"I am," he confirmed. "Why does that bother you so much?"

"I never said it bothered me," she shot back.

"It seems to, a whole lot actually. Or maybe it's just logic in general."

"What's that supposed to mean?"

"It means maybe you don't like rationality and realism. It bites into all your little fantasies too much."

She scoffed. "How about we talk about why *you* have such a big problem with how *I* think?"

"I only have a problem when it interferes with my job or when you use it to come at me. Remember I'm not the one gunning for you every chance I get."

"Oh, really? Because you always seem to want to make every argument about that the first chance that you get."

"And you always wanna make some kinda remark about the way I think."

"I simply stated a fact!"

He waved her off, but she only stepped closer, prepared to cut off any attempt to leave the room. He suppressed a smirk and a growl all at once.

"Have you been drinking?" he questioned.

"Oh, fuck you, Hephaestus," she spat. "You're a realist, but having a real conversation sends you into a panic. If we aren't talking about guns and security measures, you're a fish out of water."

"This isn't a real conversation by any standard, and you didn't seem too eager to have a 'real' conversation with my brother today, so is that really the stone you want to pick up right now?"

She pointed a finger at him. "You have no idea what conversations I've had with him every day before this, so don't you dare act like you understand."

"Don't I though? You wanna sell everyone this fucking bullshit about a mushy happy ending, but you run from it every chance you get."

"Because a happy ending isn't just about plugging in the first guy to propose. I can want something good without lowering my standards or abandoning my self respect."

"And I can have a happy ending that doesn't look like yours."

"Oh yeah, you look really happy all of the time."

He took a step closer. "Maybe not around you, but that's a special circumstance."

"Because you hate seeing things that you want and can't have."

He barked a laugh, and he almost missed her flinch. *Almost*. "You think that's you? Don't flatter yourself, Princess."

Her hands balled into fists at her sides, visibly shaking. "That - isn't what I meant! You want to be around people, and you don't know how. You're - you're like a fucking robot that doesn't let itself process human emotion."

"A robot? Seriously?"

"Yes! That's exactly what you are! Do you even feel anything? Do you experience shit?"

"I don't reserve all my emotions for the likes of you, Aphrodite, and I damn sure don't owe you any of them. I'm not one of your devout little dogs that comes running every time you hold out a bone. Get the fuck out of here with that."

"You act like you're too good for everyone! Like you're so above being here or talking to me ever! And maybe it has to do with your fucked up childhood and your fucked up parents—"

He stepped forward so fast that he nearly stumbled, but it effectively silenced her. With his eyes boring into hers, his voice dropped several octaves and just as many degrees in temperature.

"Or maybe it has to do with the fact that I can't stand to be around you."

Something shifted in her eyes then, something he didn't quite comprehend, and it was so sudden that it startled him. Her brows smoothed out slightly, the wrinkles in her forehead fading, her lips parted. He moved back an inch, unable to process what it was he was seeing. Before he could even begin to try, her face morphed into something twisted and spiteful again, her lips curling into a snide smirk.

"You can't break me, Hephaestus."

He huffed and rolled his eyes. "Trust me, Aphrodite, if I wanted to, I'm certain I could."

But he could see the venom collecting on her lips now, a malignant glint in her eye, and he knew what came next. He was all too familiar with that glint, perhaps not from her but familiar nonetheless. She was going to find the first soft spot she could and drive a dagger through it.

"What is it, Heph?" she hissed. "What are you so afraid of that you just - exist like this?"

"Aphrodite..."

"Are you alone because you want to be or because you don't know how to be anything else? You were so much like your uncle, right? Mr. Mystery, the town's urban legend. You followed his shadow around like a little puppy. And now he's in love and thriving, and what are you doing?"

"Right now? Trying not to finish what the enemy started."

A bitter laugh left her lips, and he forced himself not to wince. "You wouldn't dare, and you know why? Because between you and I, who would the city mourn? And who would they throw from the cliffs without any questions asked?"

The words touched not just one nerve but all of them. Every single one of them sparked beneath his skin, his vision blurring and his head pounding.

"I've accepted who I am," he snarled, his voice like ice and shattered bone. "But you will never accept the fact that they love you for who they think you are, not for who you are when you're alone. But you don't like her much either, do you?"

They both moved at the same time, but he managed to press her back against the wall even with her blade pressed against his throat. His cane was now flipped, bottom up, with its hollowed end fitted beneath her chin. He didn't flinch now. He didn't give.

Surprise and disorientation clouded her face for only a moment before she bared her teeth.

"Did I touch a nerve?" she asked, slightly winded. "Maybe you *do* feel something."

"And you got what you wanted. Me letting *you* feel something."

Her eyes flashed. "Do you fuck the same way you do everything else, going through the motions until the mission is complete?"

He paused then a sharp chuckle left his lips. "Of course that's what you really care about, isn't it? Is that what you need to feel something? Or are you afraid it's the only thing you'll ever be good at?"

"Fuck you, Hephaestus."

"You stay saying that. Is that what you're after, Princess?"

Her eyes widened, anger flaring her nostrils. She pulled back her blade just enough to shove against his chest, but he didn't budge, not a single inch, despite the tremors racking his legs. She moved to step around him, but he grabbed her around the waist, pulling her closer. Adrenaline coursed through him, anger and embarrassment clashing with it beneath his skin. He fought to break free of the fog plaguing his mind, but all he could think about was that vicious smirk on her lips and the sharp cut of her words. She glared up at him, but she didn't push away again. Instead, there was - *challenge* in her eyes. And he was up to it. She said he couldn't break her. He would put that to the test.

He surged forward and crashed his mouth against hers.

Pliant lips gave way to harsh teeth and rabid tongues, and each of them had a hand in the other's hair before it was done. He was soon submerged in the chaos of her reluctant moans and his cane clattering against the bedframe before it hit the floor. It was irrational and illogical and everything he was not. It went against his very nature, the stark spontaneity of it, but it shut her up and proved her wrong. Because he felt *everything*.

He didn't know who pushed who away first, but when he opened his eyes again, there were several feet between them and a thick cloud of tension. They simply stood there, staring at one another, trying to catch their breath. It seemed to last a decade.

He swore he could reach out and clutch the uncertainty in his fingers, but instead, he ran them through his hair before leaning down to pick up his cane. He stared at the hammerhead for a moment, waiting for any sign of reaction —or reprisal— from her, but when none came, he stood again. Without sparing her another look, he turned away and exited the bedroom with steady steps, all but holding his breath until he collapsed on the couch in the living room. Only then was there impact. The reality of what he'd done hit him square in his chest, knocking the air clean out of his lungs. He had set out to break her, but he wasn't certain of his success. Instead, he was worried that trying may have cost him more than he was willing to bet.

And yet, he couldn't find the strength to regret it.

Chapter Eight

APHRODITE

Sleep was no friend of Aphrodite's tonight. She lay awake staring at the ceiling, her lips still buzzing with the memory of Hephaestus's kiss emblazoned across them. If she focused really hard, she could pretend to hear his breathing out in the living room. Though how could she really when her heart was pounding at max volume?

She hadn't expected it. The moment she believed she had him all figured out, he threw her for a loop and uprooted every presumption and predilection she'd come to him with. There had been nothing robotic about it, the way he'd kissed her, as though his life had depended on it. She could call it a spark, and it would be correct, but the word did not seem to encompass the sheer size of what took shape in her chest. It was more than a curiosity. It was a hunger. It was all of the things she had chased her whole life wrapped in the one thing she had sworn to steer clear of.

She couldn't wash his taste from her mouth.

She wasn't sure that she wanted to.

She rolled over for what must have been the millionth time with a huff, grabbing her phone off of the bedside table and opening up the first social media app her finger landed on. She hadn't checked anything of the sort since the attack and for good reason. An assassination attempt, and on Aphrodite at that, was the kind of news Khaos Falls held its breath for. And in such a temperamental climate, which tended to follow a change in leadership, every story like this was like bait on a line for those who revelled in chaos and disorder.

In all of the years she'd been combating local traffickers, none had ever been bold enough to try and retaliate, but here they were thinking they had spotted a weakness. While she didn't get too involved with the investigation, allowing Hephaestus and his people to handle it, she knew one thing for certain—once she had a name, she would be the one to deliver justice. She would be the one to save herself, and she wasn't open to negotiating it.

Currently, there was a whole lot of love for her on her timelines, an outpouring of support from her district and others across the city, but every now and again, there were the rare hateful and bigoted comments that she was far too used to by now. They meant very little in the sea of divine worship she was exposed to each day, but they still nicked at some nerve in the back of her mind that she remained at war with. That was the one negative byproduct of loving yourself. There was always someone trying to talk you out of it. And sometimes that someone was you.

As she scrolled, she bookmarked some of her favorite messages from people she was familiar with, mainly regulars at her pleasure dens and clubs that she interacted with often as well as many of her employees. However, as she perused the subsequent comments beneath someone else's, one in particular made her stop in her tracks.

It seemed offhanded and inconsequential out of context, but within the context of her attack, it made just enough sense to cause a distinct discomfort. There was no profile photo, and the name was just a bunch of letters strung together followed by several numbers, but the comment read "There are snakes in the grass, but no one ever watches for the ones in the trees". Beneath it was a picture of Lush's front exterior although it looked like it had been taken with an older camera phone rather than off of the internet.

She screenshotted the comment then clicked on the profile, but there were no other posts and no kind of identifiable information anywhere on the page. She chewed her lip, staring at the grey silhouette that sat in place of a picture. She considered going out into the living room to ask Heph if maybe someone could track down the commenter or hack the profile or whatever else they knew how to do, but then she remembered what happened earlier, and she decided against it. Besides, it may not mean anything at all, just a troll who wanted to throw himself in the mix.

Then again, how many people knew the more intricate details of the attack? As far as she knew, the fact that her own men had been involved was being kept under wraps, but the comment seemed to directly reflect that knowledge. Therefore, she had no choice. She would have to bring it to Heph's attention.

As if sensing her distress, her phone buzzed in her hand, the blank profile picture eclipsed by Persephone's smiling face. Aphrodite exhaled slowly, glancing over her shoulder as if to make sure the vibration hadn't summoned Hephaestus, and answered the call.

"Girl, why you up so late?" Aphrodite drawled.

"Um, actually, I'm up early," Persephone shot back. "Have you not slept?"

"Naw, I haven't."

"Is everything alright?"

Aphrodite's teeth sunk into the flesh of her inner cheek. She turned onto her back, eyes darting up to the ceiling as she tried to unpack what she was willing to divulge to her best friend. Truth be told, she wasn't up for saying a damn thing, at least not about Heph and his stupid lips and how soft they had been against hers or how possessive his hands had been on her body or—

"You there, 'Dite?"

Aphrodite blinked, focusing on Persephone's voice. "Yeah, yeah, I'm just - it's been hard, you know. Sleeping and shit. I'm - surrounded by people I'm not sure I can trust."

"Yeah, I get that. I bet you never thought Hephaestus would be the most trustworthy guy in the building with you, huh?"

"Not even close."

Now that she thought about it, it was honestly so wild that this was a fact. She hadn't even questioned it, trusting Heph. Even before she thought she could tolerate him, she had trusted him, and now she trusted him with her life undoubtedly. What an oddity.

"You two are coming tonight, right?" Seph went on.

"To your show? Absolutely. I wouldn't miss it."

"Maybe we can get drinks or something after. You need to get out for a bit. Feels like you're living in a damn snake den over there."

Aphrodite's mind jumped back to the comment. "That's exactly how it feels. All this time, I've treated this place like a fortress, like nothing could touch me here. Turns out it's the most dangerous place I could've been."

"Heph will figure this out before you know it."

"Maybe so, but we'll still have to get brand new guards, which means a bunch of strangers coming in here that I have to learn to trust all over again. Even if Heph and Hades are vetting them, it don't matter because I vetted my folks too. I still got burned."

"Look, if all this shit is nothing else, it's a lesson. We'll figure it out, and we'll be better about it next time. They took advantage of your trust, 'Dite, but that don't mean everyone will."

"It's just a little hard to believe right now, you know?"

"I do know. I worry about you every single day. You're the strongest woman I know, but that doesn't mean this didn't affect you. Of course it did. It's like - a home invasion. They invaded your fortress, your safe place. No one goes through that unscathed, but we learn our weaknesses and we strengthen them. That's what we gotta do, alright?"

Aphrodite smiled to herself. "You a motivational speaker now then? Okay."

"Girl, shut up."

They chuckled, the sound reverberating through Aphrodite's body and pushing some of the anxiety out. Until Persephone got to talking again, that is.

"And - thank you for being civil with Hephaestus," she said slowly as though she feared triggering something. "I was worried we'd have to stop y'all from killing each other by day 2, but you've both impressed me. If I didn't know any better, I'd say you were getting along."

Aphrodite could feel the flush clawing up her neck, and she cleared her throat. "We are adults, you know. We're capable of sharing space without showing our asses."

"Mhm." Something in Persephone's tone made Aphrodite squirm, but she didn't address it. "I'm still hopin' y'all can overcome whatever bullshit you're always butting heads about before this is over."

"Don't hold your breath. He's still annoying as hell."

"And you're still a brat."

"Excuse me?"

Persephone snorted, but whatever she was about to come back with was severed by a hum that Aphrodite could all too easily identify. Moments later, Hades' voice came through the phone, bidding her good morning in confirmation. She returned it with a soft smile. It never failed to warm her, seeing the love between him and her best friend on display. It was difficult to remember that fairy tales didn't exist when couples like them did.

"I'll let you two go," Aphrodite sighed. "I should get some rest anyway."

"Yeah, you better," Persephone retorted. "Because we *are* dancing tonight."

"Don't you ever get tired of dancing?"

"Never. I'll see you tonight though. Love you, girl."

"Yeah yeah, love you too."

Aphrodite hung up the phone and set it back down on the bedside table. Just like that, her mind dipped back into the memory of Hephaestus's ruthless kiss like a claim on her skin that she couldn't wash off. The room suddenly felt hot even though her sheets felt far too cold, but she wasn't about to try and unpack that. Whatever had happened, whatever he'd sought to accomplish, it didn't matter. She had to forget about it, and if she was lucky, he would pretend it never happened so that she could do the same. This was the last kind of complication she needed when everything else was falling apart. Hephaestus checked off several boxes she should not even be thinking about fucking with, and she had to remember that. At the end of the day, he was still who he was, meaning he was still no good for her.

REGARDLESS OF HER RESOLVE, APHRODITE STILL DIDN'T SLEEP MUCH. Hephaestus roused her from a superficial slumber with his routine check of her room, but she hadn't been at all interested in interacting with him. After that, he'd waited quietly in the living room until she came out just before noon, and they headed downstairs together on a silent elevator ride.

Once they reached the second floor, he proceeded to do a thorough sweep of her office as well before she was permitted inside. From then on, he more or less kept his distance, posting up outside of her door or sitting quietly in the corner while she pretended to work. It wasn't like she could get a damn thing done, her thoughts running a thousand miles a minute and the tension thick enough to cut with a heavy breath. She hated it. She also succumbed to it.

"Hey, can I show you something?" she said abruptly as he stood up from the chair, preparing to take up his post outside the door once again. "It's - I saw it last night online, and I don't know if it means anything or if I'm just being paranoid, but I figured I should show you anyway."

"It's good to be paranoid under the circumstances," he grunted, changing his course and approaching her desk. "What is it?"

She suppressed her surprise as he dragged a chair over to sit directly beside her, staring at her computer screen. Opening her social media platform on the desktop, she scrolled through the comments section again. However, when she found the original comment the weird one had been under, the latter was nowhere to be found.

She raised a brow, scrolling back up then down again to ensure it was the right comment even when she knew in her heart that it was. She could feel Hephaestus's eyes on her, but she didn't look at him, instead picking up her phone from the desk and pulling up the screenshot she had taken. Handing the phone over to him, she then tried to search for the profile, but it too was gone.

"You said you saw this last night?" he questioned.

She nodded. "The profile was a dead end too. No pictures, no posts, nothing. Does it mean anything to you?"

"No, but it seems to have a whole lot of meaning to someone. Your security's involvement isn't common knowledge. Once Achilles and I secured the scene, the only ones that knew were us, Artemis, and my uncle. Plus Persephone and Eros, but that's a given. Have you talked about it with anyone?"

"No. I mean, I mentioned it to Psyche to make sure she didn't let anybody into Twilight House, but I figured she had to have an idea with Artemis there."

He nodded and handed back her phone before scooting his chair closer, pulling the keyboard and mouse over to him. She could only watch as he stretched his hands as best he could over the keyboard, a slight tremble evident in them. She noticed that his voice was softer today than it usually was. Even when they discussed the current predicament, he carried the slightest tinge of sarcasm in his voice, a subtle reminder of what he thought of her, but that tinge was gone right now. She forced herself not to read too much into it. They didn't have time for any of that.

"This looks similar," he said suddenly, and she realized she was staring at him. "Same sequence of letters, just different numbers."

Turning back towards the computer screen, she focused on the comment he was highlighting. It was another blank picture, but the comment was far more cryptic. It read, "You keep snakes in your garden to chase the rats away. Your compassion does not grant you immunity to their nature." A chill ran down her spine as she read it over and over, memorizing it word for word.

"How does this work?" he asked.

"What?"

"This - the platform. You don't have to approve these?"

She shook her head. "No, it's called Optics. It's like an open forum. I have a page up, but I mainly promote my businesses, keep up with the folks in my district."

"Is this the only platform like this you have?"

She scoffed. "No, Hephaestus, I promote on every platform I can.

There are at least a dozen. I only have one personal page, but it's under a fake name, and I only have my close friends on that. I—"

"Close friends like your security guards?"

She swallowed hard but didn't answer, and he didn't wait for her to. Instead, he reached across the desk for a notepad and a pen, placing it down in front of her.

"I need you to list them all out for me, usernames and passwords too. I'll get Achilles to look over the traffic on a secure network, see if we can get anything."

"Will it matter if they just keep deleting?"

"Everything matters, and the more accounts they create, the more likely they are to leave a trace somewhere along the way. If we can monitor the traffic, we might be able to follow these back to an IP address or at least a general area."

She eyed him warily but didn't question him further, picking up the pen and beginning to list out all of the platforms she was active on. The comment continued to roll around in her head, leaving her more confused with each round. The thing about it was that she wasn't sure if it was taunting her or trying to warn her.

It would take one arrogant bastard to risk being tracked like that. Part of her wanted to believe that it was Kleon, regretting his treachery and trying to make amends for it. It would mean very little as far as regaining her trust went, but at the very least, it might mean he was willing to help. She berated herself for the thought quickly after though. She couldn't trust anyone to come to her rescue, least of all those who had put her in danger to begin with. The sooner she could accept that she had been played, the quicker she could learn the lesson it entailed. And she would certainly need that lesson soon.

Once she finished writing down each of her accounts, she slid it over to him. He didn't notice right away, his eyes fixed on the desktop screen, and she took the opportunity to sketch over his profile. The light furrow of his brow was the only indication of any frustration he may have been experiencing, but beyond that, he was as calm as he always was. His jaw wasn't clenched, his tanned skin wasn't flushed, and he had not a single dark hair out of place. She wondered just how early he woke up each morning or if he slept at all, what with him always coming into her room smelling clean and looking immaculate in that day's black shirt.

It was odd how many things she had never noticed about him before like the lighter scar below his left eye that looked like an X in the sand or the way his lower lip jutted out as he read something to himself. Her eyes drifted down to his hands, the fingers hovering over the mouse shaking slightly while the other hand tapped against the surface of the desk. He was always moving even when he looked like stone, and she doubted he even realized it. Either that, or he'd grown used to it.

"Do I have something on my face?"

He didn't look at her when he said it, and the sudden sound of his voice made her jump. Turning back towards the computer screen promptly, she warred with whether or not to ask what the hell had happened the night before. That war was still waging on when he stood up, leaving her floundering for some solid ground to stand on. In a panic, she stood too, and he turned to look at her with a brow cocked.

"What's wrong?" he questioned.

There was a beat of silence, and then a flash of white hot anger tore through her without warning. It didn't last long, but it served its purpose, reminding her who it was she was looking at. Hephaestus, who was standing here acting like he hadn't kissed her into a stupor last night, like it had no effect on him whatsoever, like *she* had no effect on him whatsoever. And suddenly, her desire for him to pretend it hadn't happened was washed away by her disappointment in him actually doing so. She ground her teeth together and shook her head.

"Nothing, I just - wanna figure this out sooner rather than later," she managed with a sigh.

"You and me both." He picked up the list, clenching it hard in his hand as if he feared someone might take it. "I'll get this to Achilles."

She nodded, her eyes crawling up his torso. She wanted to fist the front of his crisp shirt and wrinkle it to the point of ruin, the urge so strong that her fingers twitched at her sides. She was as angry as she was hurt, and she abhorred the fact that he could inspire two different emotions so severely without doing anything at all. When their eyes met, there was something in his that stalled her, a quiet kind of concern bubbling beneath the surface of his grey irises. His hand started forward, reaching out for her, but he seemed to think better of it, his arm going limp again at his side. Her heart stuttered.

"We're gonna figure it out," he said, his voice so stern that it left no room for debate. "Odds are these comments are just someone fucking around. They might even be Kleon or one of the other rats trying to throw us off their scent."

"And - what about Nikolaos? Where is he?"

"We have him down in the security office with one of my guys. We have to make him believe you still trust him, and giving him a front row seat to everything going on is the best way to do that."

"What are the risks?"

"Well, to start, he can track your movements if he pleases, and he can also map out the locations of my detail, but like I said, I've got one of my guys down there. He won't be causing any trouble."

"You have a lot of faith in your guys."

"I do. I have to."

"I had a lot of faith in mine, and look where that got me."

"We don't..." He groaned under his breath. "We have a different process. You had a rat at the top. There was very little you could do about that, and he wasn't a rat when you hired him. You're right though." She almost gasped. He had never said that phrase before, but she simply savored it in silence. "I know I have to be more careful with them, especially when we don't know who we're up against. They have a long reach, whoever it is, and I'll be mindful of that."

Somehow, that soothed a whole lot of her worries. "Okay."

"Look, you may not like me, but do you trust me?"

She chewed on her lip, and she could swear his eyes snagged on it. "Yeah, I trust you."

"Good, then stay put. I'll be right back."

She rolled her eyes, and yet somehow she still managed to catch his smile. She nearly choked on her own spit at the sight of it, out of place and yet so at home on his face. He didn't give her a chance to react any other way, turning and making his way out of the room. She watched him disappear into the elevator, a thoughtful look on her face. She hadn't lied. She did trust him, more than she had ever expected to, but that didn't change the fact. She wanted her own answers. She no longer wanted to feel like an outcast in her own club, so rather than stay put, she waited until the coast was clear, and then she headed down to the security office.

Chapter Nine

HEPHAESTUS

Hephaestus leaned against the cool wall of the car park around the corner from the elevator, smoke curling from his mouth in thin wisps. He balanced his cane on both of his palms, looking over the sleek cobalt finish and the shiny chrome hammerhead. It was a consistent comfort, taking the time to focus on the details of his weaponry, thinking of what he could have done better or what he could do next.

He had forged his first cane with a dagger hidden under the head when he was thirteen or so. That was the first time Charon took him to the armory in the River Styx District and taught him how to use the tools necessary for blacksmithing. After that, the elder had told him that those tools were at his disposal whenever he pleased, and from then on, Hephaestus had spent most of his time in that workshop until he was old enough to build his own.

By then, he was already selling his swords and daggers all over the city, and Medusa and Nyx had both recruited him to build weapons for their coastal defenses. The guns came later, and although they weren't his favorite, he understood that they had become necessary if only to defend against those with more bloodlust than sense. Although now that Hades was in charge, firearms dealing had been scaled back immensely, and it was helped along by Hephaestus abandoning his former work in those deals for city security. If nothing else, no one could say that Khaos Falls wasn't safer under his uncle's rule, but Hephaestus was convinced there was a lot more honor too.

The cane he held now had been fashioned as a gun, but the ammunition for it was more likely to paralyze someone than kill them. It also kept any target from shooting off a last-minute bullet, the toxin in Hephaestus's darts shutting down all motor skills in less than a second. The fact that it was something Dionysos and Hecate had cooked up made him glad that they both used their skills for good.

This cane wasn't quite as balanced as his other canes, but it was much lighter, which had become crucial with as much as he was on his feet these days. It was also far more inconspicuous than his others, and it had a few extra bells and whistles. Being that they were expected at Asphodel tonight, he wanted to make sure he had a weapon with versatility. The casino may be the most secure establishment in Khaos Falls, but it had only been a few months since its weaknesses had been put on display, and people didn't forget things like that very quickly. That meant that tonight wasn't simply about protecting Aphrodite but all who would be stepping into the line of fire. Like his entire family.

Footsteps echoed across the cavernous asphalt, the steps both heavy and quick. They weren't quick in the way of someone in a hurry but rather someone bouncing on excitement, making it rather distinct and easily distinguishable, for Hephaestus at least. Moving away from the wall to get a look at the approaching figure, Hephaestus smirked as he confirmed his suspicions. Dionysos was coming towards him, his arm still in a sling, but the rest of him buzzing with anxious energy.

He was substantially taller than his older brother, his skin a few shades darker and his eyes several shades lighter in a vibrant brown. Dio grinned wide when he saw Heph, picking his pace up into a jog and wincing when he jostled his shoulder. Hephaestus winced too, the memory of Dio laid up in a hospital bed pale as a ghost flashing through his mind. Yet another good reason for his excessive caution, he knew one thing for certain: he never wanted to be in that position again, watching someone he loved nearly fade beyond his reach. He couldn't do it.

Dio didn't seem at all bothered by his current inhibitions, wrapping his free arm around Hephaestus's neck and dragging him into more of a chokehold than a hug. Heph rolled his eyes but hugged him back around the middle, something he would never do with anyone else. He had never been the type of person that liked to be touched when he was younger, but once Dio became a staple in his life, that preference had devolved. At first, it was invasive and overwhelming, and Hades often had to remind Dio that not everyone showed affection the way that he did, but eventually, Heph realized how much it meant to his brother as well as how much it had come to mean to him.

"Aren't you meant to be guarding the lady of the house?" Dio hissed as he released Heph.

"She's up in her tower," he chuckled. "I needed some air and some time to get my thoughts straight."

"That bad, huh? I knew Uncle was taking a risk sticking you two together, but I still wasn't sure if one of you would strangle the other or not."

Heph shoved at his good shoulder. "Actually, we've been pretty - civil."

Though as soon as he said it, his mind rolled back to the night prior, to his momentary recklessness and the lasting effects of Aphrodite's tongue in his mouth. He had been doing everything in his power to pretend it had not happened all day, and Aphrodite hadn't forced him to do otherwise, but damn if he didn't think about it every time he closed his eyes. He still had no clue what he was thinking or what he had hoped to accomplish with such a brash move, but it had certainly done more harm than good. It stuck to his skin like a thorn, maybe more like dozens of them, and he wasn't sure how to dig them all out. He wasn't even sure he wanted to.

"That's why Uncle trusted you," Dio assured him, clapping a hand on Hephaestus's shoulder. "He knew you could be a big boy about it. I'm glad it's you though. I know you'll keep her safe."

"Of course I will. Otherwise I'd have an entire city at my throat, and I don't want that."

Dionysos chuckled and shook his head. "How is she anyway? Can't imagine this is all that fun for her given the circumstances."

"She's - doing her best. We discuss developments, and that's about it. I know she's worried and frustrated, but she's trusted us so far."

"You'll get 'em, Brother. I know that for sure."

Heph nodded. "What are you doing down here anyway? Shouldn't you be getting ready for the show over at Asphodel?"

He grinned bashfully. "I should be. I left Hermes in charge, but I had to come see Eros. We're receiving a couple shipments for him this week."

"The new port can't be ready yet, can it?"

"Fates no, but we had a bit of a special arrangement. We figured we'd help Aphrodite's district any way we could while things settled, and Uncle agreed. He says having someone she knows checking her goods was more comforting than anything else right now."

Hephaestus could see the appeal of such an arrangement. Usually, Aphrodite and Eros brought their shipments through Demeter's port, but Demeter had nowhere near the numbers to be as thorough as they should be, especially at the moment. Her Harvest District was currently expanding into the Olympus District, which had been one of the stipulations of her agreement —coerced or otherwise— to accept Hades' leadership. This meant that her security forces were currently stretched thin and preoccupied with that whereas Hermes and Dionysos could spare the time and personnel to ensure nothing odd made its way into Aphrodite's hands...

A thought struck Hephaestus then.

"Have you taken any other shipments before this?" he inquired. "Like under the Lush District's books?"

Dio's brows knitted together. "No, this will be the first."

"But you have access to everyone's records, right? From the other ports?"

The Market District, which was run by both Dio and Hermes, was the trade capital of Khaos Falls if not the entirety of the Aegean, and almost everything had to go through them even if it was only in name. Hades had granted them permission to build a new port for the southern coast, but Hermes hadn't been willing to finalize plans until Dionysos was released from the hospital. Once it was built though, they would make Khaos Falls more profitable than anyone had ever dreamed of.

"Yeah, we've got everything logged," Dio answered. "Why? You need something?"

"I wanna know if there were any other shipments that were logged for the Lush District, even if it wasn't under Eros. Especially if it wasn't under Eros."

It was evident that Dionysos wanted to ask more questions, a slew of them if Hephaestus were to guess, but instead, he simply nodded. Heph was grateful for it too because discretion was as crucial as any information his brother might be able to offer. If Kleon or anyone working with him had accepted shipments of any kind and signed for it on behalf of the Lush District, they may have found the most ideal way to traffic people. Who on Earth would ever think that Aphrodite's people would be involved in the one cause she had dedicated her life to combatting? Certainly not Hephaestus.

Plus, Aphrodite was a daughter of Demeter in everything but blood. Of course, Demeter's people would be lax on accepting her deliveries. If Kleon or his higher ups had gone through any or all of these thoughts, they would have come to the same conclusion.

"Actually, Eros has access to the logs," Dio suddenly said. "Or I mean, I can access them on Eros's system. We can go get them right now."

"Perfect." Heph patted his arm then gestured to the elevator doors. "Come on."

Dio nodded but didn't immediately move, his teeth sinking into his lip. For a moment, he looked every bit like the small boy Hades had introduced Hephaestus to over a decade ago, excitable and anxious all at once. Heph quirked a brow.

"What is it, D?"

Dio shrugged, looking down at his shoes. "I don't know. I just..."

He trailed off, and it was evident that he was attempting to come up with the words to convey whatever was plaguing him. Hephaestus waited quietly although Dio's rare worry certainly afforded him a wave of unruly discomfort. At last, Dionysos looked up at him again, clutching his wounded arm closer to his body and clenching his fist against his chest.

“Do you think that - that Zeus has anything to do with any of this?”

Hephaestus shifted, immediately standing up straighter. In the months since the shooting, Dionysos had not once expressed any kind of worry regarding Zeus’s whereabouts. Heph had been more angry that the bastard was still alive than Dio had been, and the latter had immediately returned to his old self the moment he’d been released from the hospital much to the chagrin of Athena and his brothers. However, Hephaestus could see it now. Dio wasn’t over it. He wasn’t completely healed, physically or mentally, and he was struggling to admit it out loud.

He, like Hephaestus, had spent half his life justifying Zeus’s hatred for him, the other half spent trying to convince himself that he wasn’t the problem. Dio had certainly made more progress in that regard, or so it seemed, but when the father who didn’t want you shoots you — whether on purpose or on accident— it was difficult to come to terms with.

But while his brother lay in a hospital bed and Zeus had disregarded the harm he’d caused because he “hadn’t been aiming for him”, Hephaestus had come to the realization that Zeus didn’t hate them. Hate would have been far more clean cut and easier to swallow. No, Zeus was indifferent to them. He loved only himself, and no one else had value beyond what they could do for him. As far as he was concerned, his children were merely a rancid aftertaste of the games he liked to play. Not even Athena, his chosen ward and the heir of all of his affection, was immune to that reality, and they were all learning to cope with it.

And Dio, at his core, was as sensitive as they came. He had only ever wanted to please and to gain people’s approval, including Zeus’s. However, that bullet had torn through more than tissue. It had opened every wound Zeus had inflicted since he had kicked Dio off of his doorstep as a kid. It had opened some of Hephaestus’s as well, but none would ever cause him more harm than the thought of losing his baby brother.

Cupping the side of Dio's neck despite the strain of his own shoulder, Hephaestus met his eyes.

"No, brother, I don't think he does," he assured him. "And even if he did, Uncle gave him a warning. He steps back on Khaos Falls soil, he's fair game, and guess what?"

Dio grimaced. "What?"

Heph smirked, pulling Dio down to press their foreheads together. "I don't miss."

Dio's smile grew as he exhaled a heavy breath, his eyes closing and his shoulders slumping. He remained there for a moment longer before standing upright again and wrapping an arm around Heph's shoulders. The two headed for the elevator, climbing inside as Heph continued to consider Dio's concern. While he was certain Zeus had no hand in this particular situation, it didn't mean the elder would heed Hades' warning forever. That was the point of Heph's new position though, to protect the city from any and all threats, including Zeus.

For all of his reckless arrogance, the man was a slick bastard who knew how to manipulate people, and they had to keep that in mind. For now, Heph had to focus on the matter at hand, which was far out of Zeus's range at the moment. No, this was something much larger and far older than his expulsion from Khaos Falls. This was a consequence of Aphrodite's eager need to follow her heart without looking up to see where it was leading her, and whoever was at the source of this had figured out how to use it against her.

They stepped out of the elevator and onto the second floor of Lush together, Dio leading the way towards Eros' office on the opposite side of the main floor below. Eros sat at his desk, a bag of chips open beside him while he scrolled over something on his computer. He beckoned them in when he noticed them in the doorway, grinning at the two of them. He was about as excitable as Dionysos at all times, so it didn't surprise Hephaestus that they got along so well. The two of them got along with everyone too though, equally as eager to please and altogether in love with being the center of attention.

"I've got the checklists for you, Dio," Eros assured him, dusting his hands before reaching for a folder at the edge of the desk. "There should be five shipments altogether, but two of them are due on the same ship. Just check off the items and let me know if anything is missing and also of any excess. We usually call up the company, and if they don't want to pay to have it sent back, we'll donate it if we can or just get rid of it if it's no use to us."

"What do you usually get in excess?" Dio questioned, his eyes gleaming with curiosity.

Eros shrugged. "Depends on the shipment. If it's for the bakery, we get a lot of different doughs and pastry fillings, and I'll take them and just pay the extra costs if they want me to. If it's non-perishable, we donate it to the homes y'all got set up or we take it to Twilight House."

Dio nodded as he took the folder. "Beautiful. We need something else though. Do you mind if I get on your computer to access the city shipment logs?"

"By all means." He quickly stood up. "I actually wanted to talk to Big Mama. Do you know where she is?"

"In her office," Hephaestus informed him. "At least she should be. I told her to stay put."

He grinned again. "Fingers crossed."

He left the room with his bag of chips as Dionysos sat down in his chair, clicking and typing away on the keyboard. Hephaestus took the time to look around Eros's office, which looked every bit as eccentric as the man who occupied it. Bright colors, neon lights, and a large digital painting in which the background slowly changed from daytime to nighttime behind his notorious club, Emerald.

"There were three shipments like the ones you were looking for," Dio stated now, drawing his attention. Heph moved to stand at his brother's shoulder. "Just in the last six months. They were spread out a whole lot. The first one was last summer, then another in mid-fall, and another about four weeks ago."

"And all of them went through the Harvest District?"

"Yeah, but they weren't signed off by Eros."

"Who signed for them?"

"Uh, it looks like - Kleon did. For all three of them."

"Does it say what was in them?"

Dio read further down the document on the screen before pointing at it. "It says armored vehicles for the first one, two it looks like. The next one says it was - well, actually, all three of them claim they were vehicle shipments. Usually, that means bulletproofed SUVs or cars, maybe a security van."

"I've never seen any security vans in Aphrodite's lot. How were they paid for?"

"Let's see." Hephaestus tapped his foot against the floor. "That's odd. The invoices weren't attached to these orders."

"What does that mean?"

"It means whoever picked them up or signed off on them didn't enter the invoice into the system. Usually that would be Eros, but if he didn't sign off—"

Just then, Eros came back into the office, and Hephaestus immediately turned to him.

"Do y'all have new armored vehicles registered here in the district?"

Eros raised his brows. "I - not that I know of, no. We do have a couple vans that we use to transport survivors, but they're both at Twilight, and we've had them for years. Actually, I think you were the one that provided them."

Yes, he was. "Okay, apart from those, have you ordered any new armored vehicles? Did you sign off on any shipments for them?"

"Absolutely not."

"And all orders for the district go through you, correct? Like - even the security team's."

"Yep, all the orders come to me, and I put them in. No one should be doing that outside of me, and they definitely shouldn't be signing off for the district."

"Print this out for me, Dio."

Dionysos obliged with haste, sensing the urgency in his brother's voice. Eros was staring at him with a worried look, and truth be told, Hephaestus didn't know what to say. Kleon had truly used every possible backdoor to his own advantage, and if Heph's hunch was correct, he had used them to do horrific things. If that was how the victims had been transported and there were other shipments like it, he doubted the people Aphrodite had rescued the other night were the only ones brought here. Meaning there were most likely others still in the city.

"Are there any other shipments like that, any further back?"

"Yeah, I found three more. The earliest was almost two years ago for two armored vehicles. Again, that's the only details on the order. After that, there was a break for about a year before the rest were scattered out over months."

There were definitely more victims in the city then.

Dionysos handed Hephaestus the printed documents, and Heph thanked him before turning back to Eros.

"I'm going to Aphrodite's office"

Eros seemed to remember what he'd come back for. "Actually, she wasn't in there when I went in."

Of course she wasn't.

Hephaestus left the room without another word, heading quickly for her office. Even in his haste, he was once more submerged in the memory of the night before against his own will and his innate need to bury whatever feelings that memory invoked. He wasn't an idiot. He knew she wanted to ask, to encroach upon it in a way that ensured he couldn't worm his way out of it, so he hadn't given her the chance. They still had several hours before they had to leave for Asphodel though, and even if that weren't the case, he had to face the fact that eventually, he may need an explanation for the foolishness he'd pulled last night. He just hoped it wasn't right this moment.

At least he *had* hoped until he reached her office to find it indeed still empty. Now, facing her hardly seemed so bad. Before he could begin to process the space before him and the magnitude of her absence, Achilles' voice came from behind him.

"Heph." Hephaestus turned around to face him. "We got something."

Chapter Ten

APHRODITE

Since the night of the attack, Aphrodite hadn't been down to the security offices at all beyond the few interrogations she had sat in on. It had been too hard, like walking into a snake pit where every set of fangs was searching for somewhere on her to bite. No one looked familiar anymore even when she knew them all by name, and even with Hephaestus's guard littering the corridor, she was at a loss as to how to find comfort in that. Security was the last thing she found down here.

Nonetheless, she kept her head held high as she ventured down the hall into the main security room where all the camera monitors adorned the wall. When she pushed the door open, there were three people inside, two of which she recognized — Hector and Nikolaos. The other woman wore a silver patch on her shoulder, and Aphrodite didn't need to make out the shield and dagger upon it to know it was the insignia of Hephaestus's security forces. From what she had gathered from him, there were also plain-clothes guards on the premises at all times, and Hephaestus himself didn't wear his own insignia although in her opinion, it was difficult to overlook the authority he carried himself with. It was why even though she had every right to be here asking questions, she shivered at the thought of his reaction if he found out.

"Hey, Aphrodite," Hector greeted her with a smile that made her feel slightly calmer.

He was a good guy, and she still believed that. He didn't seem like the type that could put up a facade this well, and while she was sure Hephaestus would give her a stern talking to for falling into that trap and giving anyone the benefit of the doubt, she would leave the profiling to him.

"Hey," she returned. "I just wanted to come down and see how things were going."

She nodded to the woman, who returned it and stood to offer her hand. She was tall and muscular with deep brown skin and soft eyes, and it took Aphrodite a moment before she realized she recognized her.

"Callisto, right?" she questioned, and the woman lit up. "You worked with Artemis before we had the city forces."

"That's right," Callisto returned with a smile as she released the other woman's hand. "It's a pleasure to finally be introduced to you in person."

"Thank you for being here. I truly appreciate it."

Before she could even address Nikolaos, he was standing up and heading for the door.

"I should do my rounds," he muttered over his shoulder.

Aphrodite raised a brow as he exited the room, the move only making her more eager to question him. Following him out, she called for him until he stopped a few feet from the office door.

"Hold on, Nikolaos, I just wanna check in with you real quick," she stated, trying to keep her voice even and absent of suspicion. "I know things have been a bit hectic, and you're relatively new. Plus, you usually answer to Kleon, right?"

He scratched the back of his neck as he slowly turned back to face her. He was young, perhaps not younger than her or even Hephaestus but no older than 35 or so. His hair was thick and wavy, cropped around his ears, and his eyes were a lighter shade of brown. He wasn't very large, and the way he refused to make eye contact made

Aphrodite think he wasn't anywhere near the top of whatever hierarchy he worked in. He was way too fidgety for that, meaning Kleon had abandoned him, and he was probably unsure of what to do next.

"Yeah, but - I mean, he taught me a lot before he left," he managed.

"Left? You say that like he's gone for good."

He glanced up at her, eyes widening slightly. "Well, no, I just mean that - you know, before he took his leave or whatever, he taught me a lot."

"Oh, of course, but I'm sure he didn't teach you how to deal with a mutiny, did he?" She chuckled, but he didn't seem to find it funny. "You worked at the Wild Rose for us before this, yeah?"

"That's right."

"What about before that?"

"Uh, I worked back home, in Thassos."

"Oh, really? What made you come to Khaos Falls?"

He shrugged, but the vein of his temple was beginning to show. "The work. Kleon offered me a full-time position here for more money after the Wild Rose, and - so I took it."

"You didn't like the place you worked for before? Did they treat you badly?"

"No, nothing like that, but - you know, Thassos is a rough place."

"Working in security is a rough place, and I think that goes for anywhere." He raised a brow, and she feared he may have been catching onto something, so she quickly continued. "I have heard Thassos is a bit of a wild city though, so I get that. I'm sure it at least prepped you well for this job, right?"

"Oh, yeah, definitely."

"Have you heard from Kleon lately? I haven't had much time to call him with everything going on, but I'd hoped to hear how his vacation is going. Out there."

Now he looked uncomfortable. "I - no, I haven't. Not lately."

"It's crazy he left us out here with everything going on though. Got all these snakes in the grass then some in the trees. We need all the help we can get."

She watched realization wash across his face like a glass of cold water, and she knew then that there was no other way to go but forward.

"Look, I should really get going," he managed, looking down again. "I gotta relieve one of the perimeter guys soon."

"Don't even worry about it. You're with the boss lady. No one's gonna—"

Her words were severed suddenly by the sight of Hephaestus appearing at the end of the hall. Even from this distance, she could see the anger in his face, his forehead so red that the white scar tissue was visible the closer he came. Nikolaos didn't wait, trudging down the hall with his head down. He shrank against the wall as he passed Hephaestus, but the latter didn't spare him a glance. His eyes were fixed on hers, and they were filled with flame. She resisted the urge to roll her eyes, but before she could say a word, he was gripping her arm and steering her into the nearest detainment room. She squeaked in surprise, ripping out of his grasp as he closed the door.

"What the fuck, Hephaestus!"

"What the hell are you doing? What did you say to him?"

"I didn't say anything! I was just asking—"

"You shouldn't be asking him anything! I asked if you wanted to come with me to his interview yesterday, and you said no!"

"I changed my mind!"

"And I told you to stay put!"

"I'm not your fucking pet, Hephaestus! Don't forget who runs shit here."

"Yes, and you're running this investigation right into the fucking dirt!"

"No, I am not! You—"

"Those accounts that have been commenting on all of your platforms? Yes, all of them. They came from here in and around this building. We were going to watch Nikolaos specifically to see if it was him, but how can we do that if you scare him off!"

"Okay." She squeezed her eyes shut and rubbed her temples before going on. "Fuck the comments, okay? He isn't in charge of shit."

"And how do you know that?"

"The boy was skittish as shit. He couldn't even look me in the eye, and he tried to run the moment I walked into the room. If you were some kind of seasoned anything, you wouldn't be rushing out like that. Kleon abandoned him. He's scared because his boss left him here."

"He could be playing you. He can't let us know if he's important because he knows the punishment will be worse when we catch him. Do you even think before you do this shit!"

"He was not playing me. Maybe you're the best at reading people or whatever, but it doesn't mean the rest of us are incapable. I know what I saw. That man doesn't run a damn thing."

Hephaestus glared at her for a long time, and she was surprised smoke wasn't coming out of his nose with the way he was huffing. She stood her ground nonetheless, raising her chin and staring him down. She had as much right to search for answers as he did, more so really, and she wouldn't be scared into sitting silently in her office until a bunch of strangers figured shit out.

"You think Kleon is heading this?" he questioned slowly.

"You said he hasn't left that hotel."

"Because he'd been cut off."

"But what if that isn't the case? He left because he failed. He needed me out, and he must have done something that would have led to him in the end. Maybe he has connections at that security place so he can recruit people he can trust. Maybe the whole thing is a front. I don't know, but I do know that Nikolaos is not the one we need to be worried about."

His nostrils flared again. "That doesn't change the fact that he could have led us to who we should be worrying about."

"I just told you—"

"You don't know that for sure, Aphrodite! What part of that do you not get? You wanna work on assumptions and first guesses, and it's that reckless bullshit that got you in this predicament in the first place!"

"Stop talking to me like I'm a child!"

"Then stop acting like one!"

The hall seemed to grow smaller, the walls closing in around them, their heavy breaths mingling between them. It was far too familiar to the tension of last night and yet all too different. Rather than feel angry and spiteful the way she usually did when he spoke to her in that condescending way, she only felt embarrassed. He had never yelled at her before, certainly not like this. Of course, his disappointment had always been enough to subdue her, and she'd hated that more than anything, but the wrath in his eyes now was far beyond what she was used to from him. It scared her, not because she thought he would harm her but because it seemed like he was scared too.

But of what?

"So where does that leave us?" she ground out, unable to let herself fixate on that prior thought.

He didn't answer right away, pinching the bridge of his nose and shutting his eyes. He stepped back, leaning heavily against the wall, his weight shifting off of his weaker leg. Only then did she notice the papers in his hand, crushed between his palm and his cane. A strong urge to reach for him gripped her by the throat, but she suppressed it, pressing herself into the opposite wall.

"Do you need to get ready for the show?"

The question caught her off guard, not at all what she had expected. His voice was calm again, not entirely absent of emotion but at a normal volume at least. He didn't look at her, instead digging a hand into his pocket and pulling something slim from it. His vape pen. She had seen him use it a few times, and as he inhaled it now, she watched his shoulders lower from his ears at a gradual pace.

"That's it?" She blurted it out before she could think twice, and she had to choke back the desire to slap a hand over her mouth. "You yell at me then—"

He stepped forward suddenly, and she paused, but instead of heading for her, he moved towards the table, setting the papers down and tapping them with his fingers.

"He was accepting shipments on behalf of the district," he explained, and he suddenly looked much older than he was. "Shipments that aren't in the records and have no verifiable details, and I'd bet all I have that he was moving victims, bringing them into the city like that."

"Kleon? Kleon was - he moved them here? Under my name?"

"He accepted six shipments, meaning there are probably other victims still in the city that are in real danger because their plans are fucked up now. But it also means he wasn't finding those victims himself. He wasn't the one sending them over, so he isn't the only one we should be worried about."

"Heph, that's—"

"There is nothing more that I can say to you that you don't already know, Aphrodite. When I left you upstairs, you said you trusted me. Obviously, that was a lie you told to get me out of your way."

"That is not true, Hephaestus. I do trust you, but I don't want to sit around and wait for you to save me. I want to help."

"Is that what you think you did?" He lifted his gaze, and she struggled not to shrink beneath it. "You went behind my back and—" He stopped himself, holding his hand up. "I asked you to come, to help me, to be involved. You didn't want to... But this is your safety, Aphrodite, your life on the line. I can't make that any clearer, and I can't make you care more than you do right now. Just remember the rest of us that you're putting at risk when you do the shit you do."

Turning back towards the door, he yanked it open and stepped out into the hall, his foot hardly coming off of the ground. She wondered if he had been looking for her that whole time, if he had panicked when he didn't find her, and usually those things might make her smile, but right now? They did anything but.

THEY LEFT LUSH WITH AN HOUR TO SPARE, AND BY THEN, Hephaestus had reverted back to the cold demeanor she had come to associate with him. He had said the day prior that he had arranged for a car, but when they entered the parking garage, he led her to his own personal vehicle, opening the passenger door for her before getting behind the wheel. She suspected it had something to do with their discussion about his men earlier, but she wasn't about to ask. Just because he was calm now did not mean he was approachable.

Still, it was odd to think just how much trust she put in him without thinking about it despite the turmoil that existed between them. Despite what he believed, she had been honest about that trust as well, and their argument hadn't at all altered that. At the moment, as they sat beside one another, it felt more awkward than antagonistic. Though when he spoke, a chill ran down her spine, fully expecting another lecture.

"Dio is going to let us in through the theatre backdoors once we get there."

"He'll be there?" She looked over at him instinctively.

While she knew Dionysos had been released from Asklepios' care, she wasn't sure just how much work he was up to doing so soon after taking a bullet to the back. Not that it surprised her at all if he had already returned to all of his prior activities and duties. In all the time she had known him, he had never held the ability to sit still.

Hephaestus nodded, his eyes remaining on the road ahead. "Yeah, I saw him earlier. He'll be happy to see you too, I'm sure. He says he tried calling, but I told him you'd been busy."

She stared at him. She couldn't help it. His words seemed to possess a different weight than they had before. They didn't scrape against her skin like sandpaper. Somehow, that was more unsettling. Rather than any trace of venom or vitriol, all she found was the timid tiredness of a man defeated. And she hated it, so much so that she wanted to scream at him, to poke the bear until he rose up on hind legs and fought back, but she knew it wouldn't end well. If anything, it would prove his point.

As if she hadn't done that already on multiple occasions.

She was still throwing him glances when they arrived at the lot behind the theatre and he climbed out of the car without a word. She opened her door before he reached it, but he still offered his hand. She took it before she had the time to consider refusal although she swore to herself it was a conscious decision. Fortunately —or unfortunately— he let go soon after to call Dionysos, who must have been right on the other side of the door because it flew open immediately.

"'Dite!" Dio's voice cried as he came bounding out, though he stopped himself just short of sweeping her up into his arm and instead gingerly embraced her. "Tried to one up me, huh?"

"I could never," she giggled, wrapping her arms around his waist with measured caution.

Of all of Hephaestus's brothers, even Ares, she was certainly closest to Dionysos. Few, if any, could match his jubilance, and she immediately felt better than she had in days. He still had his arm in a sling, and she imagined it had been one of the stipulations of him returning to work. Once they parted, he moved to wrap his arm around Hephaestus, who didn't fight it. Dionysos was several inches taller than him and nearly twice as bulky, and Hephaestus was careful as he wound his arms around the younger man. Aphrodite realized that these were the only times she had ever seen Hephaestus genuinely soft—when he was around Dionysos.

"Sorry, I haven't had the chance to stop in and see you," Dio went on as he led them towards the door. "Everything's been hectic, and Hermes doesn't let me do too much to begin with."

"Don't even worry about it," she assured him. "We'll make the time up eventually."

"I put you two near the front of course. Uncle's there too. He likes those seats."

"I can't imagine why," Aphrodite smirked.

She still struggled to make sense of the fact that Hades was not only real but a fixture in her everyday life. His myth had prevailed and preceded him since she was a kid, and it had only turned a few months ago when he and Persephone had begun dating. Even when she would see him at events or meetings that required the attendance of them both, it was always shocking. Now, it was just a common occurrence.

She followed the two men inside, and Dio ushered them through backstage and out into the seating area. Persephone was back in the dressing areas, so Aphrodite wasn't able to catch a glimpse of her, but she was looking forward to drinks at Club Elysium after, which was just down the hall and up the stairs from the Pantheon Theatre. Aphrodite and Hephaestus greeted Hades, who was already in his seat, and she settled in between uncle and nephew after Dio raced backstage once more.

"How are you feeling?" Hades asked, his eyes on the stage.

"Much better," she replied. "Glad to be out for a while."

"Persephone was excited that you were coming." He lowered his voice, his lips twitching. "And how has your security been thus far?"

She'd anticipated the questions. "Effective."

"I'm glad to hear it. I also hear we're making good headway on figuring this out."

"I'm sure it won't be long. Hephaestus is good at what he does." And she meant it, but saying it aloud only renewed the shame of their earlier argument.

"Don't I know it."

As the lights came down and the show began, Aphrodite allowed herself to get lost in it, to escape Khaos Falls entirely and venture through the story the performers weaved before her. Persephone had always been a soothing presence, the big sister who shielded her from the worst things in life, but watching her fly through the air above and glide across the stage before them was an entirely different experience. It took her to places she could not be reached, places no one could touch her or harm her. It had been so since they were kids, when the older woman would put on shows in Demeter's grand hall or ballroom with only Aphrodite as her thoroughly invested audience.

That was back when they had to make their own dresses and steal Aunt Hestia's makeup, always on the lookout for Persephone's dad due to the sheer danger of him discovering them dressed up like that. Now both of their fathers were long gone, no longer a threat to them, but Aphrodite still looked to Persephone for strength. She always would. And to see Persephone back where she belonged after months away from the stage due to the fire damage in the theatre was inspiring, a comfort she had yearned for all week.

When she looked over at Hades, she found a familiar look of awe as though this was the first time he was seeing Persephone, lips parted and gaze fixated. She smiled, grateful for a man who looked at her best friend like that, an innocent sort of envy outlining her satisfaction. She found herself turning her gaze to Hephaestus soon after, but she couldn't—or wouldn't— find a viable reason why.

His lips were pursed, but his eyes followed the story on the stage without fail, flickering away to check their surroundings every now and again. She didn't expect them to meet hers, yet they did, and she couldn't look away fast enough. If anything, it felt like some magnetic pull keeping their gazes locked. Neither of them said anything. Neither of them smiled. They simply stared at one another, unwavering. She didn't know who looked away first when the sound of applause erupted around them. Maybe they both did, but once it was over, warmth pooled in her stomach. It was tempered by the heat of her own frustration with herself. She had to pull it together.

After the show finished, the three of them waited for Persephone in the entrance hall beside the theatre. Aphrodite immediately embraced the taller woman once she came out, congratulating her on another flawless debut. They didn't say much else until they got to Elysium where Hephaestus and Hades retreated to the elder's luxury box upstairs to presumably talk business and take up an eagle-eye view of the club. The two women grabbed a drink at the bar before taking up a table at the edge of the dance floor.

"How is it going?" Persephone questioned, raising her brows.

She didn't specify, but Aphrodite knew what she was after. She sipped her drink liberally to try and combat the heat creeping up her neck.

"I'm alive, aren't I?" she shot back, a perfectly shaped eyebrow raised in challenge.

"Ooh." Persephone held her hands up. "Okay, so we got an attitude. Is it that bad?"

Aphrodite sucked her teeth. "No, it's fine. It's just - it's a lot is all. All the questioning, the distrust. People I've had around me and shit."

Persephone seemed to veer away from her initial concern. "Hades said it was bad."

"That doesn't even begin to cover it."

She glanced around them, suddenly feeling far too bare. It was such a rare occurrence that it startled her. Her eyes were inevitably drawn upward, and she found Hephaestus's steady stare upon her. She held it for far longer than was necessary, but even once she looked away, it stuck to her and seeped down deep into her chest, pooling in her gut. Once upon a time, that stare would leave her squirming uncomfortably in her skin. Now, it served as a reminder that she was safe. Even if he was angry with her, even if he hated her, she knew he wouldn't let anything happen to her.

"I fucked up today."

The words were almost shoved out on the edge of a heavy exhale, the disappointment and embarrassment once more cutting through her like a fine blade.

"What do you mean?" Persephone asked slowly.

"I - I went behind Hephaestus's back and talked to one the guys they suspected was in on the attack, Nikolaos. And I know I shouldn't have. I know, but - I just got so sick of sitting around."

"'Dite." Aphrodite only noticed her own tears when her vision began to blur, but she looked up at her best friend anyway. Persephone reached down and took her hand. "You gotta trust him. I know that's fucking hard considering what you're going through right now, but he's the one person in that building we know you can trust without a doubt."

"I get that, and I - I feel so fucking stupid for doing it, but..." Her voice broke. "I'm scared, Seph. I've never been so scared, and it's not that I'm scared of getting hurt. It's that -" She gestured wildly with her free hand. "How am I supposed to trust people again? Kleon, of all people, was - he's been there since the beginning. If he can turn on me, who couldn't?"

"Look, I can't promise you it won't happen again, and we both know that, but you can't lose faith in everyone, 'Dite. If the only people you can trust is us right now, that's absolutely fine. Do that for as long as you have to, but don't let these bastards win. They were corrupted by greed, but you got a whole lot more people who love you than those willing to turn on you. I know that for a fact. This whole city would go to war for you."

It wasn't that she didn't believe that. Aphrodite certainly did, but rejection had never been something she coped with all that well, and betrayal felt a whole lot like extreme rejection. She hated how deeply it touched her, climbing inside of her and making a home behind her ribs until it began to rot. She had done all she could to make the people under her employ happy, but she had also wanted them to be good too, and she had failed in that regard. Maybe it wasn't her responsibility to guide their morality, but that didn't soothe her heart much. Right now, she wished she could think with her head the way Hephaestus and

Hades did so seamlessly. At least maybe then, this shit wouldn't hurt so much.

"Have they gotten any updates on Kleon?" Persephone pushed softly.

Aphrodite sighed. "Heph is watching him. Apparently, he's still holed up in that hotel, but honestly, I don't know. When I talked to Nikolaos today, something told me that he was just Kleon's mole, like Kleon left him here for a reason."

"What makes you say that?"

"He was ready to run the moment he saw me. Big dogs don't play like that."

"That is true." Persephone huffed, tossing her straw and drinking straight from her glass. "This is crazy shit though."

"Tell me about it."

"I don't wanna stress you out further, but you should probably call Mama. She's a little ticked off that we rerouted your shipments, but we explained it was for your safety. You know how she is though. She worries and makes it look like anger."

"Yeah. I haven't even talked to Auntie. I wouldn't know what to say. I don't wanna lie, but I don't wanna tell them I'm scared either. Everything just feels so out of place."

"Just check in with them." A slight smile graced her lips. "Because trust me, you don't want Mama kidnapping you out your own club."

Aphrodite snickered, remembering when Demeter had sent Adonis to more or less force Persephone to go see her once Demeter found out about Persephone working at Asphodel with Hades.

"I definitely do not need that right now, you right."

Seph squeezed her hand before pulling away. "You want me to go stay with you for a few nights? Keep you company?"

Aphrodite smirked. "I think the whole point of Hades giving me Hephaestus was so that he didn't have to spend nights without you."

"Naw, he gave you Hephaestus because you and I would already be kicking doors down and getting ourselves in some more trouble."

They laughed as Aphrodite chipped away at the ice in her glass with her straw, once again wading into the deep end of this situation. When she looked up, Persephone's gaze had strayed towards the luxury box. It soon fell to Aphrodite again, who saw the glint in her best friend's eye, but it was too late by the time she read what was coming next. Not like she could've stopped it.

"You and Hephaestus seem - comfortable," Persephone expressed, lips curling.

"You mean civil?" she returned.

It wasn't the lie that numbed her lips but a memory, reigniting the flame he'd scorched her with a night ago. She hated him for doing it. Or more accurately, she hated him for making her want him to do it again.

And she hated herself for wanting it anyway.

"Why are you blushing?"

Aphrodite's vision focused on Persephone's face, which was now adorned in a cheshire grin that made her damn near cringe. She rolled her eyes.

"I tolerate it," Aphrodite stated. "That's all I can do."

"Mhmm."

"Imagine you had to spend every waking hour with Zeus for a minute."

Persephone did shudder. "First of all, that isn't the same thing. Hephaestus is not Zeus."

"Not entirely." Though her certainty had substantially dwindled.

"What is it with y'all seriously?"

Aphrodite shrugged. "We don't get along. That's the beginning and the end of it."

"The way you're acting, I would think there's a bit more to it."

"Every time he opens his mouth, I wanna punch him in it. I think that's enough of a reason."

"Okay, so he's a bit like Zeus."

They both chuckled again, but Aphrodite was not at all willing to travel further down that road, especially after last night. She'd already passed her judgment on this man. Any alteration to that would only conceive confusion, and she hated confusion. She may desire a fantasy or a fairy tale, but neither was synonymous with a lie or suspension of belief. She knew who he was, and he was no one she needed an attachment to.

"I'll tell you who was acting like that man yesterday though," she offered instead, and Persephone was immediately engaged. "Ares came into my office. With demands."

"Girl, he did not. What demands?"

"Me moving into his district so he can 'protect' me. Complete with a marriage and all that."

Persephone covered her mouth and shook her head. Aphrodite nodded. She was glad she could finally talk about the stress that event alone had brought on atop everything else, and she was also grateful that Persephone hadn't switched up now that these *boys* were practically her nephews.

"And what did you tell him?"

"The truth," Aphrodite asserted. "I told him that isn't what I want, at least not right now and not with him. I may have been a little - rough about it, but he kept pushing, and I was already so overwhelmed. Heph saved me though. He came in and said he needed to talk to me, so Ares left."

And she had snapped at him as well, but he never brought it up again. She wasn't sure why she was thinking about that now, but the memory of the encounter all ran together in her head.

"Don't even stress about it. You were honest, and there's nothing wrong with that."

"The wild thing is I wasn't completely sure I *didn't* want it until he asked. We have fun and all, but - he isn't just like his dad. He's a lot like Adonis too."

Persephone rolled her eyes at that because they both knew exactly what that meant. In fact, she was the only one who could truly understand the meaning. Adonis had tried pinning them both down so that he could step on their shoulders to make himself bigger than he was. Aphrodite had been so naive back then, eager to please him even after Persephone left. However, it was Adonis who had shown her what love wasn't, and once she figured it out, she vowed never to settle again. She imagined that if she hadn't been through it with Adonis, she would probably be marrying Ares right now.

She shivered as her eyes climbed up to the second floor balcony of their own accord. Hephaestus's gaze struck hers like a match. He had already been staring.

"Look, I never said nothin', but..." Persephone shrugged as she trailed off, reclaiming Aphrodite's attention.

She snorted. "Yeah, yeah, hush up. You were all for it in the beginning."

"I'm not saying I wasn't, but I know him now. Don't get me wrong. I love him, but he does have some of Zeus's worst tendencies. Like that temper, and Hades has mentioned it a number of times."

"So I guess he and Athena aren't working too well together."

"They're getting better now, but those first few weeks felt like the dawn of war."

"I figured as much. They're like - complete opposites but two sides of the same coin."

"Exactly that, and you know Athena's been stressed since the shooting with Dio in the hospital all that time, but she's kept busy, and Ares was steady trying to overstep the boundaries she'd set before Hades had to step in. She and I have lunch every now and again though, and she seems to be doing better. She's a little unsettled by Dio going back to work so soon, but you know."

Aphrodite raised a brow. "Somethin' goin' on there?"

Persephone arched her own. "You serious? Have you seen them together? *Everything* is going on there, and both of them act like they don't see a damn thing. It's frustrating."

"Don't start trying to play matchmaker now just because you got your first boyfriend."

She scoffed. "He is not my first."

"Um, I think he is. The others were not worth the count."

"I guess you're right, but don't even worry. I'm staying out of it."

There was a beat of silence before they both said "for now" in unison and burst into fresh laughter.

The two of them don't stay much longer after that, both of them exhausted and in for another long day tomorrow, but Aphrodite enjoyed the time she managed to get with her best friend. She remembered back when they were all but inseparable, but once they had to grow up and go their separate ways, that had drastically changed. She'd learned to cherish every moment they were able to scrounge up.

Persephone and Hades walked Aphrodite and Hephaestus out to their car with promises of checking in the next day. Aphrodite looked back as they drove away, watching Hades wrap his arms around Persephone. Even from the increasing distance, she could see the glow of her best friend and the stars in his eyes. She suppressed a smile and turned back around.

"Did you have fun?" Hephaestus inquired, catching her off guard.

"I did," she eventually replied with a nod. "Did you?"

"Yeah." She had expected him just to grunt and wave her off. "I like the show."

She pushed it. "And the club?"

"I didn't mind it. It's not much different from Lush. I enjoy the atmosphere, from a distance."

"Only from a distance?"

He lifted a shoulder. "I prefer it. Just another one of those - artificially intelligent things I guess."

She chuckled. "You still mad about that?"

He looked over at her as they pulled up to a stoplight, laying his head back against the seat, and she immediately sobered, swallowing hard and trying not to look at his lips when he licked them.

"I'm not mad. I'm just stating a fact in a way you understand."

"Why not show me somethin' else?"

Now he laughed, the sound rumbling through her frame. "You wouldn't know what to do with it, Aphrodite."

He turned his eyes back to the road when the light turned green, leaving her speechless and squirming in her seat as she processed his words. They thrummed against a specific chord in her chest, echoing vehemently in her head. She felt raw, like an exposed nerve, searching and pleading for something she could only get from him, something he continued to deny her. The issue was that she did not have a name for it, and even if she did, she doubted she would ask for it outright.

When they reached Lush, Hephaestus had her stay in the car until he swept the area and ensured his people were properly positioned. Once he did so, he opened her door, helping her out. She didn't shy away now, even when he released her hand in favor of placing his own at the small of her back. They approached the doors, stepping inside the elevator where she punched in her code. They reached the penthouse and removed their shoes before proceeding to the bedroom. Only then did he remove his hand.

She let her hair down as he began his sweep, focusing on the mirror rather than his movements. She knew now when he grew tired, the way his favored foot barely left the floor. Beyond that, it was difficult to tell that he struggled at all even with the cane in hand, the only other tell being the subtle tilt of his shoulders beneath his clothes and the occasional tremor she would catch by complete accident. He didn't seem to be lacking any strength though, that was for sure.

This whole thing all seemed so routine now, and she refused to examine just how comfortable she was with it. But when he took a gentle hold of her arm, turning her to face him, she lost her breath.

"I have to go down and check something with Achilles," he said. "I'll check on you when I get back, so be ready for me."

She wet her lips before she started to speak. "Don't be too long, and don't you dare wake me up if I'm out already." She won't be. "I'm tired."

He smirked, dragging his hand all the way down her arm to her wrist before letting go. "Don't worry, Princess. I'll be quick."

A chill ran down her spine as he retreated, but before he could leave the room, she called out.

"Heph, wait." He stopped at the door, turning sideways to look at her with a keen gaze. "I'm - I'm sorry about today."

She watched his eyebrows slide upward into his hairline, lips parted in silent surprise. However, he didn't say anything, and the silence clawed at her like thorns, so she continued.

"I should've trusted you the way I said I did, and I shouldn't have talked to him without you."

He sighed. "Look, I get it. If it were me, I wouldn't wanna sit around and do nothing either, but I need you to hear me when I tell you something. I'm not doing it to piss you off or hurt you, but if I have to be an asshole to keep you safe, I will."

"I - okay, I get it. Thank you."

They stared at one another for a long beat before he nodded and turned away, disappearing through the door and closing it behind him. She didn't exhale until she heard the elevator ding.

And she was *trembling.*

Her skin was ablaze. Her clothes were too tight. The room was too humid. She stripped out of her gown, tossing it on the nearby chair and moving into the bathroom. She took a short shower, but it did little to soothe her, anxiety rising behind her eyes without reason. She paced her room in her towel before moving out into the living room to ensure he hadn't returned yet, and she was as disappointed as she was relieved to confirm it. She went back into her room, shutting the door and biting her lip. She looked down at her arm where his hand had touched. She had hoped to scrub off the sensation of it. The attempt had been futile, and devastatingly so. She felt it now as though he was still holding her.

And it wasn't enough.

She glanced at the door, multiple emotions waging war within her ribcage. She didn't know when he'd be back. Minutes or hours... She seemed to stand still in the center of the room for ages, contemplating, considering, questioning. Then she removed her towel and laid down across the comforter, dragging her hands down her bare body and pretending they were his instead.

Chapter Eleven

HEPHAESTUS

"He's gone."

Hephaestus sat quietly opposite Achilles at one of the interrogation tables in the very room he'd pushed Aphrodite into earlier that day. He wasn't surprised at the news Achilles was serving him. He had expected Nikolaos to run the moment he left Aphrodite in the hallway, but there was something about it all that was nagging at him. He simply wasn't sure what it was yet.

"He hasn't left the city yet, so he must know we're watching the ports," Achilles went on, "but he left halfway through his shift, and no one can get ahold of him."

"Aphrodite thinks he works for Kleon, not the other way around."

"That tracks. In all the time I spent with him, he never struck me as a mastermind."

"Yeah, but I'm still not sold on this Kleon thing. Those shipments he was receiving, someone else was sending them, and Kleon was the perfect in. The Lush District as a whole was. Are we sure he's still in that apartment?"

"Pat has had people surrounding the place nonstop. He even rented out one of the open apartments to place some guys inside. Kleon hasn't left that apartment much less the building."

"Is he alive?"

"Heat imaging says so, unless whoever *is* in there killed him."

That didn't seem so farfetched. Nothing did anymore. They had gone too many days without putting any vital pieces together, and Hephaestus was beginning to wonder if he was out of his depth. Running security was one thing. Running an investigation to uncover an assassination plot that spanned across more than one island? This wasn't something he'd trained properly for. Nonetheless, he wasn't about to throw in the towel. He couldn't. Aphrodite was counting on him.

He squeezed his eyes shut but immediately snapped them open, the image of her on the dance floor with Persephone invading his thoughts. He didn't have time for this.

"What about the landlord?" he asked. "Did Patroclus say he was suspicious or anything?"

"Naw, he said the guy was pretty lenient with the place."

"We need proof of life, and we need to get into his phone. I think he has someone at Labyrinth Security. Kleon didn't get into trafficking on his own, and he isn't the one that's running this ring. There is no way."

"Here's what I don't get: How did he not know Aphrodite was making that move that night? He's head of the night shift. Wouldn't she have told him?"

"No, he must've known. He knew she would act on the tip the moment she got it, and he knew he would be able to swap out the security team on the premises."

"So you think the raid was a distraction?"

"What else could it be? He was at Twilight. He knew they were going there even though Aphrodite hadn't been able to find him that night. Plus, he sent Nikolaos, which put eyes on her while they moved things around. Then he made himself scarce. It would have been really difficult to play dumb if the entire night team got subbed out under his nose, you know. If she had died—"

He couldn't even go there, the thought falling apart on the tip of his tongue, dissolving like ash. Achilles huffed his own frustration, and Heph felt in his chest. What he wanted to do was go to Thassos himself, but he couldn't risk taking Aphrodite with him, and he damn sure wasn't leaving her here. Patroclus could handle this though. He was smart with good intuition, and Heph trusted him. It was just that sitting here doing nothing was tough. He hadn't lied when he told Aphrodite he understood, and while he was still agitated about what she'd done with Nikolaos, he had a hunch she was right. He wouldn't have been doing something as foolish as posting anonymous comments from inside her building if he were of any value. Heph's guess was that he was now a sitting duck, and his overseers had all but cut him off the way they'd cut off Kleon.

Still, they couldn't risk losing whatever loose threads may be attached to Kleon, meaning they could not let him know they were watching him. But he had to make a move eventually. He would need food and supplies if nothing else, and they had to be prepared to take what they could get when he did.

They called it a night after another half hour of tossing around fruitless theories, Hephaestus on the verge of grinding his teeth into dust and unable to concentrate. He was eager to get back upstairs, but to consider the reason was to send himself into a spiral.

He was convinced that he was too comfortable, and the reality of that was acidic. Nonetheless, it failed to burn away the residue now lining his lungs and burrowing into his bones. Each time he had touched her tonight, it had been because he had wanted to touch her. It had been because he'd had a taste and could not refrain from wanting another. It clawed at his throat, shameful and surreptitious, and he lacked the means to tame or temper it. He berated himself on the elevator ride up to the penthouse, leaning heavily on the fact that this was temporary, and she only just tolerated him. What good could ever come from that?

He knocked twice on her door before entering. Her light was on, and his eyes first went to the bathroom door immediately to his right. It was open and absent of light. He didn't need to check the rest of the room however. Her sounds drew his attention to the bed, and he had no clue how he'd managed to miss her in the first place. She was splayed out upon the sheets, head propped against her pillows, her bare legs spread. One hand worked between her thighs. The other palmed a breast. Her head was tilted back, but he could make out the shine of her eyes as they fell upon him. *Divine.*

He leaned against the doorframe, trying to control his breathing and suppress the sudden acceleration of his heartbeat. Truth be told, he wasn't sure he trusted what he was seeing, but he wasn't willing to question it aloud. After spending the entire day combatting his own wayward thoughts about her though, he had no fight left in him. Even if he did, he wasn't sure he would be willing to spare it.

His gaze traced over every inch of her, memorizing the shape of her thighs and the fluid movement of her arm as her fingers danced between them. Her neck was flushed, the scarlet heat encircling it like a necklace before reaching out along her throat and cheeks. Rather than speed up now, his heart slowed, its rhythm falling in sync with her moans. He wasn't sure which would be worse—drowning in desire or drowning in denial.

But he could never possibly be sure without trying both.

"I told you to wait for me," he chided, although it lacked the usual bite.

"What do you think I'm doing?" Her voice was honey thick and just as sweet.

He hummed. "What did I tell you? In the car?"

"Mm, remind me."

His hand tightened around his cane. "You can't handle it."

She turned her head towards him. "And I'm just supposed to take your word for it?"

"Do you really want me to prove it?"

She spread her legs wider, wide enough for him to watch her fingers sink inside of her as a wanton song spilled from her lips. He clenched his jaw. It did nothing to soothe the ache.

"Figure it out, Hephaestus. Use that - *logic* of yours."

Their eyes locked, and his knees felt ready to buckle. He wondered if it was a trick or a joke or a way for her to point at him later and say she was right about him, whatever that might mean. And he decided he didn't care.

Setting his cane against the wall, he unbuttoned his shirt. It failed to relieve the tightening in his chest, but he removed it nonetheless. It slipped from his shoulders before he unbuckled his belt, his movements slow and calculated. She never took her eyes off of him beyond watching every piece of clothing hit the floor, and her hands never stopped working.

Once he stepped out of his boxers, he moved towards the bed with cautious and careful steps, still at odds with his desire to please her and his need to teach her a lesson. His eyes snagged on her fingers as she dragged them through her folds, which were swollen and shining with what he assumed was arousal. His eyes raked back over her frame until they found hers again, a mirror image of his own dark pools shimmering with hunger. She sank her teeth into her lip. He bit down on his tongue. Then he snatched her hands from their positions and pushed them above her head out of the way as he straddled her chest.

Shock colored her face momentarily, but she soon recovered, leaving a look of quiet curiosity in its wake. He slid forward, his cock falling heavy between her breasts.

"This is what you're into?" she questioned, her voice hoarse.

"This is the start of it," he returned. "What? Were you expecting vanilla?"

"Maybe."

"Is that what you want?"

She seemed to consider it for a moment before she slowly shook her head. "I told you to show me, didn't I? So show me."

He licked his lips. Then he licked his palm and took hold of his shaft, slicking it up as he stroked it from base to tip. Her eyes tracked the motion, and his eyes didn't leave hers. Once he was satisfied, he let it rest against her chest once more before palming her breasts and squeezing them between calloused fingers, flicking her nipples with his thumbs. She arched into his touch, her hips winding against the bed. He made note of every movement, every reaction, every whimper and gasp he pulled from her lips. He would need them. He was going to build a blueprint to breaking her.

"You're gonna earn it first." His voice cut between them like a cruel wind. "Hold 'em together."

She didn't hesitate to obey the command, replacing his hands with hers and squeezing her tits together around his cock. He grunted, immediately rolling his hips as one hand found her neck, the other curling around the intricate metal frame of the headboard as precum collected across her chest.

She played with her own nipples, her body in constant motion beneath him and her breathing growing heavy. Soon, her skin was slick with him, and he slid in and out of the valley of her breasts with ease. She casted her gaze down, watching his swollen head disappear and reappear with each stroke until her tongue was damn near hanging out of her mouth. And he couldn't say he didn't like the sight of it.

He committed the image to memory in high-def clarity, knowing he would be thinking about it for days and weeks to come. Who knew her mouth could ever look so inviting while open? Usually he couldn't wait for her to shut it. But right now? Well, he could think of a much better way to shut her up. He just needed a reason.

"You like that, don't you?"

Her gaze darted up to his, tongue folding back into her mouth before she pursed her lips. He could see the cogs turning, her need to strike back at him brewing behind her calm facade. He wasn't about to let her go back to the bullshit though. Not yet. She asked for this, and she was going to take it the way he gave it or not at all. Shoving a hand into her hair and tangling his fingers in the thick tresses, he moved her head back so that she couldn't look away.

"I asked you a question." His voice was as commanding as ever and twice as deep. "You wanna earn somethin', right?"

He didn't miss the clench of her jaw, but he didn't relent either. He expected her to act out, to be bratty and petulant, and if he was honest, he was looking forward to it. This was the one place where he had all the control, and if she hadn't figured that out yet, she would very soon.

At last, her head moved beneath his grasp in a short nod. A growl rumbled in his chest.

"Naw, I wanna hear you say it, Princess. You like it, don't you?"

Her lip twitched in a soft snarl as his hips slowed to a stop. "—Yes."

He released the headboard and took a firm hold of her jaw. "You better talk to me like you know who's in charge here."

She gritted her teeth harder, and he gripped her hair tighter, waiting for her to relinquish the last of her perceived control. If he was going to do this, he was going to do it so that there would be no question of it later. She would never be able to pretend that it didn't happen, that *he* didn't happen, nor would she be able to lie and say it hadn't affected her. She would hear these words and every word after each time she looked in his direction. He would make her repeat them until they were branded on her sly little tongue. And the next time she touched herself, she wouldn't be able to picture anyone else but him.

She hesitated because of course she hesitated, but he was patient, sitting atop her chest with his dick throbbing against her skin. Although he swore he could feel her heart beating beneath it too, anxious. He savored that.

Then, after another beat of silence, "Yes, daddy, I like it."

It wasn't entirely what he had expected, and the sudden look of smug satisfaction on her face told him that she knew that. However, it had the desired effect, his cock twitching hard between her tits, his hips shifting forward as he grunted. Fighting to retain his own control, he freed both of his hands and took hold of hers again, pinning them above her head as he moved further up her body.

"Then be a good girl and open your mouth."

She tested his hold on her wrists, her fingers stretching out until they grazed the headboard. His grip failed to give despite the faint tremor in his hand. She stared up at him through her lashes, her eyes alight with desire and her forehead gleaming with a thin sheen of sweat. Then she slowly parted her lips.

He closed the distance, letting his swollen tip rest upon her tongue. He did nothing else, and she took the opportunity to swirl that tongue around it at a sluggish pace, letting him feel every single sensation she could create for him. He suppressed a shiver with substantial struggle, leaning more of his weight forward. Only once she halted her ministrations did he ease into her mouth further, getting about halfway before pausing. He did so only for a moment. Then he pushed down into her throat.

She gagged around his girth, and he retracted some, watching the moisture gather in the corners of her eyes with growing mirth. When he pushed in again, she relaxed her throat to the best of her ability, taking him as deep as he could go. Her lips touched down against his groin, and he groaned as she swallowed around him. She wasn't holding out on him. She wasn't withholding her talents, and he wouldn't let her regret it either no matter how hard she would undoubtedly try to in the morning.

He hit a stride, watching her every reaction through his hooded gaze. Her tongue slid along the underside of him, teeth scraping over the length of his shaft, only adding to the stimulation that had his toes curling against the mattress. Even as it tired him to hold himself up, he kept stroking until spit and precum were spilling out the side of her mouth and down her cheeks. The sight of her like this did something irreversible to him, burrowing beneath his skin in a way he didn't have the tools to defend himself against at the moment. Not that he wanted to. It felt too much like it belonged there.

She relaxed her throat once more and loosened her jaw, allowing him to use her mouth in any way he saw fit. He didn't squander it, fucking her throat with strong thrusts, releasing her hands so he could reclaim his hold on the headboard. She kept them above her head nonetheless, her fingers finding one of the lower bars to grasp at as her eyes rolled back. She choked hard around him, gagging again and again, the sound more arousing than anything.

"Aph—"

He didn't get any further, pushing up onto his knees and stroking straight down the back of her throat, burying his cock to the hilt. He rutted and ground into her, her cheeks puffing out then hollowing with desperate haste. Then he was cumming before he truly committed to it, shamelessly filling her throat with his seed.

He found himself anchored only by her hands now braced against his thighs, but she didn't push him away, instead sucking him deep and swallowing down every drop. His legs trembled around her, a guttural groan lodged in his throat as he bit down on his tongue. It had been a long time since he'd cum like this, surrounded by a warmth that wasn't his sweaty palm. This was brand new. And a little addictive.

He rode it out slowly, fisting as much of her hair as he could in the process. It was a feeling he had never received in his few one-night stands —which only served to show him he abhorred one-night stands

— or short dating stints, his lackluster trysts or late-night romps meant to pass the time and dull the ache. What was she doing? What were *they* doing?

He didn't give either of them time to consider that, reaching a hand back and pressing two fingers against her clit. It pulsed beneath his touch, her hips bucking upward into his hand as she gasped around his cock. He stroked her with a thoroughness that had her breathless all over again within seconds, gasps turning to panting breaths and her nails biting into his thighs. He shuddered at the added sensations, sliding his fingers down to her entrance and letting his thumb take up the work against her clit.

She wasn't quite as wet as he had expected, his digits meeting a decent resistance as he made a shallow entry. He massaged her with caution, coaxing her open without scraping her up, but then her face fell before him, enough so that he eased out of her mouth with haste, a thread of saliva and cum strung out between them.

Her eyes widened slightly, mouth still hanging open, as she looked up at him. Then she threw a hand out, fumbling over the bedside table and knocking things over before she reached the drawer at its front. He slowed his ministrations, concern overtaking him. For the first time, she looked almost - nervous?

"There's—" Her voice was suddenly high, higher than he'd ever heard it, her face flushing a deeper scarlet than it had been mere moments before. He raised a brow, but before he could ask, she spoke again. "There's more lube. I - I don't - I just have trouble—"

Frustration suddenly flared across her face as she turned it away from him, her brows now down and knitted together. If he didn't know any better, he'd say she looked like she was on the verge of tears...

Oh. It wasn't frustration with him, but with herself.

She huffed. "You know what? Just—"

"Hold up."

She glanced back at him, but he didn't offer anything further, at least not verbally. Instead, he took his time maneuvering himself, sliding down her body until his head was between her thighs. He knew she was following him. Of course she was, and he wanted her to. He wanted her to know exactly what he was about to do. Because as much as he liked pissing her off and getting under her skin, he knew this wasn't something to joke about. This was serious for her, and he would treat it as such.

When he looked up, their eyes met, and his breath ghosted over her slit. The scent of strawberry wafted up to meet him, and he now assumed it was the lube she was using. His mouth watered, but he held off a bit longer. Instead, he turned his head, brushing his lips over the skin of her inner thigh. Her chest rose high and fell fast, and he focused on the descent of her breasts, the part of her lips. He moved to the other side, dragging his mouth with a bit more pressure. She reached for his hair.

"Please," she muttered.

He glanced up. "Please what?"

She rolled her head back, her free hand groping her breast, tugging at the nipple. His mouth hovered over her clit, waiting.

"Look at me," he demanded. There was a pause, and then she obeyed. "Please what?"

"—Please, Daddy. Touch me. Taste me."

His smirk was fathomless when he flashed it at her. She inhaled just before he smothered her clit with it.

Chapter Twelve

APHRODITE

She was in trouble.

She knew it long before this moment, but it was now solidified as she watched Hephaestus eat her pussy with unmatched fervor and an unyielding hunger. And to think she feared he could never have an attraction to a woman like her. But now that he had his face submerged in her folds like he'd never been fed in his life, she couldn't even fathom such a thing. She'd climaxed mere minutes into his tongue swarming her clit, but now that tongue was buried inside of her, and she was grinding up into his face in endless desperation as if her life depended on it. And fuck, it might.

She had never come so fast. She had never been stimulated so thoroughly. Just a moment ago, she was panicking, unable to admit to him of all people the truth of her struggle with getting wet on her own despite being absolutely and completely turned on by what he'd done to her mouth, to her breasts. It was the one thing about her body she was self-conscious about when it came to sex, the one thing she couldn't tone in a gym or get cosmetic surgery for, and he was the one person it would have physically pained her to admit it to. But he had waved it off like it meant nothing to him despite her unyielding certainty that he would clown her for it, and then he'd made her forget about it altogether.

Minutes. That was all it took for him to make her toes curl and her walls constrict so quick that she had whiplash. He was good at this, too good, and she didn't know how she was going to survive the night. Especially when she still felt him in the back of her throat.

He was of average length, but he was thick and weighted, and the way he'd fucked her face had her needy as fuck, so much so that if he had made her beg any longer for this, she would have done it without putting up any resistance whatsoever. Any doubts she may have had about how this might play out had been laid to rest. He'd already exceeded expectations twice over, and he wasn't even finished yet. She wasn't sure how long she might last, but dammit if she wouldn't do her best to keep up. She wanted to see what else he had. She wanted to see it all.

"Heph - fuck! I'm gonna—"

He didn't need more than that, nor did he allow her to proceed. He buried the full of his face in her folds once more, the bridge of his nose braced against her clit as he twisted and curled his tongue inside of her, two fingers hooked into the bottom edge of her heat. She rocked against him, hips jerking as she all but sat up before him. Both hands seized his head. His nails bit into her thighs. She toppled over the edge in a crescendo of moans that broke like waves against the rocks, devolving into shrieks of pleasure.

He lapped it all up, smacking his lips and slicking her up with his spit as he went. *Fuck*. The world tilted before her as she collapsed back on the bed, her hips still moving in time with his tongue and her body writhing in overwhelming pleasure. It was marvelous. It was devastating. It would be her undoing. And she wanted it to be.

He kissed up her body, taking his time on her tits with that Fates forsaken mouth before he left it suspended over hers, teasing. He was beautiful, and with all of his layers shed, she found more beauty than she knew what to do with. From the ink that decorated his skin to the scar tissue that accentuated the art to the unique way his body moved and settled, she adored every inch of him. Her hands found his neck, but when she tried to drag him down or crane her neck up to reach his mouth, he resisted.

"I didn't hear a thank you for that one," he noted, his voice smug.

She gritted her teeth. He had her doing things she had never done for anyone, in bed or otherwise, including offering her gratitude for her orgasm. And he hadn't even fucking kissed her again yet. What the hell would become of her when he did?

Resistance was a hopeless endeavor, futile in practice with him and just as unfulfilling. Her body reacted to his mere existence, not simply to what he was doing to her but to all the things he *could* do, which was a very new sensation. She yearned for him, and all she could do was relent. Anything for him to keep pleasing her. She felt his cock, hard once again, pressed against her folds, and she squirmed, eager, a whimper leaving her lips. He didn't budge.

"Thank you, Daddy," she forced out, digits tangling in his hair as she wrapped her leg around his hip.

He took a firm grasp of her jaw, and not for the first time. "Say that shit like you mean it, Princess."

She bit back a sigh, pushing out her lower lip. "Thank you, Daddy."

"That's a good girl. Now tell me what you want."

She groaned now, impatient. "Heph, please."

"You know what you need to do. So go on and do it."

"Please. Fuck me. I want it, Daddy. I want it. I need you inside me."

Even amidst her own endless urgency, she didn't miss the flicker in his eyes, how they seemed to ignite and burn brighter with a comparable longing. He liked that shit. He liked hearing her call him daddy, begging him to turn her out — or continue to, and she was far too needy to fight him any longer. If she had to plead with the bastard, she would, so long as she got what she craved.

Still, she fed on his reaction, taking pride in knowing she had a similar effect on him, that she was not alone in this, that he would not leave this room unscathed.

He smothered her mouth with his, a hand sliding beneath her head to tangle in her hair, and she fisted his in her hands, surrendering every drop of air in her lungs to his cause.

Then he pulled away.

In the haze pressing in on her, her immediate thought was that he might have changed his mind or realized what he was doing and who he was doing it with. Panic rose in her chest, and she did her best to wade out of the fog plaguing her mind so that she could find some way to defend her dignity. She forced her eyes open, but he didn't climb off of her completely. Instead, he reached over to the bedside table she'd all but destroyed earlier and peered into the drawer. Then he extracted the small bottle of lube she had been searching for.

Sitting back on his haunches, he didn't say a word, but he kept his eyes on hers as if to assure her all was well. It did the trick, pacifying her worry and leaving room for a newfound need as she watched him squeeze some of the clear liquid into his hand and then start to stroke himself. He tossed the bottle on the bed beside them, making sure he slicked up every inch of his shaft before he reached down and massaged the rim of her entrance, earning a grateful purr. Once he was satisfied, he retracted his hand and lowered himself down over her again, capturing her lips with his own. She wasn't sure what had her heart threatening to beat out of her chest, how sexy he was with his cock in his hand or how charming his concern was for her comfort. Probably both.

She felt his hand slip between them, fumbling for his erection before the tip slid through her folds. She yelped, and he caught it between his teeth, growling as he teased her entrance. She raised her hips, trying to catch him, but he made her work, moving back up to slap the head against her clit. Only when she groaned her frustration did he plunge every slick and swollen inch into her, her muffled cries echoing against his mouth.

One hand scrambled to grasp at his back, seeking purchase as he found his rhythm, ramming mercilessly into her. So he was concerned but not too concerned, just the way she liked it. While she may need a bit of help taking him to start, she didn't want him to go easy on her. She didn't want to be treated as though she were fragile. She never had. No, she wanted him to wreck her cunt the way he wrecked her throat. She wanted him to leave every inch of her sore.

It appeared he had the same goals.

He seemed to expand further inside of her, filling her up, the heels of her feet digging into the backs of his legs. As soon as his lips left hers in favor of attacking her neck, her sultry sounds filled the air uninhibited. He touched each and every nerve between the hand cupping her breast and his mouth on her throat and his other hand slipping beneath her to claw at her ass. She'd been wrong, so very wrong, and she was grateful for it. All she wanted now is more.

"Yes! Daddy, please. Don't - don't stop. Don't—"

Not that he needed the direction. All she could do was hold on as he drilled into her, much of his weight concentrated on his left side and much of his attention focused on her neck. How he managed to have her on the brink of her third orgasm in no more than two hours was beyond her, but she was powerless to stop it. And just as unwilling to as well.

He hit every spot with every thrust, spots she feared didn't exist for her, and her feet shook and curled against him. She clawed at his shoulder and back, hard enough to break the skin or break a nail although she wouldn't be able to confirm which until much later. His hand moved from her breast to the side of her neck, gripping it hard as he wrapped his mouth around the other side. She knew he was going to leave a mark, most likely multiple, but she could not find the strength to stop him. In fact, it only enticed her further. She wanted to be marked by him. *Fuck.*

Her cries grew louder, falling in time with his rugged grunts that sent additional vibrations through her trembling body. Sweat poured from his forehead, his own body glistening with it, and she knew he was giving it his all. By this hour, he was usually struggling to move, hunching over his cane, and yet he was fucking her with the kind of vigor she longed for. How long had she been missing out? How long had she fooled herself? The truth of it was all too clear to her.

He would satisfy her tonight, but she would never get enough.

She was blinded by the brightest of lights when she came this time, her body convulsing beneath his weight. Her eyes rolled into the back of her head as she forced out scream after high-pitched scream of unadulterated pleasure. Even as she came down, he didn't stop. And he didn't slow. He didn't even seem to notice she'd climaxed. He was too focused on getting himself there.

Despite her sensitivity, she drew her knees up, spreading her legs as wide as she could just to let him keep going. She watched the way his face screwed up in concentration as he finally pulled away from her neck, the veins in his own defined against reddened skin. Another pulsed in his temple, the exertion evident, and she gripped his hips and guided him into her again and again. His wild eyes found hers, and her breath caught. He had never looked more dangerous than he did right now. Yet she had never felt safer.

Or more turned on.

"Give it to me, Daddy," she whined, nails biting at his ass. "Please. I - I want it. I—"

With a grunt, he pushed himself up further, his hips punishing hers with rapid thrusts. She created a chorus of wanton sounds, guiding him towards climax, her walls still spasming around him. She knew he was close. She saw it in his face. She heard it in his snarl. She begged and pleaded, requested and demanded, anything she could to get him there. It was as though he were fighting to hold out, which only made her more determined to see him come undone, to do to him what he had done to her thrice over now. Gripping the sides of his head again, she dragged him down until her teeth could tug at his earlobe, her breath hot against the shell.

"Cum for me, Daddy. Please."

She felt it almost immediately; the jerk of his cock, the shortening of his strokes, the way his body went as taut as a bowstring. His arms trembled around her, the last of his strength threatening to abandon him, and she cradled his head against her chest. Then she was flooded with heat. She held him close, squeezing her walls around him and milking him until he was empty. It felt too good. She didn't want it to end. She didn't want to face what that ending meant either. She was right. She was certainly in trouble.

It was a destructive series of tremors that racked her body and left her a shaking and shivering mess. He collapsed on top of her, his seed spilling out of her and onto the sheets as they sank deeper into them. Too tired to help it much less unpack the meaning, she allowed herself to soak up his warmth and savor the satisfaction he had bestowed upon her, combing a hand through his hair as she brushed her lips across his temple.

He nuzzled his nose against her neck in response, his softening shaft still pulsing faintly inside of her in the most delicious way. She couldn't even open her eyes, the fatigue settling in her bones with haste. She didn't mind it. She wasn't ready to get up, to speak, to shatter this moment they had created out of some twisted mixture of spite and curiosity. So she lay there, reveling in his soft breathing against her neck and the flames still flickering in her belly.

Chapter Thirteen

HEPHAESTUS

The sound of a phone ringing somewhere near the door roused Hephaestus from sleep. It took him a moment to register that it was his phone and yet another moment to register his current location. He was still in Aphrodite's bed, his arm thrown over her waist and their legs tangled beneath the cool satin sheets. Memories of last night flashed behind his eyes, the soreness in his muscles amplifying the images...

The phone rang again.

His body reacted with surprising haste, and he quickly disentangled himself before it woke her up too. Climbing out of bed, he made his way over to his piles of clothes by the door despite the protest of his legs. For the most part, he could make due without his cane, but his left knee was prone to buckling without warning, and the tremors that plagued both were just as unpredictable over longer distances.

It was his muscles that were the trouble, weakening over time in the most subtle ways. It was an odd thing, how he could still lift heavy objects and do the same workouts as his brothers and uncles. Hell, he could run if he had to, but he could never tell you how far he would get. That was up to the disease and the disease alone. He had coped since he was kid with the help of Asklepios and his specialist

Hippocrates, and the degeneration moved slow enough that it didn't worry him too much most of the time. They weren't used to this type of exertion however, and he had to admit it, at least to himself. Aphrodite had worn him out.

His phone began to ring again, and he quickly snatched up his pants, digging it out of the pocket. Achilles' name flashed across the screen, the time of 9:00 in the morning glaring angrily back at Hephaestus. Silencing the tone, he gathered his things and stepped out into the hall, shutting the door silently behind him. Rather than answer the phone, he returned to the guest bedroom to wash up and get dressed before heading downstairs to speak to his second in person. He needed to get out of the suite before he ran himself ragged trying to come to terms with what they'd done, with what *he'd* done. He didn't know how it happened. He wasn't sure how it had evolved — or devolved— into what it had. All he knew was that he couldn't deal with it right now.

Achilles was coming out of the main security office with Hector when Hephaestus found him, the two of them not speaking but looking equally concerned. Achilles brightened when he saw Heph though, throwing a hand up in greeting.

"Late start?" he questioned.

"A bit," Heph grunted. "What's up?"

Achilles dismissed Hector with another wave of his hand, and Hector didn't linger, continuing on down the hall on his own. Achilles then opened the door to the interrogation room door to their left, and Heph followed him inside as he fixed the collar of his shirt.

"Kleon is alive and well," Achilles began eagerly. "One of our own confirmed it."

"They got into the room?" Achilles nodded. "How did they manage that?"

"Flooded the room above him. Sent a 'maintenance guy' in, then they moved his room."

"They moved his room."

"Yup, which means we were able to put one of our little bugs in there so Patroclus could get into his phone."

"And did he?"

"We did. No audio or anything yet, but we got call and text logs. He's made a whole lot of calls to Labrinth, but it looked like those calls were getting rerouted each time they came in. We checked it out and got a name for the, uh, head of security over there. Guy named Perseus. Ring any bells?"

Achilles stared at him as if it definitely should, his lips twitching. Hephaestus raised a brow, combing his mind for any memory of the name. Achilles offered some mercy, clicking through his phone before turning its screen towards Heph. A man stared back at him, conjuring a recollection in an instant.

"He used to come to Khaos Falls to buy weapons for Thassos," Heph muttered, more to himself than to Achilles. "A lot of weapons."

"Yes, meaning he had legitimate means of moving large shipments to and from Thassos before you stopped selling to him. His grandfather was the city leader until he got pushed out. Now Perseus apparently runs this place."

"You found this on Kleon's phone?"

"Naw, he was really discreet in his messages. Patroclus sent someone into the security office asking about a job. He was told they weren't hiring right now because their boss was out of town. Our guy asked who that was, and they gave him the name and a card."

"Convenient that he's out of town, right?"

"Very."

"We have to get a location on him. Maybe that's why Kleon hasn't left the apartment. He's waiting for Perseus to get back from wherever he is."

"I doubt the people he left in charge are gonna know. If they were in on his main business, they probably wouldn't be giving out his name like that, right?"

"Yeah, you're—"

He was interrupted by a sharp knock on the door, and his blood ran cold. He was certain it was Aphrodite, and he could say for certain he wasn't at all ready to face her yet. However, when Achilles opened the door, it was Artemis who slipped inside.

She was tall and willowy, her chiseled biceps a testament to her weapon of choice, a compound bow Hephaestus had designed for her years ago. Her black hair was short on top and completely shaved on the sides, an arrow inked into her dark skin above her left ear from the temple to the back of her head. It was the innocence in her eyes and the purity of her smile that drove many to underestimate her. It was why she was the city's greatest weapon with or without her bow. Of course, Heph preferred her with it.

She crossed the room to the table without a word, dropping a folder on its surface. It was evident to Hephaestus that the past few days had taken its toll on his friend, who was as tough as they came without sacrificing any softness in her heart. She carried the pain of those rescued with her, and he couldn't fault her for it. He imagined he would too.

"We managed to find family for about half of them," she began at last, turning to them. "All of them agreed to stay at Twilight until we caught those responsible."

"Could any of them give a description?" Heph questioned.

She shook her head. "They said they were kept in the dark, and the voices changed often. Most of them haven't even started to speak. There was one girl, Leda. She tried to give us a description of one of the men who took her on her way home in Thassos, but it wasn't much. She's upstairs with Psyche actually. She wanted to work, keep herself busy, so we thought Aphrodite might have something for her."

Hephaestus nodded, crossing his arms over his chest. He hadn't expected any eyewitnesses among the rescued, but there was still some measure of disappointment. It also scared him to think just how many people were involved in this and if he would ever be able to grab every single one. More than anything, he couldn't even begin to imagine how the survivors felt. They were once again in a house packed together and unable to leave. Would they ever truly feel free again?

"I *was* able to find out who owned that warehouse Aphrodite rescued them from though," Artemis went on. "Technically, it belongs to Demeter."

"What do you mean 'technically'?"

"There's no lease to the building, and there's no deed to the land, meaning it belongs to the district as a public property."

"Meaning we probably won't find anyone's name on anything else here."

Hephaestus chewed on his lip. It was hard to believe that Demeter had an entire trafficking ring under her nose without anyone the wiser, but he also didn't want to consider the possibility that she too had rats in her kitchen. Either way, they hadn't picked the building by accident or on a whim. Someone had to know that it was vacant, meaning they had done their research.

"How many other properties are there like that in the city?" Heph asked now. "Public buildings with no deed."

"Honestly there are probably a lot," Artemis went on. "Apollo and I talked about it before, how the leaders used to be so stingy with the land and the buildings they weren't using, Demeter included. Twilight House was a property like that before Aphrodite officially claimed it, and both Atlantis and the Market District have utilized buildings like that for housing and kitchens for the homeless."

"I want a list of them, the ones that aren't being used at the moment preferably. Odds are they've got that list, and they've probably used more than just this one warehouse."

"It's kind of wild, isn't it?" Artemis quipped now. "Aphrodite running up on that warehouse the same night they planned to kill her."

Achilles and Hephaestus looked at one another.

"That's what we were talking about last night," Hephaestus huffed. "Honestly? I think they wanted her to take it. It gave them time to swap her security out. I couldn't figure out how they'd managed to do that in the hour I was inside, but now I'm thinking it started much earlier than that. It just took time."

"I can see that."

"But wouldn't it have been easier to just kill her during the raid?"

"Not if they didn't have the numbers. If we're right about these shipments, they have more than one warehouse, but they would want to keep the number of men in the city at once as low as possible. The survivors said the voices changed a lot, probably because they were rotating across locations. The point is Kleon knew we were watching that warehouse. He was Aphrodite's eyes."

Artemis snorted a laugh. "Oh, he knew alright. The night he was at

Twilight House, he said he was the one who had tipped Aphrodite off about activity at the warehouse, tried to make himself look like a hero so I'd let him stay in the house."

Hephaestus hissed. "And Aphrodite said she couldn't remember exactly who told her, but I imagine she would've remembered if it had been Kleon."

"Which could also be why they didn't try and take her in the raid," Achilles pointed out. "If they failed, it wouldn't be difficult to figure out it was a set up, and he would be the prime suspect."

"I knew he was no good the moment he walked into the house," Artemis grumbled. "I told him to leave right away. Something felt off about him being there."

"I'm glad you did. Who knows what he would've done if he'd still been inside when Aphrodite was attacked. He was there for a reason and not just as the welcoming committee."

Now that Hephaestus considered it, he and Aphrodite hadn't talked much about that night since he'd scolded her upon her return to Lush. Right before the attack. He had been arrogant about it, thinking he knew all he needed to know and she couldn't offer him anything more. That couldn't be further from the truth. He hadn't even been to the site yet, and while his forces had, his paranoia wouldn't accept that as enough. He needed to focus.

If both he and Aphrodite were losing sight of the goal, that left her half as attentive and twice as vulnerable. Whatever this was that was working against her, it grew bigger by the day, and who knew who else would be implicated or identified. Right now, they needed to start piecing together a big picture, something they could fill in as they went. Something had to give. And soon. He was done waiting around. They had to do something.

"Achilles, focus on finding Perseus," he concluded. "No confrontations. Let's just get a location for now, and if it proves beneficial to put eyes on him before he goes back to Thassos, we will. And tell Patroclus to swap out his guys. Unfamiliar faces in one place for too long might breed suspicion, and we can't afford that. Artemis, get me that list. I want naval patrols around the coast just in case they try to dock somewhere other than the port. They have to be planning another way to get their remaining victims out of the city. I'll go check out the warehouse Aphrodite hit that night. Maybe we can find something we missed before. And all of the details stay between us and Patroclus for now. I'm still not convinced we've cleaned out all the rats."

The two of them nodded in agreement, no doubt just as anxious as him standing around. Artemis wasn't used to being stationed in one place, and Achilles was still adjusting to life as a security guard with a normal schedule and a dedicated purpose. Heph didn't blame either of them for getting antsy. He just hoped he didn't lead them down into something they weren't prepared for.

They all left the room together, heading towards the main room. As they approached the mouth of the hall, a familiar figure appeared framed within it, dressed in a dark shirt and matching bomber jacket. Charon always seemed to fill more space than he accounted for, his slender build casting a long shadow as it eclipsed the hallway behind him. His dark eyes glittered under the fluorescents, the eagle tattoo on his neck looking fresh as the day he'd had it inked. Hephaestus remembered it well. He'd only been a boy then, but he had been obsessed with the way the wings flapped when Charon clenched his jaw. To this day, there was something magical and majestic about that bird, and it added to the intimidating appearance of its canvas. It was why Hephaestus got one just like it across his chest.

Charon greeted Achilles and Artemis with a slight smile and a nod before they continued on, disappearing down the hall. He then fell into step beside Hephaestus, slipping his hands in his pockets.

"I came to check on you," he stated.

"You have good timing."

"Got something?"

"A name." Charon glanced over at him. "You remember Perseus? He was one of my biggest customers when I started out."

"He bought on behalf of Thassos' leadership, didn't he?"

"Yeah, apparently it was his grandfather. Now he's running that security company our main rat has been in contact with."

"You think he's involved?"

They turned down the hall in the direction opposite of the main room, an exit door at this end along with some of the private rooms and the stairs that led down to the lower floor. As they moved further from the sounds of the front room, Hephaestus lowered his voice.

"He's currently out of town, and Kleon hasn't left that hotel room. We managed to get into Kleon's phone, but it's only surface level stuff."

"It's something. You'll figure it out."

Hephaestus turned his head slightly to look at the elder. "When you said you came to check up on me, did you mean something else?"

Charon smiled. It was odd to think that there was someone more mellow than Hades, but here he was. Unlike his uncle though, Charon remained a shadow in the Underworld, rarely seen and often felt. He was Hades' eyes and ears, the chalice from which his vast knowledge of the city and abroad originated, and Charon often shared it with Hephaestus as well. They had built a bond around metalwork and observation, and Hephaestus had cherished it deeply.

In the beginning, it had been hard to feel like he belonged when Zeus only cared for Athena, Hera was fixated on Ares, and Hades busied himself with Dionysos and Hermes, but Charon had been there to offer some guidance. He had told Hephaestus from the start that he didn't have to fear taking up space nor did he have to accept other people labeling his struggles as weaknesses, and Heph had taken it to heart. Good thing too, otherwise he probably wouldn't be here now.

Charon hummed. "Hades wanted an update, so I came to fetch one."

"You could've called."

"I could've."

"So?"

He chuckled. "Can't I just check on you?"

Heph shrugged. "Of course, but-" He paused a moment before a groan escaped him. "I'm fine."

"Are you sure? Because that sounded like an acute brand of paranoia, and I know how those things can get to you. This is your first major assignment since taking over the city forces, Hephaestus, and it's no small task. Lives are at stake. I know you never wanted to be in charge of something like that."

"You're right. I didn't, but -"

He took a moment to push the exit door open, leading them out into the side lot. It was chilly, dark clouds rolling in from the coast, but it hadn't started to rain just yet. Heph could smell it though, and lightning cracked across the sky in the distance.

"Uncle was right too," he went on, leaning against the wall. "Arms dealing was a dangerous game, and not just for me. Even if we were doing it in the name of security, we were gambling with the intentions of other people, strangers. Now, with Uncle taking over, who knows who might try something or when. Taking this job means I can actually do some good, and I can protect my brothers and Athena, my mother... you and Uncle."

"You didn't need to take on the world just for us, Heph."

"I know that, but I have a penance to pay. I've accepted that, and I'll follow through."

Charon leaned against the wall beside him. "I'm proud of you, you know. Your uncle is too."

Hephaestus wouldn't admit how much it meant to him, but that didn't matter because Charon already knew. He had long since given up trying to earn that admission from Zeus, and he wasn't expecting Hera to say it anytime soon, but Hades and Charon had always been vocal about their faith and pride in him. They had given him far more validation than he knew what to do with.

But right now, there was a question he wanted to ask, one he couldn't bring himself to voice due to the fear of it opening doors neither of them were ready to peer into. He could feel Charon's eyes on him though, reading him like an open book in a language he was far too fluent in. Heph could ice out the best of them but not Charon.

"Whatever it is," Charon started, enunciating each word thoroughly, "I'll be here when you're ready to talk about it."

Hephaestus snorted, but it was no use trying to deny it. "Add it to the list of conversations we have to have after the past few months."

"Will do. Now, shouldn't you be getting back to your charge?"

Heph glanced at his watch. It was nearing noon. "Shit."

Charon clapped a hand on his shoulder, and it was then that Heph realized how liberating the conversation had been regardless of how brief. Then again, he and Charon often communicated without speaking at all. He hadn't thought much about his role since taking it, but that was due to the immense demand that had been waiting for him on day one. He had wanted to do some good though. All of his siblings were running districts as were his uncles, and even his mother was pursuing a new career. Arms dealing had been the best money he could ever make, but it made his morality as unstable as his mortality, and he no longer wanted the responsibility of all that blood on his hands. He could still build weapons. He just kept a much better track of where they went now.

"And Heph?" Charon said now, drawing his attention once more. "You should go see your mother when this is all said and done. She has some healing to do too, but you might be surprised at what you find underneath all that mourning."

Heph licked his lips. Then he nodded. He couldn't focus on his own shit right now. There was too much on the line. Saying goodbye to Charon, he trudged back inside only to remember that he and Aphrodite had shit to deal with now too.

Chapter Fourteen

APHRODITE

Aphrodite's phone was ringing. It had been ringing for quite a long time before it finally pulled her from sleep, the slow recognition of the tone drawing her back into the land of the living. She searched blindly for the device on her bedside table, knocking over whatever she hadn't the night before until she found it. She knew who it was, the ringtone giving it away, and she was well aware it wasn't a call she would be able to ignore again. She had been doing it for days.

Blinking the sleep from her eyes, she glanced over her shoulder to find empty sheets although the rumpled imprint of a body let her know that last night had not been a dream. She sighed and put the phone to her ear.

"It is about damn time!" Demeter's voice rang out before she could even comprise a greeting, but it sounded far away as if she weren't the one holding the phone. "What does a woman have to do to get at least one of her daughters on the phone?"

"You do remember she almost got killed, right?" came Hestia's quiet voice, and Aphrodite smiled.

"I am well aware, which is why I would have liked to hear her voice to know she was alive!"

"I am in fact alive, Mama," Aphrodite managed.

Where Demeter's overbearing nature often overwhelmed Persephone, Aphrodite had learned to find comfort in it to some small degree. It was probably because she had always been far more careful with when she allowed it whereas Persephone didn't have the luxury until she was older. Nonetheless, Demeter had taken her in, had let her practically live in her house when Aphrodite was hiding from her father, then let her actually live in her house once Oceanus passed. It was impossible not to be grateful. And Hestia... well, there were not enough words to express what Hestia had done for her. She had saved Aphrodite's life.

"And hi, Auntie," she said now.

"Hey, baby, you good?" Hestia questioned, her own concern a solid and palpable thing.

"Yeah, I'm doing alright. We've just been trying to figure this out."

"I don't think I need to lecture you on the recklessness of your little vigilante missions," Demeter started in a way that told Aphrodite that was exactly what she was about to do, "but do you-"

"No, you don't, Mama, I know I made a mistake, and I promise I've learned from it."

"Do you have any leads yet?" Hestia pushed on.

"A few. Hephaestus and Achilles are checking them out as they go, and I think they're close to finding something big."

Demeter scoffed. "I can't believe Persephone would trust a son of Zeus to protect you. Then again, after her little-"

"Don't do it, Mama. You know I don't dabble in the beef y'all got in any way. And Hephaestus is head of city security forces. He is the best we have."

She could only imagine what Demeter would say if she knew just how close Hephaestus had stayed to her last night doing far more than protecting, but she shoved the thought to the back of her mind. She couldn't lie though. There was a thrill to the idea. She wondered if this was how Persephone felt when she started seeing Hades, knowing her mother would wild out the moment she heard.

"It wasn't like he was voted in by the city, Aphrodite," Demeter spat, her sharp cadence cutting through the phone. "His uncle put him there, and - isn't that boy a-"

"Don't." Aphrodite's voice darkened of its own accord, her tone just as cutting. "Don't you dare, Mama."

"Don't *you* get all high and mighty with me, *Daughter*. There is absolutely nothing wrong with having a disability, and I know that, but I am not willing to put faith in one to keep my girl safe."

"He is the best at what he does, and he's kept my reckless ass alive this long. I have never felt safer. He doesn't just want to protect me though."

"Oh, I'm sure he doesn't."

She clenched her jaw. "He wants to help shut down the trafficking rings."

"He was selling weapons to these bastards not a year ago!"

"He was selling them to the cities for *their* protection."

"Which weakened ours!"

"Regardless, he's doing what he can now, and he's going to figure this out. Then he's going to take things down."

"Don't depend on him to protect you, Aphrodite, and don't expect him to save everyone. That is not what he is built for. Betrayal and greed are in his blood."

"It's in mine too, and I've combatted it just fine."

There was a beat of silence before she could hear Demeter again, her voice fading as if she was walking away from the phone. "...Raising these girls, and this is the thanks I get."

Aphrodite was comforted by Hestia's laugh drowning it out, exhaling a heavy breath.

"How are you really though?" Hestia questioned now, her voice clearer. She had taken the call off of speaker mode. "It's okay to be a little scared, 'Dite."

"Honestly, Auntie, I'm not scared. I'm angry. If I were scared, this might be easier. Maybe I wouldn't be so hardheaded."

That wasn't entirely true. As she had told Persephone last night, she *was* scared, but she wasn't willing to dwell on it nor would she speak it into a larger existence.

"Girl, you've always been hardheaded." They chuckled. "But that isn't always a bad thing. You get shit done, and you don't wait around for anybody. Persephone was always hesitating, unsure of herself, but you? You knew who you were from the day you were born. Don't ever look down at that."

"I guess I just never thought that - people would want to betray me. I thought if I was just good to people and I treated them right, I would always have their love."

"Baby, it isn't always love that drives them to you. Sometimes, it's worship, and that isn't the same thing. People only call on the Fates when they need something, right? And that's a reflection of them, not of you. You could be the most perfect person in the world, and people will still find it in themselves to bring you harm because that is *their* nature. It's who they are."

"I wish it wasn't."

She knew it was childish, the kind of idealistic thinking that Hephaestus often reprimanded her for, but it was also the truth, and thinking of it made her chest tighten.

"Don't we all?" Hestia huffed. "Just remember this. Your kindness is not a weakness, Aphrodite."

"I'll do my best."

After getting off the phone with Hestia, Aphrodite scrolled the rest of the few missed calls and messages from this morning. Most of them were from Eros or Psyche, but none of them were from Hephaestus, so she assumed he must be getting an update from his people. She allowed herself a moment to lay back in bed and shut her eyes, remembering the night before in vivid detail.

The things he'd done to her, the places he'd touched, the way his mouth proved to be more dangerous than she had ever imagined. If she focused hard enough, she could still feel it between her thighs and along her neck, searching for sustenance and demanding devotion. She wished he were still in bed now where she could roll over and run her hands down his body, coaxing him into doing the same for her. He'd done something irrevocable to her last night, and she wasn't sure how to handle it.

She slid her hand down between her thighs with a whimper, her skin tender and her body sore. She was a bit disappointed that he was able to make it out of bed when she could hardly move. Her clit was more sensitive than it had ever been, and she recalled how easily he had made her cum, when usually, it took her at least an hour to get herself off once. She inhaled as she began to massage her clit, biting her lip as the image of him staring up at her while he ate her out manifested in her mind. He had certainly kept his promise, showing her something different and proving her all the way wrong. He definitely didn't fuck like a robot. He fucked like an animal, and she was addicted to it.

She quickened her pace, kneading her breast with her other hand as she arched deeper into the sheets. It still brought her a genuine excitement, the thought of him walking in on her again and teaching her another lesson she wouldn't soon forget. She missed the shape of him between her legs and the weight of him over her chest and the girth of him in her throat and the taste of him on her tongue and...

"Heph!"

It left her lips like a broken prayer as her orgasm clutched her, her fingers pressing down hard on her clit as her hips bucked against them. She shuddered uncontrollably, her body flushed with intense heat and her eyes rolling back. She rode it out, hard and fast, savoring the chills that ran through her before her back hit the sheets again. Her eyes fluttered open, and for a moment, she could see him there, watching her. She had no clue what she would do when she was actually standing in front of him again, but at the moment, it didn't matter. She wanted to live in this moment of bliss a bit longer.

But then her phone was ringing again, and this time, it was Psyche. She answered quickly, still trying to catch her breath.

"Hey, Psyche," she greeted.

"'Dite, sorry to wake you, but I've got one of the girls from Twilight House here," she said quickly. "She's looking for something to do. Maybe we could place her today?"

Aphrodite quirked a brow. Usually, they gave the rescues much longer to recover physically and mentally before offering them work. It wasn't uncommon for some to be ready quicker than others, but it had only been a few days since the raid. Still, she wasn't going to deny anyone a way to keep busy if it would help them cope.

"I'll be down in a bit," she said. "Meet me in my office. Oh, and, uh, have you seen Heph?"

"Yeah, he was down in the security offices with Artemis and Achilles. Do you want me to find him?"

"No, no, it's fine. He'll find me when he's ready. I'll see you soon."

She hung up and forced herself out of bed, stretching out her muscles and hearing the resounding pop of her joints. She padded into the bathroom and took a quick shower, scrubbing her body clean of the evidence of the night before. She had to fight not to think about it, knowing she would get herself wound up again if she allowed it, and she couldn't afford it right now. Once she was finished, she hurried to get dressed before heading downstairs for her office.

She found Psyche inside, standing near her desk and talking to someone sitting in the chair before it. It was a woman, but Aphrodite could make out only a head of long brown hair as she approached. Psyche looked up when she entered, and the woman turned in her seat, immediately standing when she saw Aphrodite. Her pale skin remained marred with light bruises, her olive green eyes underlined with dark bags. She was certainly one of the younger victims they had rescued. Aphrodite wouldn't put her a day over nineteen if she had to guess, and she must have weighed no more than a child half that age.

"Aphrodite, this is Leda," Psyche introduced with a smile, her thick hair pulled back in two braids. "She's originally from Spartan Hills."

Aphrodite offered the woman her hand, and she took it with two shaky ones, squeezing it as her eyes watered.

"It's so nice to finally meet you," Leda managed, her voice hoarse. "Thank you for what you did, for - for saving us."

"You don't have to thank me."

Aphrodite took a thorough inventory of her now that they were up close. She needed some hearty meals and some ointments for the bruises, but there was something else too, something Aphrodite had seen before. It looked like guilt, like shame, like all of the things the world told her she should bear the brunt of forever. Aphrodite despised it.

"Psyche said you were looking for something to do with your time," she went on as Leda released her hand finally. "Are you sure you're ready?"

Leda shrugged. "I don't know, I just - it's hard being in the house. I

- I bonded with some of the other girls, sure, but - they're all..." That guilt was suddenly magnified as she dropped her gaze. "Looking at them is like a reminder of everything that happened."

Aphrodite grimaced. "I get that, and we'll do what we can to make you comfortable. Is there anything you've done before as far as work goes?"

She shook her head sadly. "I was - I was still in school when they took me. I'd just turned seventeen, and then..."

"That's alright. Do you have any family?"

She didn't answer, and Aphrodite caught Psyche's apologetic gaze.

"It was her father that got her into this," she said softly.

Aphrodite nodded, her heart clenching. "Okay, listen, I'll tell you what. We'll fix you a room upstairs. I have a few spares that the club doesn't exclusively use. Then tomorrow, we'll figure out something that will keep you busy until we find a more permanent solution."

Leda nodded, glancing up at Aphrodite. "Will I have to - work in the club as a-"

The elder shook her head. "I do have sex workers downstairs in the specialty rooms and at other pleasure dens in the district, but it's always a choice, and if you don't feel comfortable in that line of work, you have no obligation to do it. We have plenty of work here in the city that doesn't involve it, and we can look for something like that. We can even help you get back into school if you'd like. Our goal is to give you the life you envisioned for yourself before all of this."

She nodded again quickly. "Thank you, Aphrodite. You really are a hero."

"I'm only trying to do some good. I'm glad I can help. I—"

She trailed off as the door opened behind her, Hephaestus entering the room with narrowed eyes. He was obviously suspicious of their strange guest, and Aphrodite's thoughts were so scrambled by the sight of him that she couldn't explain fast enough.

"Who is this?" he asked.

"Leda."

The woman herself answered before Aphrodite could react, stepping forward and offering her hand. Hephaestus stared at it for a moment before taking it, giving it one firm shake before he let it go.

"I'm one of the girls Aphrodite saved," she pushed on with a small smile.

Hephaestus nodded, looking her over, and Aphrodite took advantage of his distraction. Her breath caught as she admired him in his crisp shirt and pressed khaki pants. Last night, he'd given her the most unimaginable amount of pleasure, and she felt it tingling between her thighs as she met his smoldering gaze when it fell upon her again. It wasn't fair how absolutely gorgeous he was. It wasn't fair that her desire now outweighed her disdain.

"Um, Psyche will show you upstairs now, Leda, and I'll talk to you tomorrow," she managed at last. "If you need anything, don't be afraid to ask."

Leda thanked her once more before following Psyche to the door.

"Take a ride with me," Hephaestus said without waiting for them to leave completely, startling her.

"Where?"

"I want you to show me where that warehouse is, the one you found the girls in."

How romantic. *Bastard.* "You know where it is, Hephaestus."

"Yeah, well I would rather have you with me right now." She ignored the way her stomach fluttered at the words. "I want to see it. Maybe we missed something."

"If we did, it's probably gone. In case you forgot, the traitors are the ones I sent to clear it."

"Better safe than sorry."

"Of course."

"Will you come?"

Flashbacks of her doing exactly that for him barreled through her like a train, and she had to focus on her breathing in order to answer him. Even then, she could only offer a nod, but that was enough because of course she would come with him. The idea of being left behind suddenly stung more than it had before.

She kept asking herself what had changed and when. What was different between the two of them? They bickered less despite spending more time together, and she didn't entirely understand it, but that seemed moot now after last night. Yet how did they get there?

What possessed her to strip down and put on a show for this suave motherfucker that kissed her halfway to the heavens? ...Or is that exactly why?

She really didn't have time to reach a verdict at the moment.

They made their way out to the parking garage in silence, and Heph's car was already parked near the exit. As usual, he first opened her door before moving around to slide behind the wheel. From what she knew —both by word of mouth and prior encounters— he didn't drive all that much, but he looked comfortable behind the wheel of this inconspicuous town car. She assumed this was him trying to minimize the amount of people he brought around her, and she could appreciate that. He pulled out of the lot and headed for the warehouse, his eyes sharp as they focused on the road ahead.

"Run me through it again," he requested. "Who told you about the warehouse?"

She bit her lip, the night of the attack unraveling behind her eyes. Everything had happened so fast, partly because she had been trying to make a move before Hephaestus found out and stopped her. Part of her wished he had, but she knew she would have been furious had it actually turned out that way.

"Honestly? I couldn't tell you who told me directly," she sighed. "It was quick. We got a tip there was some traffic all of a sudden, and as soon as I got confirmation, I made the move."

"Do you remember who gave you the initial tip? Could it have been Kleon?"

"No, I couldn't find him that night, remember?

"But he could've tipped off whoever did tell you."

She didn't like where this was going. "I guess. Why are you asking all this again?"

He was quiet for a moment, and then, "It wasn't a coincidence, Aphrodite, you raiding that place the same night you were attacked. Kleon outright told Artemis he was the one that gave you the confirmation so he could try and gain her trust, and he didn't expect you to live long enough to say otherwise. The raid was the perfect opportunity to swap out your security with his guys while Nikolaos was keeping an eye on your whereabouts."

Her stomach churned. “So - he set me up?”

“How many survivors did you pull out? A couple dozen?”

“More or less.” A chill ran down her spine.

“To them, that probably isn’t much. It was easy to sacrifice them if they thought they would be getting them right back once you were out of the way, and even if they didn’t, they would at least keep you from saving the others they’re holding in the city.”

They pulled up to the warehouse, which looked empty and unsettling even in the middle of the day. It was a simplistic stone structure, the walls a cloudy grey and the open land around it nothing but dirt and gravel. Heph checked his pistol to make sure it was loaded — although they both knew damn well it was— before they proceeded inside, Aphrodite pulling her knife from where it was strapped to her thigh. Still, she swung her purse over her shoulder where Heph’s pistol remained tucked away. He was careful, vigilant, checking every nook and cranny around the building before they ventured inside. Aphrodite had to fight not to hold her breath.

The place had been gutted. Not that there had been much inside of it the last time she’d been here, but there had been a decent amount of supplies outlining the “camping area” of sleeping bags and bathroom buckets that had been set up for the individuals being kept like dogs in cages. Her stomach twisted again at the memory. It had been horrific. No matter how many times she saw it, no matter how many people she’d saved, she never got used to it. She supposed that was what kept her going.

Hephaestus tried one of the light switches, and then the room was bathed in fluorescents.

“Was there power when you came?” His voice startled her amidst the eeriness.

“I think so? But now that I think about it, Demeter has a lot of these buildings open for harvest season. Food gets separated in depots like this and sent out to the other districts. I doubt she has the lights turned off and on when the schedule fluctuates the way it does.”

Hephaestus halted. “Does she have a schedule though? One she keeps?”

“I don’t know if she does, but I’m sure the workers do.”

"Because to keep a bunch of people in here, you would have to be sure it would stay empty."

"So you would need a schedule."

"And then you would need a secondary location just in case."

They shared the moment, staring at one another, before he cleared his throat and turned back to the room. She buried her disappointment beneath thoughts of where she might be able to acquire a schedule from. She imagined Aunt Hestia could help her with ease. She made a mental note to call her back once they got out of here.

Until then, she helped Hephaestus map out the area, pointing out where things and people had been when they had come. It was common for her to accompany her guards on raids, something Persephone and Hestia had criticized her heavily for. However, she wasn't willing to budge on it. She would never send her people into a situation she wasn't willing to enter herself, and besides, she believed that the moment she turned her eyes away from the horrors of the trafficking circuit, she would start to become desensitized. Then what good would she be?

In the end, they found nothing but bloodstains, which was more infuriating than Aphrodite expected it to be. She had hoped he was right, that there was something there they could use to figure this out. Truth be told, the fear of an assassination was getting old rather quickly, and she wanted this weight lifted off of her chest. One thing was for certain. This proved that there remained other evils apart from Zeus that could do as much, if not more, damage than he ever could. She didn't know what to do with that just yet.

As they made their way back towards the door, there was a loud bang from behind them. Before she could blink, Hephaestus had swung around, dropping to one knee with his cane aimed like a rifle at his shoulder. Both of them breathed out heavily when a rat scurried out of the bucket it had run into, crashing it against the wall.

"So that is a gun," she said before she could stop herself, watching him push himself to his feet once more and dust off his pants. "I mean I assumed, but..."

"Yeah, it is," he returned simply.

"Is it easier for you to aim that way? On one knee?"

"To some extent, yes, but it's good to do just in case someone gets one on you."

"What do you mean?"

He looked over at her, his dark eyes scanning over the length of her form in a way that made her clench her thighs together. Fates, she could drown in those eyes if he let her. She swallowed hard, trying not to squirm too much under his scrutiny. She was so focused on that however that she didn't realize he was approaching her until he'd taken hold of her arm and turned her around so that her back was against his chest.

"Here."

He placed his cane in front of her, and she hesitated for only a moment before taking it in her hands.

"Let's say someone is pointing a gun at you." His voice is low against her ear, reverberating through her like a bassline. "They're directly in front of you, maybe a few feet away. You won't have time to aim outright, especially with a larger or longer weapon, right?"

"Right."

"So what can you do?" She let him continue without offering a suggestion. "You drop to your knee. That gives you a second."

"A second?"

"One second. One second to save your own life. They have to fix their aim, giving you just enough time to aim yours and take one shot. Where do you aim?"

"Their - head?"

"That's ideal, but - how much experience do you have with precision aiming?"

"Not much." She was surprised at how easily she admitted that. She could shoot just fine if she had to, but aiming like that in a small window of time was not something she'd ever practiced.

"So the second best option is the shoulder he's trying to aim with. You get a good hit, and it'll shake him just enough to give you another shot. Hopefully that's all you need."

"Hopefully I won't need any shots at all."

"Wishful thinking. Now try it."

"Try it?"

"Just drop. Follow your body weight." She tried to think of the motion, but he quickly interrupted. "Don't think about it. There is no time to think. Just drop. Drop."

He kept saying it, and at last, she simply - *did*. She dropped her weight, allowing herself to sink down to one knee before him as she pulled up the cane and aimed it like a gun. When she looked back up at him, he looked almost pleased. Or maybe that was as close to pleased as he could look.

"You actually aim pretty well, and your movements are fluid. Trust your instincts. You'll know what to do."

He offered his hand and helped her to her feet, taking his cane back from her. Her heart was thrumming fast, the sound of it echoing in her ears, adrenaline rushing through her veins. She hoped he was right. She wanted to believe she could do it if she had to even if she really hoped she never needed to.

"You hungry?" The words came rushing out of his mouth as they approached the car a few minutes later, and it sounded as though he'd made the decision a second *after* he'd asked. "Like you wanna stop and get somethin'?"

She appraised him over her shoulder, suppressing the urge to tease him. "What did you have in mind?"

"Anything really. I'm just not ready to go back."

"You got cabin fever or something?" She smirked. "Or you just scared to be alone with me?"

He didn't say anything, and her irritation flared so quickly that it caught her off guard. However, before she could turn around, he was gripping her bicep and ushering her towards the car.

"Hephaestus, what are—"

He yanked the back door open, effectively severing her train of thought, and pushed her inside.

"Get down on the floor," he growled. "There's a rifle under my seat. Pull it out and load it. Ammunition is—"

He didn't have the chance to finish. Even if he did, she could no longer hear him over the sudden eruption of gunfire. He all but jumped on top of her, pushing her to the floor of the backseat before he managed to reach back and slam the door shut. Bullets peppered the windows and - bounced off. Of course his vehicle was bulletproof. Still, the sound was deafening, and she couldn't even begin to form a question.

Heph climbed over the middle console, tumbling into the driver's seat, his cane left beside her. He brought the engine to life, and she peered over the console. The screen on the dashboard showed the live video feed of what was behind them, which currently consisted of two dark SUVs flanked by masked men with big guns. She heard one of their tires go, but Heph kicked the car into drive and peeled out, making a hard turn behind the warehouse and going through the lot. The bullets hadn't stopped, but they began to fade. For a moment at least. Then they grew louder once more.

He was going back.

"What are you doing?" she shrieked.

"I need to try and see a license plate or - or a model or something. Just stay down."

Bullets once again sprayed the side of the car, and Aphrodite curled up behind his seat, her hand resting on the rifle still under it. She watched his neck crane towards the passenger side for only a moment before he seemed satisfied, stepping down on the gas and racing from the scene. Her adrenaline was spilling out all over the carpet. She couldn't draw in a full breath. She took her time recovering once the gunfire began to fade once more, only sitting up when silence fell again.

"Are you okay?" she whispered, looking over the seat and inspecting him. "Are you hurt?"

"Naw, I'm - they didn't get me," he confirmed. "I'm fine."

"Heph, what the fuck is going on?"

He glanced in the rearview mirror, his vivid gaze going right through her. "Trouble. A whole lot of trouble. But we'll handle it. We will. I promise."

Despite the overwhelming thudding of her heart, she believed him.

Chapter Fifteen

HEPHAESTUS

"She doesn't need more security," Hephaestus sighed yet again, sitting beside Aphrodite on her office couch. "The bigger this gets, the less safe it is. We need to close ranks."

Hades was pacing near the door, Persephone sitting in a chair in front of Aphrodite's desk, and the two of them had been trading off every few minutes for the better part of the hour they'd been here. They had arrived just after dawn, and Aphrodite and Hephaestus hadn't been able to get a lick of sleep all night, running through everything they knew so far and everything they had yet to piece together.

"Aphrodite?" Persephone said now, standing from the seat she'd only taken minutes ago.

Aphrodite looked up from her cup where Hephaestus had poured her some tea for her nerves. She seemed absolutely exhausted, and a pang of guilt rolled through Heph's chest. When she glanced over at him, he stilled. She could throw him under the bus if she wanted to, tell Persephone and his uncle that she didn't believe him capable of protecting her, and all he could do was bow out peacefully. He wouldn't blame her too much either. After all, it was her safety at stake.

"Heph did just fine yesterday," she stated, pulling him from his thoughts. "He's been doing just fine, and - with all the leaks, I think it's best to keep closed ranks like he said. Besides, he and Achilles are close. The less people we have to worry about, the quicker they can work."

Hephaestus tried to ignore the warmth of relief seeping into his veins, keeping his eyes on the floor. He was invested now, far too deeply to simply walk away.

"Okay," Hades conceded. "What do you need from us?"

Hephaestus sat forward, rubbing his hands together. What he needed was time, but there really was no way to control that. What he did know was that the only way those men could've known he and Aphrodite were there was if the building was being watched. Or if they were being watched.

"Achilles is gathering a list of properties like that warehouse," he explained. "Properties that belong to the district and have no formal paperwork attached, properties easily accessible by traffickers. When it comes time, can you spare some of your people to watch over them?"

"Of course," Hades agreed. "So for now, we close our ranks."

"Persephone, watch yourself too. We have to assume they know how close you are to Aphrodite, and we don't wanna take any chances."

"Are you kidding?" Persephone scoffed, glancing at Hades. "I barely go anywhere alone."

"For good reason, as Hephaestus has just pointed out," Hades added.

They all looked up at the sound of a knock on the door. Hephaestus saw the outline of a young woman, and he recognized her as the one Aphrodite had been talking to the day before, Leda. He glanced over at Aphrodite, who was offering the girl a tight smile before holding up a finger, telling her to wait.

"I'll send Leonidas and Atalanta over once you have the list," Hades concluded. "Keep us in the loop if anything else comes in."

Hephaestus nodded, downing the rest of his drink. He was both anxious and fatigued, and as he watched Persephone embrace Aphrodite, there was a pang of guilt as well. He would hate for her to lose faith in him, but he certainly wouldn't lose faith in himself. There was no one who could do better for Aphrodite than him, and he had to believe that.

As Persephone and his uncle departed, he heavily considered a nap. Aphrodite beckoned Leda inside while he refilled his glass with water and slumped back against the couch cushions.

"Leda, this is Hephaestus," Aphrodite said as the woman reached her desk. "I didn't get to properly introduce him yesterday."

"Nice to meet you," he grunted before his eyes returned to Aphrodite.

"We're supposed to be figuring out a way to keep her busy."

"What do you do?" Leda asked him. "Are you her assistant?"

Hephaestus chuckled, giving her another appraising look. "Head of security."

"Oh! That's awesome. You do look the part."

"How so?"

"All the muscles."

Aphrodite cleared her throat, and Hephaestus looked up at her. "I haven't come up with anything yet, sorry, I've been really busy."

"Oh." Leda kept her eyes on Hephaestus. "Anything I can help with?"

"I don't think so. Unless Hephaestus has any ideas."

Hephaestus raised a brow at Aphrodite. "I don't really have any—"

"I'll do anything," Leda confided, her doe eyes wide. "Anything at all."

He was quiet as he contemplated the request. He wasn't in a place where he could think clearly enough to find a proper solution, but they were both staring at him, and he would do anything to be free of that pressure.

"You ever deal with spreadsheets?" he questioned now.

"A bit, in school," Leda offered. "And I can learn anything I need to."

Hephaestus addressed Aphrodite now, his gaze on hers. "She can check the security radios in and out, make supply requests for Eros down in the security office. Have Hector help her out."

Aphrodite gave him a confused look at first before she reluctantly nodded. "If you think that'll work out, then - sure. I don't have a problem with it."

Hephaestus wasn't worried at all. At this point in time, Aphrodite's security was an obsolete unit, and whatever was done within it was of no concern to him. In his mind, none of them could be trusted, and he was only agreeing to this because he knew Leda would be safe down in the security offices where his people were overseeing. He doubted it would be smart to send her anywhere else for the time being. It was already a risk letting her leave Twilight, but he could understand Aphrodite's desire to make sure the girl didn't feel locked up again.

"I can do that!" Leda assured them, grinning. "I'd be honored."

"I'll call Hector," Aphrodite said, moving to her desk.

Leda sat down beside Hephaestus, clasping her hands together. He hardly noticed. Draining his glass once more, he'd all but decided to retire upstairs for a few hours. Judging by the look on Aphrodite's face, she would probably agree to it. He hoped so. He didn't have the patience for the day, but he certainly wasn't leaving her side for anything.

Still, as Leda hummed next to him, he had a thought.

"There is one condition to your employment," he said casually.

"—What is it?" She looked excited.

"All members of security have a duty, no matter what their role may be. You report any and all suspicious activity to me. Whether it's from guests or from one of our own. You got it?"

She raised her eyebrows. "Is there something going on?"

"That's what you have to tell me."

She seemed to catch on eventually. "Okay, I - I can do that."

He stood up, setting the glass down on the table before moving to the window overlooking the club floor. It didn't take long for Hector to arrive, and Heph was caught off guard when Leda gave him a hug goodbye. He patted her back once before disengaging, biting his tongue to suppress his discomfort. Once she was gone, exhaustion really began to set in. It had never caught up with him quite like this, but the attack yesterday had truly drained him.

He should've expected it, or been more prepared. How they'd managed to get a step on him had been nagging at him since, and he still couldn't figure it out. That lot had certainly been empty when they'd entered it, and it was flat land all the way around the warehouse. How had he missed them? It was possible they had come back to the warehouse to see if it was clear again and had just caught him and Aphrodite by accident, but that seemed like a foolish move on their end. Yet how else could they have done it?

"She really seems to like you," Aphrodite hissed, coming up behind him.

He sidestepped the comment. "At least this is still a haven."

"It always will be. Even when I'm dead."

"That won't be anytime soon." He turned to face her. "Are you tired?"

She was mid-yawn, but she still managed to give him a pointed look. Sarcasm dripped from her words. "I haven't had a wink of sleep, so yeah."

"How about we go upstairs for a bit?"

She stared at him for a moment, and he almost wanted to kick himself for asking. He wouldn't have done so if it weren't absolutely necessary of course. He would much rather push through it than admit to the need, but he could hardly keep his eyes open. He would be no good to her if something did happen.

"You need a nap?" she cooed, brushing her fingers over his cheek.

He rolled his eyes and pushed her hand away. "Do you want to or not?"

"Ooh, cranky too. We definitely need to get your ass upstairs."

Her eyes gleamed with something that made the hair on the back of his neck stand up, his heart knocking against his ribcage. Despite the lack of sleep, she looked gorgeous as always. Without makeup, he caught the faintest smattering of freckles along the bridge of her nose. If he were to move any closer, he bet could count them all.

He stepped away and headed for the elevator.

Yet as they stood in the car on the slow ascent up to the penthouse, she placed herself directly in front of him, so close that the scent of her body wash wafted up to meet him. He shut his eyes, soothed by the sound of her soft inhale until his thoughts were plunged into the depths of a memory. He was back in her bed, settled between her thighs with a boundless hunger ruling his stomach. Her touch still lingered on his skin. He recalled the taste of her, the look in her eyes as she watched him devour her pussy, the lacerations left in the skin of his back as he fucked her. Even in his exhaustion, the images were as vivid as the day they were created, and now he couldn't shake them loose.

He made it as far as the couch once they reached the penthouse, unbuttoning his shirt and setting his cane against the arm. He didn't often sleep in the guest room to begin with. He would much rather be in front of the door and between it and Aphrodite in case there was ever a breach. He watched her enter the kitchen, his eyes moving down her back. In the time he'd been stationed at her side, he'd never actually worried about her. He was worried about the job, yes, each and every day, but to worry about her specifically, as a person he cared about rather than simply a charge, was an entirely new sensation.

He could still hear the dance of bullets, and each time he closed his eyes, he watched those SUVs pull up just before he'd shoved her into the car. He remembered the lack of license plates and the missing manufacturer's logo. All he'd been able to give Achilles were guesses. It sat heavy upon his chest. He was making so little progress and losing so much time, and he had no excuses. Or at least none that could vindicate him. Yet she had vouched for him anyway.

She was passing in front of him when he recovered from the thought, blinking and looking up at her.

"Good night," she sighed. "Don't wake me up unless the place is burning down."

He grabbed her hand.

It was an impulsive decision. Then again, the first time they'd fucked had been an impulsive decision as well. He was tired. He did need sleep. However, that didn't change the feelings sweeping over him, through him, and the very potent presence of another need. One that wouldn't wait.

She allowed him to guide her down to straddle his lap, her hands finding his chest. She picked up where he left off, undoing the rest of the buttons on his shirt before pushing it down his shoulders.

"I thought you came up here to sleep," she breathed as he lifted up her dress.

"I did," he replied, running his hands up her thighs. "Are you complaining?"

"Did I say I was?"

He slipped one hand between them, brushing his fingers over her center. "You usually are."

She gritted her teeth. "Fuck you."

"I dare you."

"You can't just - decide to get it in anytime you fucking please."

"You decided last time."

"I'll decide every time."

He lifted his gaze and dropped his hands without hesitation. Then it was a contest of wills, all heated stares and clenched jaws and the innate need to *win*. Her thighs trembled against his or his thighs trembled between hers or they both shook with restraint, but either way, comfort fled quickly.

Until she was tearing away at his belt.

He didn't bother with anything else once she'd freed his erection from the confines of his pants, yanking her panties to the side with expert fingers. He spit into his palm before wrapping it around his cock, stroking and squeezing until his tip glistened with arousal. He collected it as well, making sure every inch of him was slick. She watched him, her lip clutched between her teeth, her hands braced against his shoulders. In the end, it was her impatience that won out.

She pulled his hand off of his shaft before slowly lowering herself down onto his dick with a stuttered cry. He reached up, unclasping her bra and ripping down the front of her dress so that he could get his mouth on her breasts. She cursed as she dug her fingers into the hair at the back of his head, arching into him and letting her head fall back. He palmed her ass, guiding her up and down his shaft with eager haste. She cried out then, and he could sense the pain in it. Slowing his movements, he looked up at her.

"You alright?"

Her eyes fluttered open, surprise written in them. "Don't worry about me. I - just-"

"I will worry about you. Am I hurting you? Do you need me to get the—"

"It's just - let me-"

He released her hips as she set her own pace, winding them at the bottom of each descent. He licked his lips, entranced by the movements, his own hips struggling to stay pinned to the couch. He leaned forward once more, ravishing her chest while his hands crawled up along her back. He hadn't realized how much he'd been craving her until right now, and it made him dizzy. It made him insatiable.

"Fuck, Heph, I —"

She shrieked when his teeth took hold of a nipple, tugging it firmly before his tongue soothed the ache. She bounced a bit quicker, holding him close as he smacked her ass and spurred her on. She no longer appeared to be in pain, her hunger winning out and his arousal in abundance.

"You miss this?" he panted, turning his face up towards hers.

"Yes—"

"Tell Daddy you missed it."

"Yes, Daddy, I missed this. I missed - this dick. Please!"

He hoarded every sound, throwing his hips up into hers as best he could before his leg refused. He attacked her neck then, nipping at the skin of her throat and dragging his tongue over each mark. She said his name, or she tried to, but she fell short with each thrust. Her walls tightened around him until he was groaning into the hollow of her throat, the pressure bearing down on him. He couldn't get close enough, deep enough, but he kept trying if only to hear her call out for him again and again.

"Daddy... Fuck."

"Does that feel good, Princess? Huh?"

"Yes, Daddy, yes!"

"So - you're gonna be a good girl and cum for me?"

"Please! I wanna - cum for you, Daddy. I do, I do!"

He fisted her hair, yanking her head back and crashing his mouth against hers. She took his lower lip hostage between her own teeth with a guttural growl. He slapped her ass again, savoring the whimper he was gifted as he caught it on his tongue. She was close, and he knew it. Moving a hand between her thighs, the pad of his thumb found her clit with ease. He barely touched down, and her body seized and rocked before she was calling out, nails biting at his skin. She convulsed in his arms, riding out her orgasm before she collapsed against him, her breath heavy against his temple.

He didn't let her rest.

He twisted his torso with as much caution as he could spare, dropping her on the couch before he pushed himself to his feet and kicked off his pants. He then flipped her onto her stomach, getting behind her on one knee with his stronger leg planted on the floor. He was inside of her again from one breath to the next, and she moaned as he stretched out her sensitive walls. He spread her open with his thumbs, bottoming out inside of her with grunt after sharp grunt, an instrumental for her wanton song.

His exhaustion was buried by this ravenous hunger, and he did all he could to feed it. He barked his obscenities as she braced herself against the arm of the couch, clawing at the upholstery. Nothing had ever sounded more beautiful than the sounds he drew from her with each thrust. Nothing ever would. Any ounce of control he had left, any lasting need to protect his pride, it all got washed out with that song she sang for him.

"You like that, Princess?" he bit through clenched teeth. "Tell Daddy you like it."

"I like it, Daddy! I like it! I - I like it, I do! I love it so much, I—Fuck!"

She moved forward, and he moved with her, keeping his rhythm. She pressed her forearms against the couch's arm, keeping her ass elevated before him. She attempted to throw her hips back in order to meet his thrusts, but it was in vain. His grasp on her tightened, slamming her back into each punishing thrust.

"Daddy, I - I'm gonna—"

"Again, Princess?"

"Yes, Daddy, yes!"

"You're a little brat, aren't you? I'm spoiling you."

'Please...Don't stop!"

"You wanna cum for Daddy again, huh? Is that it?"

"Yes! Please! Please, I - I wanna be a good girl, Daddy. I wanna cum for you..."

His chuckle faded into a groan as she clamped down around him.

He was close. He was so fucking close. He whipped his hand across her ass, the skin blooming scarlet in its wake, and the sight of his mark on her twisted up the coil in his gut tighter.

"Heph!"

Her body fell to her pleasure, thighs shaking uncontrollably around him. His name carried throughout the space before it was severed, left to something hoarse and pitiful as she writhed and wound her body beneath his. He took hold of her shoulder, ramming his cock into her with unyielding force until he too was sailing over the edge, his movements slower but not at all softer. His leg gave out, and he was pitched forward, caging her in as he held fast to the arm of the couch, emptying his load in her spasming pussy. He was at the height of his euphoria, and he could hardly see straight. His eyes slid shut before he could fully catch his breath.

What energy he had salvaged on the way up here was gone.

Chapter Sixteen

APHRODITE

After Hephaestus finally insisted on fetching proper lubrication for rounds 2 and 3, they didn't make it off of the couch again. Yet when Aphrodite woke up from a dead sleep, they lay bare and sprawled on the floor, her head on Hephaestus's chest. It was dark out, and if she had to guess, she would say it was well after midnight. This meant they had been out for quite some time. She had to find her phone. However, as she looked up at Hephaestus, she froze.

He was most gorgeous when he slept. The hardened lines of his face were softened and sanded down by slumber although his brows knit every now and again as if even in his dreams, he was looking for something. His hand rested around her waist, his breathing level, and Aphrodite traced the marks that marred his chest and neck with gentle digits.

Where there wasn't a scar, there was a tattoo —although they did often overlap— all of them an intricately interwoven tale of his rises and falls. She marveled at the massive bird of prey that spanned across his chest, its wings outstretched and its eyes fixed with intent. It looked familiar, but she couldn't quite place where she'd seen it before apart from his skin. Either way, she liked it.

She'd come to realize that she'd never really looked at him before.

She'd seen him, yes. She'd seen how attractive he was even when others would say he was anything but. Despite — no, *because of* the scars and the mismatched eyes and the uneven smirk, he was handsome in a way no one deserved. He carried himself with an air unmatched, to the point where even though they were roughly the same height, he seemed so much larger at times. But she had never dared look beneath.

After the terror Zeus had inflicted on Persephone and Hades, on Dionysos, and on all of Khaos Falls before then, trusting one of his sons —at least one that had been raised in his home for any period of time— was difficult. It certainly played into her feelings about Ares, but he had already begun to show his father's worst traits, and more than that, he's begun to justify them, watering them down so that he could say they did not look like his father's. Aphrodite knew them far too well however. They were her father's too.

Hephaestus wasn't like his brothers though. She'd said it herself many times. She just never looked at the ways in which he differed for the better. He had much more composure than any of them. He was more intuitive than Dionysos, more cunning than Hermes, and much more practical than Ares. Aphrodite had never cared for practical, and yet that was what came to mind. What the hell was happening to her?

It was much easier to focus on the physical. It was much *safer* to focus on the physical. He fucked her good and kept the nightmares at bay. She shouldn't look any further than that. She might find something she wasn't prepared to deal with.

Shifting up his body, she kissed his neck, sliding her hand down his chest, his abdomen. He stirred beneath her touch in more ways than one, and as she draped her leg over his thighs, his hardening length pressed against her.

"Mm," she hummed, nipping at his jaw. "Wake up, Daddy."

"Hm?" It was soft, his eyes still closed.

"I need you."

She made it to his ear, teasing the shell with her teeth before his hand moved down to grip her ass, squeezing. He exhaled heavily, his other hand hooking around her thigh as she kissed back down his neck.

"Needy girl," he grunted, snatching her hand up before she could slide it over his cock. "You want more, Princess?"

She did. She very much did, and in the haze of recent sleep and current arousal, she could not find the strength to tell him just how much she fucking hated him for it right now. She simply kept hoarding the friction he offered her. And he offered it all.

Once he released her hand, she sought out the bottle on the coffee table nearby, squeezing a generous amount of lube into her palm. The scent of green apple filled the air between them as she reached down and began to stroke his length, thoroughly slicking him up. He hissed, sinking his nails into her ass before pressing a finger between her cheeks. He had her so weak that it was almost pathetic, a string of pleas manifesting upon her tongue.

Before they could crawl out of her mouth however, he was rolling over on top of her, sliding into her with the ease of familiarity. The moment he was buried inside of her, she felt whole. A gasp left her lips as her nails claimed his back, her hips shifting upward into his. He didn't tease her even when she knew that *he* knew she would beg for it if she had to. She would do anything he asked just for another hit. If she weren't so eager for him to fuck her senseless, she'd be ashamed right now.

"I thought you were a good girl," he taunted, laying more of his weight over her.

"I am," she whispered, eyelids fluttering. "But - you make it hard - *Daddy*."

"How hard, huh?"

"—Impossible."

"What do you need then? To be a good girl."

She whimpered. "I need you - to fuck me. Please, Daddy. I promise I'll go back to sleep. Just - fuck me. Fuck me, and I'll be a good girl for you."

His eyes were open now, flashing with formidable need. The increase in his speed was instantaneous, and she was eager to match every thrust. They moved like that until he was once again expanding inside of her, stretching her out in the most delicious way. She was still sensitive and sore from earlier, but it only added to the sensation. With each stroke, he managed to hit every spot worth hitting, and she was powerless to hold out very long. He was ruining her, piece by fucking piece.

She was already so close when he reared up, sitting back on his haunches and taking hold of her hips. There was no further warning for the pace he established within seconds, more ruthless and rampant than ever before. She gripped his bulging forearms, searching frantically for an anchor. There was nothing, not a single thing that could keep her from losing herself in ecstasy. Breasts bouncing, pussy clenching, cries of pleasure filling the air. It took her a decent amount of time to realize her vision had begun to blur. He'd fucked her straight to tears.

"Heph - Hephaestus!"

"Tell Daddy you need this dick."

"I need it, Daddy! I fucking need it! Please!"

She crept up the floor, all while keeping her legs spread wide. He fucked her with a fervor, a passion, a rage. He fucked her in a way she'd never been fucked before. He fucked her like he hated her. And she loved every damn second of it. She was addicted. So fucking addicted. Their hips clapped together like thunder, his cock striking her walls like lightning. He had a bruising grip on her thighs, and he used it to his every advantage, leaving her immobile and at his mercy. He knew it too. He knew it, and he exploited it.

Her orgasm hit her like a speeding train. The whole room was spinning. The floor was unsteady. She arched off of the carpet, nearly sitting up at the height of it, trying to climb him even as he continued drilling her. She was sobbing now, a mess of sweat and tears and arousal, all for him. He pushed her back down, his hand closing around her throat. She clamped her own hands down on his forearm but did not try to remove it. She wouldn't dare.

How the fuck is he about to make her come again so quickly? Her thighs were still quivering. Her cunt was still spasming, warm and wet and waiting for more, more, *more*. He seemed to sense it too because next thing she knew, his thumb was thoroughly going to work on her clit, and she was helpless. With everything he was doing to her, every instance of stimulation at its peak, she was absolutely and pitifully helpless.

"Heph—"

It was hoarse, and it was faint, and it was the only word that she knew. Her eyes rolled back as did her head, back bowing yet again. A second orgasm ripped through her, a tidal wave of overwhelming pleasure that took her breath away and left her drowning in it. He bottomed out, letting her squeeze and constrict around him until he was coming too, relinquishing his hold on her neck in favor of holding her waist. They were a mess of moving parts, ruled by their pleasure and engulfed in one another. He toppled, and she caught him, holding him to her as they soaked up every drop of nirvana.

When it all fell quiet, she shut her eyes, pressing her lips to the side of his head. It was soft. It was intimate. It was an unruly mistake.

She did it again and closed her eyes. If she stayed really still, maybe they could live in this moment forever, pretending they were the kind of people that belonged in it.

THE SUN WAS ONLY JUST RISING WHEN APHRODITE WOKE UP AGAIN although she didn't come to on her own. The elevator alarm was ringing through the apartment, and Hephaestus jumped up, sweeping up his cane in the process. Aphrodite climbed to her feet, rubbing at her eyes as she went for her purse on the counter.

"It's probably—" she began, but she halted.

She had dozens of missed calls. From Psyche, Eros, Hector, and even Persephone. They'd been unreachable for nearly 24 hours, and she couldn't even imagine what was going through everyone's mind. She looked up at Heph, who was struggling to pull on his pants.

"Heph, go—"

She was cut off by the elevator bell ringing. The doors opened behind her. Hephaestus raised his cane, aiming it at the elevator as Persephone rushed in. She stopped cold in her tracks with a loud gasp. Hades stepped out behind her, but he too came to a halt as he took in the scene before them. Aphrodite faced the couple, not at all inclined to cover herself up. Hades' gaze was fleeting, and it didn't move past her eyes.

"Oh," Persephone managed, the color draining from her face.

Aphrodite could admit she was relatively embarrassed, uncommon as it was, although she didn't show it. This was not how she wanted Persephone to find out she had been sleeping with Hephaestus, who she'd all but hated just weeks ago. She also imagined this wasn't how Hephaestus wanted his uncle to find out.

If she was being honest, she wasn't sure either of them wanted anyone to find out.

Hephaestus lowered his cane, and Aphrodite calmly walked past him into her bedroom to fetch her robe. She heard him greet his uncle and Persephone in that gruff voice but nothing further. What could he say? What could any of them say? It was quite obvious what had happened, and even if it wasn't, Persephone was going to grill her later anyway.

Hephaestus was sitting on the couch when she came back, and she sat on the arm beside him. She decided a united front was best.

"Sorry, uncle," Hephaestus muttered, looking down at his hands. "For not answering, I mean. I assume you called."

"Everyone in the city called," Hades said at last, and Aphrodite could tell he was holding back his own frustrations. "It's no secret that Aphrodite has been targeted twice now. Everyone knows."

Persephone did not hold back. "I had Mama calling me, 'Dite! She knows everything that happens in her district, and Auntie does too. Then we get a call from Eros that you guys disappeared, and you didn't say anything? No one could get a hold of either of you? I thought I was gonna come up here and find bodies! And - well, I guess this is better than that, but what the fuck, y'all?"

"We're sorry," Aphrodite offered once more, breathing out. "We lost track of time, and - honestly, we caught up on a lot of sleep. It was just a lot. I wanted some time away. I didn't intend for it to be this long, but— well, we're sorry."

The two women locked eyes, and an entire conversation played out between them. Aphrodite could read the lecture all over Persephone's face. As reckless as Aphrodite could be, it was rarely so blatant, but she seemed to be on quite the streak at the moment. Persephone would not let it go on much longer.

Aphrodite wasn't lying however. She'd yearned for the escape, the one she found in him, and she wasn't apologizing for that. She couldn't. She could only apologize for not warning everyone they would be off the radar for an entire day.

Hades exhaled. "Persephone is right. This is better than finding bodies, and - you two are grown. We were just worried."

"And would appreciate a warning the next time you wanna disappear for a day," Persephone added, her tone biting. "At the very least, let Eros and Psyche know. They were both on the verge of a heart attack. Eros still feels bad about not seeing the signs last time."

"I'll talk to them," Aphrodite assured her. "But - can we keep this between us?"

"Of course," Hades nodded.

"Thank you."

Hades and Persephone stared at them a bit longer, and Aphrodite could tell her best friend was torn between leaving now and screaming some more. If it didn't occur today, it would eventually, but Aphrodite would definitely prefer the rain check. Persephone seemed to sense that, and she simply stepped forward and hugged her for a long moment.

When they parted, Seph and Hades returned to the elevator, her steps slow and reluctant. Aphrodite watched the doors close, attempting to gauge just how bad this outcome was. She weighed the pros and cons —or she tried to, but the thing was, there were no pros. There weren't even that many cons, but the few that existed were rooted in pride. She decided she wasn't interested in possessing them.

Turning around, she opened her mouth to speak to Hephaestus, but he was gone. She heard the door to the guest room shut, a resounding slam that nailed her to the floor in shock. Was he that embarrassed? That ashamed? And was it because it was his uncle or was it because it was her? Aphrodite stared at the entrance of the hall, wrapping her robe tighter around her. For the first time in a very long time, she began to doubt herself.

Chapter Seventeen

HEPHAESTUS

Hephaestus made his way down to the security office via the service hallway, unwilling to encounter anyone on the main floor. After yesterday, he'd been intent on avoiding anyone and everyone that he could. It was one thing to be caught with Aphrodite. It was another thing entirely to be caught by his uncle, one of the two men he respected the most.

And it wasn't that he was ashamed, at least not of Aphrodite. That was far from the truth. However, Persephone had already been weary of allowing him to continue this job on his own, and he would hate for anyone to think ill of him for falling prey to his own desires. He prided himself on being stronger, tougher, wiser than those around him. More than anything, he prided himself on being an immovable object, a title long tried and tested, a title he still held onto. Yet he'd merged personal and professional with eyes wide open, and he hadn't thought twice about it. *That* was something to be ashamed of.

And it was Aphrodite. She was the apple of the city's eye, the fantasy of all. Most would be proud to be in his place, but instead, he was only aggrieved by the fact that he'd stooped to the level of the average and mundane. If anything, he felt as though he'd done

Aphrodite a severe disservice. Differences aside, he'd always respected her. He respected who she was and how she conducted her business. Now it felt like he'd taken advantage of all of it, and while she may not see it the same way, he knew her well enough. She wanted a fairy tale. He could never give her that.

"Hephaestus!" the girl at the front, Leda, gasped as he entered the office.

He had almost forgotten that she was working down here now, and it took him a moment to recognize her. She looked different from the day she'd arrived, cleaned up and dressed in a simple blue dress. Gathering his bearings, he greeted her with a polite smile although it felt more like a grimace.

"Leda, how are you?" he asked, leaning over her desk.

"I'm alright," she responded, her smile bright and glittering.

"How do you like it down here?"

"I like it a lot. Everyone down here is really nice, and the job is easy enough. I really appreciate you recommending it, Hephaestus. I know you didn't have to do that."

"It was nothing really. You should be thanking Aphrodite. If it weren't for her, I wouldn't have had a place to recommend."

"Well, Psyche says you're in charge of security for the whole city. That's really neat. You're like - a hero or something." She giggled lightly. "It's very impressive."

"I'm more strategy than I am combat."

"You're just being modest."

She batted her lashes, and he traced the movement. He wasn't sure, but there was something about her that struck him, making him wary. She seemed to be trying pretty hard, and while it was most likely due to her desire to succeed in this position, there was something else too. He'd sensed it when she first came into Aphrodite's office. He wondered what kind of past preceded her ending up here, what kind of damage it had done, what may still be giving chase. She couldn't be much younger than him, but that hardly registered. Some people were born under burden, and he wouldn't discount that. Still, he was curious.

Pulling up one of the chairs stationed against the adjacent wall, he sat beside the desk backward in the seat. Crossing his arms over the back of the chair, he rested his chin upon it. She seemed delighted.

"Aphrodite said you're from Spartan Hills," he went on, his tone friendly. Or as friendly as it could be. "How was it there?"

"It was alright. Very pretty scenery and a lot of things to do, but after living there all your life, it gets a little boring, you know? I do miss it, but - it's kind of exciting to be in a new city even under the - circumstances."

"That's understandable. What about your family?"

She seemed to contemplate the question for a moment. Then her face fell, piece by piece. It was almost as though she had to manually change each facet of her expression. Hephaestus took note of every individual aspect. He'd seen it in plenty of people who had been forced to control their emotions to survive. At some point amidst the silence, she glanced up as if to see if he was watching her. He didn't push. He waited.

"Well," she sighed. "It was only my dad and I left before I... He wasn't a good man."

"Who was he?"

She looked surprised. "Oh, I - I would rather not. I'm sorry, Hephaestus, I just - I don't... I want to start over. I just - I want to start over."

He could understand that. More importantly, he let himself believe her.

He supposed his paranoia had begun to spill over into every aspect that didn't involve Aphrodite's naked form —although it was not at all immune at this rate— and he knew himself better than anyone. If he went looking for something, he would find it, even in places it had never existed before. He wouldn't apologize for the fact of the matter however. He would vet everyone who set foot inside this club, inside this district, if it meant keeping Aphrodite safe.

He tried to channel her now, that brave and compassionate woman, and reached for Leda's hand but stopped short, unsure if she would want him to touch her. He didn't know what she'd been through nor did he want to add to it anymore than he had by asking the question. She took his hand in hers on her own however, smiling softly as she squeezed his fingers.

"Thank you," she whispered, her eyes welling with tears. "I mean it. This really does mean a whole lot to me. You have no idea how much you've helped me."

"Again, it's because of Aphrodite. It's what she does. It—"

"Heph."

The voice of the woman herself cut through their quiet words from behind him. Turning around, he swiftly retracted his hand and stood up.

"Aphrodite," he managed, his voice sullen.

They hadn't talked much since Persephone and Hades had left the penthouse. He'd come up late last night, long after she'd retired to bed, and even when he'd swept her room, she'd either been asleep or faking it. Either way, he wasn't sure where they stood at the moment, but he didn't wish to discuss it either. He just wanted to do his job.

Her glare moved between him and Leda then back again before she raised her chin and focused on his face. He straightened up a little further, suddenly nervous and altogether confused. He'd been under her scrutiny plenty of times, sure, but not since they first fooled around. Not since he started caring about her opinion of him. It was an odd feeling, and he didn't like the look on her face right now.

"I have to go to Twilight House," she said coolly. "I assume as my guard, you'll want to accompany me."

"Oh, uh, yeah, of course."

Leda's hand landed on his bicep, and he looked back at her as she gave it a squeeze. She was smiling.

"Thank you again," she offered, her cheeks red as she leaned up and pecked one of his. "I'll see you later?"

He didn't know what to say to that, so he simply nodded. She then released him and waved at Aphrodite, who waved back albeit not nearly as enthusiastic about it.

"Bye, Aphrodite!"

Hephaestus followed Aphrodite out and back down the service

hallway, the tension thick between them. The only sound was the clack of her heels and the tap of his cane, the music fading away behind them. A chill winter wind swept through the parking garage as they exited Lush, the clouds overhead blanketing the sun and threatening a downpour. She slowed her steps then, allowing him to lead her to where his car was parked. He couldn't determine what it was she was angry about or how long she had been angry, but both questions plagued him as he opened her door. She didn't even look at him now, her face set with the slightest annoyance sitting on the otherwise calm surface.

The drive to Twilight House was much of the same silence, but she seemed to perk up when they reached the wrought iron gates that protected the place. While it was called Twilight House, it was actually a collection of two large buildings surrounded by several smaller ones. Hephaestus had never been inside, but he knew it was much like a safehouse for the girls and boys Aphrodite brought in. One of the larger buildings acted as a halfway house for survivors before they were given a job or permanent housing while the other building was for those who needed more dedicated help mentally, emotionally, or physically. She had nurses and counselors who helped with addiction issues and that of the like, and Hippokrates made weekly visits to check in on them.

It was very much a house though, a comfortable place nearly as vast as Zeus's estate with more than enough room to accommodate everyone and anyone who needed it without piling them on top of each other. Artemis had put together the long-term guard for the site, meaning many of those who watched over the place were women. Atalanta, who had worked for Hades for a long time, had recently come over to take charge of the guard. She was highly skilled and deeply trustworthy, and Hephaestus had learned a lot from her when he'd first started out.

It was Atalanta who met them at the front of the house when they arrived, greeting them with a hand extended and a curt smile. She opened the door for them, and they stepped inside the entrance hall of the main building where the newest rescues were currently housed.

Hephaestus looked around, making note of the layout, a habit he had when entering unfamiliar places. It was elegant and clean and every bit like Aphrodite's other establishments despite the obvious lack of club music and neon. Still, there was no doubt about who ran it. Her mark was everywhere from the fluffy furniture to the deep red carpets.

A nurse came up to them as they reached the first hallway, and she offered them a big smile.

"Aphrodite," she said, shaking the woman's hand. "It's good to see you."

"You too, Iris," Aphrodite replied. "How are they?"

"They're doing very well. All of them. Some of the younger girls still struggle to sleep, but we're making progress. They're about to break from group sessions right now for lunch. Would you like to see them? We can bring them into the day room."

"That would be great, yes."

"Good, I'll be back."

The nurse headed off, and Aphrodite moved towards a large archway opposite the main doors. They stepped through it, and Hephaestus found himself in what he assumed was the day room the nurse spoke of. The large bay windows looked out into a well groomed garden of flowers and hedges that stood between the two large buildings. Where there might usually be warm, natural light flooding the room, there was only the dull grey of a winter day. It washed over the white leather furniture, making the couches and chairs look darker than they were.

The walls were covered in paintings and pictures, and the fireplace sat decorated with banners sporting Aphrodite's insignia, the outline of a heart with a dove inside it, a rose in its mouth. He tilted his head to look up at the high ceiling, impressed with the architecture. Of course, it was not at all surprising. All of Apollo's work was impressive. Hephaestus had no clue how the man kept up with the demands of the city, but he did it well.

Not at all up for socializing and eager to avoid making any of the survivors uncomfortable, he found a vantage point at the top of the stairs on the second-floor balcony. Over the low wall, he could still see the entire dayroom. And Aphrodite of course. She stood at the center of the room, and as people began to enter, they all had much of the same reaction. A surprised gasp or sharp shriek, the call of her name like a prayer, and then they were rushing over to hug her or hold her hand or lay out their gratitude at her feet. Or all of the above. Hephaestus found himself mesmerized. The chill that had burdened her on the way here seemed to have subsided as she looked each of them over and conversed with them. They looked up at her in awe, and yet she treated them like family she hadn't seen in awhile. It was obvious to Hephaestus that she enjoyed this and not in the way people who liked playing the hero would enjoy it. She didn't simply enjoy receiving love. She enjoyed giving it. He never thought that was possible. There, right before his eyes, she came to life.

Something deep inside of him ached.

"Just so you're all aware," she called out before gesturing up to him. He fought the urge to hide. "That's Hephaestus, my bodyguard, so don't be afraid if you see him up there. He's a very old friend, and he's here to protect me."

He almost scoffed at that, mainly because he would have never called them friends before this. Even now, it seemed off. He didn't know what they were, but he doubted there was a word for it, much less one that would make sense to anyone else.

Luckily, the eyes on him didn't dwell long, all of them eager to move back to Aphrodite as she checked in with them. Yet Hephaestus still felt like he was being watched. Glancing over his shoulder, he scoped out the hall at his back, lined with doors that were closed. Except one. It was cracked just slightly, but when his gaze fell upon it, there was movement then the door quickly closed. Raising a brow, Hephaestus moved quietly towards it, listening for any sign of disturbance as Aphrodite's voice faded behind him. When he reached the door in question, he placed his ear against it. He was met with a staunch silence. Trying the doorknob, he found that it remained unlocked, and he carefully turned it, pushing the door open.

At first, he saw no one. It was a standard bedroom with a closet on the opposite wall flanked by a desk on one side and a dresser on the other. A bed sat in the center, and a TV was mounted on the wall across from it. He stepped inside, straightening his leg as best he could in case he needed to raise his cane, but he stopped short when he noticed the small figure sitting in the chair in the corner that the door had been blocking when he first opened it.

They shivered as he approached, and he noticed that it was a young boy, no older than his early teens with a cast around one arm as well as one on his leg surrounded by a metal cage of screws and rods. His head had been shaved recently, no doubt by the people here to protect against any diseases, and he was scrawny and small. He reminded Hephaestus of Hermes when he'd first shown up in Khaos Falls years ago, covered in bruises and wounds from literally fighting for his life in Heraklion before he managed to hide away on a ship.

Hephaestus didn't get too close to the boy, instead taking a seat at the edge of the bed. The boy shuddered again, and Heph could see how hard his jaw was clenched.

"I'm Hephaestus," he said slowly. "I'm a friend of Aphrodite. I protect her."

The boy seemed to consider it for a moment before he turned slowly in his seat to look Hephaestus over, his eyes narrowed and his lower lip jutting out. His cheeks were hollow, brown skin stretched thin over the bones, but there was still life in his dark eyes that Hephaestus was insistent on drawing on and drawing out. There was also a suspicion to them, which he could relate to.

"What's your name?" Heph asked now.

The boy stared at him for a bit longer, eyes darting between his face and the cane at his side, and when he spoke, his voice was hoarse and raspy as if it had been out of use for a long time.

"Phobos."

"Why didn't you go down to meet Aphrodite?"

He shook his head. "They don't like men here. Well, they're afraid of them, and - I don't blame them. Men did this to us. They make them fear me and my brother."

"Your brother? He's here too?"

He nodded, his face falling. "Deimos. He's - in the other house back there. He has nightmares, so they have to separate him from everyone else."

Hephaestus nodded his understanding. "What happened to your arm?"

He dropped his eyes. "They - one of the men broke it when I wouldn't help beat one of the girls."

"And your leg?"

The hint of a proud smile peaked over his lips. "He stomped on it when breaking my arm didn't work."

Heph smiled too. "So you're a protector. That's good. Did you ever see the man's face?"

"No. They always wore masks."

"How old are you, Phobos?"

"I'm - fourteen. I think. I stopped counting the summers. My brother and I both. We're twins."

"You have any family?"

He shook his head again. "We never knew our parents. The men who took us, they found us at the port in Thassos a few years ago, said they had a job for us that could set us up for life. We didn't know."

"That's how they work. They prey on those who are in vulnerable situations. You did nothing wrong, Phobos."

Phobos looked at him again before once more looking at his cane. "Are you hurt too?"

"No, I was born like this. I have trouble with my muscles sometimes. They're weaker than they should be, but I still do my job."

"How?"

"I never let weak muscles be a weakness." He smiled again softly. "Don't ever let anyone label your weaknesses for you, Phobos. When people find out what happened to you, they might try to do that, to tell you you're weak or whatever, but don't listen to them. You and your brother survived, and you didn't stoop to the level of the people who did this to you."

"I tried to protect them. I tried, and - they're still scared of me."

"They're not scared of you. They're scared of what you remind them of, and that's not your fault or theirs. They will heal in time, just like you."

"Do you - do you think I could do what you do when I'm better? Me and my brother, we guarded storage containers at the port. It's not as hard as guarding people, I know, but..."

"You can do whatever you want once you're healed. I'll tell you what though. You work on getting better, and once you're up and running again, you come see me. You and Deimos. I'll find work for you, even if it's just guarding storage containers until you're ready to guard people."

He lit up at that, grinning so hard that Hephaestus feared his cheeks would tear. "Really?"

"Yes, really. I have a lot of people working for me that came from rough places just like you, and they are some of the strongest people I have ever met. You'll fit in just fine. But know this: you can still be a kid first. You and your brother. Aphrodite and I, we'll make sure you have food and clothes and a place to stay as long as you need even if you don't work until you're a little older."

"Really?" His eyes were wide as saucers.

"Absolutely. You don't have to grow up so fast anymore, I promise you."

"I - I think we would like that. We just want to help."

"And you will, but first, you have to help yourself. And those women, they'll see that you're giving them space to heal, and maybe they'll come around to trusting you, but if they don't, just know it's nothing personal. Healing takes a long time."

Hephaestus reached into his pocket, pulling a card with his phone number out and handing it to him. Phobos immediately tucked it in his own pocket and stood up.

"You call me if you need anything, even if it's just to talk or - if you need to get out of this house once we've caught the men who did this to you, alright?"

"Can I - can I go tell my brother?" he asked, his voice cautious.

Hephaestus nodded. "Go on, and tell him I said to hang in there."

Phobos picked up his crutches, tucking one gingerly under his hurt arm before moving to leave the room. Hephaestus waited a moment, staring blankly at the floor before him. It was humbling to look into the eyes of the people he was sent to save and protect, and while he did that with Aphrodite each day, this was different. Aphrodite had held her own for as long as he could remember, but these kids never had a chance. Now, they could give them one, and Hephaestus wanted nothing more. He didn't want to be a shield and only a shield. He wanted to help them the way Aphrodite helped them, in any way he could. It could have been him or his brothers in their place instead if it weren't for Hades. Hephaestus wouldn't overlook that reality again.

Chapter Eighteen

APHRODITE

Aphrodite quickly moved away from the door as the boy, Phobos, headed for it, hurrying back down the stairs and into the day room. It was difficult to keep up her anger with Hephaestus when he was going around doing decent shit like this, but she clung to that anger nonetheless. She had more important things to worry about beyond a foolish crush stemming from incredible sex, and she refused to lose sight of that. Certainly not for Hephaestus.

The girls were still in the day room where they were brought lunch, many of them no older than their early 20's according to Psyche. Yet there were some that had been held captive much longer than the others, their entire lives passed in a cage. She sat by one of these women now. Her name was Alcmene, and her dark hair had begun to grey, her olive skin sullen and marked with years of abuse. Aphrodite took her hand in hers and squeezed it.

"I never thought I'd see freedom again in this lifetime," Alcmene sighed. "They took me when I was just seventeen. I had-" She paused a moment, squeezing Aphrodite's hand tighter. "I'd just had a son. His father had run off, and - I just pray to the Fates that he got to grow up."

Aphrodite had no idea what to say to that. What could she possibly say that would ease that ache? All she could do was tighten her grip on Alcmene's hand, and the older woman seemed grateful all the same.

"The younger girls, they looked up to me," Alcmene went on. "I think that's why they kept me around so long. I kept the girls calm. I always asked myself how they could possibly look up to me when I was still a child myself." A hoarse laugh escaped her. "You don't grow up in places like that. Even when they rob you of your innocence, they keep you young. Or at least, they keep you helpless."

"You kept these girls strong though," Aphrodite assured her. "You didn't let them break you."

"Oh, they broke me. Many times."

"Well then you showed the others that you, and they, could be mended."

Alcmene smiled at her. "You're a good person, Aphrodite. There aren't many good people left, but you are certainly one of them. We'll all be grateful for you until the day we leave this world."

Aphrodite shook her head. "My entire district was built by the hands of sex workers, people who love our work and respect it. I couldn't possibly live with myself if I pretended the dark side of it didn't exist. I just want to help those who weren't given a choice."

"You've definitely done that. I know there are - others out there. I've certainly seen many people come and go out of these places, but your work is gonna save a lot of lives. A whole lot of lives."

It clicked then, everything Hephaestus had said to her the night of the attack, his countless lectures about doing things right and not rushing their moves. *Eventually, those we lose will outnumber those we save*. She didn't want that blood on her hands. She didn't want to fail anymore people.

"I hope so."

Psyche appeared then at the doorway, beckoning Aphrodite, who patted Alcmene's hand once more before standing. She followed Psyche out of the day room and into a hallway off of one of the kitchens, exhaling heavily as she leaned against the wall.

"How's Leda doing?" Psyche questioned, leaning against the opposite wall.

"Oh, very good."

Aphrodite hated how bitter she sounded. How could she be jealous of a girl, and one she had saved at that, just because she seemed to take a liking to Hephaestus, who definitely did not belong to Aphrodite. It was pathetic.

And yet. "She seems to be taking really well to Hephaestus."

Psyche snorted. "For real? That's not what I was expecting to hear."

"Yeah, he put her down in the security office checking in radios. She's fine."

"And she caught a little crush on the head man, huh?" Psyche raised a brow. "Why do you sound so upset about that?"

Aphrodite scoffed, perhaps too harshly. "Girl, I am not upset."

"Hey, maybe you just don't like sharing your bodyguard. That's okay."

"Please."

They both chuckled, but once the laughter died down, the air around them grew dense. Psyche had questions she wanted to ask, questions Aphrodite wasn't sure she knew how to answer, but Psyche was on the frontlines too. She put her safety on the line every day to protect these girls. She deserved something.

"Just answer me this," she started. "Are they safe here?"

"I'd like to think so," Aphrodite sighed. "I'd like to believe this is the safest place in the district with all Artemis's forces here, but honestly, Psyche? This whole thing is so much bigger than me. I can't imagine where we would be right now if Hades hadn't given the city its own security. They might've got me that night to be honest."

"Look, I trust you, alright? I always have, and I always will. I'll do what I have to in order to help you every single time, but I need to know the deal."

"Our security was compromised down to the root, Psyche." Aphrodite straightened, meeting her eyes. "From top to bottom, I got stabbed in the fucking back, and - how was I supposed to explain that to you, to Eros? That somehow, I missed the signs? That I put all of us in danger? And with the same kind of people I saved him from to begin with?"

Psyche stepped forward, folding Aphrodite into her arms. "You know we've got your back, 'Dite. Eros loves you more than anything to start, and so do I. We wouldn't have blamed you. I mean, Eros figured that someone was compromised with the way everything was at the club now, but we just didn't know how bad it was."

"Kleon. That's how bad it is."

"Kleon?" She pulled back enough to look her in the eyes. "Are you serious? But - he was here that night. The night they brought in the rescues."

"Yeah, dead serious. And we know. Artemis said as much, but now we're thinking he set up the whole raid so he could swap out my security and set up the attack. I think he's running this entire thing, so when I tell you not to let anyone in here, I'm not exaggerating. We can't trust any of them."

"Then we won't. If we are all we got, so be it, but they won't win."

"I don't know what I'd do without y'all."

"Luckily, you don't gotta find out." Psyche smiled, but it quickly fell. "But you should talk to your boy sometime soon."

"Eros?"

"Yeah, he's worried for you, and after whatever scare you gave him yesterday, he's worried you might not trust him or something."

"He's-"

But what could she say? She would think the same thing if she were being iced out the way she was icing him out, whether on purpose or not. It wasn't that she didn't trust him though. He was one of the few people she did trust and one of the people she loved most. She just didn't want to look like a failure in his eyes nor did she want to put him in any more danger than she already had. She wouldn't lose him to the cycle she'd pulled him from nor did she want him to have to revisit memories long buried.

"I'll talk to him," she vowed.

"You better."

"I'll call you though, okay? And take breaks. Don't spend all your time worrying about everybody else, Psyche. I told you about that."

"Alright, alright, I'll take my breaks. I promise."

Aphrodite moved to head back towards the main doors when she halted. "Wait. There was a boy Hephaestus was talking to upstairs. Phobos?"

"Oh, yeah. He's - quiet, doesn't talk much, keeps out of the way. He has a twin brother though who seemed to step in and take a lot of hits. We have him over in the 24-hour care ward. He has really bad nightmares, and they can manage his sleep a bit better there. Plus, the girls are still jumpy around the more masculine figures."

"And they're the only males?"

"Uh, we have two others, one of them trans, but they're also in the care unit. They had some more long-term injuries that required full-time nurses."

Aphrodite nodded. "And the twins, they have to be separated?"

Psyche looked apologetic. "Phobos goes to see Deimos when he can, but when they're together, Deimos refuses to sleep or they end up sharing the nightmares."

"Well, once they're doing better, send them over to Lush. We can get them a room there so they don't have to worry about making the girls uncomfortable, and Phobos seemed to bond with Heph."

"So you wanna share him even more then?"

Aphrodite rolled her eyes. "Hush your mouth. Just send them over, okay?"

"Okay, okay."

While Psyche headed back into the day room to check on the girls, Aphrodite searched for Hephaestus. She found him near the main doors, peering out the windows. He straightened as she approached, turning to face her. Her heart jumped up into her throat, but she couldn't find the energy to berate herself. She also couldn't find the will to let her guard down again.

"You ready?" he asked.

She simply nodded and pushed open the doors, leading him back out to the car. By now, the wind had picked up, and the smell of rain hung in the air. The sun was all but lost to the horizon, the hills that ran between the Lush District and Poseidon's Atlantis District rising up before them.

She opened her own door before Hephaestus could make it around the car, and she watched him change directions abruptly before he slid behind the wheel beside her. She almost felt bad about it. *Almost.* However, her emotions were so knotted up, constricting her heart to painful degrees, that she couldn't even begin to showcase that guilt. There were so many other sensations she would have to sort through first.

"You hungry?" he inquired as he pulled out of the long driveway leading from Twilight.

"I'll get something back at the club," she returned, her tone clipped.

"Okay. Do you need to go anywhere else?"

"No, let's just-" She paused, checking her phone for the time. "Actually, stop over at Emerald. I have to talk to Eros."

She settled back in her seat, staring out the window as they headed for Eros' main club. Neon lights blurred together before her, the district alight and alive as though it had no idea what was happening within it, what its leader was up against. That was good. It meant no one would see the cracks in her facade, the weaknesses in her armor. No one would question her.

Emerald could be seen from a block away, what with the vast neon green sign that unfurled across the sky, beckoning everyone and anyone to its door. It differed from other establishments in the district in that it was strictly a queer club. It was the kind of place Aphrodite would have given anything to have when she was younger, and Eros had put his heart and soul into it these past few years. Hephaestus pulled up to the front of the building, putting the car in park.

"Go ahead and go in," he instructed. "I'll park and meet you inside."

She didn't bother arguing, climbing out of the vehicle and making her way in. The place was already packed damn near from wall to wall with bodies, dance music blaring through the speakers so that the ground buzzed beneath their feet. The bouncer at the front greeted her with a shallow bow before letting her in, and she immediately sought out Eros.

He was usually out on the floor on the nights he dedicated to Emerald, threading his attention through the crowd and ensuring everyone was having fun. She didn't see him out there tonight though, and when she flagged down one of the servers, they gestured towards the second floor balconies. That made Aphrodite uneasy, but she ascended the stairs regardless.

She found him on the exterior balcony outside of his private box, which overlooked the pool out back. His hair was a faded blue color, so she could tell he hadn't touched up the dye in awhile. His shoulders sagged beneath an ill-fitting suit jacket, and he looked like he'd aged a decade since she'd seen him last. Guilt flooded her instantly.

"Eros," she called.

She watched as his shoulders rose, the sound of a deep exhale reaching her ears. He turned around, plastering a smile on his face although it didn't quite reach his eyes.

"Hey, Mama," he greeted. "I wasn't expecting you. What's up?"

She shook her head, a slight smile on her face. He was a good boy, always looking out for her and always putting her feelings before his. She reached out for him, cupping his cheek and immediately watching him melt into his true form. He frowned, tilting his head to look at her with questioning eyes.

"We need to talk," she declared.

He nodded, moving to go back into the box, but she stopped him, grabbing his hand and guiding him back to the wall that enclosed the balcony. She carefully sat down against it, and Eros chuckled but eventually sat down beside her.

"I'm sorry for how I've been acting," she began, taking her hand in his. "I didn't want you to know how bad things were because I didn't want you to worry."

"I was already worried to be fair," he pointed out. "You almost got killed, Ma, and I was, what, down the stairs? That's it. Just down the stairs, and I couldn't help."

"I didn't need help, Eros, and I never would've let you put yourself in danger anyway."

"You're my family. I'd do anything to protect you."

She reached up and ruffled his hair. "Which is why I tried to shield you from all this. When I pulled you off that ship, what did I tell you?"

He rolled his eyes. "That you would always protect me."

"Exactly, and nothing has changed. I don't care how grown you think you are, boy, I keep my promises."

"Alright, fine, but you can't protect me when I don't know the whole truth. I know for a fact things are not all good. Our entire security team practically disappeared overnight, so..."

She contemplated it for a moment, resting her head back against the stone. She knew he was right, but it still wasn't easy to talk about. She couldn't bear it if Eros ever stopped looking at her as if she could do no wrong, and while she knew it was irrational, that fear remained palpable. Of all the love she'd experienced in her life, nothing compared to the love between her and this sweet, thoughtful boy she'd more or less raised. And his trust meant just as much as his love, so with a sigh, she began to explain the entirety of their situation to him, sparing him very little details.

He listened quietly, resting his head against hers and squeezing her hand, something he'd done since he was young when they had to have hard conversations. It reminded her that he would never change on her. At least not much.

"We gotta be honest with each other, you know," he said softly once she'd wrapped up, "because we had another vow too. We said we would take care of each other."

"I guess you're right."

"Of course I am." She playfully smacked his chest as he laughed. "And hey, I could be very useful around the club. I could listen into conversations and keep tabs on folks."

"Yeah, don't do any of that."

"What, why?"

"Because I said so, boy, who do you think you are, questioning me?"

He put his arm around her shoulders with a grin. "Listen, it doesn't have to be me, but - take all the help you can get, alright? And before you ask what I mean, I'm sayin' let Hephaestus help you."

"Oh, Eros—"

"No, listen to me, Mama." She looked up at him. "I know you don't like him much, but he's really smart."

"You sayin' I'm not smart?"

"Yes, but your means of utilizing it are flawed to say the least, and I say that outta love. Point is, he can help. He can help everybody if we let him because y'all would make a good team. You don't always gotta do it all yourself."

"What is it with you? You crushin' on him or somethin'?"

He rolled his eyes now. "Don't get me wrong. He is very handsome in that bad-boy, pit-fighter kind of way, but no. I do like him though. I think that he, just like you, has his heart in the right place. He just isn't always good about going about it when it involves other people. You two are some kinda opposite, but - I think you work."

"We are talking about actual work, right?"

Eros smirked. "Yeah, Mama, actual work. Like you don't think he's cute too."

"That's beside the point."

"You think I'm a fool, and that's fine, but-"

"Hey, I do not! Why would you say that, Eros?"

"Because you don't think I know what y'all were getting up to when you disappeared on me? Now that I know y'all were just upstairs together? Please."

She wasn't even sure what to say to that. All she could offer was an appalled scoff, but he merely tapped a finger against her nose and hugged her tighter.

"I'm not judgin' you," he assured you.

"Yeah, because you like him."

"Ain't I supposed to like my stepdad?"

"Okay, that's enough of that." She clambered to her feet, and he followed.

"Look, at the end of the day, I just want you to be happy, and if whatever board games y'all are playing every night have you glowing like this, I'll take it."

If only he knew. However, all that pleasure still had yet to outweigh all of her doubts. Nor could it outweigh the fear of the possibility that she had tripped and fallen for this apathetic asshole who wasn't all that apathetic at all while he would walk away from all of this unscathed.

"Just - have a little faith in him, professionally too. And if you can't do it for you, then do it for me because I'm not willing to risk losing you for anything."

"Alright, I hear you," she agreed, patting his cheek. "I'll try and trust more."

"Good. Don't let these bastards take that from you. If nothing else, trust your gut. Then you'll know who you can let in."

That's what she was afraid of.

Chapter Nineteen

HEPHAESTUS

Hephaestus took a parking spot as close to the door as he could find, but it was still several rows back and far too much of a distance for his liking. His eyes were fixed on his rearview mirror, watching as another pair of headlights pulled slowly into the lot. They belonged to a dark sedan although he couldn't make a definitive identification of a make or model, and they had been following Hephaestus and Aphrodite since their departure from Twilight House. He hadn't wanted to alarm her until he was certain, but as the car crept down the aisles in search of his vehicle rather than a parking spot, he knew it was no coincidence.

The sound of his ringtone cut across his thoughts, and he tried not to lose track of the tail as he answered the call.

"Finished putting together that list of properties you wanted," Achilles informed him.

"How many are there?"

"There are seven in the Harvest District alone, and then there are 22 total in all the other districts. Most of the ones in the Market District seem to be actively used by your brothers though."

"I need surveillance on them, all of them. Two bodies each at least, and be discreet. If they see something, they report it via radio to our private channel immediately, and we can go from there, but we need to know if any of them are being occupied or utilized right now. If they're supposed to be empty and they aren't, I need to know."

"Should I reach out to the district leaders?"

"Call my uncle. If he asks for information on those properties for himself, they'll give it to him, and we won't have to worry about someone talking. No one can know."

"Alright, I'll set up the teams right now. Where are you?"

"At Emerald. Aphrodite wanted to check in. Have you heard from Patroclus?"

"No news good or bad yet. They still haven't located Perseus, and Kleon hasn't made a single move. Neither has Nikolaos."

"If I were him, I'd be laying low here in town. Who knows what's waiting for him back there if his superiors find out he fled. Just keep eyes on the security building and see if they can dig up any other associates of Perseus. If his grandfather used to run the city, my guess is he has help."

"A whole lot of it."

"Yeah, well it still won't be enough to protect him from me."

Hephaestus hung up, his attention returning to the car tail. It had parked at the end of the row directly behind him, which meant it was slightly closer to the door and much too close for comfort. He weighed his options, catching the main entrance in his rearview with a slow breath.

It was evident that their enemies, like them, were becoming more urgent in their endeavors. They wanted Aphrodite dealt with quickly, and he wanted every single one of them identified yesterday. At this point, he had no clue who had an edge or who held the upper hand. All he knew was that he didn't feel like they did, and that was enough to have him on edge.

Looking down at his phone again, he clicked on Aphrodite's name and called her. It would be much smarter for him to wait out here and meet her at the doors than it would be for him to go inside. They would still have to make it back across the lot, and that left them both vulnerable. Not to mention the fact that the sky had at last opened up, the rain growing heavier by the minute, and the chill was paining his leg. She answered on the third ring.

"I'm almost ready," was what she said first.

"Tell me when you're coming out, and I'll drive up to the door," he instructed her. "Do not come out until you've told me."

"Why?"

"We're being followed. They've been tailing us since we left Twilight. I'm not sure who it is, so I'd rather be safe than—"

"Okay, I'll be out in ten."

She hung up without another word, and he tried to choke down the agitation. While it may have been the best thing for them, having their little sanctuary torn down, it didn't mean it wasn't frustrating. On top of that, everything was awkward and confusing. He wasn't sure what she was angry with him for specifically, but he could hazard a guess. She'd been caught with him after telling anyone who would listen how she couldn't stand him, and while Persephone and Hades wouldn't tell anyone, they would still know. Her best friend and the leader of the city would know, and if they knew, who was to say no one else would ever find out?

Aphrodite, the pearl of Khaos Falls, was fucking the security guard with the scarred face and the cold heart. The image was hardly becoming, especially when one considered the fact that she had his brother, an actual district leader and the prized son of Zeus, as an option. In comparison to Ares, Hephaestus was surely a downgrade. It was why she hadn't wanted them to tell, wasn't it? Why she'd insisted. Not that he had wanted everyone to know himself, but nevertheless, it stung. Because what good could ever come from a secret such as this? Especially when it wasn't the kind of secret that could be kept.

He drove up to the door ten minutes later, and like clockwork, Aphrodite came rushing out. She climbed into the passenger seat, and he immediately locked the doors once she closed hers. The car in question had yet to move from its spot, but it was only a matter of time.

"Dark blue sedan in the second row," he told her, pulling away from the curb.

"Did he see you?" she asked.

"I'm sure. I don't think he knows I saw him though. Just - watch our backs."

Yet mere seconds after they pulled onto the road, the car appeared behind them. The headlights were no longer on, which only made it more conspicuous, but Hephaestus could recognize the shape of them now. He maintained his composure, heading for Lush at an even speed and only glancing in the rearview mirror every now and again. The car kept its distance, but with so few others on the road at this time of night, it was easy to keep track of.

"Did you tell anyone we were going to Twilight?" he questioned.

"Just Psyche, but you said my line was secure."

"It is secure. That isn't how they found us."

Someone else had to know they were going over there though just like someone had to know they had planned to go to the warehouse. Yet in both instances, Psyche was the only other party privy to their plans, and if somebody was watching them around the clock, Hephaestus couldn't figure out their vantage point. His perimeter guards had been clocking every car that came into the garage, and they had spread out across the entire square block to ensure no one was spying.

"Is it possible—"

"Don't even, Hephaestus. Psyche is as loyal as they come."

He raised his brows. "I was gonna say, is it possible someone may have hacked into her phone?"

"I don't know. How would I know that?"

He once more choked down his frustration, realizing she wasn't going to be much help tonight. Pulling his phone out, he sent Artemis a text, asking her to check Psyche's phone for any bugs although the more he thought about it, the less likely it seemed. They would have likely found far more useful information than today's itinerary if they had bugged her phone, and more than that, they would have been able to manipulate far more situations with that access. He doubted they would risk that "in" by getting caught tailing them.

They turned onto the street that led to Lush, the other car doing the same, and Hephaestus dropped his phone in his lap and grabbed his radio instead. As foolish as it would be to follow them into the lot of the club, he put nothing past them anymore. They were desperate, and they knew their chances of getting to her were slim, the opportunities few and very far between.

He brought his radio to his lips as they turned into the parking garage, but before he could make the call, the other car passed behind them, keeping straight on the main street. Hephaestus slowed down to watch it, but again, he was unable to make out a license plate or any other identifying factors through the rain. He had to wonder where they were getting all these vehicles from. And where they were stashing them.

"Probably thought we were going somewhere else," he concluded.

He parked and checked his watch. It was nearing midnight, the downpour obscuring the signs of the aging evening with clouds and curtains of rain.

"We going upstairs?" he inquired.

"I am," is all he got before she exited the car.

At this point, he'd take it.

They were greeted by Hector and Leda as soon as they entered Lush, the two of them standing near the door talking. Hephaestus watched Aphrodite's demeanor change twice over as she approached, but he ignored it.

"What's going on?" Aphrodite addressed Hector.

"Oh, some of the radios weren't working too well because of the storm, so we came up to warn the perimeter guys."

"Make sure you're checking in with them frequently until it clears up then," Heph instructed, and Hector nodded his understanding.

"I'm heading upstairs," Aphrodite informed him as if Hephaestus hadn't spoken at all. "Call if you need to."

"Oh, Hephaestus, we didn't get to finish talking earlier," Leda chirped now, hopeful. "Maybe you could stay down here with me? I'm almost done with my last shift."

Aphrodite immediately stalked off towards the penthouse elevator. Hephaestus bit back a scoff and instead offered Leda a smile.

"Sorry, but duty awaits," he said. "I'm supposed to stick to Aphrodite like glue, but I'll see you some other time. Good night to you both."

He didn't allow Leda another word, moving as quickly as he could to catch up to Aphrodite despite his aching leg, a tremor racking his knee. He barely made it to the elevator, slamming his hand against the sensor in order to force the doors open again. She stood there staring at the keypad, failing to acknowledge his presence as they were sealed inside. He stood against the back wall almost directly behind her despite the vast car, staring up at the ceiling. He was at his wit's end however. He had lied. He couldn't accept things as they were whether they were better for the job or not. This dense silence, this uncomfortable tension, he was fed up with it.

"You know you're jealous of a child, right?" he questioned nonchalantly.

She scoffed, but she didn't look at him. "What would I have to be jealous of, Hephaestus? Don't flatter yourself."

"I didn't see you walk away from any of those other girls today."

"I'm tired."

"Okay, and what's your excuse for the rest of the day?"

"What are you talking about?"

"You've been upset all day, and don't tell me you haven't been because you've never been great at hiding your feelings, so it's kinda been written all over your face."

"Fuck off, Hephaestus."

"Why can't you just answer the question?"

"Because I don't have to answer the question."

"So you're just gonna act like this for the rest of the night?"

"You won't have to see me for the rest of the night."

"And tomorrow?"

"I guess we'll see."

"Just answer the fucking question like an adult, Aphrodite."

She whipped around. "Don't you dare start that shit. I'm not doing this with you, Hephaestus!"

"Doing what?"

"This hot-and-cold shit. One minute, you want me. The next minute, you want to avoid me. And now you think *you* are entitled to some answers? Fuck you!"

He didn't know what to say to that. Livid as he was, he had no clue what to say because she was right. That wasn't to say he was sorry. He wasn't sorry, but they'd had an arrangement, a professional one and one he'd failed to honor. He'd disappointed both Persephone and Hades, and while they hadn't said it aloud, he could read it right off of their faces. And her... Well, she'd wanted them to keep the secret. Now there was no secret to keep.

Except that wasn't true at all.

"Yeah, that's what I thought," she spat.

The doors opened, and she turned away, but before she could step over the threshold, he grabbed her arm. It was a mistake. He knew it was a mistake from the moment he did it, but he seemed to be making a lot of those lately where she was concerned. They should be able to discuss this, to talk about it like adults without making those same mistakes, but that wasn't them no matter how much logic he carried around.

She spun on him again, her other hand raised, but before she could whip it across his face, he dropped his cane and grabbed her wrist. He half stalked, half stumbled forward, pressing her into the wall and pinning her hand to it. Then he pinned the other. Her eyes shone with violent delight, and while she bared her teeth, she said nothing. They stood like that, motionless, long after the doors closed again. The moment he relaxed his grip however, she ripped away from his grasp.

Her hands found his chest, and she shoved him away. He tripped over his feet, nearly falling onto his back, but she snagged him by the collar of his shirt. Their eyes hit one another like live wires, sparking dangerously between them. She yanked him forward and smothered his mouth with hers.

Her back hit the wall again, and his hands found her waist, pulling up her dress as she wrestled with his belt. His trousers hit the floor at the same time the tatters of her panties did, and he hiked up her leg and anchored it around his good hip. She got her fingers between the lapels of his shirt and pulled, tearing it open so that buttons rained down onto the elevator floor. He smirked.

"I can't - fucking stand you," she growled as his mouth cascaded down her neck, her nails merciless against his scalp. "You bastard."

"The feeling's mutual," he grunted, pulling back to suck his fingers into his mouth before he buried them between her thighs.

She yelped as he entered her, squeezing her thighs around his hand. He spread his fingers, forcing them open again and massaging what moisture he could around her entrance.

"Then why do you care if it hurts?" she hissed, venom drenching the words.

He looked up at her, a sneer twisting his face into something unrecognizable. She didn't back down, her eyes flashing with challenge. He removed his fingers, placing his hand around her throat instead. Then he crammed every inch of his cock inside of her tight cunt.

She howled, tearing into his skin as he bit down on her shoulder hard enough to bruise. Each and every thrust was a rehash of that reciprocated emotion, brutal and unforgiving as she arched against the wall. He raised her leg higher, stroking deeper, her moans and his grunts the soundtrack of their downfall. They fucked like it was meant to be an affront to the other. It was petty, it was rash, it was absolutely disrespectful, and it made him want her more than he ever had. What did that say about her? What did that say about him?

"Say it again," he growled, punctuating another rough thrust. "Tell me you hate me."

She gasped for breath. "I fucking hate you!"

"Again."

"—Fuck you, Heph."

He raised his head, snatching her hands up once more and pinning them on either side of her head. She snarled at him, but he stepped closer anyway, positioning his thrust at a new angle. What was there to be afraid of now? She had already made him fall for her.

She shuddered and gritted her teeth as her head rolled back against the wall.

"Do you hate daddy?" he accentuated each word as he tangled his fingers in hers. "Do you?"

"—Yes."

"Liar."

"I do! I hate - you! I - hate you. I hate—"

She bucked her hips and fought against her restraints, but he didn't loosen his hold. His leg was weak, threatening to buckle, but he didn't slow, pounding into her pussy with reckless abandon. Her nails dug into the backs of his hands, her chest pressed against his, but she knew she was stuck. Her pride reared its head, making this all the more satisfactory. He wanted to break her. He would accept nothing less.

"Liar," he asserted again.

"No," she panted, eyes squeezed shut, but her voice had lost some of its power.

"Then say it. Tell daddy you hate him."

She fought. She fought as hard and as long as she could, even as he demanded it again and again. And he came to realize why. She was getting what she wanted.

He halted his movements.

Her eyes snapped open with a whine. She attempted to wind her hips, but he pinned them to the wall with his own. Firmly.

"Beg for it," he demanded, brows drawn and eyes glittering. She whimpered. "Like a good girl. You want it, you gotta fucking beg for it. I'm not asking."

She bit down on her lip, and that alone stoked the flames in his belly, but he kept his hips still. Even as they shook. Her leg tightened around him, but he was, as always, immovable. Up until he wasn't.

"Please," she managed. He gave nothing. "—Please, Daddy."

"Please what?"

She growled in frustration, throwing her body against his. "Fuck me!"

It was automatic. He fulfilled her demand, allowing them both to sidestep the previous question. She pressed herself back into the wall with a new series of cries. Sweat licked down his temple and along his spine, his adrenaline at newfound heights. He fucked her harder, faster, enough to forget how he'd felt the day before, enough to put off how he'd feel the day after. He released her hands, slipping his own under her ass to keep her in place as he drove into her. She clawed away at him, her mouth hanging open although her moans were severed by a choked silence. All that remained were his guttural sounds and the collision of their bodies until she slid up the wall, screaming at the peak of her orgasm.

She wrapped her arms around his neck, clinging to him as he continued. Her walls clamped down around him, drawing him towards his climax. He pursued it with a vengeance until he was cast over the edge, his roar shaking the car. She shook in his arms as he rode it out, vaguely wondering how it was that each orgasm was more devastating than the last. At the forefront was the thought that perhaps, they may just be stuck in this cycle forever, fucking each other unconscious to avoid talking about the things that mattered.

But how long could they keep that up before one of them opened their fucking mouth? He was angry at the very notion. Because he knew better. He knew this wasn't simply a cycle. It was something more or something else entirely, and the only thing worse than finding out what it was? Never knowing at all.

Chapter Twenty

APHRODITE

Aphrodite traced the sharp lines and jagged edges of Hephaestus's face as she mounted him, her hands braced against the ink of his chiseled chest. His scars glistened in the candlelight coloring her bedroom, but rather than deprive her of the beauty beneath, they enhanced it. His fathomless gaze stoked the flames still burning in her belly, and as she slid down onto his shaft, it flared up and threatened to engulf her. She knew it would in time. It always did.

She hated him. She swore that she hated him, but when he looked up at her like that, features softened into a silent awe, it was difficult to believe it. Still, she rode him like she hated him, slamming her hips down against his and clawing her way through the skin of his chest.

"I can't fucking stand you," she forced out, more as a reminder to herself than an insult to him, wrapping a hand around his throat.

"Well," he managed, his voice thick with lust, "at least you seem to ride me just fine."

Before she could even think to retaliate, he was yanking her down hard onto his engorged cock, a cry ripped from her throat in the process. His grip bruised her thighs in a way she would revel in tomorrow, but for now, she focused on the way he filled her. He was of average length, but his girth was something to gawk at, and he knew how to use it to his advantage every chance he got. She was learning to use it to hers as well, her moans flowing freely from parted lips with every swirl of her hips. She wanted him. Even when she had him, she wanted him to the point of insatiable hunger, and he was never close enough. What did that mean for them? What did that mean for her?

She'd been jealous. She could admit it to herself in the throes of passion that she hated watching another woman flirt with him so shamelessly regardless of who that woman was, but once that subsided, the shame would plague her in a most painful way. She fucked him harder if only to chase off the thought, unwilling to ruin her own pleasure for the sake of self-awareness. His hand cracked against her ass, causing her to jump forward, banging a fist against his chest as she cursed his name. Before she could warn him against it in any fashion, his other hand snaked between her thighs, pinching her clit so that she bucked brashly in place, nearly pulling off of him entirely.

"Fuck, Hephaestus!" she shrieked."I fucking - hate you!"

Not that the lie held water anymore. He only proceeded to work his fingers against her in time with the upward roll of his hips, multiplying and magnifying her pleasure, maximizing it to the point of overwhelming intensity. It wasn't simply pleasure for her sake either. It was a reminder that even when she was on top, he was in control. He held the key to her satisfaction in his hands, quite literally.

She came before she knew what was happening, eyes rolling back with his name lodged in her throat. She convulsed atop him, his hands the only thing holding her in place as light after bright light flashed behind her eyelids. It was madness. It was ecstasy. It was heavens and hells. She could do nothing in the aftermath but collapse against his chest, his hard cock throbbing inside of her.

He was patient, his hands loose against her thighs, and if she were any less fatigued, she would reprimand him for it, for relishing in her weakness. Instead, she dragged her tongue up the center of his chest, over his neck, until she could sink her teeth into his lower lip in revenge. His fingers splayed out over her ass, stretching her open. He pulsed harder inside of her in a way that echoed through every bone in her body.

"What?" she asked because that was all she could manage to ask.

He didn't answer, not verbally, instead sliding two fingers between her cheeks and teasing her hole. She shivered in his arms, whimpering against jaw, and she wanted it. It surprised her to the point of breathlessness, but it was the truth.

"No," she breathed.

"No?" he repeated.

"Fuck..."

"What?"

"Please."

"Make up your mind, Princess, and tell Daddy what you want."

"I want it, Daddy. I want it."

What passed between them as he slipped out from beneath her and flipped her onto her stomach went unspoken, but it lingered long after she'd buried her face in the pillow. She groaned as his heavy erection fell between the seam of her ass, but he took his time making any further moves. Apprehension turned to anticipation, her hips grinding down against the sheets as her fingers curled into them. She could feel him, teasing her entrance, legs straddling hers and keeping her in place. She bit down on her tongue if only to keep from pleading with him. She did so until she tasted blood.

Then he was moving again but not into her. Instead, he was moving away. She whipped her head around to look at him over her shoulder, his naked form sliding down along hers. He pushed her knees apart before lowering himself between them, his hands sliding up the backs of her thighs to squeeze and spread her asscheeks open. She gasped when his lips touched down against her inner thigh, featherlight and teasing. His hands trembled slightly, the sensation making her toes curl.

"Heph—"

"You said you wanted it," he said, his voice low yet strong enough to vibrate through her core. "That means all of it. Now be a good girl and lay still."

It was damn near impossible. His tongue was snaking its way up at an agonizing pace, his fingers creeping closer to her hole. There was no room for her to be self-conscious, not when he refused to shy away. Despite all the shit they still talked to one another and all the vitriol they continued to throw around, despite all the ways he still made her blood boil, he was good to her when it mattered.

And she fucking hated him for it.

It would be easier if he just fucked her, came, and left. It would make more sense if he treated her like something to do rather than someone to respect, but no. Of course he had to prove her wrong. He lived for it.

"Heph!"

Her back went rigid as his tongue swirled around the rim of her hole, but the cry of his name was met with a hard smack of his hand against her cheek.

"Who are you talking to?"

She gritted her teeth. He was growing bolder by the day, by the moment, and she loved it as much as she despised it. She yearned for it as much as it annoyed her.

"Say you're sorry," he demanded.

She screwed her eyes shut. He delivered another sharp smack, dislodging another cry from her throat. His growl sent shivers through her.

"Tell Daddy you're sorry."

"I'm - sorry, Daddy."

"Like you mean it, Aphrodite."

She whimpered. "I'm sorry, Daddy."

"Good girl." He spread her open once more. "Now put your face in the fucking pillow."

She hardly had time to process the command much less follow it before his tongue was slipping into her ass, stretching and expanding even as she clenched around him. His mouth was a menace she had no defense against, and she was learning to accept that. This sensation in particular was brand new to her, never having allowed anyone else the privilege, and the fact that it was Hephaestus introducing her to it had her in her feelings.

She couldn't dwell long on the thought though, not when he was sliding his hand beneath her so that she had something solid to grind her clit on. He crooked his fingers, letting her rut against them in shameless desperation. Of course it still wasn't enough. Fates, would anything ever be enough?

His mouth was there one minute and gone the next, her eyes snapping open at the edge of a sharp inhale. Before she could look back at him, his hand was at the side of her head, pressing it into the bed. Her eyes found him regardless in the mirror of her vanity. She saw him rearrange himself atop her. She heard the click of the lube bottle opening. She felt the cool liquid drip over her entrance. Then his slick cock was once again resting heavy against her, causing her eyes to flutter closed and her mouth to fall open. She fought to keep her hips still.

"Please, Daddy," she breathed, her pride stripped away.

"You want it bad, huh, Princess?"

"Yes! Yes, Daddy, please!"

"You gonna be a good girl for me and take it?"

"Yes yes yes - Daddy, just - please! Fuck me. I want you in - ah!"

Her words were clipped by his shallow entry, stretching her open and stealing her breath. He sunk into her inch by torturous inch, hardly allowing her to adjust before he retracted almost completely and pushed back in. She groaned out, reaching back to grasp his thigh as his hand slid down to the back of her neck. She could feel every flex of each one of his muscles, every spasm and tremor that passed through him as he kept himself upright. He was determined to ruin her. She knew that now, and if she were a better woman, she would forbid it. Then again, if she were a better woman, she would not be here to begin with.

"By the Fates, I— Daddy!"

Her back bowed upward, or at least attempted to, but his hand pinned her firmly to the mattress. His other hand was still on her ass, his thumb holding her open so that he could plunge deeper into her. His grunts pooled in the valley of her shoulder blades, an added pressure that seeped into her skin and stimulated every nerve it touched. She was almost ashamed at how deeply she had underestimated him. In all of the time she'd known him however, he had never seemed intrigued —much less attracted— to her, to anyone. She never would have guessed the things he was capable of doing with her, *to* her. She welcomed the surprise now though. Eagerly so.

"You like that?" He was fully slamming into her now. "Do you?"

"Yes—"

"Yes?"

He delivered a particularly deep stroke, and she called out. "Yes, Daddy, fuck!"

"That's my good girl."

She purred as if on instinct, leaning into his praise and yearning for more. She didn't just want to possess him. She wanted to be possessed by him, in every way one can be possessed.

"I - wanna be your good girl, Daddy," she breathed, his eyes catching hers in the mirror.

She felt it rumble in his chest, the possessive and predatory hunger that drove him into her deeper and harder and faster. He leaned over her, lower until his breath pressed in against her ear.

"You are my good girl, baby." She shuddered under the honey sweet tone of his voice, throwing her hips back into his. "You take this dick so good. You are such a good girl."

"Oh, fuck—"

The words died in her throat as he shifted, replacing the hand on her throat for a forearm across her shoulders as he lay flat atop her. His other hand slipped around her hip and beneath her, and she realized what he was going to do only a second before his fingers touched down upon her clit.

A withering cry ricocheted off of the headboard as she bucked against his hand, his name a curse upon her lips. She sensed her orgasm coming upon her like a rogue wave, eager to wash away the last of her anger and agitation she'd held beneath her tongue all day. Most of it had been left on the floor of the elevator after her first orgasm, but he seemed intent on cleansing the whole of it. She would dare not complain.

She had no defense or means of suppression for the shriek he tore from her throat, shaking violently under his weight as the orgasm racked her again and again. He rubbed her clit faster nonetheless, and she felt like she might simply turn to ash in his arms, the friction overwhelming and all encompassing. Removing his arm from her shoulders, he moved it beneath her instead, holding her to him as he plunged into her at a rapid pace.

She squeezed around him mindlessly, desperate to be filled. Between one moment and the next, their hands were clasped against her neck, and he at last showed mercy —or perhaps another kind of cruelty— relieving her clit of his touch. He pushed those fingers into her mouth, and she sang around them as he continued to pound her into the mattress so hard that she was certain they would leave a lasting imprint. On the edge of his own climax, he swelled inside of her, and she had to force herself not to bite down, too hard at least, tears streaming down her face.

"That's a good girl." His voice sounded foreign in her ear. "Take this dick. Take it!"

He came with a resounding roar and a fractured rhythm, his hips battering hers until she felt the warmth spread through her. In that same instant, another orgasm ripped through her with no warning whatsoever, leaving her breathless and trembling hopelessly in his hands. Then his mouth was on her neck, and she was fighting to turn over enough to reach it with her own. Once she was able, she kissed him with the fire of every sun she had ever seen rise or set in her lifetime. He returned it just the same.

In the back of her mind, the truth burned like a brand. This was no longer hatred. And that lie may no longer hold up.

Chapter Twenty-One

HEPHAESTUS

Aphrodite was quiet for so long, her steady breaths gliding across his chest unhindered, that he assumed she was asleep. He stared up at the ceiling, his mind running away with him as he attempted to track their path, the one that had led them here. He still didn't know where it started, and he damn sure didn't know where it would end. All he knew was that it was much too late to turn back, and the only option left was to see it through, no matter what that entailed.

His fingers combed through her dark locks absentmindedly, his nails scraping over her shoulder blade each time.

"Still awake?" she asked, startling him so bad that he froze for several distinct seconds before he resumed the motion. "I thought you were out."

"Can't sleep," he grunted, trying to control his breathing. "Did I wake you up?"

She shook her head against his chest. "Can't sleep."

They lay in silence for a while more, Hephaestus contemplating the reality that this was more than what it appeared to be. If it were just sex, he would have returned to his room by now. At the very least, he would have turned over. Instead, he held her to him like a secret, one he was eager to hoard and expecting to lose.

"I wasn't jealous," she said suddenly.

He snorted. "Of course you weren't, Aphrodite. What would you have to be jealous of?"

"Exactly."

He said nothing more, thinking that was the end of it, but then she spoke again, and her voice had lost some of that edge that had shone through not a moment ago.

"Are you - attracted to her?" she questioned softly.

He didn't know whether to laugh or not, but there was an underlying irritation there too.

"If I were, I wouldn't be in bed with you," he pointed out.

"You can be attracted to me too. They aren't mutually exclusive."

"I'm not attracted to her, not in the least. And again, even if I was, I still chose you. I followed you up here, didn't I? Knowing damn well you were gonna be a pain in the ass."

He huffed in indignation, certain that this was the beginning of a fight. He would indeed have to return to his room after all, it seemed.

"Actually," she said softly, her fingers moving over his collarbone. "*You* were the pain in the ass."

There was a beat of quiet before he was subdued by laughter, the sound shaking his frame until she was laughing into his skin as well. Shaking his head, he rolled his eyes.

"I can't stand you," he sighed once the laughter subsided.

"Lucky for you, I don't require much standing as of late," she shot back.

He continued to push his fingers through her hair as her lips brushed his chest. "Do you even know why you hate me? Like do you have any idea, or did you just decide because I don't kiss your ass, I'm worth hating?"

"Again, you *just* kissed—"

"You know what I mean, brat."

She hummed, seemingly in thought before she replied. "I've come to realize that - maybe I didn't hate you so much as - feared you."

His hand paused at the top of her head. "Feared me?"

"Yeah." He waited. "I mean, you... you're your father's son."

"Not the only one."

"But I know Dio and Hermes. They weren't raised by him, and they're nothing like him. And - Ares, well, he's proven lately that he's very much his father's son, but before that, he had his redeeming qualities. He was passionate and spontaneous and—"

"As reckless as you?"

"Yes, he was as reckless as me," she conceded with a roll of her eyes he caught in the corner of his. "But you-" She took a breath. "You were always a wildcard because it always seemed like you existed solely to put me in my place. You always made me feel like - like I wasn't good enough to be around you or that you were above me and the things I stood for. And I know you're a lot more like Hades than anyone, but you're different too. You're... I don't know what you are. I could never figure you out, so I figured there were other pieces of your father hidden underneath all your judgment and your cynicism. And after everything Zeus has done, what he put Seph through, I just—"

"I'm not his son."

He croaked it out before he could even consider the repercussions of it, and they both froze.

He'd never told anyone, and he rarely thought about it. Zeus had been inconsequential to his existence for a long time now, and while Hephaestus grew up, Zeus didn't. As far as he knew, only Hades, Hera, Zeus, and his real father knew the truth of his birth, and he'd never thought it necessary for anyone else to. Plus, unveiling that secret while Zeus was still around would have done more damage to Hera than anything he had ever done. And he had done a whole lot.

Even now, Hephaestus didn't know what would happen to her if others found out, but it had never been an issue before. He hadn't cared for the fact because the only facts that mattered were this: Hades had been his guardian, Charon his guide, and Hecate and Thanatos had filled in any other gaps in his parenting. That had been what mattered. Despite how young he and Zeus were when Heph was born, Hades had never run from caring for him, and Charon had taken to him with a quickness he wouldn't fully comprehend until much later. That was what Heph remembered when he chose to recall his childhood. Everything else was white noise and unfortunate supporting detail.

Aphrodite propped herself on her elbow so that she could look at his face. "What?"

He sighed, staring up at the ceiling. "My mom was - she was pregnant before they were married. She had been promised to Zeus, but - she was already with someone. But instead of breaking the betrothal, her parents worked it out with Zeus's parents so that they could keep the arrangement, after they knew she was having a son at least. But Ares wasn't born long after, so it was easy to believe they'd have a kid that young."

"Are you serious? I - I mean, Demeter always said the whole thing was... She said they were young, really young."

He nodded. "They were kids. My mom was sixteen, and Zeus was even younger than that. It was a bad look, but the truth would've been worse. At least that's what they said."

"And Zeus didn't hate you for it?"

He laughed now, deeply. "Of course he did. But - he had other things to hate me for. Not only was I a bastard, I was a disabled one. They didn't even think I'd live long enough to leave the hospital, but I did, and I think he was more disappointed than anything."

"I'm sorry, Heph, I—"

He shook his head. "You got nothing to be sorry for. I know what people think of me, and I've used that to my benefit, so it's as much my fault as anyone's."

"I'm still sorry, for calling you a robot and saying you didn't care about anything."

"And I'm sorry I ever made you feel like you were beneath me. You aren't, Aphrodite. I've always respected you. I always will, but you know. We just never gave ourselves a chance I guess."

"Do you... What about your real dad?"

He fell into silence again for a moment, chewing the inside of his cheek. While he had never received direct confirmation from either party, he had a hunch. It may have been one downfall to his observational nature to some, but to him, it was soothing.

"I think protecting that secret is the only thing protecting my mother and what's left of her reputation, so - no one's ever said his name out loud or pointed him out to me, but..."

She stared at him until he finally turned his gaze on her, and once he did, she brushed her fingers against his jaw. It was soft, softer than anything he expected and certainly more so than he was used to. He didn't know what to do with that. He never had.

He took hold of her hand, pulling it from his face and resting it against his abdomen.

"Don't pity me," he instructed her.

She smiled. "You must not know me very well if you honestly think I would ever pity you."

He knew it to be true. Never once had she offered him anything but the truth, blunt as a hammer with that sharp tongue of hers. Maybe that was why he liked her amidst all the agitation she inspired. He knew that when he looked into her eyes, he may not see something soft, but he would also never see pity. To him, pity was the worst thing he could find there. He would gladly take her hatred any day.

But there was no hatred there now. There was indeed something softer, and maybe... Maybe pity wasn't the only soft thing the world could offer him after all.

"But just to prove it," she went on, a mischievous grin on her face. "I gotta ask. What is it? I mean, what-"

She gestured to him, and he chuckled.

"It's something degenerative," he explained. "My muscles are deteriorating. Slowly, very slowly, but deteriorating nonetheless."

"So... what does that mean?"

"It means that one day, I may or may not lose the ability to do things I already struggle to do now. My legs will get weaker, my arms too, but there are ways to slow it down, and Asklepios says they're developing more effective treatments every year. Either way, he's sure I'll live a long life. Or at least a full one, so there's nothing to worry about immediately, but - it's something I have to be conscious of, especially in my line of work."

"So your canes then. Are all of them-" She wiggled her eyebrows. "*Weapons?*"

It was his turn to roll his eyes. "Yeah, and it has its benefits. For one, they're lighter, so they're easier for me to wield, to hold steady. But I prefer a blade or staff because while I struggle to hold things steady or lift things sometimes, my movements are still pretty fluid if I move fast enough. Does that make sense?"

"I think so. I mean it doesn't seem to stop you so much as hinder you a bit, right?"

"Exactly. Nothing is impossible. It's just a little more difficult. I have to drink a lot of water. That usually keeps the tremors to a minimum, but it can be frustrating at times, especially because one leg is substantially weaker than the other."

"I think you do just fine."

"Oh, we're moving up to flattery already?"

"Shut up."

She lifted her hand to smack his chest, but he caught it in his own, threading their fingers together and resting them on his stomach.

"Come to my uncle's with me tomorrow." It sounded more like a request than it needed to in his opinion. "It's our monthly family dinner, so."

She raised a brow. "Heph, you can go. I'll be fine by myself for a couple of hours. I'm not—"

"I'm not asking you for work." He only just realized that as he said it. "Come with me tomorrow. You're family anyway. Persephone's there."

"So you want me to go because Persephone's there?"

He rolled his eyes. "I want you to go because I want you there. Do I really need to spell everything out for you? For Fate's sake."

He had no clue what he hoped to accomplish by asking, but it felt right at the time. It felt like the logical result. Now, he wondered if there was something else keeping her from simply agreeing.

"We still don't have to tell anyone about this," he assured her, remembering what she had requested of Hades and Persephone. "We can play it off as a work thing for everyone if you want. No one's gonna ask any questions. Well, maybe Persephone after the fact, but that can't be avoided. She'll probably be angrier if I don't take you."

She leveled him with a glare, but her lips twitched. At last, she nodded before settling back down against him, her head resting just over his heart.

"Lucky for you, she already insisted," she admitted, fiddling with his fingers. "I said I'd think about it because I have work to do, but since you asked so nicely."

"Glad I could sway your interest."

"And what about your brother?"

"What about him? Like I said, we play it off as work. Ares is gonna think whatever he wants no matter what we do, and you know that."

"Yeah, I guess that's true." She sighed, quiet for a moment before she went on, her voice a higher pitch now. "But if I do go, do I get dessert after?"

"Yeah, I'm sure my uncle will have something waiting."

"That's not what I meant."

He smirked. "If you're a good girl."

"Mm." He hissed as she tugged his nipple between her teeth without warning. "Deal."

"Not a good start."

"Quit playin'." She soothed the area with a tender kiss. "You only care about the ending."

He fell asleep adamant that it was best he never asked what that meant, what any of it meant, lest he find himself severely disappointed. When they awakened in the morning, still wrapped in one another, she seemed to have made the same commitment. They renewed it again when he ate her out against the wall in the shower an hour later, and by the time they made it downstairs, he could pretend he wasn't nervous about tonight. Still, he found himself struggling to focus on work, his eyes consistently drawn back to her.

It was also becoming increasingly difficult to maintain his distance when they were in public. It served as a reminder of the nature of the arrangement, or lack thereof. When it became too much, he told her he was going downstairs to check in with Achilles, and she hesitated only a moment before nodding. He hesitated another moment before moving.

Once he was on his feet, he left the room as quickly as he could, taking the elevator down to the first floor and heading for the security office. As usual, Leda was at the front desk testing radios or putting them on the chargers. She immediately stopped when she saw him approaching, putting the radio in her hand and standing with a large grin.

"Hephaestus!" she squealed.

Before he knew it, she was hugging him around the middle, and all he could do was pat her back as he nearly fumbled his cane. Once she released him, he cleared his throat.

"How are you?" she questioned, batting her lashes.

"I'm good," he reported. "And you?"

"I'm alright. Just another day at the office."

He managed a slight smile. "Is Achilles down here?"

"Uh, yeah, I think so. I can check if you—"

She cut off at the appearance of the man himself behind her, stepping between the two with a boisterous bark of Heph's name in greeting. Hephaestus let out a sigh of relief as they shook hands.

"You got any updates?" he asked.

"Well, not great ones, not right now," Achilles replied with a grimace. "Patroclus' hack failed overnight. We got shut out. He must have missed something on the way in."

It took a moment for Heph to remember they were talking about Kleon. "Do we have a location on the big guy yet?"

"No, but Pat thinks he might have a lead. He said he'd call me tonight. Will you be around?"

"Uh, late, yeah. We're going to the Styx District for dinner though."

"Oh?" Achilles' lips twitched upward, and Hephaestus breathed out through his nose.

"Family dinner, with my uncles and my brothers. And Hecate and Persephone of course."

"Ah, well while you're down there in your uncle's district, how about you check out one of those warehouses? The ones you wanted a list of? It's on—"

"Let's go to your office," Hephaestus suddenly said, realizing how exposed they were out here. Leda's staring made him uncomfortable enough, but he also didn't trust the radios on the desk or the doors lining the hall. "I want the whole list."

Achilles only shrugged and turned around, leading the way, and Hephaestus followed him down the hall to the office he'd taken over from Hector. Hephaestus closed the door behind them as Achilles gathered his documentation.

"What were you saying about the warehouse?" Hephaestus prompted.

"Yeah, so it's on the southern coast." He turned around and handed him a folder. "Looks like a leftover building from before your uncle's reign. The address is in there. There are two others listed too, but Dionysos and Hermes are looking to start using them once they have the new winery up and running."

"They already have the leases?"

"Not sure. I just know they listed the addresses on the documents for the land."

"I'll check with them tonight."

Achilles leaned against the desk. "Taking her home to meet the family, huh?"

Hephaestus rolled his eyes. "She knows the family, Achilles."

"Right, but have you taken her to a family dinner yet? I don't think so."

"I'm taking her, so I don't have to leave her here with you."

"Mhm." Achilles clapped a hand on his shoulder. "The energy is changing. I can sense it."

"What does that even mean?"

"Oh, come on, Heph. I've known you both for years."

"And you're still full of shit."

He chuckled. "Yeah, sure. Facts are facts though."

Achilles walked him back out of the office, and Heph tried to focus on the task at hand rather than how he felt about taking Aphrodite to his uncle's home. He hadn't lied. She'd been friends with his brothers far longer than they'd been doing what they were doing, and she was Persephone's best friend. Her showing up to family dinner was not at all weird, and while she'd never come before, they'd only done it a few times thus far. Besides, Persephone had invited her first.

He knew Hades and Persephone both might have a few questions on standby, but as he'd told Aphrodite, they were inevitable. Ares might have his own suspicions too, but that wasn't something Hephaestus had to answer to. He refused to feel bad about what he was doing. The only regret he had was that he didn't know how to admit she was more than a hate fuck.

"You gonna check out that warehouse before dinner or after?" Achilles asked as they approached the security office entrance.

"I'll probably do that first, before nightfall since I have her with me."

"Alright, check in with me. Let me know how it goes."

"Will do."

Hephaestus left the office with a curt goodbye to Leda, who watched him approach and retreat without blinking it seemed. As he reached the second floor landing, he met up with Hector, who gave him a friendly smile. Hephaestus had vetted him thoroughly in the beginning, and he'd come to believe that Hector was loyal enough, specifically to Aphrodite. He'd put forth a lot of effort since the first attack, and Heph had a lot of faith in him, which he utilized now.

"Do me a favor," he instructed, leaning in so that his mouth was near Hector's ear.

"Yeah, anything," Hector agreed, raising a brow. "What is it?"

"We're getting ready to leave. Do a sweep of the parking lot and surrounding area, make sure no one's waiting around, trying to tail us, alright? And - keep it off the radio." Hector pulled back to look at him, but Hephaestus shook his head. "I just - need to see somethin'."

Hector nodded. "Alright, you got it."

"Text me, let me know when it's done. We'll head down then."

Hector patted his shoulder before continuing towards the stairs, Hephaestus making his way back to Aphrodite's office. She stood at the window overlooking the club, dancing in place to the music being fed through the speakers. His eyes raked over her frame, fingers twitching at his sides as he thought of all the things he could do to her in this office right now, all of the things he wouldn't mind putting on display for any and all to see. Freeing himself from the wayward thought and the surprise it inspired, he entered her office and came to stand beside her.

"You ready to go?"

"Now?" She turned to him, confusion on her face. "You said dinner was at 7. We have like 3 hours."

"Yeah, but I wanna check out one of the warehouses in the Styx District."

She nodded. "Okay, but I wanna go up and change."

He knitted his brows. "What for? You look fine."

She bit her lip. "Oh, yeah? How fine, Daddy?"

The answer was instantaneous. "Fine enough that I wanna bend you over that desk right now and fuck you until you cry, so you better hurry and do what you're gonna do."

"Mm, you're saying that as if I wouldn't let you."

"You'd beg for it. I assure you, but we don't got time, so come on."

Her tongue swept over her lips with a hum before she turned and headed for the elevator. He followed, the heat in his gut threatening to swallow him whole. He maintained his distance somehow all the way up to her suite, and even as she swung her hips in the most provocative way possible, he refrained from following her into her bedroom. If they started now, they would never make it to dinner. He vowed to make it up to both of them after though.

He received an "all clear" text from Hector just as she resurfaced, and they headed down to the parking garage immediately after. Despite the assurance, Hephaestus remained alert and aware every step of the way to his car, his eyes scanning the garage before he got behind the wheel. It was still early in the evening, so it wasn't yet filled to capacity the way it would be come nightfall, but the cold didn't seem to be keeping anyone away.

Over the past week, he'd memorized many of the license plates that were consistently parked on their level, but he'd mapped out people's particular parking spaces the first night he'd stayed here. Aphrodite seemed to sense his tension because she looked over at him with brows drawn together.

"What's wrong?"

He refused to worry her with a hunch. He didn't want to plant a seed if he was wrong. As of now, he wasn't sure that the current suspicion plaguing his mind was even warranted, so he tucked it away for the time being. Either way, he would see soon enough.

"Just - the same anxiety every time we leave the club," he replied. "It's nothing."

"You haven't let them get me yet."

"And I won't."

When she didn't respond right away, he turned to look at her. She was staring at him in a way he didn't understand, and it felt far too fragile for him to ask about. Instead, he turned his gaze back to the road and pulled out of the parking garage. He nearly flinched a moment later when she placed her hand on his neck, brushing the skin there with an uncanny softness that made him tense. She didn't stop, and her hand remained there as they made their way south into the Market District then across the river into the Styx District. He relaxed into it with every street they passed, but he refused to think about it. He couldn't. It was all becoming too real.

As they pulled up to the warehouse though, a more promising tension immediately returned. Before she could open the door, he put his arm out to stop her, his eyes trained straight ahead.

"What?" she asked, confused.

"Someone's here," he immediately said. "Or was."

"How do you know?"

"Look at the air. The dust is still settling, like someone just peeled out of here. Multiple people. My guess is multiple people did, but someone's still inside waiting on us."

"So they knew we were coming." He didn't answer, and she looked over at him. "Who knew?"

"Just Achilles."

Although that wasn't entirely true, he left it at that. Looking in the rearview mirror, he surveyed the area. That was when he spotted the car.

It was not at all suspicious from a glance. Grey and old, parked at an angle in the corner of the lot. However, given the circumstances, he would say it was anything but innocent. He had a choice to make now. He doubted the car was simply a tail, and if it was empty, it only enhanced his theory about an ambush waiting inside the warehouse. It would be foolish to traipse around the Styx District like that. Then again, he had to keep reminding himself that these people were outsiders. They didn't know the dangers of the city like the residents did. Or they didn't care.

He gritted his teeth. After days of this, they still hadn't established a viable lead, and while he thought he may finally be able to turn the tide, he would rather have multiple pieces by now. Besides, in order to find that lead, he'd sacrificed whatever advantage they may have had, and that stressed him. He thought himself better at his job than this, distractions aside. He couldn't get ahead of himself now though. That was just looking for trouble.

He drove away.

He was trusting his gut on this one, and while he'd like to know who was in that car or who was waiting inside, he wasn't going to gamble with Aphrodite's life. That defeated the entire purpose, didn't it? Besides, it was hardly worth picking up a few expendables when he now had a better lead to follow.

She didn't question him, but he glanced over just as her eyes landed on the car parked at the other end of the lot. It didn't follow after them as they made their way back onto the street, and Hephaestus was only mildly disappointed. He wasn't surprised though. Whatever, *whoever*, they were dealing with, they weren't amateurs. He refused to underestimate them.

Chapter Twenty-Two

APHRODITE

Fear was no longer something Aphrodite was acquainted with. With her life on the line and snakes in her midst, her mind fled from the very suggestion of such a thing, eluding the element of surprise that came with terror and dread. Yet when she looked at Hephaestus, she feared losing him far more than she had ever feared losing herself. Whether by death or disengagement, the idea of parting ways with him had begun to bury an pain in her belly that she didn't know how to treat. She didn't fear her own demise. She never had. When the assassin had buried that blade into her sternum, she feared nothing and no one. Now? She feared running out of time.

Dinner was difficult. Suddenly sitting beside him without contact came with a physical discomfort she was helpless against. It was severely exacerbated by both Ares' angry glare and Persephone's probing gaze catching her across the table, the latter filled with questions Aphrodite had no clue how to answer. Nonetheless, she didn't regret coming. Dionysos seemed like his old self, and he filled the silence with fresh bottles of wine when necessary.

If it wasn't him, it was Hermes, telling some tale about his many trips across the Aegean. All this joy didn't keep her from sensing

Hephaestus's tension however. Even as he smiled at his brothers' jokes and had a riveting conversation about naval forces with Athena and Hades, his worry radiated off of him in waves. She swore she could inhale it. At the very least, she was getting a contact high.

As Athena and Hades began speaking of something else, Aphrodite reached beneath the table and slipped her hand over his thigh. She felt him blanch, but he didn't react otherwise, shoving a forkful of potatoes into his mouth. She suppressed a smirk against the lip of her glass, and what started off as an innocent comfort evolved into anything but quite quickly. She slid it up further as he snatched up his wine, taking a long drink and gulping loud enough for her to hear. She knew that he knew someone would suspect something if he reached for her hand now. She put her bets on that fact alone. She also knew she would pay for it the moment they were alone.

She couldn't wait.

"How are things going with the investigation?" Hades asked him now, and Aphrodite tried to stifle her laughter as he choked down the food he was still trying to chew. "Any news?"

"Uh, not much," Hephaestus managed, wiping his mouth.

"What's holding you up so long, brother?" Ares asked now, obviously waiting for a chance to jump down his older brother's throat. "Seems like you haven't made much progress at all since this started. You can't drag her along with you forever, you know."

Hephaestus didn't seem at all bothered by Ares's antics, but that could be due to her *distraction*. Either way, it certainly bothered her. He spoke about her as if she weren't sitting right there.

"These things take time, Brother, and these are delicate matters. I want to make the city as safe as possible for her, not just lock her away in a tower to guard." Ares' face reddened as Heph turned back to their uncle. "We've been checking into a few warehouses in each district, and... ACTUALLY." Hephaestus nearly yelled the word as her hand skated up against his crotch, and he shifted in his seat. "Uh, I - the warehouse on Delos. Do you - have you - used it recently?"

"On Delos?" Hades raised his brow. "No, I can't say I have. I gave your brothers access to two warehouses on the westside, but the one on Delos hasn't been used much for a number of years. My father used to operate a brewery there, but—"

"A brewery?" Dionysos gasped, eyes wide like he'd just been given a gift. Aphrodite giggled. "Now that's what we need. Wine is great, but no one likes a one-trick pony, you know."

"You make whiskey," Ares shot at him, momentarily tearing his gaze from Hephaestus.

"Okay, well no one likes a two-trick pony either." Dionysos shrugged.

"You are anything but, baby brother," Hephaestus assured him.

Aphrodite caught Heph's lopsided smile in response to Dio's bashful grin, and she smiled too. This was the first time she had really seen him interact with his family in a setting so casual, and he was much softer than she would have imagined despite seeing how sensitive he was with Dio. While she'd seen a glimpse of it here and there, it was pure in this space, and she savored it.

"Why do you ask?" Hades questioned, steering the conversation back to the initial topic.

Hephaestus sobered, turning his gaze on his uncle even as Aphrodite's fingers dusted over the outline of his length. He cleared his throat almost in warning.

"We went by there before we came here," Heph pushed out. "I could tell there was someone there, but - I didn't wanna chance going in. Didn't want a repeat of last time."

"Were you followed?" Persephone asked now.

"We—"

"We weren't followed, not this time," Aphrodite immediately interjected.

While she hated lying to Persephone, she didn't wish to worry her right now in front of everyone. Besides, it wasn't really a lie. No one had followed them. Someone had simply tipped off those they were pursuing, most likely someone in Lush. Ares was still red in the face with all of the things he could not say, and the thought of having everyone else speculate about what was going on made her stomach churn.

"I had the entire block swept before we left," Hephaestus added.

"No one followed, but I could tell someone had just left the warehouse before we got there. I don't know if they were alerted somehow, but I let Achilles know when we got here. He'll make sure it's swept."

"Maybe it's best not to take Aphrodite *into* the danger," Persephone hissed at him.

"Yeah, that sounds counterproductive," Ares growled.

"He's my bodyguard for a reason," Aphrodite shot back without thought. "No matter where we are, I'm safest with him."

A fork clattered against a plate, and Aphrodite assumed it was Ares', but she didn't bother to look. As Dio refilled her glass, she and Persephone locked eyes. The latter looked away first, but Aphrodite knew that reckoning would come as swiftly as Hephaestus's would. She simply wouldn't enjoy it as much.

She was right too. Before she could really torture him, Persephone was beckoning her from the table and out onto the balcony, no longer caring for propriety. She hesitated only a moment before standing, drawing Heph's gaze to her like moth to flame. She didn't miss the way it bled into her back as she retreated from him. Until the doors closed behind her of course. Then she missed it very much.

"I'm not even gonna ask," Persephone immediately huffed, leaning back against the railing. "You're just gonna start talking."

"Am I?" Aphrodite returned innocently.

"Girl, don't play with me. If you think I'm over what happened the other day-"

"Oh, don't worry. I don't."

"Good, because I'm not, and you're not doing yourself any favors right now, so talk."

She shrugged, standing against the railing beside her. "What do you want me to say?"

"Oh, I don't know, something about how you went from hating a guy to fucking him for 24 hours straight to the point where I thought you were dead."

"We didn't fuck the whole time." Persephone glared at her, and Aphrodite's resolve began to splinter. She huffed. "If I had the answer to that, I'd give it to you, but I don't. I don't know what happened. I just know that it did, and I'm not sorry about it."

"And what are you gonna do when all this is over?"

"I'm just trying to survive 'all this' first, okay?"

"And that has to involve fucking him?"

"How are you mad when you were the one always teasing me about him!"

"I was kidding! I only did it to annoy you. I never thought something would actually happen!"

"Well it did!"

They stared at one another, Persephone's anger clashing with Aphrodite's agitation. She wasn't sure what her best friend hoped to gain from this conversation, some kind of vow that she wouldn't do it again, but if that was the case, she would be sorely disappointed. Even so, Aphrodite wasn't sure she was able to explain her evolving feelings for Hephaestus just yet.

"And Ares?" Persephone pushed on though her voice had lowered again.

"What about him?"

"They're family, Aphrodite. Family who already almost lost a brother. Hades' family. *My* family."

Aphrodite's brows shot up into her hair. "And what am I?"

"Aphrodite, don't—"

"Don't what? If you honestly think I did this to ruin your little family—"

"I didn't say that! All I'm saying is to be - more responsible!"

"Well, I'm sorry not all of us find our true love so easily."

Persephone opened her mouth to retaliate but seemed to think better of what she was going to say. She paused, staring at her best friend for a long beat before she deflated. Aphrodite looked away. She felt ill with it, the idea that Persephone would be more concerned with a feud among brothers than with her best friend's feelings, but at the same time, it put into perspective just how bizarre this development was.

"Is that what you think Hephaestus is?" she inquired cautiously as if she feared Aphrodite might run off at the implication. "Or is that what you want him to be?"

Aphrodite scoffed. "You think I want him of all people to be? Really?" She turned away though, looking out over the Styx District. "The fact you think that I would just - abandon all my standards for him is a take, I'll tell you that."

"'Dite..."

She held up her hand. "Look, I don't know what he is. All I know is that - I like being with him. When we're together, just the two of us, it's not messy or complicated or filled with pointless expectations. The only time that it is is when we have to take everybody and everything else into consideration. I don't know what happens after all this, and I don't know how he feels about me. For all I know, it's all just - revenge sex or something for me being so much trouble. What matters to me right now is that he doesn't ask anymore of me than what I give him."

"Unlike Ares."

"Unlike everyone."

"Everyone?"

Aphrodite shook her head. "Forget it."

Persephone reached for her arm. "No, I'm not gonna forget it, Aphrodite. You are my family too. Don't think I could ever forget that."

"It sounded like you just did."

"And that was fucked up for me to say, and I'm sorry. But you're my other half, girl. You know that. And - look, I just don't want my family, including you, to fall apart if something goes wrong."

Aphrodite chewed her lip. There were many things she dared not say, most of which she had buried beneath her success and motivation, but that did not make them any less true. Saying them out loud felt like a curse however, one she wasn't certain she could overcome, not before the damage was done. But Persephone's expectant stare bulldozed through her defenses, and she was left with nothing but those truths.

She sighed. "—You left your mama's house, on your own, and all you have to do is drive through the Harvest District to remind yourself. But I - I never left my daddy's house, and I don't need him alive to be reminded of that. It fell in on me, and I had to rebuild it. The building is new, but - the bricks are not. Just because he doesn't scare me anymore doesn't mean he has no effect. I'm still trying to live up to his expectations."

"But, 'Dite, you don't have to."

"And logically, I know that, but - my heart doesn't always listen to my head."

She smirked. "I know."

Aphrodite shoved her away, but her lips twitched nonetheless. "The point is that you want me to be smarter. Ares wants me to be softer. My enemies don't want me to be at all, and I'm starting to forget who I wanna be. But Heph - he knows who I am. He may not like all the things I am, but instead of constantly pushing me to try and change, all he's done is push himself to accept it. To see me and - and to care for me even when I'm at my worst. Even when I'm pushing him or pissing him off or making his life harder. He still won't let anything bad happen to me."

"And I'm grateful to him for that," Persephone assured her. "I really am."

"And - Heph has nothing to do with Ares. I - I honestly forget about everything and everyone when I'm with him. He drives me crazy most of the time, but - believe it or not, we've gotten along better since spending more time together."

"Oh, I believe it. I never understood why you hated him in the first place."

Aphrodite thought she may have that answer now. "He's practical. He's - he's logical. He's everything I'm not, everything I never wanted to be, but - I realize those aren't bad things. I just - don't want them to be the only things."

"And are they?"

She smiled now. "He can be - very creative when he needs to be."

Persephone gags. "Okay, shut up, Nasty."

"Hey, you asked. I'm just sayin'. He's - he's good."

"Nothing like Zeus?"

Aphrodite recalled what Hephaestus had told her the night before, how he'd confided in her so easily. She wouldn't dare say a word about it to anyone, not even Persephone, but the thought alone had her heart fluttering. He trusted her with parts of himself he had yet to entrust to anyone else despite how many reasons she had given him not to.

"No, nothing at all like Zeus," Aphrodite admitted. "A lot like Hades but - different too."

"Yeah, I thought so too. Before I mean, but being in the loop now, I see it. He spends a lot of time with Charon though, and according to Hades, it's always been that way. They bonded really well when he was a kid, and Charon is the one who taught him how to create weapons."

"Yeah, that's what he-" Aphrodite perked up, a thought striking her, accompanied by the memory of that familiar eagle inked on Hephaestus's chest.

"What? What's wrong?"

She quickly tucked that thought away. "Oh, nothing, I just - I think that's where Heph gets his observational skills from."

"Oh, for sure. The two of them are scary with how easy they read people."

They were silent for a moment until Persephone glanced at her.

"Okay, I'm just gonna ask, and you can't get mad."

Aphrodite gave her a confused look. "Okay?"

"Do you think that maybe this - these feelings for him exist because he's sort of your knight in shining armor right now?"

She inhaled slowly. "I considered that, but honestly, that part of his job irks me the most. I don't want to be saved, not by him or anyone else. I used to think so before, you know, like that was such an important part of the fairy tale, but now? Actually going through all this where I feel helpless is just - no. I wouldn't wish for this. It's agony."

"So then - you like him? For real?"

Aphrodite turned back to the railing, leaning over it with a sigh. "Yeah, I think I do."

She could feel Persephone's gaze morph from withering to observant, and she waited patiently, her eyes still fixed on the horizon. As she replayed her own responses, she came to realize —or rather, to accept— that Hephaestus wasn't just a warm body. She'd obviously already known it before Persephone started asking, but now that she had spilled it all, there was no denying it any longer. He meant something to her. She just didn't know how to put it into words. Truth be told, she wasn't sure she was ready to.

Maybe there *were* still things to be scared of.

"How bad was it?" Hephaestus asked as they got back into his car later that night.

"Not as bad as it could've been," she offered.

"So not as bad as it's gonna be when we get home for what you pulled in there."

She liked the way he said 'home'. It almost spared her the shudder that ran through her when she registered his threat. "Why does it have to wait until we get home?"

She was quick to reach for him before he could pull his seatbelt over his body, unbuckling his belt and dipping her hand into his pants.

"Hey," he hissed although his own hands remained on the belt. "Someone could see us."

"Please. No one can see us through your dark ass windows."

The truth was that she was eager and unwilling to wait. She had wanted him all night, and judging by how hard he was by the time she freed his cock from his boxers, the feeling was mutual. She gave him a few good tugs as her mouth found his neck, nipping and sucking down to his collar.

He shivered, the seatbelt crashing against the window as it slipped from his hands. He spat her name through gritted teeth, but when she prompted him to recline his seat, he did just that. As soon as he did, she bent over his lap, taking the tip of his dick into her mouth. He threw himself back against the seat with a groan, a hand slapping against the steering wheel as the other dived into her hair.

"I told you that you would - only get dessert if you were a good girl."

She was no longer listening to him. She removed her hand completely and sunk down his shaft, hollowing her cheeks and allowing her tongue to press into the velvety skin she worshipped. It didn't take long before she had him rutting up into her mouth, and she reveled in it, bracing her hand against his thigh as she bobbed her head. Watching his control fracture and wane, even from this angle, was a magic in and of itself. While she would much rather have his hands all over her, his fingers yanking at her hair before guiding her back down would tide her over. For now.

The way he used her for his pleasure, foregoing his commonplace composure for this carnal need, had her panties damp after all the tension at dinner, which was brand new to her and turned her on even more. She moaned just as his head hit the back of her throat, causing her to gag until spit dripped down into his lap. He hissed before speeding up, and chills rolled down her spine at the revelation that it had turned him on too. She was eager to unravel him, to see him lose all semblance of control on behalf of her will.

She didn't have to wait long.

He forced her all the way down until her nose was pressed against his thigh, pumping up into her throat as her eyes watered. Still, she choked him down, and as she did, he pulsed and broke apart, coating her throat in his thick load. Though she tried hard to swallow it all, some managed to spew from the sides of her mouth. Between that and the roar he filled the car with, she was already so wound up, rubbing her thighs together in a desperate search for friction. She busied herself by licking him clean once he let her up, regaining her breath in the process.

"Fuck," he groaned, laying back limp against the seat. "It was supposed to be a punishment, not a reward."

"Sorry, Daddy," she purred, not at all apologetic. "I just wanted to be a good girl."

"Mhm."

"You can just punish me twice now." She sat up and wiped the corners of her lips. "Preferably soon."

He tucked his softening cock back into his trousers and buckled them up before raising his seat and putting his seatbelt on. "Yeah, you can wait. That's part of the punishment."

She rolled her eyes but sat back regardless, pulling her seatbelt on too. Resting her head back, she looked over at him as he put the car in reverse. Her eyes moved over his trembling hands wrapped around the steering wheel and his narrowed gaze as he focused on the street.

Everything she'd confessed to Persephone and herself came flooding back, and her heart thudded in her chest. Even sucking his dick in the front seat of his car couldn't eclipse the truth of the matter. There they were, her feelings for him, like stars in the darkest sky. Impossible to ignore, impervious to condemnation, she brushed her fingers along them like a priceless jewel. She could not tell him. She could not ruin this.

"What?" he asked suddenly, yanking her violently from her thoughts.

"Nothing," she shot back defensively.

Still, there was merely a beat of silence before she moved a hand to the back of his neck once more, playing with the hair there. He didn't tense this time. Instead, he placed one hand on her thigh, and she exhaled a breath that left her feeling lighter than she ever had. Maybe she need not tell him at all. Maybe this was enough for now.

They arrived back at the club to find it quickly filling for the night, but she was eager to get upstairs and take her punishment as he saw fit. She reached for his cane from the backseat and handed it to him before sliding out of the car and rounding it to his side.

"I have to talk to Achilles," he sighed. "I'll meet you upstairs."

Usually she would simply nod and pretend she wasn't bothered, but something in her had tilted, and she was unable to do such a thing.

"Uh uh." She shook her head firmly. "And that's an order. You're going upstairs with me right now, and you can talk to him after."

She waited, staring up into his concrete expression and fully expecting to be reprimanded for stepping out of line, for challenging Daddy. Not that she wouldn't still try and goad him into fucking her in the elevator. But at last, the left side of his mouth curved upward. He reached out with his free hand, brushing his knuckles under her jaw. Her knees felt prepared to buckle, but she did not relent.

He did though.

"Okay. Lead the way, Princess."

She did, as quickly as she could, taking his hand and dragging him into the elevator, scraping her card against the keypad in a hurry. She was thrilled when he swept her into his arm, kissing her hard as the car ascended, his tongue swiping through her lips until she parted them. She kissed him with a hunger unbridled and unbound, the taste of him still tickling the back of her throat.

"I need you, Daddy," she admitted through harsh breaths as his lips scaled down her neck. "Please."

The moment the doors opened behind her, he was stalking forward, half carrying her into the living room. He was heading for the bedroom, but she dragged him down onto the couch where they rutted against each other like teenagers who had never known touch. His cane fell beside the couch as clothes were discarded, and her hands smoothed over his skin like a map once he was hovering over her, tracing the majestic feathers of the eagle staring back at her.

How could she miss having him against her, inside of her, after so few hours apart? She pleaded with him again, and she felt him inflate between her thighs, lathering his cock with her faint arousal. It would be enough. It had to be. She wasn't letting him leave this couch.

She reached down between them, taking him in her hand and stroking him thoroughly before guiding him to her entrance.

"Punish me, Daddy," she hissed against his ear as his teeth scraped across her collarbone. "Hard."

"Is it really a punishment if you're begging for it, Princess?" he countered.

"If I tell you no, can you pretend I didn't beg for it?"

He grinned at her. "Naw, I like when you beg for it."

He didn't hesitate further nor did he disappoint. The moment he was in range, he pushed into her, glancing off her clit with each thrust and sending her scrabbling back up the couch with a shriek. She floundered to find purchase, wrapping her limbs around him as best she could. He drew his knees up, angling his stroke so that it hit a new spot, and she was immediately opening fresh wounds across his back.

"Daddy! Yes!"

"Are you sorry?" he grunted. "Tell me - you're sorry for being a bad girl."

"I'm - sorry! I'm - so sorry I was a bad girl, Daddy, fuck!"

Before she could continue, he claimed her mouth, biting down on her lip before soothing it with his tongue. She returned the kiss fervently, her shoulders now braced against the arm of the couch. He fucked her so good, it was damn near disgraceful. In all of her past relationships or trysts, in the few years she had worked in her own clubs, never had she been exposed to a stroke game this good. Would he ever stop surprising her?

She really fucking hoped not.

"Now be a good girl-" he breathed as their mouths parted. "And cum for Daddy."

His voice seeped into her skin, low and seductive, and every nerve in her was touched by it. He sped up his thrust, leaving her helpless as her orgasm crept up on her with the mercy of a natural disaster. He reached down, palming her ass as he plunged into her, bottoming out with each stroke. She could take no more. She opened her mouth, but nothing came out as her body gave itself up to the immense ecstasy he bestowed upon her.

Climax came at an alarming rate, an out-of-body experience that left her little more than a shuddering mess beneath him. He kept fucking her, his grunts growing louder until his back locked up and his cock jerked inside of her. He came with quick, punishing thrusts, her name filling the air as she clung to him.

She shivered as his warmth filled her, and she felt whole. She kissed up his neck and jaw, eager just to be close. He fell against her, and she held him tighter, her lips brushing over the side of his head softer now. She settled into her soreness, swearing she would live in this moment forever if she could. At the very least, she would keep him here permanently.

"Come on," he huffed after a long while, kissing the side of her head.

"Where are we going?" she groaned.

"To bed."

"You're not gonna leave, are you?"

"No, I'll text Achilles and talk to him tomorrow. Come on."

"Why can't we stay here?"

"It's harder to stretch my legs here, and - your bed is much more comfortable."

She blinked up at him before a smile crossed her features. "Comfortable for what?"

He gave her a defiant smirk. "Sleeping."

"Mm mm. You're not doing any sleeping tonight."

"Oh? Is that an order?"

"It is."

He rolled his eyes. "Needy girl."

"And it's all your fault."

"I guess it's my responsibility to handle it then, huh?"

"Now you're getting it."

He pushed himself up before helping her to her feet, and she followed him into the bedroom once he grabbed his phone. As he texted Achilles, she moved to collapse atop the bed. As soon she did, Hephaestus's sharp eyes turned on her as though she'd thrown something at him. He was immediately alert. She raised her head, giving him a confused look.

"What?" she questioned.

"What was that?" he hissed back.

"What?" She was confused as to what he meant. "I - don't know. I didn't hear—"

He put a hand up before she could sit up. "Wait. Don't move."

She watched as he carefully got down on the floor beside the bed, peering beneath. Then there was dead silence. She couldn't even hear him breathing. As if he was holding it.

"Heph?" she said slowly. "What is it?"

When he emerged again, his gaze was dark, so dark that it scared her.

"Listen to me," he said, reaching for her but not touching her, almost like he was afraid to. "Do not move. Do not get off of this bed. Do not shift, don't lift your body. Nothing. Do you understand me?"

"What is it?" she asked, furrowing her brow. "Heph?"

He visibly swallowed. "I need you to trust me, Aphrodite. Can you do that? Please?"

The look on his face chilled her to the bone, and she wasn't sure what to think or what to do. But there was really only one possibility for what was happening here, wasn't there? And that possibility put her, and him, in grave danger. Therefore, there was only one option.

She nodded.

"Relax, Baby," he said softly, so soft she could cry. "Just do as I say, and I swear, I will not let anything happen to you."

And she believed him.

Chapter Twenty-Three

HEPHAESTUS

He'd known the click the moment he'd heard it, his ears attuned to any and every possible danger even in the midst of passion. He berated himself, lowering himself onto his belly upon the carpet. The one time he hadn't swept her room first, and all because he was thinking with the wrong fucking head coming in here. One little mistake, and it could have cost him everything.

As he surveyed the charge attached to the underside of the bed, his mind went through a million different outcomes and possibilities, probing and poking at the few ways this could have happened, but none of them seemed concrete. How someone had gotten up here while Lush was crawling with his forces was entirely beyond him, and he was ill with it. He couldn't help thinking what would have happened if he hadn't heard it, if she would have investigated the sound, getting on and off the bed before he had a chance to stop her, to save her. That thought alone plagued him with a level of fear he had never known. He couldn't lose her, not like this, not now. Not ever.

She trusted him too. He knew she trusted him because she hadn't asked another question since he asked her to do so. She lay there, tense but patient, waiting for him to save the day, the woman that didn't want to be saved. He was more grateful for her composure than he could ever express.

He carefully maneuvered himself beneath the bed, his phone in one hand and one of his blades in the other. He hadn't disarmed too many explosives in his short life, but he believed he'd put enough together to figure it out. He wasn't about to call anyone up here though. Getting a bomb into her sanctuary took skill, but it also took access beyond any normal level guard, and he trusted no one. Even Achilles would have to be considered, and while it insulted Hephaestus himself to even think it, he must. They had been taking risks with her safety for too long. This had to end, and it had to end soon.

He took his time inspecting the charge. It was by no means an amateur project, and it certainly wasn't homemade. That was good news. Industrial charges generally followed the same design, and any extra bells and whistles were a signature of its creator. He knew the signatures of many arms dealers and explosive experts, which meant he could eliminate the known ones in Khaos Falls. This charge was too intricate to belong to the Cyclops and far too simple to belong to Prometheus. Still, once he managed to get the faceplate off, it looked far more familiar.

And every moment he spent under the bed with it, his anger grew into something feral and ferocious. He'd always been good at separating business from pleasure, but that was not the case right now, and he wouldn't waste energy trying to deny it. This was fucking personal. He knew what that meant in a matter of moments, what it said about him and his feelings for her, but he didn't care. He would protect her regardless. It just hurt more now. That fear, he felt it all.

Sweat collected upon his brow as he drew the white wire out from the bundle, slipping the blade beneath it. With a swift movement, he severed it. There was a beep, but he could now hear the faint ticking of a clock. A failsafe. He had expected as much, carefully isolating the blue wire now and cutting it as well. The charge beeped three times aloud before the lights on it shut off completely. He breathed out a sigh of relief, and he heard her do the same, signaling she must have figured out what was occurring.

He carefully inspected the rest of the device, making sure there were no further failsafes or other traps before he detached it from the bedframe. Slipping out from beneath the bed, he placed it on the bedside table before turning to her. He held out his hand, and she quickly took it, standing up and throwing her arms around him at the same time he wrapped his own around her. They embraced for the longest time, and he kissed her head and cheeks until his lips were sore. The worry bled from his body like poison, and he sweated out the anger like a fever. For now. There would be time to collect it later. At the moment, he had to act.

"Get dressed," he finally said, pulling back and pressing his forehead to hers.

"What - who could have-" she started, but he shook his head.

"We're gonna figure that out, and we're gonna stop this. I promise you. They are not gonna take you from me. Not today, not ever."

And he meant it. That theory he had conceived earlier evolved further, but it would take more than a theory to put this to rest. Still, this was arguably the riskiest move their enemies had made thus far, and yes, 'their' because they were his enemies now too.

It took some time for Aphrodite to pull herself together. Hephaestus didn't hurry her. He knew how deep the endless betrayal cut into her, and he knew it wasn't easy for her big heart to take. While she might have hidden it well for any and everyone else, he could see right through the facade, and not because he had feelings for her. It pained him in a way he never thought it would, but he did his best to focus. For once, his superpower felt more like a burden.

They made it downstairs within the hour, sitting in his car with the doors locked as Hephaestus inspected the device now laid in his lap. She wouldn't look at it, and he didn't blame her. He tucked away his own frustration, hoarding it beneath his tongue to chew on later when he need not hide it. Frustration wasn't even the right word. No, what he was feeling was far worse. It was fury, white hot and ruthless, and it would be shaped into a weapon that would be wielded against the enemy when he exposed them.

There was a tap on the window, and Aphrodite jumped slightly beside him. He placed a hand on her thigh as he unlocked the back door for Achilles, who slid in behind him.

"What's going on?" Achilles immediately asked as Heph locked the door again.

Hephaestus answered by handing the device over the seat to him. Achilles hesitated before taking it, and Hephaestus watched him in the rearview mirror. Nothing in his face suggested deception, but more importantly, nothing about it implied prior knowledge.

"Is this-" He turned over the device, pulling out the wires and looking over them. "Where was this? Was this on the car?"

Hephaestus' jaw clenched. "No. It was under her bed."

Achilles looked up. "What - that's impossible. How would it be under the bed?"

"That's what I would like to know."

"No one has been given access up there. Not a single person."

"But someone could have added access if they used the computer in Hector's office. *Your* office. Has anyone else been in there?"

"Not since I've been here and not since we changed the codes and made new key cards. I lock it up every time I leave, even for a moment. And even if someone had gone in there, they would have needed to get into the system, create the access codes, and put them on a card. There's no way."

"There was some way!" she suddenly shouted.

Hephaestus reached for her hand, squeezing it in his own. That theory now took root in his mind and began to bloom, and he knew that now was as good a time as any to pluck it.

"I want you to review the tapes," he instructed Achilles now, meeting the other man's eyes in the mirror. "I doubt you'll find anything, but I want to have a window. They know that we know her security has been compromised, and they're using it to their advantage. Messing with the tapes won't be such a big thing. If anything, it proves their reach, and it makes me doubt my own men."

Achilles' face paled. "Me?"

"If I truly doubted you, you wouldn't be in this car right now, Achilles."

He took a breath before nodding. "Well, this doesn't give me much confidence in my workplace either. No one has access to that office."

"We'll talk about it tomorrow." Hephaestus needed the night to think through his next move, and even if he trusted Achilles, he would handle Aphrodite's safety on his own. "Tonight, you sweep this place. And I mean you, not anyone else. Her office, the conference rooms, the garage. Then I need the last of the warehouses checked. If any of them are occupied, they are to be left alone until we speak again. No tails, no scouts, nothing more than a confirmation. I just need to find one that's occupied by someone who shouldn't be occupying it. My guess is one of the two my brothers are supposed to start using."

"Why? I thought we were focusing on the ones not being used?"

"I asked Hermes after dinner tonight. They haven't signed the leases. My uncle doesn't really need them to. It's more a formality, meaning whoever's been using the warehouses doesn't know they're set to be taken over. Plus, the safest place to be is the Styx District."

"Because it's the most dangerous to infiltrate."

"Exactly."

"You don't think they've infiltrated your uncle's district, have you?"

"No, I don't. You keep this between us, and tomorrow we'll talk. I'll meet you in the security office at noon. Tonight, we're staying elsewhere, a place I'll share with no one." He felt her shift in her seat. "Text me once you review the tapes."

Achilles nodded before getting out of the car, leaving the device on the backseat. Once the door closed, Aphrodite looked at him.

"You really trust him?"

"I do," Hephaestus assured her.

"Where are we going?"

He didn't answer, instead putting the car in reverse and pulling out of the lot.

"Are you hungry?" he inquired instead.

"I'm tired," she replied.

"I assume this was a bit of a mood killer too?"

She glared at him. "Don't joke about it, not right now."

He nodded, pulling her hand to his mouth and kissing her knuckles until he felt her relax. "I'll call my uncle, let him know we're on our way."

Her sigh was that of pure agitation. "Please don't. Just - please. I can't have Persephone more worried than she is right now."

"We'll be safest in Asphodel."

"Well - go to the second safest place then. I can't handle that right now, Heph."

He didn't argue further. There was only one other place he could take her, and while he knew it was just as secure as his uncle's casino — in fact, more so considering he was the only one with access and knowledge of its existence save for the two people he trusted most in the world— it was always the last resort. He had never taken anyone there, not even Athena or his brothers. Desperate times and all that, he supposed.

"I bet she regrets putting me at your side," he chuckled darkly.

"She does not, Hephaestus," she shot back.

"What did she say to you then? On the balcony?"

She scoffed. "It wasn't about work, I assure you."

"She made it pretty clear that my current methods of - taking you to crime scenes isn't allowed."

"I'm a big girl. I go where I please. I know I'm safe with you, and that's what matters."

"If something happens to you—"

"It will be my fault!"

"But I'll have to live with it!"

The sudden rise of each of their voices seemed to shock them both, silence falling amidst the echoes of their words. Still, the reality of it seemed to sink in, the fear that came with it. She pulled her hand from his, but before he could panic, it found the back of his neck. He placed his own in her lap.

The Lush District soon morphed into the Market District outside the windows, neon and pearl giving way to high rises and billboard advertisements. He turned onto the coastal highway, which rose up over the land it stretched across, the obsidian waters of the Aegean visible in the distance despite the dark. The moon glittered upon its glassy surface, full and bright. Dense clouds surrounded it idly, and judging by the thickness in the air, Hephaestus guessed it just might snow. It didn't happen often, but he remembered what his mother used to say about snow so early in winter.

It was a bad omen.

Hephaestus made sure they weren't being tailed, doing a few laps around the block before he pulled into the deserted lot of the Khaos Car Dealership. The windows were currently shuttered in thick, metal curtains, and the place was undoubtedly empty. He drove around and behind the building, parking his car right up against the door of the attached garage.

"You're gonna hide me in a car dealership?" Aphrodite blurted, shooting him a confused look.

He only smirked in response before reaching beneath his steering wheel and popping open the compartment beneath with the pad of his index finger against the discreet fingerprint scanner. He extracted a slim, black remote from within and hit the button at the top. The door before them slid up and open, allowing him to drive forward into the garage, which currently housed several cars, some of them lifted and others covered in tarp. To their right, through large glass windows, the showroom was visible albeit dark and absent of life. Heph parked the car among the others then reached back to retrieve the device and his cane. When Aphrodite only stared at him as he stepped out of the car, he beckoned her to follow suit.

"Come on," he instructed simply. "We're almost there."

Eventually, she clambered out of the car as well, grabbing her bag and shutting the door. He pulled a tarp from one of the shelves and tossed it over his car, circling it and fixing the blue plastic so that it covered the entire vehicle. Then he took her hand and led her towards the showroom, unlocking the door with a key on his car keyring.

He locked it behind them again then led her deeper into the room and straight up to one of the show platforms where a black sports car currently sat. Utilizing his remote once more, he unlocked it, opening the door for her. She only glanced at him once before getting inside, her bag on her lap, and he quickly rounded to the driver's side, sliding in beside her. One more click of the remote, and the platform began to sink into the ground, drawing a gasp from her.

"What the—" Her eyes were wide as she turned to him. "Are you serious?"

"Hey, I offered to take you to Asphodel."

She merely gawked at him as the car descended into another garage, *his* garage.

When the platform stopped moving, he instructed her to get out, and this time, she didn't question it. After sending the car and the platform back up, he led her across the dark space to what appeared to be nothing more than a rock wall.

"We come back with our shield or on it," he said, loud and clear.

"What?" Aphrodite asked.

But he wasn't talking to her. Before them, the wall cracked and split, revealing a steel door beneath. He pressed his palm and all five fingers of his left hand against it, green lights flickering through the metal as it collected his prints. Once it cleared those, a large red dot appeared above his hand. He moved closer, allowing the retinal scanner to sweep over his eye. Only then did the door swing open.

"Where the fuck are we?" she whispered, although she sounded more bewildered than angry.

"The most impenetrable place in Khaos Falls," he said with the utmost certainty as the door closed behind them. "Embedded in the cliffs on the border of my uncle's district and my brothers'."

He had no doubt of his claim because he had made it so. He had found the place long ago, remnants of a reign long before his time and his uncle's. He spent years fortifying it into a formidable fortress with only Charon's help and Hades' knowledge. It was his workplace. It was also his home.

"Wait," she said, looking around. They were now in a normal looking living room with a normal looking kitchen on the other side of a counter. "Is this your place?'

"And the safest place in the city," he conceded. "I have another house near Dio and Hermes. That's my official address with everybody, but this is my place. You're only the fourth person who's ever been inside and knows it exists. Let's keep it that way, alright?"

"Who were the other two? Since I'm assuming number one is you."

"Charon and my uncle."

Overall, the place was nothing inherently dazzling. He lived a simple life. He always had. The furniture was picked for comfort rather than show, and the majority of the place was dedicated to his workshop. Hephaestus himself was barely here anymore even before he'd become Aphrodite's personal guard. Since becoming head of city security, he spent more nights in the headquarters than anywhere else. When he did come, it was to his workshop where he built the weapons that protected the city. It dwelled beneath the apartment, the walls and ceiling thick and more impenetrable than the walls of the city itself.

"It's exactly what I expected," Aphrodite hummed as they entered the living room.

"And what's that?" he asked, turning on the light.

"Bare walls and dark colors everywhere."

"I'm not here much, and I don't care for bright colors."

"You must hate the club then."

He flinched at the thought of the bright red walls. "I've - grown accustomed."

She smirked over her shoulder at him. "I'm sure."

He led her towards the hall and all the way down to the master bedroom, setting her bag on the bed. He took a moment to soak in how nice it was to be home, away from the crowds and the noise of the city. He'd begun to build these walls at a time in his youth where he'd come to realize Zeus would rather see him dead, and his mother wouldn't mind that much either if it made the man love her more. Athena had just come to them shortly before, and Hephaestus had known then that there was no place at Zeus's table for him. While he knew they weren't kin by then, it still hurt. Even with a seat at his uncle's and his bond with Charon, he felt out of place, so he'd decided to build his own. One covered in armor.

"Bathroom's right there," he informed her, pointing to the door on the adjacent wall. "Make yourself comfortable."

"Why didn't you bring me here before? If it's the safest place in the city?"

"Would you have come?"

She stared at him a moment before shrugging. "Maybe."

He thought back to her argument with Ares. "Naw, you wouldn't have. You wouldn't want to look weak, hiding away while your district needed leadership. I respected that, and I knew I could keep you safe anywhere."

"Cocky as always."

"Have I not earned it?"

She rolled her eyes. "Maybe a little, but keep it to a minimum."

"I'll do my best, Princess."

She moved around the room, taking it in as she went. There wasn't much apart from the TV mounted on the wall, the game console Dionysos had insisted on giving him for his birthday one year, and the sound system Hephaestus had taken a liking to. Beyond that, there was the bed, a chest of drawers, and the walk-in closet. He watched her open the latter, lips curling as her fingers brushed over the collection of dark shirts. Worry drew his brows together beneath an air of curiosity. She was obscuring her stress once more, and he was willing to let her. She plucked one of his shirts from the hanger and brought it out, laying it on the bed.

"I also expected all of your shirts to be black, but I saw a bit of blue in there, so that's refreshing," she said, pulling off her shirt and unclasping her bra. "A red one in the back too. Is that for special occasions or something?"

"My uncle bought it for me, but I've never found a reason to wear it."

"I'd like to see it on you sometime. I bet you'd look sexy."

"And - what are you doing?"

"Hm?" She bit her lip as she pulled his shirt on, buttoning it halfway before kicking off her pants. "I forgot pajamas."

"Mhm, I'm sure you did."

"Do I get to sleep in your bed?"

He tilted his head. "Only good girls get to sleep there."

She moved towards him, placing her hands on his chest before moving them up to cup his neck and whispering against his jaw.

"But I listened to you, Daddy. I stayed still and didn't move, like a good girl."

He didn't know what to think of her speaking about it like this, but he wasn't going to scold her. Besides, he had to be honest with himself.

He wanted her close, as close as she could be. And then he wanted her to remain there forever.

"You're gonna sleep next to me every night you allow it," he returned, winding his arm around her and pulling her closer. "Because I can't wake up wondering if you're safe. I need to know the moment I open my eyes where you are."

"As part of your job?" she questioned.

"No." He left it at that for a moment before he kissed her, *hard*. When he pulled back however, his eyes were stern. "You know I won't let anything happen to you, right?"

"You haven't yet." She grew serious too, her hands soft on his cheeks. "I trust you, Hephaestus."

His lips twitched. "And - do you still hate me?"

She answered with a kiss that melted away what was left of the frost protecting his heart. He held her tight, and as they fell into bed, he thanked the Fates he'd been enough today. That fear seeped into his bones, reminding him just how close death could linger. He would not forget it.

She undressed him, but that was all she did before settling down in his arms. He rested his forehead against hers, running his fingers down her back.

"Do you still hate *me*?" she inquired now, fingers skating along his jaw.

"I never hated you," he admitted. "You piss me off, and you probably always will, but I don't hate you. I think I might like you a bit now though."

She rolled her eyes. "You think?"

"Yeah, I'll let you know another day."

"I'll be waiting."

"So will I."

They fell asleep like that, holding one another as close as possible beneath the warmth of his sheets. He didn't mind it at all, the simplicity of it, finding comfort in her breath on his neck. He'd lied. He knew it now, and he knew it in a way that it could never be unknown. He didn't like her. Or at least he didn't *just* like her. No, he was far beyond that.

He came to slowly at her beckoning. She had turned around at some point in the night, and now, her ass ground against him at a deliberate pace. His arm remained wound around her, and through his haze of sleep, he dragged her closer. Palming her breasts, he let his mouth find her neck, eliciting a moan that brought him into full consciousness.

He hardened against her, his hips meeting hers in these teasing rolls. Her hand found the back of his head, nails scraping his scalp as his tongue traced the column of her throat. He kneaded the supple flesh between his fingers, his shirt having found its way off of her frame sometime before he'd been aroused. He wasn't at all complaining.

She pushed back against him, closer, quicker, and he welcomed it. She gripped his hand, wrenching it from her breast and guiding it down between her legs. He needed no further instruction, his fingers seeking out her clit, and she stretched out like a cat against him.

"I need you," she breathed, reaching back to push down his boxers and release his cock from their confines. "I need you right now, Daddy, please."

She pushed her hips up higher, parting her legs enough to catch his erection between them. He groaned, slipping against the lace of her panties in the most tantalizing way. He licked his lips. Relieving her of his fingers momentarily, he pushed himself up to search the room.

"Where is your bag?" he questioned.

"On the floor," she said, obviously confused. "Why?"

He reached over her, seeking out the bag and unzipping the side pocket. "Lubrication."

"I didn't put any in there."

He pulled out the bottle. "I did."

"So you knew you were getting laid?"

"No, I knew your needy ass would want me to fuck you senseless at some point."

She paused, and he could hear her inhale sharply. Then, "—Thank you."

He pressed a kiss to her temple. "You should know Daddy will take care of you, Princess."

"Mm, yeah, I should. Sorry, Daddy."

"You're gonna be."

He laid back down, turning on his back to slick up his cock. Her grumbling was cut short by a gasp when he yanked down her underwear enough to give him access to her entrance, tracing it with his wet tip until she was moaning aloud. She tried to impale herself, but he matched each movement, remaining just out of reach until her whine echoed through the room. Once her hips stilled, he thrusted up into her, eliciting a hearty cry that tickled his spine. He returned his digits to her clit, stimulating it as he stretched her out and filled her up.

Each stroke pulled him further from sleep until he was wide awake and wanting, plunging into her with growing desperation. Her hand hooked around his hip, nails digging into his ass, and his leg spasmed in response. He pushed through it with a grunt, nearly rolling her on her stomach as he moved that leg between her thighs, parting them further.

Sex had never been too high on his list of priorities and needs, but it was quickly climbing the ranks with the way she made him feel when he was buried inside of her. He slipped his other arm beneath her, placing his forearm over her chest and palming her breast once more. She wound back into him to the best of her ability, dragging him towards the edge.

"That what you needed, Princess?" he snarled against her ear before sinking his teeth into the shell of it.

"Yes," she choked out. "Yes, Daddy, don't - stop. Please."

He wouldn't dare. Every single time they collided, it felt like the first time. It also felt so much better than the last time. And each time they collided, he lost more of himself in her. Whatever mark he left on her skin was layered with a piece of him he would never get back. He only hoped she kept each of them safe.

He felt her walls beginning to constrict around him, and he applied more pressure against her clit. She relinquished her hold on his hip in favor of bracing her hand against the mattress, moan after precious moan spilling out into his sheets. Silently, he hoped they would remain there forever. He fucked more out of her just in case, savoring the melody as he pinched her nipple and dragged his teeth down her neck.

"Heph— Daddy..."

"Cum for me. Right fucking now. You better cum for Daddy."

And just like that, she was falling apart in his arms, her thighs trembling and her pussy spasming around his cock. Still, he stroked faster, her hands scrambling for purchase anywhere they could before a scream ripped free from her throat. He chased it relentlessly, slamming into her again and again until he came on the cusp of a loud shout. She kept grinding back against him, her fingers once again threading into his hair as he rode it out. It was the only thing that anchored him to the earth, his mind going blank and his head obscured by a haze of euphoria. He could wake up like this everyday if given the chance.

As soon as he relaxed into the bed, she slipped off of him with a whimper and turned around in his arms. His mouth met hers immediately as he folded her into his chest, her weight against him somehow making him feel lighter. The events of the evening before came back all at once, that fear clinging to the edge of his mind. He could've lost her. And that wasn't a fucking option.

He brushed a hand through her hair as they parted, his eyes boring into hers.

"I'm gonna leave for a few hours," he informed her softly. She opened her mouth to argue no doubt, but he shook his head. "It's not a negotiation, Princess. I'm not letting you set foot in that club until I make sure it's safe. I promise to do that as quickly as I can, but I need you here, out of danger."

"And if I refuse to stay?" she asked, but her voice was more curious than confrontational.

He smirked. "I'm gonna put you over my knee and show you who's in charge today."

She bit her lip. "Don't threaten me with a good time."

He pressed his lips to hers. "I'll give you a real good time if you're a good girl for me today."

"Mm, you always say that."

"And have I ever disappointed?"

Her lips curled. "I suppose not."

"Then I meant what I said."

She ran her hand over the side of his head. "On one condition then."

"Apart from the good time?"

"Yes."

"What's that?"

"I get to take a shower with you first."

His eyes rolled, but he smiled nonetheless. "Brat."

"Are you complaining?"

"Did I say that?"

"Do we have a deal or not?"

"Yes, Princess, we have a deal."

Chapter Twenty-Four

HEPHAESTUS

It was well into the afternoon when Hephaestus arrived back at Lush on his own. Rain had begun to blanket the city sometime during the night, persisting through the morning until the chill at last turned it to slush and fog. Thick clouds now hung low over the land, threatening snow at any second. It was almost as though the sky were holding its breath, waiting for the perfect moment to unleash its ammunition.

He'd left Aphrodite in his living room, lounging in his shirt and pouting about having to stay there alone. He would have given anything to be with her now, cuddling in bed away from the chill. As much as he hated being apart though, he knew there was no place safer for her right now. But if today went as planned, he could bring her home by nightfall.

He headed straight for the security office where he found Leda at her post as expected.

"Hephaestus!" As per usual, Leda jumped up and rushed to give him a hug, which he had learned to brace for. "It's good to see you. Where's our fearless leader?"

"Errands," he returned with a curt smile.

"Oh? I didn't see you guys last night. You went out, didn't you?"

"Yeah, we ended up staying with family. Didn't wanna drive around drunk, you know."

She giggled although the sound failed to carry as far as it usually did. "That's - Good for you. That's smart. I'm glad you're safe."

"Yeah. Where's Achilles?"

"Doing rounds I think. Do you need me to call him on his radio?"

"Uh, yeah, if you don't mind. It's kind of urgent."

"Should I be worried?"

"No, you're safer here than you could ever be anywhere else. I won't let anything happen to you."

She grinned wide. "My very own protector."

"That's right."

Luckily, Achilles returned mere minutes after she paged him, looking almost relieved to see Hephaestus. He was dressed in the same three-piece suit from the night before although his navy blue tie hung loose around his neck and his white dress shirt was untucked beneath his vest. His eyes were red, exhaustion underscoring them, but he looked cheery all the same.

"We got one," he proclaimed, walking past Hephaestus towards his office. "Come on."

"Wait, a what?" Hephaestus asked, stopping him in his tracks.

"A warehouse. In use." Achilles accentuated the last two words as he turned back around.

"Which one is it?"

Achilles gave him a questioning look, eyes darting towards the back of Leda's head, but Hephaestus didn't yield.

"The one near the river on the Market District border, meaning your assumption was correct. Our guys got multiple vehicles in the immediate vicinity and a decent amount of activity early this morning."

"Okay, good. Clear out the area. I don't want them getting a whiff of us before we're ready to go in. I'll call my uncle, bring in his guys so we got the numbers, and we'll go in there at 3 a.m. Not a moment earlier. They won't see us coming."

"Shouldn't we keep a scout nearby? What if they move again before we go in?"

"Why would they? They must have been there awhile, and they have no clue we're coming. Besides, even if they did, I'd rather miss them than get our guys slaughtered on enemy lines."

Achilles nodded his understanding. "Alright, I'll clear it right now."

"I have to run up to Aphrodite's office real quick, but meet me up front when you're done."

"For what?"

"We're going to Twilight."

"What for?"

"I know who's been feeding information. We're gonna go pick 'em up."

Achilles looked even more lost than before, but he didn't question it. He merely nodded and retreated towards his office, Hephaestus watching him disappear down the hall before turning back to Leda. She was toying with one of the radios, but she looked up at him again as he stepped back in front of her desk.

"Sounds like a lot is going on," she commented with a nervous laugh.

"There is, but it'll be alright after today." He leaned over the desk now, close enough to whisper in her ear. "But if anyone comes into this office after we leave, I want you to call me immediately, alright? And if anyone asks where we went, you don't know."

She nodded immediately. "Of course. You can count on me."

"I know I can. You can get into Achilles' office, right? In case you need a safer place to go."

"Oh, uh, yes. Yeah, I can."

"Good."

He patted her shoulder then turned back the way he'd come, making his way to the elevator and up to Aphrodite's office. Several of his men had kept their station around the second floor, but it was obvious Achilles had swapped out the usual guys for people he was most familiar with.

Callisto stood closest to the office doors, giving Hephaestus a curt nod when he stepped out of the elevator. He returned it before entering the office, immediately moving towards the window. He was eager to see what kind of activity would kick up after he and Achilles had planted that seed in the open hallway, but before he could discern anything at all, the door opened behind him.

"Sorry," Eros's voice called, causing Hephaestus to tense. "Ares is - oh. Heph, where's Aphrodite?"

Hephaestus turned to him just as Ares came barreling into the room, looking around with narrowed eyes.

"Aphrodite isn't here," Hephaestus informed them, his voice filled with nonchalance.

"Where is she?" both Eros and Ares asked.

"Safe. What did you need?"

Eros deferred to Ares, and Hephaestus gave him a nod, permitting him to leave. He didn't wait around, rushing back out of the room and leaving the two brothers alone.

"What do you think you're doing?" Ares growled.

"I'm trying to work, Brother, do you mind?"

"I do mind."

"And I don't care. I have a job to do, and the longer you keep me from it, the longer Aphrodite has to stay hidden, so I—"

"She should have been with me. She would have been safe with me."

"She didn't want to go with you, Ares. She said it to you multiple times, and I'm not here to argue it with you. It's truly none of my business."

"Don't think I didn't notice you two at dinner, Hephaestus. What are you playing at?"

Hephaestus sighed, scrubbing a hand down his face. He didn't want to be having this conversation. He would never want to, but he certainly didn't want to now, and his frustration was already at its boiling point. He and Ares got along as well as two polar opposites could. They always had, but before Athena, Ares had been pitted against his older brother from the day he came into the world, eager to show him up and put him down so that Zeus would name him as his predecessor rather than Hephaestus. The elder brother had never minded. He knew Zeus would give him nothing once he had an actual son of his own. However, Ares had been cruel, honing his father's worst qualities and wielding them against Heph until Hades' careful countering dulled them enough.

But by then, the damage had been done, and it turned out not to matter in the end because Athena became the favorite and Hephaestus had forged his own path, literally. Now, they were brothers, and they were blood, and Hephaestus loved him enough to fight beside him or protect his neck if need be. That affection ended there however. Because Hephaestus knew what lurked beneath the surface of his brother's soft features—a weapon carved by Zeus and enforced by Hera. And it was not a weapon that should ever be underestimated or overlooked.

"Just like your relationship with her is none of my business," Hephaestus started slowly, "My relationship with her is none of yours."

"So you have a relationship? You're saying you—"

"I'm saying that whatever happens or doesn't happen or may happen between Aphrodite and I, or Aphrodite and anyone else in this city, is none of your business, Ares. She told you the truth. Accept that."

"I love her."

"Do you? Because you're standing here throwing a fit instead of letting me work. You only wanted her to go with you to Olympus so you could rope her into a marriage she doesn't want and decisions you made for her. I'm here trying to make sure she can still do what she loves, to protect her for her not for me. So do you really? If you do, you better go back to square one and find a new way to show it because I'll tell you this, Brother. You're not showing it now."

"What would you know about it? You don't know anything about loving anyone!"

"Trust me, I wish that were true."

"You know I'm right, Hephaestus. You know it, and everyone else does too. And you try to act all tough and shit—"

He barked a laugh. "I try to act tough? Mr. 'Come with me. I'll protect you, helpless woman'? Please, Ares, spare me. I guarantee you this though. If I didn't care about anyone, you wouldn't still be standing right now."

"You stay away from her! You know damn well she deserves better than that, Hephaestus! Than all your apathetic, emotionless bullshit!"

"But she doesn't deserve better than all your selfish, macho bullshit?"

"Fuck you, Heph! You don't know shit about us!"

"And I don't want to, so please, Brother, take this up with her at a later date. I—"

"Heph?" Achilles peered at him from around Ares' large form with a questioning look. "You ready?"

Hephaestus nodded before looking back at his brother. "I have to go, Ares, and I need you to leave this office."

"You can't make me do anything!"

"I can. Right now, I am the authority here, and I am not above having you tossed out on your ass, so please. Make this easy for both of us."

They stared one another down, Ares huffing with rage and Hephaestus standing with quiet composure. At last, Ares surrendered, turning and trudging out of the office. Achilles raised his eyebrows, but Hephaestus merely waved him off and led him out of the office as well. He didn't have time to get into it nor did he want to. He had more important things at hand.

They didn't speak again until they were exiting the parking garage in Achilles' SUV, and Achilles let out a rough laugh.

"What the hell was that?"

"What?" Hephaestus said, innocence in his tone.

"Oh, trust me, I wanna ask about your brother's issue, but I doubt we got the time for that, so what was that in the hall with Leda?"

"A plant."

"What do you mean?"

"We're not going to Twilight. We're going to my uncle's place first, and while I get him to gather his men, you're gonna tell ours to stay in place. If anyone leaves that warehouse, they call us immediately."

"Okay, you lost me the moment you started."

"There was nothing on the tapes, were there?"

He pauses a moment. "No."

"And Hector hasn't been in that office. He's barely been in the building. If you would've gone back to the beginning of the day, I bet he was nowhere near the office that day because I made sure he wasn't." Achilles opened his mouth, but finding nothing more to say, he simply listened and waited for understanding. "Who has access to the office unfettered? Who is in there every single day and has been since we started investigating the warehouses? Since the day Aphrodite and I got shot at in the Market District? Who's there right now with no oversight?"

Hephaestus watched Achilles as that understanding he was waiting on slowly began to dawn. Once it did, his eyes widened and he slapped the steering wheel.

"Are you fucking kidding me?" he howled. "That little girl has been finessing us this whole fucking time? How - how did you figure it out?"

"I wasn't sure at first. But when we went to that warehouse yesterday in the Styx District, there was a car there waiting for us. Like it knew we were coming, and whoever had been in the warehouse had left in a hurry. We didn't go inside, but I assume they left an ambush in there waiting on us to go in. But once I found the charge under the bed, I knew. I knew Leda was the only person that could have gotten access to the elevator without your knowledge. We gave her free reign over the fucking office, and I bet that's exactly what she wanted. I put her in the perfect position."

"How the fuck were you supposed to know?"

"I was careless. I never should've put anyone new in there. Even charging fucking radios."

"There's no way any of us could've foreseen that, Heph." He ran a hand over his head. "But how did she get into the elevator to begin with? We have people guarding it."

"Yeah, the one inside the club, not the one in the parking garage. Our guys do rounds in there, so they don't have eyes on it 24/7."

"Shit. And you think she took folks up there to set the charge?"

"Naw, I think she set it herself. It would've been too risky having multiple people go up, and she had no clue when we would be back. It wasn't a difficult charge to set. All she had to do was put the velcro on the bedframe and turn a knob. Aphrodite would do the rest."

"I can't believe that shit."

"I barely could. I locked up all the detainment rooms and set up a camera in the office to see if she would make a call when we left to relay the information. It would have been risky to send a message or make a call out in the open."

"And she made one, right?"

"Yeah, she did, and I confirmed it. I never thought she would be able to make an access card though. Like you said, the system isn't easy."

"But if she's working with these people, maybe she worked at Labyrinth too. They probably have a similar system."

"She also got a second call, which I assume was from whoever brought her the charge. That means she has people close. Or still in the building. And they had a charge ready to go. They were just waiting for an opportunity."

"Damn. So you wanted her to hear us. You want her to tip them off, so they'll move."

"If they're moving and they expect us in the morning, they won't expect us this afternoon. Plus, if they're moving, it means I'm right."

"And if you are? What are we gonna do?"

"Question her, see what we can get. She may be brave, but I don't think she's stupid. Her best bet is to talk to me."

"Are you sure she doesn't know you know?"

"I told her we didn't come home last night, and she immediately got nervous. She doesn't know I found the charge, so we have that to our advantage. We can't let them get past us this time though. We need to get ahead of these guys. I'm not risking Aphrodite's safety like that again."

Achilles looked at him but said nothing more, turning onto the bridge that ran over the River Styx. Heph didn't like this any more than he did. He hated having to make a move without seeing the big picture, without having all the pieces, but they had to do something. And they had to do it now. He had to keep his word.

Chapter Twenty-Five

HEPHAESTUS

Hephaestus had just crossed over the threshold of Hades' office when his phone rang, Patroclus's name flashing across the screen with as much urgency as the man himself displayed when Hephaestus answered the phone.

"Kleon left the hotel." Patroclus sounded as though he had just been running, his breathing heavy. "A dark vehicle, no plates, pulled up around back and got him. Before we could get a tail on him, he made us."

"So he's gone?"

"We were able to stay with him for a few blocks, but we lost him. I think he was headed for the port. But that's not all. Perseus is here."

"There in Thassos?"

"Yeah, he showed up at the security HQ about an hour ago, but he looked like he was in a rush."

"Like he was gonna leave again?"

"Yeah, like that."

Hephaestus screwed his eyes shut. They were out of time and low on options. He had a decision to make, one that could make or break this entire operation, and he couldn't be brash about it. He weighed pros and cons quickly in his head, pinching the bridge of his nose. He could sense his uncle and Persephone now standing from their seats, seeing the distress all over him.

"Okay, forget Kleon, we'll track him down later," Hephaestus instructed slowly.

That was the easy decision, considering it had more or less already been made for them. However, without a certainty as to Perseus's role in all of this, taking him in now might do more harm than good. That meant there was really only one way forward. Hephaestus would have to break Leda. He would have to make her talk.

"I want everybody we have in Thassos on that HQ. Call in our friends there if you have to. If he tries to leave the city, you stop him at all costs. Odds are Kleon is tipping him off if he hasn't already. We cannot lose both of them, Patroclus, do you understand?"

"I got it."

"But again, and I cannot stress this enough. Do not make a move until he makes a move. We have to be sure he is the end of the line. We cannot gamble with that."

"I got you."

"I'll call you back once I have confirmation."

He hung up quickly, pocketing his phone just as Thanatos and Charon entered the room behind him.

"What is it?" Persephone questioned first.

"They lost Kleon, but they have eyes on Perseus."

"And you think Perseus is the one running all this?"

"I have a pretty good hunch, but I'm about to go find out for sure."

"How?"

"Questioning our mole."

"Mole?" Hades and Persephone echoed at once.

Hephaestus nodded. "There was a girl that was among the survivors. She came to Aphrodite asking for a job in the club but not on the floor, and..." He shook his head. "Look, I can offer a play-by-play later, but we have literal minutes to work with. Achilles."

Achilles came in from the hall. "Yeah?"

"I need you to run this raid. I want that warehouse cleared out and everyone in it detained. I also need to know if they were tipped off beforehand."

"You got it. What are you gonna do?"

"I'm gonna go talk to Leda, and if we're right, I'm going to Thassos."

"I'm going with you," Charon added, and while his voice was calm, Hephaestus knew he wasn't asking and there was no negotiating.

"Persephone and I will coordinate with Achilles and call in Athena and Ares if need be," Hades offered.

"Have them ready to go just in case we manage to find out if they're occupying other locations," Hephaestus said. "Achilles, call Artemis, and tell them to lock down Twilight for the time being. No one goes in, and no one goes out."

"Where is Aphrodite?" Persephone asked.

"I promise you she is in the safest place she can possibly be, and I am the only person in the world who knows where that is."

"I appreciate that, but if you're going to Thassos, I wanna know where she is."

"If I go to Thassos, that means we know for sure who's in charge of this, so I'll take her back to Lush the moment I have that confirmation. Does that work?"

Persephone seemed to consider it for a moment, Hades placing an arm around her waist in an attempt to soothe her. At last, she nodded.

"Thank you," Hephaestus breathed out. "Let's move. We don't have time to waste."

Leaving the office, Charon followed him to the service elevator closest to Hades' office. At the moment, adrenaline coursed through Hephaestus, hardly utilizing his cane and moving as quickly as his muscles would allow. He let Charon drive them back to Lush, going over the information they currently had in his head.

For him, the warehouse raid was obsolete apart from saving any and all rescues that they could. He had hoped one of the perpetrators they found within would talk so that he could keep Leda as a last resort. Thinking back on it now, nearly none of his plan for this operation had gone as he'd hoped, but if they could just bridge the gap between fact and speculation in regard to Perseus, it wouldn't matter.

One thing he knew for certain was that he wouldn't give Perseus the opportunity to slip through their fingers. He would deal with the man himself if he proved to be the party putting a hit out on Aphrodite.

Every step he took as they entered Lush had his heart pounding, but just before he turned into the hall of the security office, his phone rang again. Aphrodite's name flashed across the screen, but he ignored it for now. The sooner they did this, the sooner he could give her the good news and bring her home where she belonged.

Charon branched off, heading towards the stairs as Hephaestus continued down the hall. To Heph's relief, Leda was sitting at her desk, swapping out radios on the docks. She looked up as he approached, that commonplace bright smile flashing across her features. Hephaestus had to force himself to return something similar.

"Did you - find who you were looking for?" Leda questioned, voice upbeat as he stopped before her.

"Hm? Oh, yeah. Yeah, we did, but - there's a complication we have to deal with, which is - why I'm here talking to you. Do you wanna help me with something?"

Her eyes lit up. "Of course! Yeah, what is it?"

He glanced over each shoulder then down the hall before he beckoned her to follow him. She did so with haste, and they headed further down the hall. The door to the armory lay at the end, but just before it was another door. It led into a holding room. She followed him inside before he turned around and shut the door.

"Sit down please," he stated.

The room was barren apart from a few standing shelves that comprised the lost and found, a long table with metal legs and a plastic top, and several chairs. The lights bleached the whole scene in an eerie white. Of course, it was made to be absurdly uncomfortable.

Yet she took a seat on the edge of the table, leaning back on her palms as she stared at him with wide eyes. She looked different in that moment, the image of innocence soiled by a raw look in her gaze. He momentarily feared that she knew what this is about, but he didn't divert from the path he'd drawn.

"In a chair if you don't mind."

She raised a brow but didn't argue, moving to sit in the seat nearest her. He moved to take the chair opposite her, placing his cane on the table before him. He stared at its sleek, black frame for a long while, as if he was waiting for something.

They sat in silence for over ten minutes before his phone rang. It was a text from Achilles.

"You were right. They were tipped off."

He exhaled a breath of bittersweet relief. Still, he didn't speak right away, considering how best to go forward. Of all the mannerisms he'd learned from his uncle, tact wasn't inherently one of them. Uncomfortable silence was. The former was hit or miss in most situations, and in this particular situation, he couldn't quite focus on finding any.

"So what did you need help with?" she prompted, an expectant look in her eyes.

He inhaled sharply as he lifted his head. "Nothing too big, but - tell me. Where was it you came from again? Before you came here?"

Her face fell. She looked surprised for only a moment. Then she looked defensive. "Why is that important?"

"I guess it isn't. The outcome is the same. I know you're from Thassos, so... What I need to know is the name of the man who sent you here. I have a hunch, but I need a confirmation."

"I - I don't know what you're—"

"You, I don't have a hunch about. I had a hunch a few days back, but I received confirmation today when the guys in that warehouse tried to move early. We got them though, and you did exactly what I expected you to, so no worries at all."

"Heph—"

"Who sent you here, Leda? Just give me a name, and I will send you on your way with enough money to start over wherever you want. Anywhere you want. Except Khaos Falls."

She glared at him, but he was unwavering, the reins of his rage clasped tight in his grasp but only just. She stood up, making a move for the door, but it opened before she reached it. Charon stepped inside, followed by Callisto, who shut the door behind them and locked it. There was a bag in Charon's hand, and Leda gasped.

"That's mine!" she shrieked.

"I know," Charon stated, moving towards the table.

He dumped the contents of the bag before Hephaestus, revealing several items including squares of velcro similar —no, identical— to the one used to attach the charge to Aphrodite's bed frame. Heph picked up some folded up papers, unfolding them to find blueprints of Lush and several other properties in Aphrodite's district. Charon then extracted a phone from his pocket, which Leda tried to snatch from his hand, but his other forearm stopped her. Hephaestus took it.

"There was only one contact, but there was no answer, no answering machine set up, nothing," Charon explained. "It just rings."

"Who is it?" Hephaestus asked again.

When Leda didn't answer, Charon gripped her shoulder and steered her back into the seat across from Hephaestus. She was defiant now, eyes alight and arms crossed.

"What is it that keeps you from giving me the name, Leda?" Hephaestus' voice softened. "I'm offering you money and a fresh start, which I imagine is how he roped you in to begin with. I don't want you. I want him, and if it's loyalty, I respect that, but if it's something else—"

"I'm not gonna tell you anything," Leda shot back.

"Is he family? Or is he a lover?" She scoffed. "He must be. Why else would you risk your neck for a guy who sent you in here? He must have been aware that it could cost you your life, coming here." She said nothing. "Here's the thing though. My people are headed for him right now. With or without your cooperation, I'm taking Perseus down tonight, and you'll both get your due."

She perked up now. She tried to fight it, but he watched the sudden bunching of her shoulders and the widening of her eyes and the reddening of her cheeks. That was all he really needed.

"Last chance to be cooperative," he offered her.

"—You're gonna kill him anyway!" she suddenly shouted, slapping the table.

"That may be what you're used to, but that's not how we do things here. And besides, when I reach Thassos to talk to him, I could just tell him you gave me his name regardless. How do you think that will affect your - 'relationship'?"

"Fuck you."

"Mm, at least I can say I tried."

"You don't know who you're dealing with! You think it'll be so easy taking him down? That you have all this figured out? You have no fucking clue."

"I gotta tell you, the acting? Impressive. I'll be sure to tell him that you did your best."

He stood, picking up his cane and following Charon to the door. Callisto opened it for them, and once they were isolated in the hall, Heph turned to Charon.

"Take her to Uncle," he instructed. "He'll be able to put her in a more secure holding until we get back. While you do that, I'm gonna go get Aphrodite and bring her home. Then we head to Thassos, alright? The ferry leaves at midnight."

Charon nodded, placing a hand on his shoulder. "I'll meet you at Harvest Port. Be safe."

"I will. You too."

The two shook hands before they departed, and Hephaestus's heart was again beating a mile a minute. By this time tomorrow, it would all be over. He didn't know what that meant for him and Aphrodite, for what they'd shared, and he was far too much of a coward to probe it at the moment. But with every bit of relief came several drops of anxiety about it. He choked it down. No matter what she decided, he'd done it. He kept her safe, and in the end, that was what mattered. He'd done his job.

Chapter Twenty-Six

APHRODITE

Under any other circumstance, Aphrodite would be having the time of her life, picking and probing through Hephaestus's humble abode and uncovering the man behind the mystery. She would explore all the doors lining the halls branching off of the living room, and she would go through his movie and music and game collections. She would peruse his cabinets, medicine and kitchen, and she would find things to tease him about later. But this was not any other circumstance.

Instead, she paced his kitchen, chewing her nails down to nothing. She'd called him several times in the past hour without a response, and she was growing more worried by the moment. She wanted to call Hades, but that would alert Persephone, and she had no clue how much her best friend knew about what was going on nor did she want to be questioned about her whereabouts. Seeing as Persephone had a show tonight, Aphrodite didn't want to worry her, and she didn't know what she would say about the night before if she did.

She was still shaken after all. She doubted she could've slept at all if Heph hadn't been laying beside her, and each time she stopped to think about the bomb under her bed, she shuddered into a fit of pointed anxiety. It was heightened by the fact that Hephaestus had been gone for hours, and while she pacified herself with the thought that if something were wrong with him, Hades would have called her by now, she couldn't avoid the wonder. She hated being apart from him. She was learning that now, and it was honestly the worst time to do so.

She thought it clicked the night before, how invasive and indiscreet death could be. It didn't care about anything but itself, and she had thought herself immune for too long. Not that she'd ever worried much for herself. She worried for Persephone, for Auntie Hestia, even for Demeter. She worried for Eros and Psyche, for all the victims she had yet to save, but she never worried for herself. She'd never had to. They worried enough for her. Now...

Now she felt foolish for never stopping to think that maybe, just maybe, Hephaestus was right and she was still adhering too close to the guidelines of a fairytale. Being the hero did not breed immortality. And it didn't promise a happy ending.

She was just about to give in and call Hades when she heard a familiar tapping beyond the door leading to the garage. She rushed towards it as the door opened, revealing a windswept Hephaestus. He dropped his cane just as she threw herself into his arms, catching her and holding her against him. The scent of his cologne soothed her with immense efficiency, and she buried her face in his neck for as long as she could before pulling back and shoving at his chest. He caught himself by her elbows, eyes narrowing.

"Where have you been?" she demanded, gripping his shirt in one hand. "I was fucking worried."

"Finishing this," he said easily, his thumbs running gently over her biceps.

She stared at him for a moment, trying to decrypt what it was he was saying to her. He seemed to sense her skepticism because he nodded, kissing her forehead.

"It's done," he sighed once he pulled away, resting his own forehead against hers. "We got the guy."

"Who is it?"

"His name is Perseus. I used to do weapons deals with him for Thassos a long time ago. Achilles called on my way here too. They were able to clear two other warehouses, and they're preparing to raid three others they got a tip on. Altogether, we rescued 127 people tonight. We're keeping them safe until we've secured Perseus."

She breathed a sigh of relief, her hands finding his cheeks. "You did it."

"Not yet, but I will. There's - something you gotta know though." She raised a brow. "Leda was a plant. They put her here to watch us. She warned the warehouses each time we were heading there. That's how that car found us last night. That's who got access to your room."

She gaped at him, her brain struggling to catch up, before a dry chuckle leaves her. "I fucking knew it."

"Guess the jealousy was warranted."

He smirked, and she pinched his neck before smothering his lips with hers, his strong arms pulling her into him. Now that they were standing on the edge of this horrible situation, she couldn't help but wonder what came next. With him, with them. Did they end this? Did they stop seeing one another? Did they go back to being hostile? She didn't want that. In fact, she couldn't even begin to fathom it being possible.

"Come on," he whispered. "I'm taking you back to Lush."

"What about you?" she questioned, more desperate than she meant to.

"Charon and I are going to Thassos to get Perseus. We leave at midnight. I'm gonna make sure it's over, that we've tied up any and all loose ends. Achilles will stay with you, and once I'm in Thassos and have Perseus with me, you can go over to Twilight House and greet the new rescues."

"And Leda?"

"At Asphodel. My uncle will make sure nothing happens to her until we decide what to do with her, but we wanna get the big guy first."

"Alright, but - maybe I should go with you."

"Absolutely not." Before she could argue, he shook his head hard and placed his thumb against her lips. "There are too many unknowns. I don't want any surprises, and I wanna make sure we don't take more risks than we need to."

She eyed him warily. It scared her, letting him go again, and while she was sure he would be just fine, the doubt remained. It felt like now that she loved him, he was no longer invincible either.

And she did love him. *Fuck*.

She was still adjusting to just how terrified she was of losing him. The idea that she had to go back to her life, to her penthouse, without him... It was the worst kind of horror. She didn't know how to express that either however. She didn't know how to admit it out loud.

"Well - come see me as soon as you get back," she commanded.

"It might be a couple days," he pointed out.

"I don't care. Come see me."

His lips quirked. "Is that an order?"

"It is. And before you get smart, you work for me until you bring home the assurance that this is over, so you have to do what you're told."

His lips spread further into a smile. "You got it, Princess."

That got her, and she sobered. "...And what about us?"

His expression did not change, but she saw the flicker in his eyes. "Why don't we add that to the agenda of talking points when I report back to you?"

She took it as a win. "Sounds good."

He kissed her again, and she felt every ounce of passion he possessed poured down her throat. She took it like a glutton, ravenous for the taste, and she only released him when she could no longer breathe. She only realized she was crying when his thumbs swept across her cheeks too, capturing the moisture.

"Come back to me." It sounded like a plea on her lips.

"You know I will."

She held his neck the whole drive back, and she held his hand on the way up the elevator to the penthouse. He seemed just as eager to hold onto her as she did him, and it relaxed her substantially. Yet not enough to stop worrying about the fact that he was leaving her. She wasn't ready to let him go.

The moment the elevator doors shut, she pressed herself against them, pulling him back into her and seizing his mouth. He didn't fight it, his hands roaming her body and tugging at her blouse until they reached the hem of her skirt. He yanked it up, squeezing her ass and teasing her slit through her panties as she moaned into his mouth. She knew he had to go, but there was still an hour before midnight, and she was going to make the best of it. If she couldn't go with him, the taste of her would.

"I have to go," he hissed.

"First, I have to come."

He chased the words relentlessly, smothering her mouth with his, and she drank from his lips like the deepest well. Still, she could not get enough. She didn't think she ever would. But damn if she wouldn't keep trying. She'd fallen in love with the trying.

By the time he pushed her down onto the ottoman, she was bare, a trail of fabric tracing their journey. He folded her in half on that ottoman too, her toes touching the couch behind them as he dropped her bag and sunk to his knees to push his tongue inside of her. She froze up, her breaths short both due to the constriction and the overwhelming sensation of his mouth on her pussy. He was sloppy with it, messier than she had ever seen him, pushing his face between her folds. She gripped her thighs, nails piercing the backs of them and her moans permeating the air like a thick cloud of smoke.

Before she could adjust to his rhythm, he was up again, digging through her bag for the lube bottle he'd put in there because he cared so much about her comfort. How many times had Adonis conveniently forgotten some? How many times had Ares complained? How many times had men refused to wait? How many times had they walked out instead? But not Hephaestus. No, the bastard she couldn't stand the sight of just weeks ago never complained and never forgot. And she loved him.

She was only pulled from the delicate sentimentality of that thought by his pulsing cock plunging into her cunt. She yelped, releasing her thighs and reaching for his. She buried her nails into his skin, anything to bring him closer, deeper. She felt empty when he was away from her, but once he was inside, that feeling fell away with unbridled ease. The entire world fell into place, and with him to keep her whole, it felt as though nothing could harm her. None would dare try.

She latched onto him as he thrusted, and he never broke his stride even as she felt his leg shake in warning. His calloused hands clenched the loose leather of the ottoman before he laid his weight over her, her breathing restricted in a way that brought infinite euphoria. Light-headed though she may have been, he was hitting a depth that he never had, that no one ever had, and she was so close to coming undone that her lungs delayed their protest.

"Don't - you fucking - stop!"

"You better ask nicely," he snarled.

"Please, Daddy! Let me cum! Let me!"

"That's Daddy's good girl."

Her voice was hoarse beneath the intense pressure, but she welcomed more of his weight regardless. He buried his face in her neck as he drilled her, his breath hot against her skin and his lips sucking at a place above her pulse point.

His weaker knee eventually ended up on the cushion, but that didn't slow him down in the slightest. If anything, it adjusted his angle just enough to force her back to arch up off the surface. He never ceased to amaze her nor did he fail to surprise her, and admitting she had underestimated him came easier each time. He fucked her like he had something to prove, and she wasn't about to correct him if this was the result.

Fuck, it was so good.

"Yes, Daddy—" she moaned, her nails claiming the meat of his ass. "Please. Please!"

Even when she couldn't vocalize what it was she was pleading for, he delivered, pounding her harder until the ottoman was inching across the floor. She doesn't know what would come first, her or the couch, and then...

It was her. Of course it was her. She cried out, slapping his ass before gripping it hard and holding his hips to hers as she bucked and convulsed, her legs clenching around his shoulders. Her orgasm was both shameless and merciless, a blinding light overtaking her vision despite her eyes rolling completely back. He was unperturbed, failing to give her a moment to catch her breath. No, he kept fucking her, and she was far too weak to offer any resistance.

As if she would have anyway.

He made her cum again, and she knew quite quickly that had been his goal all along, the way he slowed down just when he began to throb inside of her. With every roll and grind, he hit all her spots as though he'd mapped them out, and then he hit them again. He assaulted them until she was begging for mercy, the pleasure overwhelming, threatening to swallow her whole. She had just adjusted to his rhythm when he sped up again, and her orgasm disrupted every single function she possessed, unexpected and unforgiving. Only then, as she laid there limp and longing for revival, did he cum too.

He spilled out of her in thick streams of white, wetting the seam of her ass and soiling the furniture beneath. She didn't fucking care. He would leave his mark all over this suite if she had her way.

They wound up on the floor, his mouth on hers and her legs tangled with his. They grabbed at each other with a relentless eagerness. Or a fear. Although she wouldn't acknowledge the latter. She couldn't.

Until she had no choice.

"Come back to me," she whispered against his lips. "Promise me - you'll come back to me."

His eyes were closed, but he was wide open, the truth falling from his own lips with ease. "I promise, Princess. There is nothing in this world that can keep me from you."

Chapter Twenty-Seven

HEPHAESTUS

The trip to Thassos City was roughly half a day's ride via ship from Khaos Falls, but it felt longer under current circumstances. While there were city airplanes that were often utilized for emergency flights, it was frowned upon for city and district leaders to fly due to the very real possibility that a plane could be shot out of the sky.

After several city leaders from across the Aegean were eliminated this way, Khaos Falls all but abandoned their local airport in the Market District. Although he was now considered a city leader, Hephaestus still might have opted to fly if Charon hadn't come with him. Dangerous as it would be to fly into Thassos unannounced, he was too eager not to at least consider it.

Aphrodite's touch lingered on every inch of his skin, but it only enhanced his anxious impatience. He didn't know what they were. He had no clue what it meant. All he knew was that he wanted to —no, needed to— make it back to her. With the assurance that she was safe.

Beyond the distance between them, there were chasms between Thassos and Khaos Falls. Thassos would like to think of itself as more advanced and evolved than its southern neighbor, a bustling city built on absolute power and zero tolerance. Everyone in Thassos answered to a single leader, and any step out of line was handled with swift punishment.

However, this pattern was often upended by the continuous cycling of leadership, very few lasting more than a year in the position before they were usurped or taken out. To Hephaestus, Thassos was just a bunch of pretty skyscrapers built over blood and bodies and painted with denial.

He had taken to cleaning his weapons in his cabin to pass the time, but he could hardly sit still, the seconds slipping by slowly. His watch seemed louder than it ever had, a taunting tick that pounded against his wrist. Eventually, he set down the blade in his hand, getting to his feet and heading up to the deck. As he stepped out into the hall however, Phidias, one of the ship's permanent men, called to him from the opposite end of the hall leading towards the captain's quarters.

"Hephaestus," he said softly. "Someone's on the radio for you."

Raising an eyebrow, Hephaestus changed directions, making his way down towards Phidias and the radio room. He assumed it was Patroclus. They had been waiting for news about Perseus's capture, and Heph had instructed them to radio the ship the moment he had been secured. While he worried about the dangers of having his people take down a security head, it was the last card they had left to play. There was no Plan B now. There was only this.

The radio room was a small space just off the bridge with dark yellow walls and a single counter bolted into one of them from end to end. Atop the counter was the large radio system consisting of seven or eight separate devices that could be utilized at once or that would provide a failsafe in the event one broke. There was also one in the bridge where the captain steered the ship as a precaution.

Phidias gave him a nod and disappeared down the hall as Heph entered, seeking out the machine with the green light blinking. Once he found it, he picked up the radio.

"Hello?"

"Heph?"

His heart lurched up into his throat before swan diving into his stomach, elation and exasperation clashing behind his ribcage. He shook his head, his lips twitching.

"What are you doing awake?" he questioned. "Are you okay?"

"I missed you," Aphrodite said simply.

"You know this radio is supposed to be for an emergency, right?"

"This *is* an emergency."

He rolled his eyes. "Reckless as always."

"Mhm, but apparently you like that shit."

"Yeah, I guess I do."

"So are you alone?" Her voice dropped lower. "Can we have hot radio sex?"

He chuckled. "No, we cannot. At least not right now, but I'll tell you what, we can keep the hand radios when I get back."

"Do you promise, Daddy?"

He let his head fall back with a groan. "You're killing me, you know that?"

"The feeling is mutual."

He was quiet for a moment, biting his lip. It was all so new. The giddy emotion, the butterflies in his stomach, the missing her. These were things he had never truly experienced, and if he was being honest, he had started to fear he wasn't able to. He had started to fear that she had been right, that he was some robot that had no clue how to care correctly, at least about people outside of his family. Odd how she herself proved her own theory wrong.

"I miss you," he admitted. "More than you know."

"Oh, I think I have an idea. Are you almost there?"

"We've only been gone a couple hours, Princess."

"Yeah, well, it feels like a lifetime."

"How are things there?"

"They're great. Achilles is standing right outside the door as he promised. Twilight is still on lockdown, but Psyche said all was well, and Persephone and Hades will be over tomorrow if you're not back yet. They were gonna come tonight, but I told them not to worry. I'm safe and sound."

"That's my good girl."

"Mmm, do I get rewarded for being a good girl when you get back?"

"Immensely. You better take the day off."

"You don't gotta tell me twice."

As much as he wanted to stay here and talk to her all night, it would do neither of them any good, and it would only make him more antsy. He hated being able to hear her voice and not being able to touch her. It was torture.

"Listen though, get some rest, okay?" he said softly. "I'll call you tomorrow as soon as we're done here, alright?"

She seemed to have the same feeling because she didn't argue. "Okay. It's hard sleeping without you though, you know."

"I know. I haven't been able to even consider it, but I'll try if you try, yeah?"

She exhaled heavily. "Yes, Daddy, I'll try."

"That's my good girl. I—" He stopped himself, clearing his throat. *Not now*. "I'll talk to you soon."

"Okay. I'll talk to you soon."

He paused only a moment more before setting the radio down, forcing himself to walk out of the room. He scrubbed a hand over his face as he walked down the hall, his steps heavy against the hollow floor. It creaked beneath his weight light as a whisper, and yet in the silence of the ship, it seemed to carry.

He took the stairs up to the deck at a slow pace, holding the railing and picking up his cane, following the sound and smell of the sea. There was no one else out there, the crew bedding down for the night and Charon presumably doing the same. They hadn't brought anyone else. Hephaestus had full confidence that they could handle business alone. He would rather have everyone else on watch back home. It was the only way to convince himself that leaving Aphrodite wasn't a mistake.

He leaned against the railing of the deck, looking out over the calm sea surrounding the vessel. He felt offended, the gentle waters lapping carelessly at the ship's side triggering a sudden burst of irrational anger in him. How could the sea be so calm when Aphrodite's life was at stake? How was it not as riotous as his heart?

He inhaled a deep drag from his vapor pen after pulling it from his pocket, the chill in the air seeping into his muscles and making them feel rigid and uncooperative. Despite that, it kept him awake and uncomfortable, just like Aphrodite had been all those nights while danger lurked in every corner of her sanctuary. He vowed he wouldn't rest properly until this was all over. Until he was back in her arms.

"You should get some sleep."

Charon's voice carried like a cold wind of its own across the deck, washing over his shoulders. Hephaestus waited for the elder to appear in his peripheral, Charon placing his inked hands on the railing beside him with a slow exhale.

"I couldn't even if I wanted to," Hephaestus concluded.

"There's a whole lot of weight on your shoulders right now, and you have to let yourself rest, Hephaestus. Even if you don't sleep, just put it down for a bit."

Rather than argue, he changed the subject. "Do you remember when you would tell me stories about the siren and the blacksmith?"

Charon's chuckle was a pillow soft sound. "Of course I do. I didn't think you would take to it as well as you did. I had to struggle to make up more each week."

"They never really had an ending, did they?"

"They did."

Heph shook his head. "You would always get distracted by something else and leave them there, wherever they were."

"Yes, but what did you do?" Heph raised a brow, looking over at him. Charon smiled. "You would go into the workshop and become the blacksmith, and you would act out that story either in your head or in the shop, but you always wrote an ending, Hephaestus."

"So you did that on purpose?"

"I did. Because I never wanted you to think your future was set in stone. The ending is what you wanted it to be. It was often happy, and it was often heroic."

"I thought it was supposed to be."

"Then it was. That's the point. The only person who could determine that was you."

Hephaestus turned his head back towards the water, chewing the inside of his cheek. He didn't know why it struck so vigorously now, the memory of Charon's storytelling. It had always just been one of those things they did together, but now it felt so much more pivotal.

"You wanna know if you're allowed to write this ending," Charon went on, and Hephaestus remembered then who he was talking to, the very source from where he inherited his skill of reading people from. "You can, but you don't have to. This can be a beginning, Hephaestus, and in the real world, you don't have to do it alone. You don't have to be the siren *and* the blacksmith."

"I never thought that was the story I would act out when I grew up. I thought it was someone else's story. Even when I made it up myself, it was somebody else's happy ending."

Charon laughed again, wrapping an arm around Heph's shoulders. "You're the blacksmith, are you not? It was always your story, Son. Just know that it is hers too."

"You don't think maybe I'm making a mistake?"

"I don't think that, but I don't know that either. Neither will you unless you try."

"Ares will hate me."

"Ares will survive. He's your brother, and he loves you. Besides, what Aphrodite chooses to do with her heart is up to her and her alone. Respect that, regardless of her decision."

He nodded, glancing up at him once more. "Is that why you never told my mom's secret?"

Charon smirked, pulling Hephaestus's head against his chest and hugging him. "I didn't need to tell anyone. I knew, she knew, and you knew eventually. Then, of course your uncle figured it out pretty quickly, but the people who needed to know did. I didn't want to hurt your mother. I only wanted to be able to be there for you. She knew that. It's why she let you come live with Hades when she did. She knew you would be taken care of."

"I just thought she didn't want me."

"Oh, we wanted you, both of us, but we were foolish kids. We thought you would save us, keep us together, and that didn't happen.

Your mother was depressed for a long time because of how trapped she felt, and I tried to help her. Then she convinced herself she loved Zeus, and so I stepped back. I still wanted you though." Hephaestus wrapped an arm around Charon's waist. "You are my son, Hephaestus, and I would not trade you for anything."

It was the first time either of them had ever said it aloud despite the fact Hephaestus had known the truth since he was a kid no older than ten summers. They never needed to though. Despite Hades leading everyone to believe he was Hephaestus's main guardian in order to protect Hera, Charon had always been there for him. His actions spoke louder than any words ever could, and Hephaestus loved him for it.

Never had Charon looked down on him or made him feel weak. He never treated Hephaestus any differently than his brothers, and he taught him everything he could to survive in a world not made to accommodate him. It was why it was so hard to think of his mother now and who she had become, who Zeus had made her into. He wished he could meet the woman that his father loved.

"You haven't spoken to your mother yet, I'm assuming," Charon hummed.

Hephaestus screwed his eyes shut, feeling like a child again. Or for the first time. "I will, as soon as we wrap this up... Will you?"

"What? Talk to your mother?"

"Yeah, talk to my mother."

"I don't know if she wants to open old wounds when she's still licking her new ones, Son."

"Well, will you eventually? I think you should. I think - we should all talk really."

Heph lifted his head, and their gazes met. Then Charon nodded.

"I suppose that's fair. You two should talk first though. Then we can go from there. Just know that while I do believe your mother made a lot of mistakes where you were concerned, she isn't beyond saving, Hephaestus. The Hera I knew is in there somewhere."

Hephaestus smirked now. "That's something the blacksmith would say about the siren."

Charon matched his expression. "Maybe I do have an ending to write after all."

They fell into a comfortable silence, but it was soon disrupted by heavy footfalls coming up the stairs from the lower deck. Phidias appeared at the top of the stairs soon after.

"Patroclus just called in over the radio," he said quickly, foregoing pleasantries. "They have Perseus."

Chapter Twenty-Eight

APHRODITE

It felt good to be back. Lush operated in the same way it always had, as though it hadn't been infiltrated and under attack the past few weeks, and Aphrodite was grateful for it. Hephaestus's men remained in the halls, and Hades and Persephone would be there later that night to keep her company until Hephaestus came home. What they would talk about, she had no clue, and she felt kind of nervous. Honestly, even though Persephone was her best friend and closest thing to a sister she had, it almost felt like she was meeting Heph's parents alone. Although she supposed meeting Hera would be far more nerve-wracking.

But she was getting ahead of herself.

The club welcomed her back with an unmatched enthusiasm, and she reveled in it. She was home, and that was all that mattered to her. Well... Okay, that was not *all* that mattered to her. What really mattered to her was currently on a boat headed for Thassos City, and so as she stood in her office overlooking the activities below, she felt bare. She felt - alone.

She missed him; his focused gaze, his silent movements, his possessive touch. She missed it all, and she had decided that once he returned, she was never going to let him go again.

A knock on her door drew her attention. She had expected to find Achilles there, letting her know that he had arrived from the last warehouse raid to take up his position as her guard. Instead, she turned to find Psyche standing outside of it with a man beside her. He looked tired and mildly disoriented and - scared. He looked scared. It was a look she knew all too well. Aphrodite beckoned them in, putting on her best smile.

"Aphrodite," Psyche greeted. "This is Cris. He's - he is here to seek your help."

"Come on in," Aphrodite urged. "Thank you, Psyche."

The man waved bashfully, his light brown hair wild and his dark eyes sunken. His lip trembled as he moved into the room, stopping before her desk with a polite smile. Psyche left the room, shutting the door behind her and leaving them in privacy. Aphrodite took a seat, inviting the man to do the same, which he did eagerly.

"I'm - I'm sorry to bother you, Miss Aphrodite," he managed, his voice high and hollow. "I - I was told I could find help here, with you."

"Help with what?" she questioned gingerly. "I can promise I'll do everything I can."

"I - I tracked my daughter here."

He reached into his pocket, extracting a photo which he handed to her. It was a young brunette girl with bright brown eyes and an even brighter smile.

"She - she was taken nearly a year ago," he went on, "and I've been searching ever since. I found someone that said he'd seen her at the port in Deucalion Heights, that she'd been sold to people here. So I came, and - I found her. I saw her. She's - She's at a house - across town. I've seen her there, and I - I saw the man who has her. He was talking to another man. They're moving her again, tonight, and I need to get to her. I'm afraid I'm gonna lose her if I don't get to her tonight."

Aphrodite looked up at him. "What's her name?"

"Kyra."

"And you know she's there for sure?"

"Yes. Yes, I'm sure, but - I don't know when they will move her."

Aphrodite stared at the photo, her heart aching for the child staring back at her. She couldn't be older than fourteen, but her father looked as though he'd aged decades in the past year. She didn't know how many men she still had in-house that she could trust, and while Hephaestus's men were there, she doubted they would be too thrilled with escorting her out of the building when their captain had given strict instructions about keeping her in the club until he returned word that all was well. He hadn't waited around to let her argue it either. Although she imagined she may be able to get some of them to listen if she had evidence of the predicament. Therefore, all she needed was proof.

"Do you have - pictures of the home?" she questioned. "Anything like that?"

"I - I'm sorry. I didn't think to take any," he said, ashamed. "I - I just - I saw her, and I—"

"It's okay, Cris." She set down the photo, reaching for his hand on the desk. "I want to help you. I will. Can you show me where the house is?"

"I - yes. Yes, I can show you where it is. Thank you so much."

Aphrodite smiled and stood up, sliding the picture back to him. This was what she needed, to get back to the real work. She wanted to help, and she wanted to prove —to herself and everyone else— that she was still capable of doing so. This was her livelihood, and she would be damned if she let it die.

She managed to rope one of Hephaestus's men into her little field trip at the door, stating that she would call the captain herself once they were on the road. Of course, both of them knew he probably didn't have service at the moment, and the only way to reach him would be the radio in the security office. The man, Orion, pretended as well as she did though and followed her to the car with Cris in tow.

Cris eagerly gave Orion the address and directions from the backseat, Aphrodite sitting in the passenger seat with her heart thudding. She stared out the window at the passing buildings of her district until they morphed into that of the Harvest District, its usual lush green landscape lost to the cold. It had been a long time since she'd paid attention to the astounding simplicity of the city, taking it all in without any ulterior motive. It was soothing. Maybe when Hephaestus came back, they could just go for a drive.

The directions led them to a house on the southern border of the Olympus District. It didn't surprise Aphrodite at all to find that people in Zeus's former district dabbled in this horrific trade, but it still angered her. It worried her too though. Who knew how many individual sales were going on outside of the large trafficking circles. She feared she may never truly put a stop to this problem in the city.

At least she had the head of city security on her side now though.

"This it?" Orion asked.

"Yes," Cris confirmed.

Orion put the car in park across the street. "We'll do a bit of surveillance first, make sure we—"

A large bang filled the car, eclipsing the sound of his voice. Aphrodite's ears were suddenly ringing, her vision blurring as disorientation took her. She squeezed her eyes shut, waiting for the ringing to stop or for her vision to clear or for her stomach to stop churning. When she opened them again, she turned in her seat only to find Orion slumped against the steering wheel. If she didn't know who it was to begin with, she never would have been able to identify him now. There was blood everywhere, on him and on her, and it blotted out the window beside him.

Before she could react, she felt the cold barrel of Cris's gun against her temple.

"Don't move," he said coolly, the nervous father completely washed away.

Time seemed to slow, her heart hammering in her ears as the ringing died down. In her peripheral, she watched as a dark SUV pulled up beside them and the back doors opened. A man stepped out, yanking Aphrodite's door open before pulling her out of the car and herding her into the other vehicle. Cris followed, slipping into the passenger seat while the man who grabbed her slid in beside her. Then the car began to move, leaving behind a crime scene she couldn't yet comprehend.

Nonetheless, she kept her calm. She asked no questions and made no demands. In her heart, she knew. She knew she'd made a mistake, and she knew who was sitting in the seat in front of her. And all she could do was worry about Hephaestus. He should still be on the ship heading for Thassos, meaning he should still be safe, but what was he walking into? What was waiting for him in Thassos?

"I'll admit, I didn't think this would be so easy," Cris commented as the car got onto the highway. "If I would've known you were so gullible, I would have just done this to begin with. Then again, I thought my assassin was more than capable, so that's on me." He smiled over his shoulder at her. "Your bodyguard really wedged himself in the way there for a while. Made a mess of my business too, and for what? I got to you regardless."

"And for what?" she returned, her tone acidic. "Now you're a dead man walking."

He chuckled. "I doubt that, but you? Feel free to roll the window down, enjoy your last ride down the coastal highway. In your next life, I would caution you against sticking your nose in other people's business."

"And I would caution against—" She stopped herself, shaking her head. "You were stealing and trafficking *people*. You were selling them and making a profit off of their pain, their family's pain."

"People are a commodity. You of all people should understand that."

"I don't force people to work for me. Those who do stay out of loyalty."

"Loyalty didn't really work out for you this time though, did it? Kleon understood the business. You really were wasting his talents. He knows where there's money to be made, there's a business to be run. I took the responsibility."

"You can try and justify it with all your morally grey bullshit, but if you think this ends with me, you are sorely mistaken. Where there are people like you, there will always be people like me."

"And I'll find them too."

Aphrodite recognized the neighborhood they got off the highway in. Of course she did. This man was going to execute her in her own backyard because not only was Hephaestus not coming, no one else was either. No one was looking for her because no one knew that she was missing.

It would take far too long for them to find Orion's body. Even once they did, and even if it were Ares himself who might recognize the car, they still had no clue who took her. This man was not from Khaos Falls, and while there was something familiar about him to her, she had no idea who he really was. More than that, no one would know where to look because they would certainly not think to look in her own district. In fact, the only one who would was on a fucking boat half a day away.

It was clear to her. She could not be the damsel in this fairy tale, at least not the one in distress, and even if she was? She had to be the hero too. There was no other way for this story to go. There was no other hero coming to her aid.

Her stomach churned as they pulled into a familiar grey and brown building, one that hadn't been used since her father passed. She'd been meaning to have it torn down but hadn't made it around to it yet. When Oceanus was in charge, it had been one of his many weapons caches sprinkled throughout the city. Now, it seemed every bit as run down and abandoned as it should from a distance, but there was distinct movement within as they approached. The front door opened, and two men came outside, men that Aphrodite recognized — Nikolaos and Kleon.

They pulled into the driveway, and the driver killed the engine. Cris turned in his seat to look at her.

"I'm going to make you an offer," he explained, resting the hand holding his pistol atop the middle console, "but I'm only going to make it once. You call your little Twilight house right now and tell them to let us take our girls in peace, and I'll let you live."

Aphrodite scoffed. "That's not gonna happen."

"We'll get them either way, Aphrodite." He gestured out the windshield. "That's what your boy, Kleon, is for. What I want from you is a show of good faith in our business relationship going forward."

"My bodyguard knows that Kleon is-"

"Your bodyguard won't be back to the city until at least tonight, and it'll be over and done with by then, so I'll ask once more. Do you want to live?"

"My bodyguard is gone, but his co-leaders are not. They have Twilight on lockdown. You wanna go to war with them, be my guest, but I'm not going to give up those people. Not ever."

His laugh was low and dark. "Defiant to the end, like a wounded lion. They don't know when they go from predator to prey either I suppose. The least I can do is let you watch the show."

He got out of the car, and the man next to Aphrodite did the same, pulling her out after him and leading her into the house. As she passed Kleon, he tried to look straight ahead. She sneered.

"Look at me, you fucking coward!" she demanded, planting her feet in the dirt. He wouldn't. "You're pathetic, Kleon. Whether I live or die, Hephaestus won't let you rest. He won't stop coming for you until he puts your head on a fucking pike!"

She spit in his face. She didn't have time to see his reaction before she was being shoved over the threshold. She had to think quickly. She wasn't worried about her survivors. She knew Artemis wouldn't let a soul breach those doors, but Aphrodite still had to help herself. She may not make it. She may not survive, but she had to try. Hephaestus had promised to come back to her. How could he do that if she gave up now?

Chapter Twenty-Nine

HEPHAESTUS

The trip seemed to transpire a bit quicker after Patroclus confirmed they'd secured Perseus, but Hephaestus was still anxious when Thassos came into view on the pale purple horizon. They docked at a private port Hermes and Dionysos used strictly for exports and imports, most of the people working there coming straight from Khaos Falls. Charon had convinced him to go inside his cabin and rest his legs a few hours before their arrival which was probably for the best after being on them for nearly 24 hours straight. He would need all of his strength today, and he couldn't afford any disadvantages.

The moment cell service returned, his phone was alive with several texts and voicemails. He opened the latest message from Patroclus. It was an address, and it was relatively close to the port. Two of the guards that had been assigned to Patroclus's team were waiting for them in a navy blue SUV, greeting Charon and Hephaestus with nods as they slid into the vehicle. They could sense the tension, and they acted accordingly. Good. There was no time to waste.

They met Patroclus in a housing development that was not yet finished, the multicolored houses marred by thick plastic and roofs without shingles. Fences with warning signs and caution tape surrounded each and every one, and when they pulled up to the correct address, it was impossible to tell that it was occupied. Once Hephaestus and Charon got out of the SUV, it turned around and headed off back down the street, no doubt to watch the entrance.

They had secured Perseus in the garage, a bag over his head and a gag over his mouth. After hours in this position, the culprit seemed to have surrendered himself to his circumstance, sitting quietly and only squirming in his chair every now and again. Hephaestus made his way towards the corner he was positioned in, Charon and Patroclus flanking him, and tried to calm his nerves enough to hold his composure. He couldn't have the upper hand if he was acting in anger. He had to put his personal feelings aside for just a moment and get this right.

He pulled the bag off. The man before him looked much the same as he did a few years ago although he had facial hair now and a few new scars along his bronze skin. His head was shaved along the sides much like Hephaestus's, his hair long on top and slicked back. His large eyes were filled with question. It made Hephaestus uneasy.

He removed the gag.

"Who the hell are you?" Perseus immediately spat.

"Your worst nightmare," Patroclus shot back.

Perseus looked between them for a moment before recognition dawned on his face.

"Hephaestus?" Recognition was once more replaced with confusion. "What - I don't buy weapons anymore, so whatever this is—"

"And I don't sell them anymore. I'm now in charge of Khaos Falls' security forces. Kinda like you from what I hear."

"I - I'm a private contractor. I don't work for the city anymore, not since my grandfather was ousted. There's bad blood here. What is this about?"

"You really don't know why I'm here?"

"I don't know why *I'm* here!"

Heph gripped the front of his shirt and yanked him to his feet, driving him into the wall behind the chair with adrenaline alone.

"You put a hit out on Aphrodite." His voice was cold, so cold that Perseus shivered.

"What? I—"

"You have been trafficking girls through my city."

Perseus's eyes widened. "What! No! I—"

"I shut down both of your warehouses last night, and I'm taking you back to Khaos Falls where you will rot for the rest of your life—"

"I didn't do that! I didn't do any of that!"

"Your little rat that you put in her district gave up your name."

"What rat! What the fuck are you talking about!"

Hephaestus stared into his face, taking note of every bead of sweat and flicker of fear in his eyes, each of them planting a seed of doubt. Hephaestus didn't like it. It made him anxious. It made him afraid.

"Leda," he growled. "Do you know that name?"

"Yeah, I—" Something registered in his brown eyes before he looked down at the ground, cursing. "She - she did work for me, at my security firm, but now she works for Acrisius."

"And who is Acrisius?" Patroclus questioned, but Heph already knew.

"He used to be the leader of Thassos," Charon filled in. "Not a pretty fall from grace."

"No, it wasn't," Perseus huffed.

"He's also your grandfather."

"Yes, and the worst thing to ever happen to this fucking city."

"What happened?" Hephaestus demanded.

Perseus deflated, and Heph could see things clicking into place behind his eyes. "He was - he was using his position to fund and support the local trafficking rings. The new leader agreed to let him go free if he shut it down and stepped down from his position, which he did. In Thassos."

"You're saying he's running the trafficking rings in Khaos Falls?"

Perseus looked up. "I - I don't know. I'm assuming so, because it wasn't me, but he - he asked me to. He asked me to take the girls he still had to Khaos Falls. He said that - that it was a good place to go, that each district was like a whole separate city, and as long as we didn't get comfortable, we wouldn't get caught. Plus, you all just had a change in leadership, and he thought it was a good time to strike. But the first guy he sent down there got run out within weeks, and so he wanted me to go, but I didn't want anything to do with that business. I - I do security now. That's what I do."

"You're not very good at it if you're still letting him run around doing this shit."

"Okay, look, you don't know him. You don't know how he works. Like I said, I'm a private contractor. I have no sway in this city, and I told the new leadership he was still doing it. They didn't care so long as he wasn't doing it here."

"And where is he?"

"I - I don't know. I just got back into town before your guys dragged me out of my car, and I've been at sea for weeks."

"Where were you headed?"

"I had a ship to catch back to Deucalion Heights. We're working on a contract there. I'm trying to get out of this city, you know. My grandfather's legacy is a stain on everything I do."

"And you have no clue where he is?"

"I - what's the date today?"

"Second week of winter," Charon relayed. "The 28th day of the month I believe."

"Shit."

"What?"

"He's going to Khaos Falls."

Heph halted, turning back to him with eyes narrowed.

"What did you say?"

Perseus inhaled sharply. "Acrisius, he's on his way to Khaos Falls. He didn't say why. He just asked me for a few of my men a few nights ago and someone that could drive a private boat. I was still traveling, and he never tells me shit over the phone, so I didn't think much of it."

Hephaestus's blood ran cold. "When did he leave?"

"Last night."

"What time last night?"

"Uh, seven, I think?"

Patroclus looked between Hephaestus and Charon. "So he'd already be there."

Charon was already pulling out his phone.

"We have to go," Hephaestus asserted to the room before heading for the door, but Patroclus grabbed his arm.

"If she's in danger, we will never make it in time," he pointed out.

"We still have to go. Charon will get ahold of my uncle, and—"

"He's not answering," Charon said tersely, already dialing again.

"We can't just stand here!" He could no longer wrangle his anger, panic and dread coiling around him and making it hard to breathe. "We have to go! I have to get back to her! I have to!"

"Heph," Patroclus said softly. "We—"

"I can fly you."

They all turned to Perseus, whose eyes were on Hephaestus.

"What?" Hephaestus questioned, his voice shaking.

"I have a plane. I can fly you."

"If this is a fucking joke and you're helping him, Perseus—"

"I swear on everything it isn't. It's the least I can do. Like I said, I'm trying to get out, but if I can help you take Acrisius down, I will. In a heartbeat. I'll fly you myself.'

"Where is the plane?"

"It's in Naxos, only about a half hour flight. I leave it there when I travel so my grandfather doesn't get his hands on that too. But if I call now, they can have it at the airfield close to the time we'll reach it."

Hephaestus glared at him, searching for any sign of deception, but he found none. Looking over at Patroclus, he nodded.

"Get him untied and get him a phone," he directed. "Let's go, quickly."

They worked with haste, Patroclus letting Perseus use his phone to call his pilot while he went back into the house to gather the rest of their men. Hephaestus listened to the entire call, acutely aware that Charon had yet to speak to anyone on his own phone. Why was no one answering? They knew Hephaestus and Charon might call, and he was having enough trouble standing around.

"He's on his way," Perseus assured him after he hung up.

He handed the phone back to Patroclus when the man came back into the garage, and Patroclus quickly called the car around before they all headed outside. Hephaestus hardly let his cane hit the floor, forcing his legs to move faster than they ever had. His mistake weighed down on his shoulders, whispering in his ear and plaguing him with guilt. If they couldn't get someone on the phone, if they didn't get someone to her now, all of this would be for nothing. He couldn't accept that.

THE DRIVE TO THE AIRFIELD WAS AS NERVE-WRACKING AS IT COULD possibly be, Hephaestus in the passenger seat and Perseus at the wheel. Hephaestus shut his eyes, resting his head against the glass of the window until the SUV pulled to a stop. Immediately, he shoved the door open and stepped out, fumbling with his phone as he yanked it from his pocket.

The airfield itself was nothing more than a shed and a small strip of land in the corner of Thassos, and Hephaestus almost thought it was a joke when Perseus pulled into it. He wouldn't complain though. Flying back to Khaos Falls would effectively cut the journey down by more than half, and although they had to wait a bit longer, it was still a large upgrade he refused to squander.

Charon had been able to reach Achilles, who had been on his way to Aphrodite after the last warehouse raid. He was now speaking to Artemis, coordinating another lockdown of Twilight House. Luckily, Artemis hadn't been too keen to move her forces out without Hephaestus present in the city, so it was easy for them to return to their previous positions. At least Hephaestus knew for certain that the survivors were safe. Aphrodite's work hadn't been for nothing.

Hephaestus's phone rang before he could decide who to call again, and he was surprised —but relieved all the same, at least to some extent— to see Psyche's name on the screen. He had tried calling her in the car, but she hadn't answered. Nonetheless, he hadn't expected her to be the first to call back.

"Psyche, where is Aphrodite?" he asked without preamble.

"I - I don't know. I just went to her office, but she wasn't in there. Why? What's wrong?"

"When was the last time you saw her?"

"I - she was in her office. A man came in. He wanted her help finding his daughter, and—"

"Man? What man? What was his name, Psyche?"

"Uh, it was Cris. His name was Cris."

Hephaestus's blood curdled. "How did he find her?"

"I - he came to Lush. I came by to grab some supplies from Eros, and I met him downstairs. He asked to see her, so I took him up. Hephaestus, what is wrong?"

"Where is Achilles? Is Achilles there?"

"I don't know. I—"

He could hear her rushing somewhere, her heels clicking on what he assumed was the tile of the hall where the security office was located. Then there was another voice and hers, but it was muffled. Hephaestus gritted his teeth.

"Achilles is right here," she said timidly into the phone at last.

"Put him on."

It only took a second, but Achilles was already talking. "She's not here, and we got a guy missing."

"What guy?"

"Orion."

"That-s - that's our guy." He knew that was what Achilles meant to begin with, but he was still struggling to catch up. "You're sure?"

"Yeah, he's supposed to be on the second floor. He isn't, and one of the cars in the lot is gone."

"You have to find her, Achilles. Call in everyone. Send Psyche to find my uncle at Asphodel. He took her. Acrisius took her."

"Acrisius? The old Thassos leader? I thought—"

"We don't have time! Just go!"

Hephaestus hung up, his shaking hands dialing his uncle for the third time as the shame and guilt pooled in his gut. Aphrodite hadn't answered the three times he called her either, and in his heart, he was certain he knew then. This was so much worse than he'd imagined however. She hadn't simply been taken. Against his wishes and his demands, she had left the club with a fucking stranger who had asked for her help. The moment Psyche had said his name, Hephaestus knew. *Cris*. He'd beaten them. He'd gotten to her.

Hades didn't answer yet again, meaning he was probably in a meeting or some other engagement. It was the only reason he wouldn't be answering his phone.

Meaning Hephaestus had to call Persephone.

"Pat," he called, stalling the inevitable.

"Yeah?" Patroclus answered from where he still sat in the SUV.

"I need you to try and track Kleon's phone again. Can you do that?"

"I can try. He made us though, so he might have tossed it or turned it off."

"It's the best we got. If he's back in Khaos Falls, I need to know. I need to find out where they would've..." Where they would've taken her. "Just try."

Pulling out his phone again, he took a deep breath and called Persephone. She answered on the second ring, his name filled with worry as it fell from her tongue. He choked down his guilt so he could focus. He tried to formulate a coherent explanation, to tell her what had happened in a way that didn't send her into a spiral. Yet, all that left his lips when he opened his mouth was a broken plea.

"Please tell me she's with you."

"What?" Her worry was answer enough. "No, she's not. Why? Hephaestus, what's wrong?"

He didn't hesitate now. "You have to get my uncle, and you have to go find Aphrodite."

"What? Why? I thought you found-"

"We got the wrong guy." He dropped his head. "And the right guy left for Khaos Falls last night. Psyche said he - he showed up there this morning, and he took her. I'm trying to get back, but - if he has her already... You have to find her."

"Okay, I'll call her and-"

"She won't answer. She hasn't been answering, and she's been gone awhile. I—" He was falling apart, right there on the airstrip. Charon gripped his shoulder, but it didn't help hold the pieces together. Nothing could. "Just find her."

"Okay, what - what do I - Heph." She was panicking. He was too, but he couldn't let it show. "I-"

"Listen, listen. Tell Uncle to call Achilles. He's tracking the car that's missing from the lot, and we think one of my men went with her."

"Okay. Okay, I got it."

She hung up without another word, and Hephaestus felt empty. This was his job. He was supposed to keep her safe. He swore to keep her safe. He slammed his hand straight through the window of the SUV, but no one said anything. No one could. Hephaestus tried to speak, to scream, to do something other than stand there quietly, but fear coated his throat. All he could do was worry and wonder. Is this what love was? Panic? He didn't know. All he knew was that he couldn't lose her.

He heard the plane before he saw it, gliding over the mountain that separated earth from sea before it began its descent. Hephaestus was still holding his breath when it landed, but that didn't stop him from being the first on the plane. Charon and Patroclus followed him, and he tried not to think about how he would have to sit still for the next few hours and do absolutely nothing. He felt like he might just tear out of his skin before they made it back.

Scolding himself alleviated nothing. They were racing against time, and he could only imagine what Aphrodite was going through right now. In fact, he didn't even want to try and do that. He just wanted to get to her.

Once they gassed up the plane, the pilot prepared for takeoff, Perseus taking the seat beside him in the cockpit. Charon busied himself with wrapping Heph's bloodied knuckles, carefully cleaning out the window glass from the wounds. Hephaestus felt nothing. No pain, no discomfort, nothing. He was numb to it all, and for the first time in his life, he just wanted it to hurt a little more.

"How long will it take?" Hephaestus asked.

"If I'm in a hurry?" the pilot quipped. "Four hours."

"Make it three or less, and I'll pay you enough to buy you a brand new plane."

"I think we might be able to do that. You sure we won't be shot out of the sky?"

"Not in Khaos Falls. Everybody's too busy for all that anyway."

"Where am I landing?"

"The Atlantis District." It was Charon who answered. "They're expecting us."

For the sake of something to do, he called Aphrodite's phone one more time before they took off, if only to hear her voice on the voicemail message. It soothed him and terrified him all at once. Then the voicemail box beeped. He put his mouth to the phone.

"I'm coming for you."

Chapter Thirty

APHRODITE

Oris, who Aphrodite now knew as Acrisius due to his men calling him such, was an arrogant bastard. He didn't tie her up or lock her in a room. No, he sat her at the kitchen table for hours, his hand intermittently finding her shoulder —or her thigh when he decided to squat down in front of her and gawk at her chest— as he orchestrated this plan he must have had in the works for ages.

Kleon was preparing to leave the nest now, and that worried her just enough to make her shake. Had he been careful, he would have been the perfect traitor. He would have been able to waltz into Twilight House, welcomed by Psyche and the other staff members as he had always been. It wouldn't happen that way now, but that only made her wonder what they would resort to instead. She doubted he came all this way without a plan B.

She'd left her phone in her purse. She'd left her purse in the car she'd been abducted from. Psyche might have been worried by now, but she couldn't even imagine how long it would take for her to elevate that worry to worthy of calling Persephone and Hades. She didn't know how long it would take for Hephaestus to figure out that they had the wrong guy, or at least that there was another guy, and that was assuming he hadn't been ambushed or blindsided himself. While she knew she had to figure a way out of this herself, she was still wishing he would come. Hopeless romantic to the end.

No. Not the end.

Acrisius squatted down before her once again, but her eyes remained on the window. He placed his large hand on her leg, his dark hair now combed back neatly and his eyes clear.

"I want you to watch Kleon march each and every one of those girls in here," he whispered, close enough to her ear that she could feel his breath there. "Then, they're going to watch their savior get on her knees and beg for her life."

"No," she said curtly. "They aren't."

His lips curled. "Well, they'll certainly watch her burn. If that's what it takes, Aphrodite, I will make sure the last thing they hear from you is your screams. It will live with them forever, right alongside their own once I'm done with them, with all of them."

"Is that what it takes to make you feel like a man?"

"Oh, I am no mere man."

"You're nowhere close, you fucking coward."

His hand whipped across her face so fast that she never saw it coming, but she bit down on her tongue and didn't make a sound. Even as the bruise bloomed across her cheek with a notable burn. She would not give him the satisfaction.

"I'd watch that mouth if I were you," he warned.

She answered by headbutting him. *Hard.* He roared out in pain, clapping a hand over his mouth as he fell back, but before she could use that momentum, one of his boys was pinning her in her seat with his hands. Acrisius turned back on her, growling, his lip and nose bleeding profusely.

"You better watch it," he warned, pointing a finger in her face. "Or I'll fucking skin you alive for your whole district to see!"

He stalked off, angry and out of sorts, which was exactly what she needed. She shook off the hand on her shoulder just as Kleon entered the room, and she pulled herself together. If she was going to get out of this, she had to be smarter than everyone else in the room. And in the house.

"Kleon," she called.

He looked over at her instinctively, but when he saw her, he tried to look away. She stood up before anyone could stop her, reaching out and grabbing his arm.

"I just want to know why," she stated, her eyes fixed on his profile.

He ran a hand through his cropped hair. "It's business, Aphrodite."

"Those girls you swore to protect? They're business?"

He looked her in the eye, but she could tell it was difficult for him. "Yes, and they're worth more to me in chains."

"After everything we've been through, your loyalty is that cheap?"

"You didn't see me! What I could be!"

She raised a brow, a sneer in place once more. "A slaver? Or just someone else's bitch?"

It began and ended in seconds. He lunged at her, and she stayed calm, calm enough to grab the pistol on his hip. The man who had pinned her in her seat rounded the table, but he wasn't quick enough. Aphrodite spun out of Kleon's grip, shooting him in the side of his chest and sending him careening into the wall.

Before the other man could pull his weapon, she shot him too, once in the leg and once in the center of his neck. Just as two more men rushed in, she rounded the table away from them, turning and pulling the trigger multiple times. They dropped one after the other before she reached down and grabbed the rifle the first man had dropped. She'd counted six in total apart from Acrisius. She wasn't leaving here without seeing them fall too.

She moved into the living room, cautious and vigilant, her senses heightened and her heart thudding in her chest. The front door was across from her, and she knew that the other two men must be out there. She also knew they must have heard the gunshots. As soon as it opened, she waited only a second before shooting the pistol, catching the first man in the chest just above his shirt. The second man started shooting behind him, forcing her to duck into the hall. She tucked away the pistol and switched to the rifle, aiming it the way Hephaestus had done with his cane.

She waited for the man to reload, and when he did, she moved to the edge of the hallway wall. Once he moved back into the doorway to aim, she fired. He fell to the ground with a haphazard thud. She had only a moment to celebrate before she heard footsteps behind her. She turned just before Nikolaos could tackle her to the ground, her next shot catching him square in the face. Before she could turn back around however, hands gripped her shoulders, throwing her into the wall headfirst.

Everything went dark albeit for only a few seconds, her head buzzing and her vision disrupted by bright lights. The world seemed to tilt sideways, and she struggled to find the ground to stand on. Still, she forced herself to turn around.

She came face to face with Acrisius, who immediately grabbed hold of the rifle she still clung to and tried to rip it from her hands. He shoved it right into her face again and again, blood immediately streaming from multiple places as sweat trickled into her eyes, making them burn.

Blinking vigorously, she pushed herself off the wall until they were both upright, playing tug-o-war in the center of the hall. He let go with one hand, throwing an elbow into her cheek, her eye. She kicked at his shin. His fist caught her in the jaw. She didn't relinquish her hold. She wouldn't let go. She couldn't. If she let go, she lost. If she let go, she would never see her family again.

If she let go, she would never get to tell Hephaestus she loved him.

Or maybe...

She released the rifle. Acrisius went stumbling back. He caught himself, and as he moved to aim the gun, she pulled the pistol out of the back of her jeans once more. *Just drop.* Hephaestus's voice rang in her ears, his words a mantra. She dropped to one knee. Before he could adjust his aim, she shot. Then she shot again. She kept shooting until she heard nothing but the continuous click of an empty clip. Then she shot again. It kept clicking.

Acrisius fell to the ground.

She didn't know how long she kneeled there, the gun clicking in her hands as Acrisius's body jerked and writhed and... stopped jerking and writhing. Then he was gone, and she was still there, but her ears were still ringing, and her head was still buzzing. At some point, she dug a phone out of someone's pocket, dialing in the only number she could think of and sending her location pin. Then she slumped against the wall, falling in and out of consciousness. The world simply refused to come into focus.

Sometime later or maybe moments later, she heard a car pull up, vaguely, and she reached for the rifle, fumbling into the living room and aiming at the door. They would not take her. She would not die like this, in some abandoned building in her own fucking district. She refused.

The door opened, and she placed her finger on the trigger.

"Aphrodite, don't!"

She screwed her eyes shut then opened them again, blinking past the stars and lights to reveal Hades, then Persephone, both with their hands up as he moved to shield her. It took Aphrodite a long moment to recognize them, but once she did, she dropped the rifle. Then she dropped herself, letting out a roar of frustration and pain as her blood stained the floor. Persephone was beside her in a moment, Hades' men storming the building with guns drawn.

"It's okay," Persephone croaked through her own tears. "'Dite, it's okay."

"Fuck you!" Aphrodite screamed, kicking at Acrisius's body again and again. "Fuck! You!"

Persephone pulled her into her arms, and Aphrodite all but deflated. The fear, the worry, the acceptance; it all roiled in her gut as she slumped against her best friend, the reality of what had happened collapsing in on her all at once. She still didn't feel the pain of the bruises no doubt spreading across her skin, but she felt the shame and frustration that warred within. That was more than enough for now.

Once Hades hoisted them both off of the floor, Aphrodite followed Persephone out of the building with slow steps.

"How - how did you find me?" she managed.

"I got your text," Persephone yelped, tears streaming down her face. "And - Hephaestus had already called and said they had the wrong guy, and—"

"Where is he? Where is Hephaestus?"

"He's on his way. He'll be here soon."

It was only then that Aphrodite broke into a fit of unbridled sobs, her knees buckling so that Persephone had to support all of her weight. He was alive. He was okay, and he was coming for her. He was coming. And that was the only thing she cared about right now. She didn't care if he came back and screamed at her. She didn't care if he came back and told her he was tired of all this. She just wanted him to come back.

Chapter Thirty-One

HEPHAESTUS

She's safe. Leaving Asklepios.

Hephaestus let out a heavy exhale. His emotions had been put through a blender in the past 12 hours. By the time the plane started to descend, his heartbeat no longer had a rhythm, and his mind had completed at least a dozen obstacle courses pertaining to what Aphrodite could have endured. He was exhausted. He was frustrated. He was absolutely worried and utterly ashamed, and even his uncle's text didn't soothe him the way that it should have. Instead, it angered him.

Achilles met them at the Atlantis airstrip, driving them back to Lush. Once they arrived, Hephaestus made his way straight up to Aphrodite's office, a thousand words poised on the tip of his tongue. He wanted to berate her. He wanted to kiss her. He wanted to scold her. He wanted to apologize to her. Each of these desires were at war at the back of his throat, but he kept moving forward regardless. What he needed now was to see her. He needed to see for himself that she was safe. Maybe then, it might all make sense.

The club was hollow, nightfall long past, and the silence felt fragile around him. As he approached her office, he caught a glimpse of her face, bruised and battered to the extent that it made him recoil. Acrisius was dead. His uncle had confirmed that, and he was fucking lucky for it. Had he lived, had she let him live, Hephaestus would have torn his guts from his fucking stomach while he watched. Then he would have fed them to him.

He didn't notice Ares in the office until he opened the door and his younger brother turned on him. Ares had him shoved up against the wall before Hephaestus could blink, and Aphrodite's shriek did nothing to dissuade the larger man. Hephaestus only glared. Or at least he tried to, his eyelids heavy and his face pale. He wasn't in the fucking mood for this.

"Great fucking job you did, Heph," Ares barked, digging his knuckles into Heph's chest. "You almost got her fucking killed! You had one job—"

"Take your hands off me, brother," Hephaestus commanded, his voice cold and concrete.

"She could've died! I thought you had the guy! I thought—"

Hephaestus's hand dug into Ares' abdomen, fingers curling under his rib cage until he howled in pain. He released his older brother with haste, and then Hephaestus released him, creating some distance between them. Ares leveled him with a potent stare, his large body heaving with wrath, prepared to strike at any moment. Part of Hephaestus wanted him to. Part of him knew he deserved it. Still, he straightened with the help of his cane, eyeing his brother.

"Stay away from her, Heph," Ares growled. "You can't keep her safe, and you know it. We all know it now, and for you to tell uncle otherwise for the sake of your ego is gonna get her killed. Just let her go. You can't protect her, and you can't be good—"

"Get out, Ares!" Aphrodite screamed, catching them both off guard, but Ares recovered first.

"—You know I'm right," he breathed, getting closer to Hephaestus. "She doesn't know what's best for her, but you do, and you know it's not you—"

"Get out!"

This time, when Aphrodite demanded it, Ares jumped back, looking over his shoulder at her. When he deduced that she wasn't backing down, he shook his head.

"Ares, I'm not gonna tell you again," she hissed.

"He can't make you happy, Aphrodite. And once he loses interest, you're gonna see that—"

"Get out!"

They stared at one another for the longest time. Then Ares obeyed, shoving Hephaestus into the wall once more before he left the office. Despite his composed exterior, Heph's heart was pounding, embarrassment drowning him right there at the edge of the room. Ares was right. Somewhere, amidst all that talk, he was right, and Hephaestus knew it. He couldn't keep her safe. He had failed.

Aphrodite rushed towards him the moment the door closed, prepared to throw her arms around him, but he quickly put his hands up to stop her. She gave him a confused look as he seethed with anger.

"What were you thinking!" he yelled.

She stared at him as though he'd struck her. "Excuse me?"

"You almost died! Why would you go with someone you don't know! After everything that happened! You could've—"

"Okay, I'm gonna give you a chance to tone that shit down because I know how stressful this was, but don't you dare—"

"That was reckless, Aphrodite." Despite his denial of her words, his voice did lower, but only after it cracked violently. "Why would you go with him?"

"I thought you had the guy."

"But you know damn well there could be more men. Your own men were scheming against you not hours before, and you thought it had been long enough? I hadn't even given the okay yet."

"Someone was in trouble—"

"No, you *believed* someone was! And it turned out to be you! You can't fall for every fucking crocodile tear that walks through your door! Next time, you might not be so lucky!"

"I wasn't lucky!" she shrieked. "I fought my way out!"

"How many times do I have to tell you! This isn't some fucking fairytale where the good guys always win! You can't keep running around like you're bulletproof!"

Her voice grew cold. "Is that what you think I did? I know damn well I'm not bulletproof, Hephaestus, but if you think I'm gonna stop trying to help people—"

"Who's gonna help you!"

"I helped me! I did! I fought on my own! I made my way out! I made my way back! To you!"

He opened his mouth to retaliate as she drove her finger into his chest, but he could think of nothing substantial to say to that. Wasn't that what he wanted? Wasn't that all that he wanted? As if to confirm, she swiftly moved back towards her desk and picked up her phone. Moments later, his voice filled the office.

"I'm coming for you."

"If I believed this was a fairytale, where the hero made it in time, I would be dead."

He turned away from her, resting his head against the wall in a bid for his peace of mind. She was safe. Not without bruises, but she was breathing, and that was what mattered. That should be what mattered. But it was no thanks to him, and she was still as reckless as she had always been. So yes, anger was easier. It helped cover up the anguish. It helped bury the fear.

She was at his side suddenly, her hand on his chest. She forced him to face her, but he kept his gaze on the floor at his feet.

"Look at me," she demanded.

"I can't." It came far too easily for his liking, and his vision was blurring.

"Heph, look at me."

"I can't! I can't fucking look at you! I failed, and you ran off with the guy who put out a fucking hit out on you!"

"I made a mistake! I know that!"

"And it could have cost you your life!"

"I'm sorry!"

"Sorry isn't fucking good enough!"

"What do you want me to say, Hephaestus! I fucked up! And I paid for it, and then I fixed it!"

"And what if you hadn't!"

"I did!"

At last, he looked up at her, his eyes flashing. "You have to grow up!

This is the real world! Fuck the fantasies and the romance novels and the bullshit you say you don't believe in because you do, and you keep doing dumb shit because of it! You never fucking learn!"

She sneered. "Fuck you, Heph!" She slammed her fists against his chest. "Fuck you!"

"Fuck me? Fuck you!" He let his cane fall to the floor as he snatched up her wrists. "Fuck you, you reckless, foolish woman! Fuck - you!"

"I hate you! You bitter, pessimistic man!"

"And I hate you! I hate caring about you! I hate loving you, and I hate worrying about what foolish fucking thing you're gonna do next!"

She tried to swing at him, to rip her hand from his grasp, but he held her to him until there was little more than the brittle tension between them. Only then did he hear his own words echo back at him like a war cry. His cheeks were damp, and her eyes were red, and the walls felt like they were closing in.

His nose brushed hers, eyes blistering with rage, but he honed in on her breath against his lips. He had honestly thought he'd lost her. He never wanted to know that kind of terror again. Fairy tale or not, he was in love with her. And it didn't matter if he was wrong or if Ares was right. That was the truth.

He turned his head and crushed his lips against hers, still holding her wrists although they began to relax in his hands. Damp turned to wet, but he didn't know whose tears were streaming down his face, and he didn't care. He didn't care about anything but her.

"I'm sorry, Daddy," she muttered, half cry and half moan, and his chest tightened. "I'm sorry."

"You're gonna be."

He shoved her back towards the desk, chasing her with deliberate steps driven only by adrenaline and anger. As she collided with the wood, her hand blindly found the switch on the side, the transparent windows of her office instantly opaque. He gripped her arm the moment he reached her, spinning her around before he cleared the surface with one sweep of his own. Then he bent her over it.

He bothered with very little, bunching her dress around her hips as she braced her forearms against the desk and widened her stance. He pushed her panties to the side and pushed his fears down as deep as he could, pretending he could rid himself of every apprehension that plagued him beneath the skin.

He twisted a hand in her hair, jerking her head back to elicit a sharp gasp from her gritted teeth before he pushed his cock inside of her. Even in his anger, he tried to do so slowly so as not to hurt her, but she threw her ass back, taking him up to the hilt.

"Punish me, daddy," she whimpered. "Please. I promise I'll take it like a good girl."

He grunted as he spread her open, his thrust rough, punishing in every sense of the word. He should be apologizing. He should be telling her how sorry *he* was. He should be admitting to his monolithic failures. But this was the only thing he could do. It was the only thing he knew how to do because once he said those things, he would no longer be able to convince himself he deserved her.

Their knees knocked against the desk, a cacophony of sound permeating the air. She slapped her open palms against the surface, her breasts pressed flush against it. When he looked up, his ragged reflection glared back at him from the window, each one of his strokes like a trigger shooting another wanton sound in the air.

"Say you're sorry," he commanded, his voice like broken glass.

"I'm sorry! Daddy, I'm sorry!"

"Say you're sorry for being a bad girl."

"I'm sorry, Daddy!" Her sobs ricocheted around the room. "I'm - sorry I was a bad girl! Please!"

He shifted his hips just enough so that his hand could connect with her ass, the force knocking them both forth. If her desk wasn't bolted into the floor, it would certainly be pushed up against the window by now. Her hands moved to grab the edge in front of her, and he reached down to take hold of her thigh, hoisting one knee onto the desk and leaving her wide open for him to fuck deep and hard, her screams soon loud enough that she had to bite down on her forearm. In that moment, it was what he needed. He needed that mixture of pain and pleasure, panic and relief, gratitude and shame. He needed her to know that he wouldn't let her get away with putting the woman he loved in danger.

Her pussy clamped down on him, holding his dick in a vice grip so that his thrusts grew shorter. She let out another cry, but it was abruptly severed by her orgasm ravaging her body, her back bowing upward and her legs trembling between his and the desk. Shudder after violent shudder racked her, but he kept thrusting, gripping her shoulder and forcing her back down against the wood. He didn't want it to end. He didn't want to cum. Once he did, it would all come crashing down again, and he wasn't sure he would be able to find his way out. But as her walls spasmed around him and she riddled the air with the soft sputter of his name, he could hardly hold on.

He relinquished it out of sheer self-preservation, snapping his hips into hers with ruthless force until he came with a rumbling shout, seed spilling over her walls and rage spilling over her back.

"Heph..." she mewled, looking back at him. "Daddy."

He rode it out, lost to the euphoria of being inside of her again and the weakness of his own exhausted body. Slumping forward, his panting breaths buried themselves in the valley of her shoulder blades, her hand reaching back and threading through his dark hair. As soon as he was able though, he pushed himself away, stumbling back on trembling legs. He managed to pull his pants up before he collapsed. He sat on the carpet in a daze, hands hung over his knees and head hung against his chest. As he came back down, he was greeted by the grief, the doubt, and every other dark and treacherous thing he had tried to smother between them.

She pulled her dress down before dropping to her knees and crawling over to him, kneeling between his legs.

"I broke my promise," he croaked. "I failed. I failed, and it could've—"

"Stop it. You didn't fail. You were on the right track, and I - I made a mistake. I never should've trusted him. I never should've run off like that."

"I thought I had the right guy."

"And you didn't, but you got him eventually, and if I'd just waited a few hours—"

"I should've seen it."

"Seen what?" She cupped his face between her palms, and he was forced to look at the bruising under her jaw and beneath her eye and across the bridge of her nose. "We made mistakes, but we're here. We're okay, and - the only thing I have wanted since I got out of there, since you left really, was to see you, so - please."

A self-deprecating chuckle left his lips. Even as he tried to recall his father's words and his timeless tale of the blacksmith and the siren, it all felt so helpless. Like the pen had been torn from his hands, and maybe it should be. What if he wrote the ending and doomed her to ruin? What if the story he created was not meant for this world? For them?

"Aphrodite, I'm not the brother you end up with."

She swallowed. "Isn't that for me to decide?" He shook his head, and he could feel her go rigid before him, agitation slowly corroding her. "Is that because of what Ares said? You agree with him? That I'm not capable of making my own decisions?"

"I'm not saying that, but—"

"Hephaestus, if you don't want me, don't be a fucking coward and pass it off on some bullshit assumption or expectation. Look me in the eye and tell me that you don't want me, but don't—"

"Of course I want you!" He clasped her arms and met her gaze in desperation, face ashen as he struggled with the weight of not being enough. "I want you more than anything, but that—"

"Then that's all that matters!"

"That's not the way the world works. I'm not - for you."

"Says who!" He dropped his head again. "Tell me! Says who? Because I want you, Hephaestus. I want you more than anything. I'm so fucking in love with you, foolish as that may be, and all I want right now is - is for you to hold me and tell me you feel the same way, so don't fucking say you aren't for me because that isn't up to you! That is up to me and me alone! I don't want anyone else. I will never want anyone else. So how can you not be?"

She waited, her breathing heavy, until he finally straightened, his jaw set. "Then - why did you want to keep it a secret? Why did you ask Persephone and my uncle to keep quiet about it?"

She barked a bitter laugh. "You think I was ashamed of you? I was ashamed of myself!"

"Why?"

"Hephaestus, I was just with your brother, and - Persephone thought I would start a feud or something between you two. And I couldn't even admit to myself how I felt about you yet. How could I get her or your uncle to believe me? To - to believe I wasn't just making my way through all of his nephews? I - I didn't want them to think less of me, and - I didn't want anyone to think I was just sleeping with you because it was convenient."

Confusion colored his face. "But wasn't it?"

She stared at him for a moment as though he were daft before she gave a slow shake of her head. "No. It wasn't. I - I hated you. Or I wanted to hate you, but - I never would've slept with you just because you were there. That wasn't it. When you kissed me, everything was different, and I chased it. And I'll keep chasing it."

"Because it was me or because it was fun?"

"Hephaestus, keep up. It was only fun *because* it was you."

He studied her for a moment, every single one of his doubts and insecurities eating away at him like maggots. It wasn't clicking for him. For as long as Ares had been alive, he had overshadowed his older brother. Before then, Hephaestus had been the worst kept secret in Khaos Falls, bearer of Zeus's shame and Hera's failure. He'd carved out his own path out of necessity, and he hid these burdens beneath a cold smirk and crystal eyes, but that did not negate the fact. They weighed upon his shoulders heavy as anvils, and just as impossible to break.

"Hephaestus."

She pulled him back from the depth of his thoughts, his eyes focusing on her face just as her hand found the side of his. He felt frozen, his need for her at war with his desire for the safety of solitude. If he stayed, he had one more thing to lose and one more person to let down. Yet he couldn't sit here and say it wasn't worth the risk. Because if he left, he would have nothing. Worse than that, he wouldn't have her.

"Why me?" he questioned, almost as an afterthought.

She smiled through fresh tears. "I ask myself that every damn morning." She cradled his face in both hands now, and he leaned into the touch. "You are the antithesis of everything I am, and that led me to believe that you are everything but what I need. But - that isn't true. I need you, Heph. I need your - your logic, rational thought. I need your pragmatism. I need your rough touch and your soft one. I need your annoying reality checks and your stupid rules. And I need you to love me even if you don't like me at the moment so I can do the same for you. I need you. All of you."

He shook his head again, his lips twitching sadly. "Everyone in this city, they worship you."

"I don't want to be worshipped by everyone in this city. I just want to be loved by you."

It felt foreign. It seemed surreal. Who would ever choose him? Yet... he blinked, and she was still kneeling there before him, waiting. Soon, it was difficult to remember what it was he was so afraid of. He tightened his grip on her elbows.

"Okay."

She sighed. "Okay?"

"Okay, Aphrodite. I promise to love you even when I don't like you at the moment."

A watery laugh jumped from her lips as she moved her hands down to shove at his chest, but he simply pulled himself closer to her. Then her mouth was on his like a signature on this commitment they'd agreed upon. He wasn't complaining, not in the least. If fear was the price of loving Aphrodite, he decided there were steeper prices to pay.

And he would probably pay them just as well.

Chapter Thirty-Two

HEPHAESTUS

The Sarpedon District was an intricate maze of sharp angles and dead end streets, most of its "attractions" taking place underground rather than above it. More than anything, it was notorious for its streetcar races, and people came from all around the Aegean to either watch, bet, or drive in one. Nonetheless, the landscape was a dark beauty, an intricate painting of purples and silvers and white marble. Many of the buildings flew the flag of their leader, Medusa's insignia like an omen watching over the land.

Hephaestus looked up at the carved ivory before him, that insignia brought to life in a 3D sculpture of the famed gorgon, her head of snakes reared up and ready to strike at any moment. Her mouth was open, bearing sharp teeth and a serpent's tongue, her wicked eyes bright with hunger. He had never feared the gorgon. His mother used to tell him that it was foolish to fear a woman who became what she must to survive. Unless of course you were what stood between her and survival, but then that meant you deserved what came to you.

Medusa herself was as imposing as the gorgon and far more beautiful, with silky dark hair flowing over her shoulders, complementing her rich, black skin. She too had eyes like a cobra, and her bite was just as vicious without her ever using her teeth. She was Hephaestus's godmother, and while Zeus had more or less kept her out of their lives, she had been Hera's best friend since they were children.

It was Medusa who had taken her in after Zeus's exile, offering Hera a soft place to land or a place to fall apart and put herself back together. In the months since, Hera had taken up a position as head of the historical society, which Hephaestus found quite intriguing. According to Charon, Hera had always loved to read, and Hephaestus himself knew she loved to peer back into the past even when no one but her knew what she was looking at.

He walked up the ramp that led to the grandeur library doors, gilded and golden and shining in the faint winter sunlight. The library itself was vast, seven floors of the past, present, and future colliding amidst thick oak shelves and blacktop tables. He passed the circulation desk, waving at the two women sitting there in front of their computers, proceeding through the open space and back towards the elevators. Climbing into the car, he hit the button for the fifth floor, but as the doors began to shut, an elegant hand slipped between them. In stepped Medusa herself, looking him over until she made a positive identification then sweeping him up in a hug as the doors closed behind her.

"Hephaestus." Her voice was low and perpetually alluring. Just like the many serpents she kept in her reptile house down the street. "I heard you've been busy. It's good to see you standing."

"Hey, Auntie," he returned as they disengaged, a lopsided smile on his face. "Yeah, it's been - a rough few weeks. How are you?"

"Oh, I am grand. We tend to keep to ourselves in this district, and it serves us well more often than not. How is your uncle adjusting to his new position?"

"Very well actually. You would think he's been doing it his whole life."

"Ah, and he should've been. His father was one of the most pleasant men in the city, and he led his district well. He simply never wanted more power than he had. A simple man, much like Hades. What about you? How is this new position treating you, apart from the past few weeks of course?"

"So far so good, I guess. I'm still adjusting. I liked the quiet just as much as Uncle, so."

"Solitude is an important asset, even when you cannot utilize it all the time. It's something you should always keep in case you need it."

He had never thought of it like that. "That - makes a lot of sense, thanks. How is my mother?"

She smiled now. "Thriving, but you'll see for yourself in..."

Just then, the car came to a halt, the doors opening onto the fifth floor. She gestured through them with a smile.

"I'm expected upstairs," she informed him, giving him one last squeeze. "I'll see you soon though I'm sure. Be careful out there, Heph."

"I will."

He waved goodbye before stepping off of the car, the doors shutting behind him. In front of him was a small atrium and straight ahead was a large glass wall with a set of doors set in the center. The sign above them read "Khaos Falls Historical Society". He approached the doors, and they slid open as he reached them, admitting him into a whole new world. The walls were covered in maps and diagrams, the shelves lining the wall stretching from floor to ceiling.

There were more shelves in the center of the room, tables and chairs sprinkled throughout. Another smaller room sat to his left on the other side of a glass partition, computers visible within. He took it all in with eager eyes, his steps slowing almost to a halt. He could understand how his mother found solace here. In the quiet of the room, one could cease to exist in the rest of the world, creating one of their own.

"Hephaestus?"

Turning his head to his right, he found his mother standing from a desk in the corner, a parchment unrolled in her hands. He smiled. Medusa hadn't lied. His mother was practically glowing, her glasses perched at the edge of her nose and her dark curls drawn up into a bun atop her head. Her tanned skin was flawless, luminescent beneath the fluorescents. Hera had always been beautiful even when Zeus did everything in his power to convince her she wasn't. Nonetheless, for Hephaestus, loving his mother was like loving a rose. There was no place to hold her where the thorns wouldn't tear open his skin. He didn't blame her so much anymore.

She set down the scroll and moved towards him, her lips pursed and her cheeks flushed. He imagined he looked much the same way, nervous as he was.

"Your fa - Charon called me," she started just before she reached him.

They halted a few feet from one another, simply staring, so many of his features reflected back at him although not nearly as many as when he looked at Charon these days.

"You look good," he told her. "Truly. You - you look happy, and Aunt Medusa said you're thriving. I just saw her in the elevator."

"Oh." She nodded, looking him over. "—I heard you were in a bit of trouble, but you worked it all out. They - they said you're a hero."

He shook his head. "Naw, I - I helped to some extent, but I made a lot of mistakes, and it almost cost us - a lot of lives."

"It isn't easy protecting an entire city, but from what I was told, you did well for your first big job. You'll only get better."

They were both quiet for a long time, neither knowing what to say until suddenly, without warning, she was moving forward, throwing her arms around him and pulling him into a hug. He tensed for a moment before relaxing and wrapping an arm around her waist.

"Hey, Mama," he mumbled against her neck.

"I'm so glad you're okay," she breathed. "I was so worried. Your - Charon, he said-"

"It's okay, Mama." He pulled back to look at her. "You can call him what he is. It's okay now."

There were tears welling in her eyes. "I'm sorry. I'm so sorry, Hephaestus, for everything, and I can never apologize enough. I know that. I know I made - so many mistakes with you, but - I just wanted you to - I..." She removed her glasses, fanning her face. "I knew he would look after you. I knew that."

It seemed like there was no easing into this conversation, so he went with it. "And he did, but - that whole time, I thought it was because you regretted me."

The tears fell now, and she shook her head. "I was terrible to you. I know that, but it was never because I regretted you. I could never regret you. You were - you were everything I wanted. Your father and I, we wanted a family, and... But my parents had a plan, and there was no derailing them from it. And when I looked at you every single day after I married Zeus, all I saw was your father and - all of the things I could never have. A past I couldn't save. And I didn't know how to deal with it, but by the time I figured it out, you were grown."

"I just wanted to know you cared." He could feel his eyes burning. "I wanted to know I was enough because ever since then, I feel like I never will be."

"Hephaestus." She cupped his cheeks as he bowed his head, pressing her lips to his forehead. "You are so much more than enough. You look so much like your father, so much like the man I loved more than anything and anyone. You were perfect, son. I just didn't know how to appreciate you, and - Zeus was - he was horrible. He was so horrible, but I didn't want you to stick around because you thought you had to protect me. You were born a protector, you know."

He nodded, a sob breaking loose from his lips.

"So I pushed you away, towards your father because I knew he would look after you, and he would make sure you were loved. Him and your uncle. And I'm sorry it took me so long to tell you the truth, but I swear to you, Hephaestus. You are one of the two best things I've ever done."

He couldn't speak anymore, his throat constricting as a lump formed, so he simply pulled her back into his arms. It wouldn't heal every wound he had. Nothing ever could, and much of the damage was done, but while he may have been broken in places, some of those pieces could be fixed and filled in. There was still work to do, and now that he had a future to look forward to with the woman he loved, he would do it. He would do anything to always be enough. And it wasn't up to anyone but him now.

"So - you talked?" he questioned, pulling back once more. "To my dad?"

"I did," she chuckled, wiping her tears. "For the first time in a very long time."

"Do you - do you still love him?"

She smiled. "I will always love him. He gave me you."

"But - you know..."

"No, I don't, Hephaestus. I honestly don't know. I'm still trying to figure out who I am after - everything. I still wake up most days thinking I'm back in that - Fates forsaken house with that Fates forsaken man. I still have nightmares. And - I'm doing better, but I'm not better yet."

He nodded, taking her hands in his. "I still think you should talk. Even if you can't change the past, I think you both could help each other. You can heal, Mama. It's okay to be happy. Don't think you don't deserve it just because he made you believe that. He was wrong. He was wrong about everything."

"But what I did to you—"

"I forgive you, Mama, and I won't let you punish yourself for the rest of your life. No way."

She stared at him for what felt like ages, her eyes mapping out his features, and he knew she was seeing his father there. Maybe he'd been spending too much time around Aphrodite's hopelessly romantic ass, but he did think his parents deserved to at least try to be happy. Even as friends or even just as his parents. But he didn't want Zeus to take more of her than he already had. Heph didn't want him to keep winning.

"How about we have dinner?" he suggested now, a smile spreading across his face. "I can introduce you both to my girlfriend."

She scoffed. "What girlfriend?"

He wet his lips. "Aphrodite."

"Aphrodite?" She raised a brow. "Wasn't she—"

"I promise that Ares and I... Well, I'll talk to him once he calms down."

She sighed. "I stay off the grid for a few months, and this is what I come back to."

"I love her, Mama. I love her the way Dad loves you, the way he always loved you. He used to - tell me stories, you know, about a siren and a blacksmith."

She laughed now, harder than he had ever seen her laugh, and he knew his hunch was correct. She knew what he was talking about. "Did he? Oh, he loved calling me a siren. He-" She caught herself, but a smile remained on her face. "Okay, I'll have dinner with you and your father. And your girlfriend."

"Okay, but-" He grew serious now. "You gotta be nice, alright? Nothing about Ares."

"She chose you, didn't she?"

His smile returned. "Yeah, she did."

"And not just because you had to keep her safe?"

"And not just because I had to keep her safe."

"Then I'll be nice. As long as you're happy."

"I am, Mama. I really am."

She brushed a hand through his hair. "Then that's all that matters."

HE FELT LIGHT ON HIS DRIVE BACK TO LUSH, ONE OF HIS HEAVIEST burdens lifted from his shoulders and tossed away for the birds. The whole world seemed brighter in his eyes despite winter still bearing down on the city, and for the first time, the days didn't seem so mindless. The routine of work and sleep had been broken into a billion pieces, and he had room to breathe. He was looking forward to it, whatever came next. Because Aphrodite, goddess of Khaos Falls, loved him, and he was enough.

As he stepped off the elevator onto the second floor of the club, he was greeted by two figures near Aphrodite's office door, one of which he recognized. Phobos was still on crutches, but he all but bounded towards Hephaestus anyway, wrapping his fully healed arms around his waist. Hephaestus didn't tense this time, instead hugging the boy with a chuckle.

"Got my cast off!" Phobos announced as they parted. "Well, one of them. Deimos!" He looked over his shoulder at the other boy, who looked as timid as he did tired. He inched forward, keeping his eyes on his brother as he came to stand beside him. Hephaestus offered his hand. Deimos eyed it a moment before taking it in his own and shaking it briefly.

"Hi, Deimos," Heph said softly. "I heard a lot about you. It's nice to finally meet you."

"My brother says you'll let us work," he blurted, his eyes widening.

"That's right. As soon as he's all better, I can find work for you no problem, but I also told him that it's okay to take a break. Be a kid."

"Aphrodite says we can stay in the club until then, and we get our own suite!" Phobos revealed with a large grin. "That means we can stay in the same room, and we won't have to be apart anymore."

"But you'll behave nonetheless," came a voice from behind Hephaestus.

Psyche strode forward with another woman in tow, and Hephaestus recognized her as one of the nurses from Twilight House.

"Iris will be checking in on you boys every day to make sure you're not agitating your wounds," Psyche explained. "And that you're both getting proper sleep. That was the deal, right? You could share a room as long as you slept?"

"Yes, Ma'am," both boys chirped before Phobos turned back to Hephaestus.

"Aphrodite said you live here with her sometimes, so we can see you whenever we want. Is that okay? Like can I see you even if my leg is still hurt?"

Hephaestus smiled, ruffling his hair. "Yeah, you can. We'll find something to do, alright? And - maybe you can meet my brothers soon. I think you would love my baby brother, Dio."

Psyche giggled. "I'm sure of that."

Phobos grinned and hugged him again, and Hephaestus's heart swelled in his chest. He had no clue just how relieved he would be to see this boy again, and it surprised him.

"Tell you what," Hephaestus said now. "Why don't you two go upstairs with Iris and get cleaned up while I find Aphrodite, and then we'll take you two out to eat?"

"Really!" This time, it was Deimos, and he shouted so loud that it surprised all of them.

"Yes, really. You down?"

"Yes!" The twins said.

They quickly followed Iris back towards the elevators, leaving Hephaestus and Psyche alone on the landing. They turned to each other at the same time, but before he could ask where Aphrodite was, she shot forward and hugged him. He was slowly getting used to all the surprise embraces, but this one was just as shocking. Slowly, he wrapped his arms around her.

"Thank you," she breathed, her tears seeping through his shirt. "You have no idea how thankful I am for everything you've done for her."

"She did most of it."

"Please." She stepped back, wiping at her eyes. "She's never been this happy, but also - everything you did. I know you might think you didn't protect her, but - you did. You got her through it all, and don't ever forget that."

He didn't know what to say to that, so he simply nodded. "Thank you."

She hugged him once more, and he patted her back, trying not to get lost in his own emotions.

"Hey, uh uh, hands off!"

The two of them pulled apart as Aphrodite came up the stairs, Eros on her heels.

"What is all this? And in my club?"

"Girl, please," Psyche chuckled, the sound watery. "I was thanking him for keeping you in check, so I don't have to anymore."

Aphrodite snorted. "Y'all wish you could."

"No, but we really do," Eros said.

They laughed as Aphrodite folded herself into Heph's chest, wrapping her arms around his waist. He was quick to squeeze her tighter to him, pressing his lips to her forehead.

"Did you see the twins?" she asked. "They were looking all over for you."

"I did," he answered. "I told them we'd take them out to eat. Is that okay?"

"Ooh, you wanna take them on our first date now?"

He rolled his eyes. "I'll make it up to you later."

"Mm, you promise, Daddy?"

"I do, as long as you're a good girl."

"Come on, y'all, really?" Eros groaned.

"Hey, don't talk to your parents like that," Psyche teased, Eros rolling his eyes all the way back into his head and triggering a fresh round of laughter.

"Y'all wanna come too?" Aphrodite asked now. "I guess we can take all the kids."

"Damn right I do!" Eros sang, immediately recovering from his disgust. "So now that we're family and all, Pops, does that mean I get to drive the bulletproof car?"

Hephaestus smirked. "Not a chance."

"Come on! Why!"

"Actually, ask your mother."

"Uh uh, leave me out of it," Aphrodite said quickly.

There was an eruption of arguments and debates on the topic until it morphed into Eros and Psyche arguing about the irrationality of bulletproof glasses. Aphrodite took the opportunity to turn back to Hephaestus, pecking his lips.

"Where are the twins?" she questioned.

"They are-"

Just then the elevator dinged, and they could hear Phobos talking animatedly inside. Hephaestus smirked.

"Right there."

The twins came tumbling out, and Phobos immediately zoomed towards the railing before Iris grabbed him.

"There is an alternative way to get them in and out of the club, right?" she asked.

"Yes, garage elevator only for you two until you're of legal age to enter this establishment," Hephaestus declared.

Both boys groaned, but then Eros was whispering in their ears, and they were happy again. Hephaestus assumed he was bribing them with chocolate.

"You really ready to do this?" he asked Aphrodite with a sigh.

She gave him a challenging look. "With you? I'm ready to do anything. You'll just have to stick by my side a bit longer than originally planned."

"You just wanna keep me close, huh?"

She grinned. "Now you're getting it."

EPILOGUE

It took Aphrodite weeks to be able to sleep through the night. Even in Hephaestus's arms, her mistake with Acrisius still haunted her to the point that she woke up breathless, only comforted by his warm hands and soft lips on her forehead. However, what she came to realize was that he wasn't sleeping much either, and they eventually ended up finding other ways to pass the time.

Sure, there was tons of sex, Hephaestus eager and able to feed her insatiable appetite whenever she asked. However, they also played video games and threw popcorn at each other across the couch and watched movies with the twins in a pillow fort they roped Hephaestus into building. Of course his pragmatism and attention to detail made it slightly less fun at stages, but once the fort was done, the twins' happiness was unshakeable. They started sleeping through the night long before Aphrodite, sometimes on the living room floor of the penthouse, but she was grateful that she and Hephaestus were able to help. She was still eager to do that regardless of all that had happened, and he was just as eager to aid her.

The new couple took time for themselves too. Once a week, Psyche or Iris watched the boys while they escaped to Hephaestus's place where they recuperated and simply spent time together, sharing stories and swapping traumas until they had a better understanding of one another. As time went on, he grew so much softer with her too, but she supposed the twins had much to do with that. If he wasn't working or with her, he was with them, and if she didn't know any better, she would say he was attached. The boys were surely attached to him.

These were all the things she had grown accustomed to literally overnight, and she cherished each and every one of them.

She stood at the window of her office, watching Lush come to life for the evening. Hephaestus had just returned from putting the twins to bed, and he was now on the main floor, checking in with the new recruits. After cleansing her security team, he and Hades had taken it upon themselves to construct a new one for her, one they could all trust, by taking pieces of both of their forces.

She hadn't had any complaints. In fact, the only thing she wasn't looking forward to was the fact that Heph wouldn't be at her side 24/7 come next week. He'd stayed on awhile longer for her sake and so the twins could become better adjusted to the place. Or at least, that was what he said, but he seemed as eager to be there with them as they were to be with him.

It was comforting beyond all else considering the fact she had feared he would wake up one day and realize he was making a mistake, that he didn't actually love her. It had simply been the proximity that had him in his feelings. It hadn't happened yet though, and each day, he became more open about his love for her. He still tried to hide his softest feelings, but she was getting really good at pointing them out on her own. They were her favorite.

"You know he won't disappear if you stop staring at him for a few minutes, right?"

"No, I don't know that."

Persephone came to stand beside her, offering her a drink before joining her in watching the floor below. Hades and Charon had now joined Hephaestus, and the new guards had begun branching off to head to their stations.

"And look at you," Aphrodite scoffed. "You'd stare at Hades all day if you could."

"Damn right," Persephone conceded. "He is fine."

They shared a laugh, even as Aphrodite's heart thudded in her chest. Her claim was nothing short of the truth. Every time Heph wasn't with her, she feared he would never come back. That something would happen to him or that this was all a dream to begin with. It was a nightmare she was slowly learning to combat.

"You know, looking at them now, it's kind of amazing we didn't know Charon was his father," Persephone stated.

"Right! Heph is practically a clone."

"I guess he does look a lot like Hera though too, and his eyes are very..."

"Unique," they both said in unison.

They chuckled once more. Aphrodite could admit she was relieved that she had already met one of his parents even without meaning to, and Charon was certainly a huge step up from Zeus in all the ways that mattered. She was glad to know that Hephaestus had grown up with a loving father after all, whether anyone knew it or not.

"What did y'all end up doing with the girl?" Persephone inquired. "Leda."

"Heph talked me down from throwing her into the ocean," Aphrodite quipped. "And we eventually agreed that she deserved another chance. She was a kid after all, and Acrisius - who knows how long he'd been manipulating her, you know?"

"Yeah, I thought the same thing. It was probably a lot longer than we realize."

"So I asked Mama if she had any job openings."

Persephone whipped her head around. "You did not."

"Oh, I did."

"And Mama didn't say she would rather feed her to the sharks?"

"At first, but I managed to talk her down too. Leda will be working in the fruit plant on the coast. She'll have lodging, meals, and a tutor as well as a counselor that will check on her twice a week until she's - *reformed*."

"How do you feel about it?"

Aphrodite shrugged. "I mean we helped her. That's the important thing, and - she did at least try to apologize. Like we said, she was a kid. She did terrible things, but - I don't think she's beyond help. She just needs a chance."

Persephone nodded, a small smile on her face. "I'm proud of you, you know. Not of your recklessness maybe, but I am proud. You've done a lot of good here, 'Dite, and hopefully now, you and Hephaestus can do even better."

"We will. After going through all this, now that we understand each other better, I think we're really gonna change the world, you know?"

And as Aphrodite said the words aloud, she realized she truly believed them. The situation no longer seemed so hopeless. She was making a difference, and she had someone by her side to do it with now. That was the story she was made for. She didn't need a hero. She needed a partner.

"How did it go with Ares?" Persephone asked slowly.

Aphrodite sighed, thinking back to her visit to Olympus days prior. She had wanted to try and end things on good terms with Ares, but he seemed to want anything but. His passion had shown brightest amidst his anger, but that anger was also chaotic and unchecked. He had vehemently tried to convince her that she was wrong, that she couldn't decide for herself who she should be with, and he didn't parse words. While she didn't fault him in the least and there had been no violence, it was the first time she'd ever felt entirely uncomfortable around him. But she couldn't only attribute it to his behavior, regardless of how explosive it was. Her shame had a whole lot to do with it too.

She didn't regret it of course, and she knew he was the one that was wrong. No choice had ever been easier to her than Hephaestus. She loved him, and she loved loving him, but above all, she loved being loved by him. Nothing could compare to that feeling, and she knew nothing ever would.

"About as well as one would expect, but - his reaction only convinced me of what I already knew," Aphrodite explained. "Even if it wasn't Heph, it still wasn't him."

She felt Persephone's eyes burning a hole in the side of her head, but she said nothing further. What more could she say? What was done was done, and though she hoped Hephaestus and Ares could mend their own troubles, she could only do so much to help herself. If Ares ever decided to try and understand, he knew where to find her.

"You really do love him, huh?" Persephone's voice was feather soft.

Aphrodite nodded easily, her eyes once again drawn to him. It filled her with a giddy excitement, the stark realization that she had fallen in love with the man she could not stand to be around mere weeks ago. Just like that. And now they're practically parenting twins together and working to save a city long damned. It all happened in the blink of an eye, and she was better for it. Everything was better for it. And she would go through the whole damn ordeal again just to get to him.

"I don't know, I - I always wanted love so bad that - I thought I knew what I'd do when I found it," she started without really meaning to, but she continued nonetheless. "Now that I do though, I don't - have any kinda plan or - really any idea on what to do with it. I just know I never wanna lose it. It's so much more than I ever thought it would be. Loving him feels like the most rational decision I've ever made."

"To be fair, the bar is set pretty low."

Aphrodite shoved at her shoulder as Persephone snickered.

There was a long pause before Persephone spoke again. "Hephaestus though. That was straight out of left field. I never saw that coming."

Aphrodite snorted a laugh. "How do you think I feel?"

"You must be sure though. I know you wouldn't even entertain the thought if you weren't. And y'all are out here running around with twins? This has to be serious."

"Ain't that the truth. Those boys love him though. I can see it all over their faces. I mean, they're close to me too, but the way Heph bonds with them. It's -"

"Kinda magical to see, huh?" Aphrodite nodded. "That's how it feels watching Hades and Dio, especially now after everything. Nothing could ever compare to how much he loves that boy. Athena and the other boys too, but..."

"I get it. And honestly, the fact that Heph was the one who asked if we could keep them here long term caught me off guard, but I'm glad he did. I think he needs them as much as they need him."

"They need you too. We all do."

"Well, after what I just went through, it'll be a whole lot harder to end me now."

Persephone smiled. "You finally got your fairytale ending."

Aphrodite shook her head. "That's the thing though. Before him, I thought that's what I wanted, what falling for someone would be, but... No. What I have with him, it's not a fairy tale. It's real."

Persephone seemed to understand, her lips stretching wider across her face. "Well, I'm glad you found him... I guess you can thank Hades and I."

"For what?"

"We put him in charge of your safety. If not for us—"

Aphrodite bumped her shoulder against the other woman's. "Oh, please, girl. Hush up."

"Hey, I'm just sayin'. It's the truth."

"Yeah, yeah... Thank you."

The last of the guards dispersed below, and Hephaestus sat down at a table. With one look at his face, Aphrodite could tell by now that his leg was troubling him even before he pulled the vapor pen from his shirt pocket. A red shirt, she realized then. The shirt from his closet she had asked him to wear. She had been right too. He looked sexy as fuck in it.

Persephone nudged her before kissing her cheek.

"I'm happy for you," she whispered. "Both of you."

"I appreciate that," Aphrodite returned.

She turned away from the window just as Hades entered the office, regal as ever in his carefully fitted suit. Charon trailed behind him, and it was the first time Aphrodite had seen any emotion on the man's face. He looked - happy. Or maybe proud.

"You ready to go?" Hades asked Persephone, who nodded and moved to gather her purse.

Aphrodite hugged her best friend, promises of a call tomorrow passing between them before Aphrodite headed for the door. The men idled there amidst her approach, and she halted before them, her eyes meeting Hades' first. There was a silent understanding between them, the words that went unspoken well meant and unnecessary. Still, he patted her shoulder with a small smile.

"I'm not worried."

She smirked. "You don't have to be."

She moved past him, stopping in front of Charon, who did not hesitate to pull her into a hug. Surprised as she was, she quickly hugged him back.

"Take care of my boy," he whispered in her ear.

"I will," she assured him. "You have my word."

Once he released her, she walked out of the office and down the stairs to where Hephaestus sat. His eyes were sharp as ever, scanning the room as it began to fill. She sauntered towards him, and it didn't take long before his eyes found her, climbing up her legs until they reached her waist, her chest, her face. She bit her lip, coming to a halt before him. She winded her hips, turning around slowly to give him a full view of her until she could lower herself into his lap. Stretching herself across the planes of his body, she finally heard that gravelly chuckle she loved so much, gruff against her ear. His hands found her waist, and she melted into him immediately.

"You looked so good sitting down here in that red shirt, I had to come—"

"What, bug me?"

She nearly snapped her neck to look back at him. "Oh, is that what I'm doing? Okay, don't bother coming up to see me—"

"Hey, hey." He wrapped his arms around her fully, and she struggled to even pretend to be mad. "I'm just playing, Princess. You know I'll be right behind you when you go upstairs."

"Oh, really?"

"Mhm. Maybe even after that."

"Nasty."

"You like it."

"But I don't like you much right now."

"Mm, you love me though."

She eyed him, but her heart skipped a beat as that smirk began to melt into something more sentimental. She couldn't help but smile too.

"Unfortunately."

He scoffed. "Oh, unfortunately?"

"Mhm."

"Just remember. You can have any person you want in this city."

"Yes, but unfortunately, I only want you, jackass."

"Then get used to it." He moved his mouth closer to her ear, lowering his voice. "And be a good girl before Daddy has to bend you over his knee right here in your own club."

She turned in his lap, wrapping an arm around his neck and resting her other hand against his chest. His fingers rose to dust along her jaw where most of the bruising had faded. Then there was that look in his eyes, the glossy look that gave his clouded irises color and made her stomach swan dive.

"I really am in love with you," he whispered, more to himself than to her it seemed.

She chuckled. "Don't sound so surprised."

"But I am." He smiled wider. "And that's not a bad thing."

This kiss was softer than she expected, softer than he had ever kissed her, and she could drown in it. It touched something in her that had never been touched, and she leaned into him like a flower to the sun, yearning for more.

And he delivered.

This was so much more than she had ever imagined, and she had imagined being in love a whole lot. It consumed every inch of her, every fiber and every thread, and she had never felt more alive. Every breath she took was deeper, expanding her lungs and heating her blood. She gripped the back of his head, kissing him harder, chasing that feeling of euphoria. She never thought it would be him, but she was more than glad that it was. She supposed that was the point though, wasn't it? This was worth everything.

"So..." She started slowly, brushing her fingers over his neck. "Your dad and uncle just left."

"Mhm."

She leaned forward and kissed along his jaw. "And your auntie..."

"That's right."

"And the boys are upstairs asleep."

"Yes, ma'am."

"And Eros is at Emerald tonight."

"Correct."

"Then how about I finally show you the inside of one of the playrooms?"

"Mm, public or private?"

"Whatever you want, Daddy, but on one condition."

"What's that, Princess?"

"You let me have my way with you."

"Hm, have you been a good girl?"

She dragged her tongue along his throat, feeling the groan he emitted. "I will be."

He bit his lip. "Alright. Show me. And if you want, you can show me off."

Aphrodite didn't know it at the time, but Hephaestus had come to realize something. Or rather, he had seen it from a different vantage point. It wasn't simply that she was reckless. It was that she hated to waste time. She was learning though, to slow down and live in the moment, to get everything she possibly could from it. So now, as she dragged him towards the partitioned rooms, only just giving him enough time to grab his cane, she vowed that she would take her time enjoying this for all that it was.

She scanned her key over the second to last door's lock, the space bathed in vivid red light and the heart-shaped bed in the center adorned in a comforter with a dove, a rose in its mouth. It was low to the ground, the height having been adjusted so that Hephaestus could maneuver more easily. She noticed he took some time getting on and off of her much taller bed, especially after they went several rounds, and she had planned accordingly for tonight. Plus, it gave their audience a better view of the show.

Once they were locked inside, she turned to him, taking hold of his shirt and carefully unbuttoning it.

"I thought you liked me in it?" His voice was teasing.

"Oh, I do, and I expect to see it more often, but right now, I need to see all of you, Daddy. Otherwise, how am I supposed to show you off?"

He didn't complain any further, allowing her to undress him fully before shoving him down on the feather-soft bed. He chuckled, propping himself up on his hands just as she raised her foot, pressing the heel of her red bottom into the center of his chest. He looked down at it, groaning as he admired the glistening gold buckles stretched over the black leather and the defined muscle of her calf. His eyes continued up, up, up until he caught the faintest glimpse of her bare pussy. He inhaled.

"No panties, needy girl?"

"I wanted to make it easy for you, Daddy."

He seemed to consider that explanation for a moment before deeming it acceptable, his gaze continuing its ascent until it met hers.

"You're gonna fuck me in these heels, right?" he questioned.

"Oh, I'm gonna do so much more than that, Daddy."

She pressed him down into the mattress, his body reclining into the pillows behind him. He ran a hand up along her leg, but she shook her head, wagging her finger at him.

"No touching just yet," she purred.

He dropped his hand with a sigh and a smirk as she dragged her foot down to his stomach then his semi-hard cock. He groaned beneath the pressure, lifting his hips up into her reflexively. She watched him settle under her control, and she was quickly drunk off of the power she drew from the sight of him. Months ago, it would have been far more satisfying. Then again, months ago, they wouldn't be here.

Stepping up onto the mattress, she treated him to a tantalizing sway of her hips, her red dress form fitting and accentuating the thickness of her thighs. The hem of it came to an abrupt halt at mid-thigh, and her breasts threatened to spill over the plunging neckline of the sleeveless bodice. She watched his eyes hone in on them, darkening several shades until a storm brewed within them, one she wished to dance in, to drown in. She loved when he looked at her like that.

"Can you help me take my dress off, Daddy?"

She gave him a distinguished pout, running her hands down her belly. He hummed, running a hand through his hair.

"I can," he returned, "but first, I want you to ride me in it."

Even now, on her own stomping grounds, she would deny him nothing. She couldn't. She bit her lip, a sly smile in place as she descended to her knees, straddling his thighs and immediately feeling the swollen head of his erection demanding entrance.

"I left something under that pillow for you," she said softly.

He raised a brow but slipped a hand beneath his head nonetheless, feeling around momentarily before he extracted a full bottle of lube with a smirk. Aphrodite offered her hands, and he squeezed a generous amount into her palms before she reached down and began thoroughly lathering his shaft. He grunted, letting his head fall back, the clench of his jaw making her stomach flip.

They were gathering a decently sized audience now. Aphrodite was used to having a crowd the few times she treated her clubs to a public showing of her own pleasure, but this was different. Never had she put on a show with someone she loved. Not only that, but she was acutely aware that Hephaestus had never done anything like this before at all, and he had only agreed because it was her.

He had said so several nights ago, vowing to try everything — although after she started listing things off, he'd changed the verbiage to "most" things— at least once. He wanted to integrate into her world so that it was no longer so alien to him, and she had been eager to start. She didn't think he would adjust and excel so fast however. Just two nights ago, he'd finally agreed to let her suck his dick with an ice cube in her mouth, and now he was letting her fuck him in public? He had been so wrong. He was definitely the man for her.

Once she was satisfied with her work, she pressed her hands against his chest, her fingers pinning down the wings of his eagle. Then slowly, she lowered herself onto him, her walls stretching around him as she yelped softly. He always seemed to expand once he was sheathed inside her, not that she was complaining. It felt too good, stroking along her walls and giving her the maximum amount of pleasure.

He wasn't stingy with the rest of him either, his hands grasping her thighs as she began to move. She wished she could keep her eyes open so that she could watch him watch her, gluttonous for that look on his face. It was a mixture of adoration and arousal, greed and gratitude, and she had come to realize he often looked at her that way. However, it was never more potent than when he was inside her.

"Oh, fuck, Daddy..."

She let her head fall back on her shoulders, her eyes rolling back and her fingernails biting into his skin. He pushed her dress further up her thighs until he could watch her clit glance off of him with each roll of her hips, her pussy constricting at the bottom of each movement. She pushed her hair over her shoulders, ensuring he could see every inch of skin she could offer as his grunts began to fill the room. Still, it didn't seem to be enough.

Before she could remember where they were, he was sitting up, reaching behind her and roughly unzipping her dress. His teeth latched onto her neck, drawing a loud moan from her lips that echoed around the room and through the floor speakers beneath the partition. Yanking down the fabric, he freed her tits, his mouth descending with a quickness. She arched into his touch, burying her fingers in his hair and holding him to her chest as he sucked and bit and licked her breasts. The more they fucked, the more feral he became when they did so, relinquishing his self control early on and doing and saying things she could have never imagined him doing and saying.

Like now.

"You ride this dick so good, baby," he growled, pulling her hair so she pressed even harder into him. "That's my good girl. Don't you dare stop."

She wouldn't dare, instead bouncing faster and harder in his lap until he was forced to drop back onto the mattress. His back bowed, chest rising before her even as her hands reclaimed their prior position. He bucked his hips, albeit with not nearly enough power to dislodge her, and her moans turned to screams each time he reached her spot and hit her clit. She was close, but she wasn't quite ready to give him an upper hand just yet. She wanted to make this last.

Slowing her movements, she slipped her feet out from under her, pressing her heels into the mattress as she squatted over him. He watched her with a vague curiosity, but once she started bouncing fully, hands on her knees, she knew he wouldn't last long.

"Fuck!" he yelled, throwing his head back. "That's my fucking girl!"

Butterflies assaulted her stomach before arousal drowned them out, but she forced herself to keep looking at him. She wanted to see him fall apart. She loved it. She loved watching him come undone at her hands, and she would savor it.

"Am I a good girl, Daddy?" she whimpered.

"Yes, baby," he groaned. "You're my good girl. Such - a good girl."

She withered beneath the praise but picked up the pace nonetheless, dropping her hips, clenching around him and jumping right back up to do it again. His eyes were all but shut, his skin tainted red, and the veins in his neck were threatening to burst. Faster she went, harder too, her hands moving to brace against his thighs behind her. Then he had a full view of his cock plunging into her pussy over and over, and as soon as he looked down again, his back went rigid as a board beneath her.

"Fuck, 'Dite, you—"

He ended the sentence with a sharp thrust of his hips upward, holding it there as he coated her walls.

"Yes, Daddy! Yes!"

She continued to swirl and swivel on his dick, getting herself close to the edge before slowing down and backing away from it. Slowly, his hips lowered back onto the mattress, but he remained hard inside of her, not at all softening despite the intense orgasm she'd just driven him to. She watched him stretch out, a satisfied smile slung across his face.

"Was it good, Daddy?"

"You know it was, Princess." He licked his lips, and she traced the movement with her eyes.

Fates, he was devastating.

"Mm, do you need a break before you fuck me again?"

"I'll tell you what I need." His hands found her thighs once more. "Daddy needs his good girl to feed him."

A chill ran down her spine. "Oh yeah?"

"That's right. Why don't you come up here and sit that pussy on my face?"

She need not be told twice. With a giddy laugh, she pulled herself off of his cock and moved up his body, pressing her hands to the wall behind his head as she positioned herself over his mouth. Their eyes locked, and he watched as she carefully descended, his tongue flicking out to welcome her folds. She gasped, pressing her head against her arm as she touched down.

In her peripheral, she caught a glimpse of the growing crowd on the opposite side of the window. One woman was pressed up against the glass, her body consistently being pitched forward. A man stood behind her, bunching her dress up around her waist as he fucked her. Aphrodite groaned, eager to have Hephaestus inside her again already. She was insatiable.

He violently tore her from her thoughts as he yanked her down onto his jaw, pressing his face into her folds and shoving his tongue inside of her.

She was immediately moving, rocking against his mouth, a slew of curses spilling from her lips. She reached down with one hand, tangling it in his hair while her own spilled back to brush over his chest. Pleasure built quickly, Aphrodite doing what she had to do to make sure he touched all the right places, grinding her clit against the bridge of his nose with shameless desperation and only breaking to give him a chance to breathe. He growled against her, nails anchoring in her thighs as her prayers and pleas filled the air.

"Yes, Daddy, that feels so good! Don't stop! Please don't—"

Her orgasm built at breakneck speed, her heels altogether uncomfortable now that her toes curled of their own volition. He adjusted easily each time she sped up or shifted her hips, keeping her clit stimulated as she searched for release. The world melted into the background and then away entirely, and all she knew was his mouth and the pressure building in the pit of her belly.

She teetered on the edge, clawing at his scalp and smothering him until climax seized her in its clutches, winding around her like a rope and growing tighter by the second. Her breath hitched, eyes rolling back to the ceiling as her hips stalled against his tongue. Hephaestus didn't falter now, tongue fucking her with that hostile haste he still kept reserved for her in the bedroom. And she loved it.

"Hephaestus!"

It rang out around the room as she struggled to hold herself up, her descent much slower than her rise. Once she was able, she carefully slid off of his face, moving to lay beside him. His cheeks and chin were glistening with her, the fine hair of his growing beard frosted with her arousal. He licked his lips again with a wolfish smile.

"Was it good, Princess?"

"You know it was, Daddy," she breathed, running a hand down his chest. "Are you satisfied?"

His grin widened. "Not even close."

He didn't seem to notice the bodies crowded around the window. Either that, or he didn't care. He simply got up and busied himself with setting her up for the next round. He turned her fully onto her stomach before kneeling behind her, grasping her hips and propping her ass up before him.

"Mm, what are you planning to do, Daddy?"

He picked up the bottle of lube, dousing his cock in it impatiently.

"Give my good girl one more reward." His voice was husky, climbing up her back like an extra set of hands and making her shudder. "Is that alright with you, Princess? You think you can take this dick again?"

"Yes, Daddy, please. I'll take it. I'll do anything for you. I'm your good girl. I'm — ah!"

She wasn't expecting the subtle entry, but she wasn't at all ungrateful either. He pushed all the way into her pussy, holding the position momentarily before pulling all the way back out. Then he did it again. She was used to this warmup, the teasing stroke that would soon turn into something aggressive and inebriating. And he didn't disappoint.

She clutched the sheets in her hands as his hips slammed into her the first time, a sharp clap of skin on skin ricocheting around the room. Soon, it was impossible for Aphrodite to pick out her own sounds from those seeping into the room from the audience, and she didn't care to try. Between Heph's possessive grip on her thighs and him fucking her like he was trying to brand her skin with his thrust, everything else seemed inconsequential.

"Yes, Daddy, yes!"

"That's my good girl," he grunted, reaching up to grip her shoulder. "Take this dick. Take it!"

"Yes! I will, yes!"

She was unbound and absent of control, her own body bowing to his whims and his alone. It was almost easy to forget he was in love with her with the way he rammed his cock into her, but she knew he would remind her right after. He always did.

He took care of her in a way she was not at all used to yet was very much in need of, and she had ceased doubting him. This man of hers was nothing she thought he was and everything she needed him to be, and she was so damn grateful.

And right now, he was driving her straight into another orgasm. He knew it too.

"My good girl is gonna cum for me again, isn't she?"

"Daddy..." she whimpered, unable to form a coherent sentence amidst the haze fogging her mind. "Please."

"Yeah, you are. You're my good girl, aren't you? And you're gonna cum for Daddy."

He repeated it again and again, each more aggressive than the last, and her body twisted and writhed beneath the force of his thrust and the pressure of his command until she was once more swept up by overwhelming pleasure, a high-pitched scream tearing its way out of her throat.

He was drilling her now, straight into the damn mattress, the lewd sounds of their meeting a constant song. She knew he had been holding on, holding out until he could ruin her first, but she fought to do the same now. Squeezing around him, she pleaded wordlessly, aching to be filled.

"Cum for me, Daddy." It was barely more than a whisper, but it seemed to impregnate the space. "Please."

A roar echoed from behind her, her hips snapping back on instinct. He bottomed out, holding her hips in place as he came again. Her pussy spasmed around him, contracting helplessly and milking him dry, drawing curse after precious curse from him.

He collapsed atop her almost immediately, his body all but giving out, and she reached back to run a hand through his hair. Yet before she could settle beneath his weight, he was slipping out of her, laying beside her and turning her towards him.

She gasped as his mouth found hers, kissing her with that raw passion she was gradually becoming acquainted with, a passion he seemed only to share here with her. She grabbed at him, pulling him close just as he did the same with her and enveloping herself in his warmth. She didn't care if the crowd had dispersed or if they were waiting for another show. All she knew was that she loved this man before her, and she was fit to burst with it.

When he pulled back, he was smiling, brushing his hand along her face and tracing her jaw. He looked at her as if he'd never seen anything like her before, that awe in his eyes caressing something deep in her chest. She couldn't help but smile back.

"Did you like it?" she asked softly, dusting her fingers over his lips, his chin. "Like - can we make it a routine thing?"

He shrugged a shoulder. "I wouldn't mind it every now and again. It didn't really feel all that different than being upstairs."

"How so?"

He tilted his head. "You're still the only person in the world to me when we're together like this."

A blush made its way up her neck, but before it reached her face, she buried it in his neck.

"I think I'm a bad influence," she mumbled.

"Why?" She could feel his laughter rumbling in his chest.

"Because you're all sappy and romantic and shit now."

"You're an inspiration. What can I say?"

She looked up at him again, curiosity striking her eyes. How could she be so lucky? After everything she'd done and all that she'd put him through, he loved her.

"I love you," he said as if reading her mind. "I've never been in love before, but - I can feel it in my bones. And while I've never said shit like this before, I'd never say anything I didn't mean. You know that, so - maybe this is just who I am when I'm in love with you."

"Is that a bad thing?"

"Loving you? Naw, it's the best thing I've ever done."

She felt the moisture pooling in her eyes, and he pulled her against him again, kissing her forehead before moving back down to her lips. His kiss was soft and savory and all the things she always thought a kiss should be when it meant something.

"I love you," she sighed as they pulled apart, her forehead against his.

"Yeah? You sure?"

"I've never been more sure of anything in my life."

"Good." He brushed her hair back from her face. "...because we're having dinner with my parents next weekend."

Her eyes snapped wide open. "What!"

He didn't give either of them the chance to open the conversation, crashing his lips against hers once more and rolling over on top of her. In mere minutes, she had forgotten what he'd just said, drowning in all the sensations he ignited within her. Maybe there was no fairy tale. Maybe she was the hero and the damsel. She might even be her own worst enemy at times. But it was worth it, every moment, if it meant loving —and being loved by— Hephaestus.

ACKNOWLEDGMENTS

This book was arguably one of the most terrifying, heartbreaking, funny, heartwarming, and beautiful things I've ever had the pleasure of writing. I put so much of myself into it, and Hephaestus literally carried me through to my own diagnosis and adjustment to my disability the past several months. The only regret I have is that I can't read this for the first time, but I can hope that you enjoy reading it as much as I enjoyed writing it.

I would like to thank so many people across the writing community, especially all of the book bloggers and bookstagrammers that make our little world go round. Thank you to Whit (lifewhitme), who was literally on the frontlines (my DMs) cheering me on and helping me out whenever I asked, who kept my secrets and carried my burdens with me (remember when I couldn't talk about the audiobooks!). She really held it down, and I don't think I would have survived all the late nights and early mornings and rough patches without her. I even had to fight with her about preordering the e-book even though she got one free as my first and only top tier patron on Patreon??? Anyway, I know she hates when I say "Soft" things, but YOU ARE THE WIND BENEATH MY WINGS AND THANK YOU FOR ALL YOU DO!

Thank you also to Sil (thebookvoyagers), Nicole (whopickedthisbook), Bee (YeineEssun), Taima (shadesnpages), Purabi (bierotica), Sharonda (BBrReviews), Gab B. (gabwithpurpose), Nick (nickofthebooks), Ari (daydreaminbkwrm), my favorite Literary Fairy Maliyah (LiteraryFairy_) and all my other Twitter friends for every supportive comment and word of advice and general excitement that you shared with me. A large chunk of my success is directly because of y'all. Sil is constantly cheering me on and championing my work, and Purabi really taught me a lot about how things work here when I was brand new to romancelandia and publishing. Y'all got me here for real!

Thank you to Tasha L. Harrison for looking out for me and sharing her wisdom and knowledge all the time. Thank you to Jack Harbon, Aveda Vice, Katee Robert, K. Sterling, Katrina Jackson, and every other author who offered their experience, knowledge, mentorship, and overall support. Of course, thank you also to my patrons, who support everything I do and have enough faith in my talents to support me monthly lol. I wouldn't be here without any of you, and I am so grateful to everyone who has accompanied me on this journey. I'm sure I missed people, but just know I appreciate you all!

I would like to especially thank my siblings Miranda, Devin, and Oolie for always showcasing their pride in me and holding me down the best they can. We've come a long way and have gone through a lot together, but I never had to worry about whether or not you would clown me for writing romance or put me down for writing full time. I'm glad each of you have been able to live your own romances though, and I am so inspired by each of you and how you've really become more of yourselves by loving others (Thank you Mikey, Antonio, and Reagan). I love you.

Thank you also to my father Gary who has supported me, mentored me, advised me, and done everything in his power to see me through to my success. He has never lived vicariously through me. Instead, he keeps chasing his own dreams so he can show us how to catch ours. Again, I couldn't have done it without y'all, and I am so grateful. All I can do to repay you is to keep going, and I hope you'll come with me!

ABOUT THE AUTHOR

R.M. Virtues is an independent author of dark fantasy and erotic romance. From gods and monsters to werewolves and witches, angels and demons to sinners and saints, you will find something for everyone here. R.M. is an advocate of the underdog, the antihero, and the morally grey. Many of his stories feature minority characters as he prides himself on creating narratives for his communities, writing them into places they do not often have the pleasure of seeing themselves in without also seeing their own pain. R.M. currently resides in the notorious city of Sin, a grad student by day and a creator of worlds by night. He enjoys horror films, true crime documentaries, tales of magic, and video games with riveting storylines, all of which prove to inspire.

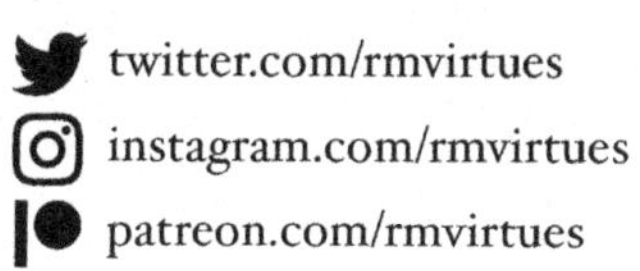

ALSO BY R.M. VIRTUES

Drag Me Up: Gods of Hunger Book 1

What Are the Odds? (Standalone)

Made in the USA
Las Vegas, NV
23 June 2022

50647756R00193